BITTER SEED

Shirley Cook

ISBN 13: 978-1499378429
ISBN 10: 1499378424

This is a work of fiction. Names, characters, places, and incidents either are the product of the author's imagination or are used fictitiously. Any resemblance to actual persons, living or dead, events or locales is entirely coincidental.

The author researched the times and locale of this story, including a three week study tour in China. Under the watchful eye of the national guide, historical facts were established. The author assumes responsibility for any errors regarding persons, places or events.

Many Thanks!

To the Write Bunch, my longtime critique group, who listened, advised and encouraged; and to the Book Buddies, who wanted to read and discuss Bitter Seed's story.

I also thank the many well-read and accomplished editors who generously gave of their time and expertise in the reading of *Bitter Seed*: E. Pomada, Carol Paulin, Greg and Carol Cook, Darla Briggs and Marilyn Schank. And of course, I thank my God and Savior for the gift of imagination and writing; and my husband, Lester, for his many decades of love and patience.

Other Books by Shirley Cook

Diary of a Fat Housewife
Diary of a Jogging Housewife
The Exodus Diet Plan
Around the House in Forty Days
Building on the Back Forty
The Marriage Puzzle
Grown-up Kids
Murder on the Fat Express
Through the Valley of Love (a novel)
The River Runs Deep (a novel)

PART ONE
CHINA 1853-1854

Chinese life in the 19th century was based on tradition and the philosophies of hard work, obedience and respect for ancestors and authority. Men retained the power and property while Chinese women had little in the way of formal education, or the power to choose their husbands.

PROLOGUE

The Kuang compound was not unlike others homes of nineteenth century China. Harmony and serenity prevailed. Sons revered fathers, and fathers revered the eldest woman, the matriarch. Every person held a place of honor, that is, every person except the daughters of the clan. Females had but one purpose, to submit to a rigorous training that resulted in marriage and the bearing of sons. And so it went, season after season.

Then Kulien, favored daughter of the Kuang patriarch came on the scene. Kulien, Bitter Seed, was unlike any female ever born into the Kuang clan. Her spirit rebelled against tradition as much as her dark green eyes rebelled against her Asian heritage. As the sixteenth anniversary of her birth approached, her restlessness increased. Not only would she soon know her future, the curiosity regarding her past would be satisfied.

A soft breeze blew through the compound that spring day of 1853, and her longing for faraway places grew. On this, her birthday, she treasured a hope that she was about to begin a new season of her life. She longed for freedom—freedom from the constraints of ancient and revered customs as well as freedom from the constant abuse of the many relatives who also lived behind the walls of the expansive Kuang compound. Although she had been walled in from contamination with the outside world, her father loved and treated her with respect. In his presence, she was truly free to express her joy and her hope for a future life beyond the walls.

The Tilling Season

"When spring comes and the pastures have an abundance of green grass, farmers turn their cattle into the pastures, but even then they keep a close watch over them. It is so with the minds of people: even under the best of conditions the mind will bear watching."

~~~~The Teaching of Buddha~~~~

ONE

It was Kuang Kulien's sixteenth birthday. She could hardly contain her excitement because today she would learn the secret of her past —and her future. When she pushed aside her bed curtains, she saw Jiang, her *amah*, standing in the center of the room, arms folded against her wide waist.

"It's about time you woke up from your nap," she said, a slight frown on her round face. "Today may be the most important day of your life."

Kulien swung long, graceful legs over the side of the bed and pushed her hair behind her shoulders. She was beside Jiang in two steps and planted a kiss on the older woman's cheek. "What do you mean *may be*? You know it *is* the most important day! Father has promised to tell me today why I look so different from all my cousins; and why I'm the only one allowed to have an English teacher come to the compound."

She was almost certain that Jiang, who had cared for her since birth, knew more than she let on. Kulien had never been told who her birth-mother was, and as the only daughter of the patriarch, Kuang Lufong, she was treated with favor and many acts of kindness. Her father had not only granted her every wish, he had raised her to be independent as well as educated in both the Chinese classics and European history. Lufong's mother, Mahwu, scowled and pointed an accusing finger whenever she saw Kulien, yet no one ever told her why. Kulien had tried to understand her grandmother's hatred, and thought it must be because her feet had not been bound into four-inch "lotus blossoms," a custom practiced by all the other women and girls in the family. Kulien was different in other ways, too. Her eyes though delicately slanted were not dark brown, but as green as imperial jade. She was taller than her cousins of the same age; and her skin had a pink tone rather than the tawny one of her relatives. Her black hair, however, was long and thick as that of any Chinese woman. No wonder she was so eager to meet with her father today.

At Jiang's impatient nudging, Kulien walked across the room to sit at her cosmetic table, while her *amah* combed and twisted long strands of hair into tight coils before pinning them to the sides of her head.

Kulien, looking at Jiang's reflection in the mirror begged, "Why don't you give me a hint at what Father will tell me? I'm sure you already know what he's going to say. Am I to learn about my mother? And how about my future? Has he arranged a marriage for me with some handsome young man? Or, as I most wish, will I be allowed to live here in the compound for many more years?"

Jiang's brows drew together, and her mouth turned down at the corners. "I've been instructed by the master to keep quiet. You will learn all you need to know after your birthday dinner."

Kulien noticed a tear form in Jiang's eye and roll down her rounded cheek. "What is it, Jiang? Why are you sad? Tell me now! Surely my father won't have bad news for me. I'm his most beloved child."

"You're his *only* child, you mean. Those twin boys, Ohchin and Sunfu are adopted sons, born of your grandfather's concubine! It's a disgrace that they are even part of this family! I suppose that with the old man dead and that woman, Yingsi, still living, it was the only thing your honorable father could do."

Kulien tipped her head, and with a mischievous smile said, "Ohchin, it's true, is mean and hateful; but Sunfu is like a true brother—a blood-brother. We've always been close."

Jiang patted Kulien's head harder than necessary. "Why you want to associate with that vagabond, I'll never know. He's always running off doing who knows what? He gave up his inheritance as the first born son because he is so self-willed. What a foolish young man."

"I like his spirit," Kulien said, rising to walk to the diamond-latticed window of her upper story room. "I wish that I'd been born a male so I could do as I please."

She raised her eyes to the high walls at the far side of the compound, feeling closed in and impatient. She had been outside the walls only once when she was twelve years old. Lufong had taken her, along with Sunfu and Ohchin, in his best sedan to the nearby city of Shanghai. She had been amazed at the expanse of the Kuang Compound as the rickshaw coolies circled the perimeter before heading down the dusty road to the city. She smiled within herself as she recalled how she and Sunfu had run away to explore the shops on their own; and how angry her father had been when they were found.

Jiang tottered over to Kulien, holding out the green silk gown Lufong had recently presented to his daughter. "And what are you smiling about, Ladybug? You have a faraway look in those eyes."

Without an answer, Kulien turned away from the window, allowing Jiang to slip the gown over her head and fasten the frogs that decorated the front. "You look lovely in this shade of green. It brings out the color of your eyes," Jiang said.

"Eyes that should be brown, you mean. I hope Father keeps his promise to tell me what has been a secret all these years."

"Hush, my pet. Your honorable father always keeps his promises. Today you will learn many secrets." Jiang blinked away another tear that had pooled in her dark eyes. "It's time for you to expect great changes in your life—and mine," she added softly. When she finished preening over the young girl, she gave Kulien a slight push. "We must hurry now to the audience hall as your father requested. The sun is sinking into the west, and he'll be waiting."

Outside, the late afternoon sun slanted through a row of ginkgo trees, washing the courtyard in a thin yellow light. Crocuses, hyacinths and tulips, all imported from Europe, scented the air with sweetness. Kulien felt an excitement fluttering in her chest as she approached the long hall reserved for greeting foreigners. Why had her father chosen this place to meet with her? Perhaps she would come face to face with one of the foreign devils she had spied on other occasions.

"*Baba.*" Kulien held out her arms as Lufong crossed the room to embrace her.

"My daughter," he answered in English. "While we're alone, you may speak the foreign language."

Kulien's eyes widened. "Truly? But Jiang is here. You don't care if she knows our secret?"

Lufong smiled at Jiang, dismissing her. "Your *amah* knows many secrets. She won't betray us."

Of course, Jiang knew of the years Kulien had received English lessons from Elizabeth Whitfield, the white woman from the Shanghai mission house; but she didn't know that her charge had become interested in the western religion. Miss Whitfield had been making regular visits to the Kuang compound for many seasons and was quite proud of her able student, and especially pleased about Kulien's curiosity regarding the Christian faith. (Her elders weren't the only ones with secrets!)

But Lufong's knowledge of the foreign devils' tongue was unknown to other members of the family. How her father had acquired the language was but one more mystery to her.

With Lufong's arm around Kulien's shoulders, he led her past lacquered ebony screens and brilliant tapestries to a low platform where two ornately carved chairs overlooked the wide hall. "Sit, child. Your teacher, Miss Whitfield has asked to greet you as a special treat on your birthday—and she brings her brother who recently arrived from Great Britain." He watched with pleasure as Kulien sat down, tall and erect. "You wear the new gown I brought from Peking. I was especially fond of the embroidered lilies. The pink and white threads reflect your coloring—which I notice is exceptionally high today." He smiled again, patting her hand. "I think this is a day you will long remember." His smile faded into a somber expression that puzzled Kulien.

"And I believe you are the best father a girl could have!" Kulien's eyes sparkled and the dimple in her right cheek made its appearance.

A rustling movement caught their attention as a houseboy, dressed in a white jacket and black trousers tied at the ankles, pushed aside the heavy blue drapery that covered the doorway. He stepped over the sill to stand at attention. In his hands he held a large red card. On it in wide Chinese characters were the names, "Elizabeth Whitfield" and "Lord Marshall Whitfield."

Lufong waved a hand. "You may present our visitors."

First through the door came Kulien's English teacher. Elizabeth Whitfield was seven years older than Kulien and, although feared by some as a foreign devil, she had become as much a friend as a teacher to Kulien. When she lifted her long bulky skirts to step over the threshold, Kulien remembered her comment about the four-inch high doorsills. "Your people believe demons travel in a straight line, but high thresholds, zigzag bridges and swooping eaves cannot deter them. There is only One who can hold back evil. That is the one true God who is written about in this Book." Along with her many history and English books, Miss Whitfield always carried the black book entitled, "The Holy Bible," in her colorful satchel.

Elizabeth crossed the room to stand in front of Kulien and her father. Her long honey-colored hair was swept up under a ridiculous wide-brimmed hat adorned with a faded pink rose. She raised dark eyebrows and fastened blue eyes on her pupil. In deference to Kuang Lufong she bowed, almost losing her hat.

Kulien repressed a giggle and smiled as Elizabeth shoved her hat back in place and winked at Kulien.

Lufong, ever the picture of severity and elegance in the presence of guests, cast a sidelong frown in Kulien's direction.

"I thank you, Mr. Kuang," Elizabeth said in Mandarin, "for allowing me to visit your daughter today and wish her a most prosperous year."

"My daughter and I are grateful for your company." He nodded. "And we are pleased to welcome your brother as well." He raised a forefinger displaying a long curved nail, a symbol of wealth. The servant, who had been standing in the shadows, responded by drawing the drapery aside the second time.

Stepping over the threshold with stately grace, Lord Marshall Whitfield made his entrance. He approached Kuang

Lufong, his eyes straight ahead, obviously careful not to make eye contact with the favored daughter of a high-ranking official. Kulien felt the breath catch in her throat as she watched his every movement. Compared to her father and step-brothers, the foreigner was a giant. A high collar of stiff fabric fit tightly about his throat, and a long dark coat with many buttons came to his knees. The man's legs were long, and his shoulders wider than Kulien had ever seen. However, it was the afternoon sun shining on his thick golden hair that caught her notice. He held a black top hat in his hands and bowed from the waist, reciting the strange words he had memorized.

"It is with humbleness that I come into your presence," he rehearsed in strained Chinese. He glanced at his sister and shrugged his shoulders. "Do you think I spoke correctly? I don't want to offend him."

Elizabeth Whitfield, unaware of Lufong's adeptness in English, directed her words to Kulien. "My brother, though familiar with many of the Chinese customs, is apprehensive to speak in your language. Would you ask your father's permission for my brother to speak English? Then I will translate."

Kulien's eyes danced with merriment as she relayed Elizabeth's words in Chinese, knowing her father understood every word. His face showed no comprehension of Elizabeth's request, and he nodded his agreement. He faced Lord Whitfield with his answer. "My daughter and I are pleased to have your social call. We are grateful to your sister who has proven to be a faithful teacher."

He waited as Elizabeth Whitfield translated, then went on. "I understand you have business in the port of Shanghai. Although the presence of foreigners in our treaty ports since the end of the Opium War in 1842 has sometimes been a problem, it is my wish that you have success while in our land."

The words exchanged between the Englishman and Kulien's father barely reached her consciousness. The only foreigner she had ever seen first-hand was Elizabeth Whitfield. After three years of lessons from the English woman, she thought she was accustomed to the difference between them; however, Lord Marshall Whitfield was another matter. This man was neither like his sister, nor Kulien's father, who was slight of build and wore a thin moustache and long goatee. Lord Whitfield was so tall his presence seemed to fill the large audience hall. His voice reminded her of distant thunder as words came from a mouth partially concealed by a dark moustache. She considered it strange that the foreigner also trimmed his beard to barely cover his chin. She pulled her attention away from his mouth to eyes fringed with dark lashes and deep blue—as blue as the sky on a spring day.

Kulien's curiosity showed in her entire demeanor. She leaned forward in the chair, her hands gripping the arms. Her father nudged her elbow.

"Daughter." Lufong's eyes bore into hers. He spoke in a low voice. "Behave yourself. Didn't Jiang instruct you to keep your eyes lowered?"

"Yes, Father," she said quickly. "Forgive me. I was overly curious."

"Remember who you are—an unmarried daughter of a first class mandarin. You are not to behave like a 'singsong' girl."

Lufong's words pierced her heart like a cold dagger. He had never spoken to her in such a way. She felt her face flush and touched her warm cheek. With eyes focused on her satin shoes, she mumbled, "You are right, *Baba.* My behavior was crude."

After several strained moments, Lufong stood and drew Kulien to her feet. Together they stepped down from the platform, and with a wave of a hand Lufong directed his guests to lead the way. "A meal has been prepared in the dining area of my private quarters. A servant boy will guide you through the compound."

Still feeling chastised, Kulien followed at the end of the single file group wending its way through the garden. Smooth stones made up the zigzag path that took them by a small waterfall splashing over jagged rocks into a pool filled with bright orange, fan-tailed carp. Spring flowers abounded, releasing their fragrance in the late afternoon twilight, but Kulien had little interest in the lush surroundings. Her mind was filled with the sight of Elizabeth's brother and the knowledge that she would soon be sitting at a meal with him. She must be careful when watching him. It would not do for her father to have to correct her again.

She lifted her eyes from the path to Lufong's thin back. He wore a black skullcap on his shaved forehead, and she noticed that the long braided queue that hung to his waist was threaded with gray. When had her father become gray? He had always seemed so young and vibrant. How proud she was to have such a man for a father. As a first-degree mandarin, he wore the official garb—a blue silk gown, decorated on the chest with a square insignia of a stork worked in silver and gold. Around his neck hung a long string of one hundred and eight amber beads, the mystic number of Buddhist theology. She remembered how, as a small child, she had played with the beads, learning to count in both English and Chinese.

Miss Whitfield and her brother stopped at the entrance to the dining hall waiting for Lufong to give them further instructions. He dismissed both Jiang and the servant, and then with a low bow, he invited the foreign guests inside.

Kulien thought her heart would burst with excitement. On only one other occasion had she dined with her father in his personal dining room—the day Jiang informed him of Kulien's first menses. This, too, was a special day because on her birthday she would finally learn the secrets that had been kept from her. However, the thought of hearing those long anticipated words paled as the Englishman let his eyes touch hers.

Kulien sat beside her father at the teakwood table decorated only with a cloisonné vase holding a single branch of almond blossoms. He smiled as she glanced at him, showing his forgiveness of her brazen behavior. With her eyes lowered to hands folded in her lap, she listened to the polite interchange between the foreigners and her beloved father.

Houseboys moved silently about the table, setting tureens and platters in the center where each person could serve himself. Delectable fragrances wafted from the dishes of meat, vegetables and rice, and Lufong pointed out the various ingredients, explaining the preparation.

"As you may have surmised," he said, glancing first at Miss Whitfield, then her brother, "both the preparation and ingestion of food are considered arts in our country."

After they finished the meal in silence, Kulien laid aside ivory chopsticks and glanced at her father who had addressed Lord Whitfield in Mandarin. "We would be pleased to hear about your journey. It is a great distance from England to the Middle Kingdom. My daughter is interested in geography." He reached over to touch her arm, granting her permission to look at Lord Whitfield.

Elizabeth nodded and spoke to her brother in English. "Mr. Kuang is extremely protective of Kulien. He wants you to explain about your voyage. But please be careful not to direct your words or your eyes in her direction."

As the man spoke, Kulien watched his every movement careful to contain her excitement. He appeared to be slightly older than his sister, and spoke with authority and knowledge. "I come in my father's place," he explained. "Our father, Lord George Whitfield, is a baron in the court of Her Britannic Majesty Queen Victoria. He had been assigned to the British Consulate here in Shanghai; but I am sorry to report that he is gravely ill." Lord Whitfield waited for Elizabeth to translate before going on.

"As for the geography lesson," he said, nodding in Kulien's direction, "my ship left from Southampton, Great Britain and sailed around Africa's Cape of Good Hope, through the Indian Ocean and the South China Sea. After many months of rough waters, we finally sailed along the China coast until we reached Shanghai." He sighed as if reliving the arduous journey.

"I am pleased to be here in my father's place, and hope to work out problems concerning the collection of customs. Our government is eager to correct the irregularities caused by the opium traffic. I will spend most of my time at the docks."

Marshall Whitfield leaned back in his chair, his eyes shifting for a moment to Kulien, then to Elizabeth. "Will you tell the young lady I hope some of the details of my travels were of interest to her?"

Elizabeth smiled across the narrow table at her student. "Kulien understands everything you said. She is an excellent pupil and speaks English with very little accent. She's not only well educated," she added, "but she also has a fair grasp of politics and world events."

Kulien felt the blood rise to her cheeks, and opened her mouth to respond, but Lufong cleared his throat reminding her to remain quiet.

"Sir," Marshall Whitfield said, "my sister and I have a small gift for your daughter." He reached into his coat pocket and drew out a delicate silk box. "I hope she will not be offended."

Kuang Lufong received the package with both hands and placed it on the table next to Kulien.

"She is honored, and will open it at a later time. *Shei, shei.* Thank you." Lufong rose from the table, an act of dismissal, and each person followed suit.

"Would you ask the magistrate if I may address his daughter?"

"I don't think that's a good idea, Marshall. Customs regarding an unmarried daughter are strict, and I don't want to insult him."

"But she *is* very beautiful. I want her to know that I admire her beauty."

Kuang Lufong glanced at Kulien, his eyes dark and stern, his chin set. "This Englishman is bold," he whispered. "You will not be in his presence again."

"Sir," Lord Whitfield said with a bow. "Would it be possible for me to have an audience with you at a later date? I do want to understand the problems of the district, and as a magistrate, you could give me great insight that would further my work."

Kuang Lufong listened to Elizabeth Whitfield translate; though Kulien could tell he was impatient with his answer.

"I travel a great deal, Lord Whitfield. I will advise you through your sister *if* a meeting can be arranged." His eyes narrowed, and his tone was sharp.

He stepped to the doorway to usher the foreigners out. Before leaving the room, he turned to Kulien. "I will escort our guests to their sedans. Please meet me in the library. It's time for you to know both your history—and your future!"

TWO

Knowing that Lufong would not return for many minutes, Kulien left the dining area, and walked past the adjacent library to stroll in the garden. This northern garden was only one of many throughout the large walled compound, though it was the most beautiful. In the spring, flowers of every color and hue edged the walkways. Trees dripped with blossoms that would soon develop into ripe peaches. Huge porcelain pots, decorated with pictures of dragons, contained fan-tailed, bulbous-eyed fish that hid behind jagged stones and small water lilies. It was twilight now, and as the sun sank into the west, Kulien inhaled deeply of the rich fragrances that wafted through the garden.

High walls kept intruders out and the feminine occupants inside. Although Lufong's vast estate was near the city of Shanghai, Kulien was not allowed to go beyond the heavy red gate that protected the family from bandits that roamed the countryside. Jiang continually scolded her for being restless and dissatisfied with her high position.

"Your aunts and cousins don't complain," she had warned. "They're contented to be cared for by such a great man as your honorable father, and to live in this wealthy compound."

"They have no brains! All they do is sit at Mahwu's feet and embroider. They're no more than slaves to my grandmother."

"They behave as proper Chinese women. You are the exception."

"I know." Kulien though pleased with her freedom to study the classics and English, often felt dismayed that the other members of the family ignored her. Mahwu especially seemed to hate her, the only child of her eldest son, though she readily accepted the daughters born of her aunts and uncles. Perhaps her hatred arose from Kulien's favored treatment by Lufong.

She continued past the low wall encompassing Lufong's quarters to walk in the central courtyard, paved with tiles imported from Italy. Statues of various gods sat beside gnarled pine trees, some smiling with beneficence, others grimly scowling their displeasure. The only lights in the courtyard were a few lanterns placed near the four gates that accessed the area.

Kulien sat on a stone bench beside a waterfall to wait for her father's return. It had been an eventful birthday, the best she could remember. As she recalled the face of the Englishman, her heart fluttered. He admired her and thought she was beautiful. She thought he was beautiful, too. But she knew she would never be allowed to see him again. Her father, though hiding it from the foreigners, had been angry at the man's boldness. She hoped he would not be angry with Elizabeth. She would die if the delightful teacher could not return.

"What are you doing out here?" Lufong sat beside her and put an arm around her shoulders. "The night air is chill. Let's go into the library. It is time for you to learn the answers to your many questions."

When Kulien entered the gracious room filled with scrolls, books and tapestries, she immediately seated herself on a straight-backed chair opposite Lufong's writing table. "No, child. Come here." The man had removed his skull cap and outer garment, motioning to a low couch near the fireplace. "Sit beside me where it is warm. My soul is as chilled as your lovely fingers," he said, taking her hands in his. He lifted her fingers to his lips, an uncharacteristic gesture, and Kulien felt a strange sense of fear wrap around her heart as she placed her hands back in her lap. What was it that troubled her father? It was surely not the Englishman, for his eyes, reflecting the light of the fire, brimmed with tears.

Kulien sat beside Lufong waiting for him to speak. His breath came in heavy sighs, and moments passed before he found his voice. "You have reached the age of maturity and want to know your heritage. Rightfully so. One must know the past to live with grace in the future."

Kulien held back the urge to respond by tightening her entwined fingers together. It would not do to interrupt him as he fought to control his emotions. She only nodded in agreement, turning her attention to the sparks that danced above the logs before they escaped up the chimney.

"Your past, of course, is also mine. I will appreciate your silence and careful attendance to my words. It is difficult for me to speak of these things, for because of my folly, your grandfather went beyond the Yellow Springs to avoid the shame."

Kulien gasped. "What do you mean?"

"Be still, child. I will say when you may speak." Another heavy sigh. "As the first-born son of a wealthy and educated mandarin, I was given the opportunity to attend Oxford University in Great Britain. It was there that I learned the English language. It was also there, while a student, that I met your mother, Marguerite Howard. She was the daughter of one of my professors." He rested a cool hand on Kulien's folded ones. "I had never met such a woman: intelligent, graceful, gentle, and beautiful. I didn't expect to—to love her because I had been pledged, when but a child, to marry a woman of the Kong clan. It was a contract that could not be broken. But remember, daughter that I was far from China, living among Europeans whose culture is poles apart from ours. I was young, only twenty-five. Marguerite loved me against her parents' plans and wishes for her as well. We became outcasts from both our races when we married."

Lufong's eyes met Kulien's as he turned to face her. "Yes, we were married secretly, and it was only two moons later that my beloved discovered she was with child. I was to return to China within the year, but I disobeyed my family once more and stayed until the birth of our child."

Lufong buried his face in his hands, stifling the sobs that struggled within his breast. "The delivery was difficult, and because the doctor refused to deliver 'a half-breed,' as he called it, an inexperienced midwife attended the birth. Marguerite gave birth to you, a beautiful baby girl. We named you Grace after her mother.

"Due to the immaturity of the midwife, complications set in. But before your mother died, I promised that I would see that you were raised to have compassion and tolerance toward those of different races. Marguerite wanted you to know the heritage of both your parents, and to be educated in China as an English woman. She also requested that I love you as I loved her, and to keep you always close beside me. I have honored those wishes as much as has been within my power. To my shame, my venerable father, Kuang Linho, was disgraced when I brought you into this compound. He saved face when he hanged himself in the summerhouse. Your grandmother, Mahwu, named you Kulien, Bitter Seed, because of my disobedience and her own ill will."

Lufong stood to warm himself before the fire. With his back to Kulien, he gave permission for her to speak. What could she say? Her mind was all tangled with her feelings. She found it hard to breathe, much less speak. Her mother was English, Caucasian. The answer to so many questions lay in that knowledge alone. Perhaps the answer to all her questions: her unusual appearance, her "unwomanly" bent for scholarship, the ostracizing from Mahwu and the rest of the family, the atypical attention of a father for a female child.

"I don't know how to respond, Father. I feel so confused. I knew I was different from other members of the family. I also knew it was a deep secret known perhaps only by Mahwu. Does Jiang know of my beginnings?"

Lufong turned and with arms folded across his waist, answered, "Jiang was a young woman exiled from a family of wealth—for what reason, I don't know. She was misused by a man who found her in the streets, and later gave birth to a child who died. I knew about her family and brought her to our compound to become your *amah*. She nursed you and loves you as her own."

Kulien raised herself from the low couch to face her father. She took a deep breath and forced her attention away from her pounding heart before speaking. "Surely you have fulfilled your obligations to my mother. And now that I have come of age, I know that you are free to do with me as you please. What is my future, *Baba*? Am I to remain here with you? Must I be sent away to marry like other girls? Oh, please, don't send me away!"

Lufong turned to stare out the window into the darkening night. Only the flicker of a garden lantern glistened against the panes. "I am not free to follow my wishes, my dear, my Grace. To me you will always be Marguerite's daughter, my lovely Lotus Blossom, but because of my folly and my father's shame, I must do what I least desire."

When he turned, Lufong's face was pale, his forehead furrowed, his eyes hard. "I not only shamed my family by marrying a foreigner, I shamed the Kong clan by disgracing the daughter I was contracted to wed. I had no choice but to promise my eldest daughter to marry Kong's eldest son. His name is Litang, and he is now the patriarch of that noble family."

Kulien gasped. "Oh, no. You can't send me away to a strange family. They would never accept a woman of mixed race!"

"It is our way. I can no longer go against tradition. It is settled. They know of my shame, but to spare our family's honor, they have graciously agreed to allow you to go through the traditional marriage ceremony." Lufong paused and glanced toward the window, gathering his thoughts. "I am grieved to say that after the wedding you will assume the place of one of Kong Litang's concubines." His last words faded into a whisper. "There is no other way." Lufong's demeanor and tone of voice changed. He had stepped out of the role of loving father to unbendable master. "I cannot change destiny. As the offspring of two races, you must adapt to the future. Before your next birthday you will go to Hangchow to become but one of Kong Litang's many concubines. I pray your deceased mother will never know this turn of events."

Kulien stared at her father, unable to speak. She reached out to touch him, to find some semblance of mercy. He had turned from her, his shoulders slumped, his head bowed. With a raise of his hand, he dismissed her. No word of sorrow. No encouragement.

Kulien, who prided herself on her strength, felt resolve drain away. Overcome with despair, she hugged herself tightly and stared at her father's back. If only he would face her and say that he loved her too much to send her away. But he said nothing. Finally, with tears pouring from her eyes, she ran from the library and through the gardens, unaware of the beauty she had enjoyed only a few moments before...or had it been a century ago?

When she reached her own apartment, she fell into the open arms of her waiting *amah*. There, snuggled against Jiang's soft bosom, she cried until there were no more tears.

THREE

After a long and restless night, Kulien attempted to open her eyes to the sun streaming through the latticed window. She blinked against the bright light and burrowed deeper under the quilt. The remembrance of her father's words and actions brought fresh tears to her eyes and she wiped them away with her fingertips. It wouldn't do for Kuang Lufong to see her like this today when she met him for morning exercise and meditation. After all, she prided herself on the strength she had shown him regardless of the treatment she suffered from other family members.

The ominous words crept through her mind like a lion seeking its prey: "Within the year, you will leave this home to become one of Kong Litang's many concubines."

She pressed open palms over her ears to silence the future destiny engraved on her mind. How could her father send her away as if she were an ordinary Chinese woman? Hadn't he seen to it that she be educated in Western ways as well as the Chinese classics? Wasn't she recognized among the clan as the favored daughter of the Kuang patriarch? Why did he raise her hopes when he knew they would only be dashed?

Now her step-brothers and cousins would laugh at her. The children of the great-aunts and uncles who lived in the compound would find another reason to taunt her; and her grandmother, Mahwu, would smirk, nod her head, and point her boney finger. How could she face them? How could she bear becoming, not a favored wife, but an inferior concubine to some old man in a faraway city? Kulien felt as if her heart would shatter like a prized Ming vase tossed aside on a rocky path.

Suddenly the bedclothes were pulled away and Jiang stood over her, forcing a smile. "Wake up, little ladybug. You've had enough sleep."

With soft, plump fingers she patted Kulien's face, swollen from much crying, and clucked her tongue. "You'll feel better after your morning exercise. Now get up, wash your face and behave like a young lady!"

"I won't. My own father disgraces me! How can he send me away as if he didn't care? He's always loved me and treated me with honor. I've trusted him completely. How can I live without ever seeing my beloved father again? I can't bear it, Jiang. Can't you do something to change his mind? Won't you please speak to him?"

"Now, now, you know that although I've been your nursemaid and *amah* these many years, I'm but a servant. I wouldn't attempt to speak to the master about this problem." She paused as if to gain new strength. "But what about the other news he gave you? He told you about your mother, didn't he? You wanted to know; now you do."

"That wasn't exactly good news, was it? You've known all along that my mother was English, haven't you? Why didn't you tell me that I'm a half-breed, a foreign devil? It's no wonder the family shuns me."

"It is a shame," Jiang admitted, "but I was sworn to secrecy. Your father wanted to tell you on your sixteenth birthday. And, at least now you know." She reached into the deep pocket of her tunic and held out a silk bag with both hands. "Your father asked me to give you this when you awoke. He said you may do with it as you will."

Kulien stared at the red silk bag, hesitant to take it. The figures of a lion and a crown were embroidered in fine stitches of gold thread. The emblem was unlike any she had ever seen among her father's many curios. She was certain it wasn't Chinese. She looked from the bag to Jiang's stoic face. Was there a tear forming in the corner of her eye? "What is it? Where did it come from?"

"See for yourself." Jiang dropped the small parcel beside Kulien. She lifted her chin and sniffed before turning away, and then added over her shoulder. "Examine it later, but now you must go quickly to the courtyard. You don't want to keep your father waiting. As an obedient daughter, you must continue to please him before your trip to Hangchow."

Kulien had no desire to see her father or to go through the movements of *taichi,* the Great Ultimate. She had no reason to please him anymore. What difference would it make? Although she and Lufong had enjoyed the morning rendezvous for many years, she could not bear to look at him. Not after last night. There was nothing left to say.

She poked at the pouch with a forefinger before picking it up. It wasn't very large, but felt heavy, and seemed to hold several articles of varying sizes and shapes. Could it be that her father had reconsidered his decree and had given her a present to show his sorrow? Perhaps she could remain in his home until she was old and wise. She certainly had no desire to marry a man as old as her own father! If she had to marry anyone, she much preferred him to be a tall, young Englishman with golden locks. She smiled to herself. *Now that I know I'm half English, maybe the news isn't so terrible after all.* She closed her eyes against the rays of sun slanting across the room. *Oh, what a dreamer I am. I'll never be allowed to see Lord Whitfield again. Not after the words he said about my beauty.*

Her hand flew to her chest. When she left her home, she would never see her teacher again, either. Tears sprang to her eyes once more, and she brushed them away with fury. She must not hold such dreadful thoughts. She would tell Miss Whitfield about her concerns and her friend would pass the message on to her God. The Christian God, according to Elizabeth Whitfield, was interested in the details of life. Elizabeth told her that He even noticed when a small bird fell to the ground. Amazing.

As curiosity overcame her distress, Kulien untied the tasseled silk string that held the sack closed, and with her breath coming in short uneven gasps, she turned it upside down and watched the contents spill out onto the quilt. There was a silver frame with a miniature painting, a jade ring set in an ornate band of gold, a rolled-up parchment tied with a red string, and a small brooch studded with diamonds and rubies. Why had her father given her such a strange collection of items? What did they mean?

She picked up the small portrait and studied it closely. Although the image was faint, Kulien could see that it was of a Caucasian woman of great beauty. Dark curls framed her oval face, and her eyes seemed to look directly at Kulien. The mouth was slightly open in an inviting smile. A dimple studded the woman's right cheek. Kulien touched her cheek on a similar dimple. Could this be the likeness of her mother? She looked closer. At the neckline of the woman's collar was a brooch—a gold circle studded with diamonds and rubies.

Kulien picked up the brooch and stared first at the picture of the woman and then at the brooch. It was the same. This very ornament had been close to her mother's face.

A mixture of joy and sadness filled her heart as she stared at the picture. "Mama. My own mother." She studied the portrait again. "Would you have sent me away to be a concubine to an old man?"

She took a deep breath before unrolling the parchment scroll, and began to read the beautifully written English words.

"In a few days my baby will be born, a child created out of a love that is not accepted by either the English or the Chinese. God alone knows what the future holds for our child, be it a boy or a girl.

"I have a dread that sweeps over me that there is great suffering ahead, but I entrust my concerns into the hands of my Heavenly Father. If my apprehension becomes reality, I pray that our child will grow strong in character and in faith, and that this citizen of two worlds will one day bridge the great gulf that separates humankind simply because of the color of one's skin.

"Though I am physically weak today and feel life ebbing from me, I gladly give my life for my most beloved child, born out of the great love between myself, Marguerite Howard and my most treasured Kuang Lufong."

Several moments passed before Kulien realized the sun was higher in the sky. She rolled up the scroll and quickly put the items back into the bag, and hid it under her pallet to examine more carefully later. Her father would be waiting, and although she dreaded seeing him, she knew he expected her to join him.

After dressing in blue cotton pants and tunic, she twisted her hair into a long, queue-like braid, forced a smile and with renewed purpose she walked slowly down the steps to her own courtyard. As she neared the meeting place, she picked up her pace and headed toward the central courtyard situated behind the family dining hall in the northern garden.

The pathway leading to Lufong's quarters wound throughout gardens filled with trees and fragrant flowers. Gardeners spent hours every day planting and digging around the plants. Sunlight and shadows from overhanging boughs created constantly shifting patterns that changed with the rising and setting of the sun. Statues of dragons and miniature pagodas flanked the walkways. Colorful flagstones of various shapes led to ponds where goldfish darted to and fro through underwater plants, the sunlight reflecting off their shiny scales. Small mountains built of rough boulders rose up beside the central pond, creating a scene of delight for those who took time to ponder the beauty.

When Kulien reached the main courtyard, her father was nowhere in sight. Either he had completed his exercise without her, or had left for his post in Shantung Province. He was often gone for months at a time, but she had hoped to see him, to seek to persuade him to change his plans for her future. She stood in the center of the courtyard for several minutes turning over in her mind the events of the past twelve hours. Her mother was English; her father had gone against his family's wishes in marrying her; her grandfather had committed suicide to save face; and her destiny was to leave her home to become a concubine in a family shamed by Kuang Lufong.

Kulien tossed her head to shake off the depressing thoughts, and stepped into the first position of *Taichichaun.* As she lifted her arms, energy and serenity began to flow throughout her body. She walked slowly, deliberately through each concentrated motion, head and neck erect, her breathing deep and even. Soft breezes tinkled delicate wind chimes and ruffled emerald leaves overhead. *Are they whispering secrets to me? Do they want to tell me how to escape my destiny?* She shifted her weight holding an imaginary ball. Her father's words from her childhood came to mind, "Make your stride as quietly as a cat walks, and your exertion as mild as reeling raw silk from a cocoon." Time passed unnoticed until she reached the final movements.

"Draw a deep breath and lower hands to hips." She brought her feet together, bowed her head and swallowed the *dew of life* that had gathered in her mouth. She had finished the meditation, and although completed only through a sense of habit, Kulien felt revived, ready to face another day.

A rustling sound near the lotus pond caught her attention and she turned, "Is that you, Sapphire Eyes?" Are you trying to snatch away another goldfish, you naughty cat?"

She skipped across the flagstone pavement to a grassy area and dropped to her knees near the black granite boulders of a miniature mountain. "Here, Kitty. Where are you?" Her eyes roved around the garden and fastened on the pond. "Sapphire, come here."

Instead of a soft "*meow*," the harsh, guttural voice of Ohchin, her step-brother, broke the serenity of the morning. "It's not your scrawny cat that comes looking for you, Bitter Seed. Get off your hands and knees and show respect to your father's son."

Kulien rose quickly and clenched her hands into a tight ball at her waist. With eyes fastened on blades of grass growing through cracks of the flagstones, she concentrated on the words of Confucius about honoring her superiors. Ohchin and his twin brother, Sunfu, were, in truth, her deceased grandfather's sons born of a favored concubine, Yingsi. After Kuang Linho's death, Lufong had given Yingsi a home; and because he had no male heirs, he had chosen to make his half-brothers step-sons.

Sunfu actually held an honored place in the clan because he was the first born of the twins, coming twenty-five minutes before Ohchin. However, he seemed to care little for the prestige, and spent more time away from the compound than was acceptable. So Ohchin, proud of Lufong's favoritism, used his position in the family to torment Kulien on any occasion.

She clamped her teeth together and imagined a giant phoenix snatching him by his long queue and carrying him off to a high mountain peak, preferably somewhere in Tibet! The thought brought a faint smile to her lips.

"What do you have to smile about, ugly goose? You bring nothing but shame to this family, and I rejoice in the day that you leave this compound forever."

Kulien slowly lifted her eyes. Ohchin's knee-high satin boots were spread apart and planted firmly in front of the moon gate entrance to the garden. He wore a blue silk gown and trousers similar to their father's. Over that was a short jacket with wide, loose sleeves. When Ohchin passed the last two of three civil service examinations, he would walk in Kuang Lufong's footsteps as a full-fledged mandarin to the Hsien Feng Emperor of the Ching Dynasty.

"You disgust me," he said in a low guttural voice.

Kulien met his pebble-hard eyes. "Why do you say that?" Her words were faint in spite of her determination to stand up to him. "Why do you hate me so? I have never done anything to harm you."

"I've always hated you!" He pointed at her shoes. "Those unbound feet of a peasant bring shame upon any high Chinese family. They're the gunboat feet of the *fankuei,* the foreign devil, who teaches you English. I hate everything the barbarian represents. I can never forgive your father for bringing that big nose into our compound." He shook a finger in her face. "And I'll never forgive him for bringing you into this family. You don't belong here—you half-breed!" His voice rose in volume with each word.

"But I find comfort in knowing you'll soon be sent away to the Kong clan where you'll be just another concubine." He lifted his nose as if sniffing the air. "And your ally and favorite step-brother, Sunfu, will no doubt give up his rights in the family to follow his so-called secret society. He's no better than you are. But that's all to my benefit, isn't it? I shall take his place as master of this clan when Kuang Lufong passes beyond the Yellow Springs."

Ohchin turned to leave the courtyard, and glanced over his shoulder. "Your father has business outside the compound today, so don't plan to whine to him about this conversation."

Kulien watched her step-brother as he disappeared through the moon gate, his Manchu queue swinging with each stride. He was so unlike Sunfu that it was difficult to believe they were brothers, much less twins.

With her head bowed, she wandered through the garden to the red crescent bridge that crossed a narrow stream. The pebbled pathway on the other side of the stream led beyond the woods to the estate's far northeastern boundary. Slowing to a snail's pace, she sauntered down the path bordering the stream. The path was overgrown with wild plants and weeds because the gardeners neglected this area of woods that held a forbidden place—the summerhouse. Now and then, she stooped to pick up a smooth stone, rolled it between her fingers, and tossed it into the shallow stream that gurgled among the rocks. Although apprehensive after hearing about her grandfather's suicide in the summerhouse, she was drawn by an unseen force. Fear and curiosity stirred her heart as she approached the small building.

Suddenly, the labyrinth of tangled trees and vines separated to reveal an open area. There it was—a place of death and evil spirits. Kulien struggled against the weakness in her knees, wrapped her arms tightly around herself and exhaled sharply. Mid-morning sun glinted off the blue tiles of the pavilion, and Kulien forced herself to take a fresh look at her surroundings before entering. Some of the tiles had fallen from the moss-covered roof, and the once vermilion paint had peeled and faded from the wooden columns leaving only a pinkish hue. Until today the deserted house had seemed beautiful, untamed and natural—a little like herself. But now she knew the full story of her birth, why her grandfather died—and where.

She stomped a foot. "I'll not allow ghosts of the past to rob me of the only privacy I can find in this busy compound. Leave, Spirit of Kuang Linho. Go to your ancestors and let the living have peace!" she shouted into the air.

Infused with courage, Kulien went up the two steps leading into the wide latticed room where the sun barely shone through twisted vines that clung to outside walls almost covering the windows. Glancing over her shoulder to be sure she wasn't followed, she raced across the tiled floor and dropped to a padded mat in the corner. She pulled back one corner and lifted out the forbidden foreign book entitled, "The Holy Bible." Miss Whitfield had given it to her, she said, as a study in literature. Kulien had never spoken to anyone about the book, but kept it for her own secret reading.

The thin delicate pages rustled as she turned to the place where she had left off. As a student of English for only three years, she found many of the words and ideas difficult to comprehend, but her favorite stories were of the man called Jesus. As she reread the story of his raising a dead girl to life, her heart warmed at the idea of a man who cared so much for an inferior female.

Kulien turned her thoughts to Lord Marshall Whitfield. The sight of him frightened yet entranced her. He was so tall, his shoulders so broad, his voice so booming. Yet his manner was gentle, and his words kind. He had said she was beautiful, and that he admired her beauty. Could it be in the plan of the gods that this foreigner would help her escape the prison Lufong had contracted for her future? A cold breeze suddenly swept through the summerhouse ruffling the pages of the book and sending a chill over Kulien. The grandfather's spirit was angry.

Kulien replaced the book under the mat and ran from the summerhouse, her long braid flying out behind her. She dared not look back in case the old man's ghost pursued her through the woods. Would this secret hideaway no longer welcome her? She must have a place to be alone, to consider the future, to plan. She would just have to think about it. After all, she had as much right to the summerhouse as the angry spirit of Kuang Linho.

FOUR

"Kulien, the sun sits on the wall, and still you sleep. What ails you?" Jiang pulled back the filmy curtains around Kulien's bed and rested a cool hand on the girl's brow. "What are you thinking about that causes you to frown so? Are you up to some mischief, my pet?"

"I was awake most of the night," she said, turning her face to the wall. "I have thoughts and plans that I don't want to share, not even with you."

"Thoughts of your marriage bed in the Kong household, I suppose." Jiang's lips curved in a crooked smile.

"How can you say that? I can only imagine that the old Kong patriarch is as ugly as a toad! I will be just a disgusting concubine!"

Kulien sat up and unwound her braid, combing her fingers through the long strands of jet black hair. "If you must know, I wasn't thinking of marriage at all. I hate the thought. I'd rather die." She glanced over Jiang's shoulder to the open window. "I was wondering what it would be like to go outside these walls. There's so much to see of the world. I suppose that even though I detest the thought of leaving home to marry that frog, I will at least get a look at the world on the journey to Hangchow."

"Oh, you will see nothing on that trip," Jiang snapped back.

"And why not? Am I blind?" Kulien tossed her head so the long tresses covered her face.

"Your face will be covered to be sure, but not with your hair. You'll wear a thick veil and the curtains will be tightly sealed on your sedan. I will be with you though. You'll be safe."

"If I can't see, I won't go." Kulien swept back her hair and lifted her chin.

Jiang sighed as she pulled back the quilt. "That's enough. It's time for your bath. And..." Jiang frowned while reaching into the depths of her tunic, "perhaps you are ready to see what the foreigners left for your birthday, though I totally disapprove of your receiving it."

The gift. Kulien, in her sorrow, had forgotten that Miss Whitfield and her brother had brought a gift. Her face brightened as she held out both hands. Jiang, expressing her displeasure with a grunt, placed a lotus blossom box in them. *How beautiful.* Kulien touched the lid covered with pink silk petals. The stitching was intricate; the artistry delicate.

"Well, are you going to open it or not?" Jiang's curiosity seemed to overcome her disdain.

Kulien smiled at her *amah.* "I think I'll wait until tomorrow. I'm not really that interested; and I know you don't approve. Besides," she teased, "who knows that perhaps *kuei,* evil spirits of the foreign devils, will jump from the box and crawl under your blouse?" Kulien reached for Jiang's soft waist and began to tickle her.

"Stop that, you naughty girl. Your attitude appears to change as the sun rises in the east." Jiang paled and she lowered her voice. "You could be right. I believe the barbarians cast a spell over you. I watched from the shadows and saw how that long-legged jackal eyed you. I didn't miss the way you pranced down the pathway either. With your big feet, you don't need to sway your hips like that!"

Kulien fastened her eyes on Jiang as she set the box on the bed beside her. "Speaking of bound feet, you promised to tell me why our women have to endure such pain and misery. I hear my cousins crying in the night as their toes are broken and bound back with tight bandages."

"Never mind that now. Open up the gift, and perhaps before your bath I'll tell you why and how the custom began."

Satisfied for the moment, Kulien's inquisitiveness about the gift overcame her long-held questions about footbinding. She picked up the box, holding it in one hand as she lifted the lid. Inside, on a bed of red satin, rested a delicately-carved ivory comb. She took it out and for several moments traced the images of roses and butterflies with the tip of a forefinger. "It is most lovely," she said, fastening it on one side of her hair. "I wonder if Miss Whitfield chose it, or perhaps the 'long-legged jackal' thought it would add to my beauty. He did say I was beautiful, you know."

Jiang bowed her head and murmured, "You'll be the death of me yet—just you wait and see."

Kulien plumped the down feather pillow and lay back smiling at Jiang's stricken expression. With a twinkle still in her eyes she lifted first one leg, then the other, twisting and turning her feet and stretching her toes. "There's time for my bath later. First you must tell me why our women bind their feet. I cover my ears when I hear my cousins crying in pain. I feel sorry for them yet they hobble around me with their noses in the air. They call me 'camel feet' and 'lotus boats' as if I should envy them. I don't. I hate them! They're jealous of my father's attention, and wish they could run and play like I do."

Jiang walked to a low stool covered with a purple cushion. She lowered herself onto it before pointing to her own four-inch slippers. "I remember the footbinding as a young child. Even though I was not born in great wealth as you were, my mother insisted on the tradition. Of course that was before my brother arrived. After his birth, as the first-born son, my family disowned me and sent me away to fend for myself on the streets of Shanghai. She glanced again at her feet. "My lotuses are not as delicate as the wealthy girls in this clan. The ideal is less than three inches long."

"I know all that." Kulien's words rang with impatience. "But why do it? It's a horrible custom and a cruelty to women!"

"Oh, you are edgy this morning, aren't you? I pity the old Kong gentleman who gets you for a bride--a big mouth along with big feet."

Jiang watched Kulien clamp her lips in a narrow slash, and began to speak with authority. "The practice (if you must know) began in the tenth century with the palace dancers. Those girls walked with tiny mincing steps, and the craze soon spread throughout the country. My mother told me that Confucians only *tolerate* women, and the crippling keeps them close to home. As you already know, the wrapping begins when a girl is four years old, and it takes about two years to permanently break the foot so the toes rest against the sole."

Kulien winced at the thought. "But why do they call them 'golden lotuses'? There is no resemblance to the beautiful lotus blossom. Those deformed feet are ugly."

"Let me think," Jiang said, lifting a small booted foot. "There's a story about a favored palace concubine who was a gifted dancer. The ruler had a golden lotus platform built for her to dance upon. She was ordered to bind her feet with white silk." Jiang shrugged her plump shoulders. "That's the romantic story, but the true reason the custom continued is because men like them. There's a saying, 'Why must the foot be bound? To prevent barbarous running around!' Men want women to stay in their rooms and remain uneducated."

"I would never do such a cruel thing to a daughter of mine."

"Yes, you will. Kong will insist. You will have to learn to be submissive and obey your master."

"Never! I will die first. Kong Litang will have to accept me as I am, a big-footed, independent, half-breed woman who reads and writes both Chinese and English." Kulien's words and tone were assertive, but in her heart, she feared the worst. What would become of her? How could she ever live as a submissive concubine?

She shrugged her shoulders. "I don't know why you didn't tell me this before. You said I was too young to know the details and 'mystery' surrounding footbinding. What's all the mystery?"

"Well," Jiang said, inhaling deeply, "it's a very personal subject, but since you'll soon go to Kong Litang, I will explain." She folded her hands in her lap before continuing. "Walking on bound feet broadens the hips and tightens a woman's *'jade gate'* so she brings greater pleasure to her man. The small foot also arouses both pity and lust. For a man to caress a woman's foot declares his ownership."

Kulien leaped from her bed and paced the room. "That's revolting. My feet are normal—and so am I. I'll not be owned by any man, especially Kong Litang. My father can't do this to me."

Jiang rose from the stool and tugged at a long satin rope to summon the houseboys to bring pitchers of warm water for Kulien's bath. She seemed to be talking more to herself than Kulien. "The Kong clan is highly respected in the great city of Hangchow. You should be happy instead of complaining."

Jiang's lips pulled downward and her tone changed. "I worry about you. It's that *fankuei*, the foreign devil teacher, who puts all these defiant ideas into your mind. Your father's preferential treatment (forgive me for speaking against my master) hasn't helped you to grow in obedience and filial duty, either. Any other girl would be thrilled to be accepted into such wealth."

Jiang continued to mumble to herself as she received pitchers of warm water from four houseboys as they filed into the room. After setting the pitchers on the floor, they backed out, their heads bowed. Jiang lifted one pitcher after the other and poured streams of fresh warm water into a large porcelain tub with hand-painted flowers. "Not everyone would be so tolerant to accept a woman with unbound feet, and a mixed race at that. You should thank the gods your honorable father could make such a contract."

"Oh, Jiang, you pretend that you don't know why Father is sending me to the Kong compound. You know he married an English woman against the family's wishes when he was contracted to marry a Kong bride. Father believes that Grandfather roams the countryside to avenge his death." She bit the edge of her lip. "I'm not to blame for what my father did in his youth, so why should I have to pay with my life? Haven't I as much right to marry a man of my own choice as well?"

At Jiang's insistence, Kulien strolled across the room to stand beside the tub of water. She let the nightgown fall around her ankles in a pool of pink silk. "I'm no more than a ransom in my father's eyes. And he tricked me into believing I was his favored daughter." Against her will, tears rolled down her cheeks as she eased her slender body into the warm water.

Jiang used a dipper to scoop up some of the bath water to pour over Kulien's head, still speaking to herself in low tones. Finally, she spoke aloud, "He didn't trick you! Your honorable father has always treated you with favor. You can't deny that."

"Not so much as he honors my stepbrothers. They're not even of his seed. I've known for many moons that Ohchin and Sunfu were Grandfather's sons born of Yingsi, *his* concubine." She sighed as she lay back, resting her arms on the sides of the tub. "Why did my Father allow Yingsi to live in an apartment of her own and make her sons, his half-brothers, heirs to rule our clan? I'll never understand the ways of our people!"

Jiang only clucked her tongue and poured another pitcher of water into the tub before leaving the room. She stopped in the doorway to glance back at Kulien. "It's not for you to understand, but only to obey!"

As Kulien watched her go, she thought, *I have two faces. I love my father and want to please him, yet I want to think for myself, and choose my own husband, just as he chose his own wife.* She sank deeper into the water and rested her heels on the end of the tub. Twisting her feet this way and that, she spoke aloud to herself, "If Confucianism teaches us to preserve our bodies intact because they're the gift of our ancestors, it's wrong for men to insist our feet be mutilated! At least my father spared me that."

Jiang hobbled back into the room. "Why do you keep harping on that subject?" she demanded as she poured the last pitcher of warm water into the tub. "It's no concern of yours. You'll never have 'golden lotuses.'"

"But if I ever have a daughter..... Oh, I can't bear the thought of that old man touching me. I will never have his children. I'll die first." Kulien twisted her long hair into a tight rope, wringing the water out of it before she stepped out of the tub.

Jiang huffed and panted her displeasure as she wrapped a towel around Kulien and began to vigorously rub her body dry. "Your words are haughty, my little one. I predict by this time next year, Litang's boy-child will be growing here." She patted Kulien's stomach.

"Well, you can take your predictions to the temple and burn them," Kulien said just loud enough for Jiang to hear. To herself she thought, *I'll think of a way to avoid Litang and his possession of me. I don't know how yet, but I'll think of a way.*

Later that day, after successfully avoiding not only her father, but also the rest of the family by hiding behind bushes and screens, Kulien returned to her rooms to meditate and find solace in her music. Dusk painted the room in a soft rosy glow, and although the air was heavy and humid, she burned incense while strumming the seven-stringed *ching*. As peace and serenity filled her spirit, she put aside worries of the impending marriage and the heartache she suffered because of her father's decision. Even thoughts of the handsome Englishman and dreams of faraway places dissipated in the rising vapors of fragrant smoke and ancient melodies.

"Kulien." Jiang came into the room, her eyes wide and her hands fluttering like moths over a flame. "Your father waits at the courtyard gate. He insists on speaking with you before he leaves for his post in Shantung Province."

"I will not see him," she said, without looking up and continuing to stroke the strings. "He has lost face with me."

"I can't tell him you refuse to see him. He will be angry with me as well as with you."

"Yes, you can tell him. I don't care if he is angry." Kulien continued to pluck the soothing melody, but her heart raced with fear. She had never defied her father's wishes in all her life, because she had loved and respected him. But now.... If he ordered her to come, she would have to obey, but until then she would ignore his request.

"This he brings on himself," Jiang muttered. "He has given you too much freedom. You've always done as you pleased, now look at the pigeon that has come home to roost!"

"You speak the truth," Kulien said, without looking up from her instrument.

"I still believe with all that is in me that the foreigner he brought in to teach you English has captured your spirit." Jiang scurried about the room on her tiny feet, her voice rising with each step. "That woman cast a spell on you. Even worse, you've been in a trance since you looked at the eyes of that brother of hers." By now Jiang's voice hung on the edge of panic. "How can I tell the patriarch his daughter refuses to see him? He'll be furious!"

Kulien lifted her chin as she walked away from the *ching* to stare out the window. "Tell him I suffer the pain of women. Tell him whatever you wish, but I won't see him. Not yet."

"Oh, dear. Oh, dear," Jiang muttered as she disappeared down the short stairway and fled to the outer court where Kuang Lufong paced.

"My daughter *cannot* see me? Or *will* not?" Lufong's voice echoed through the small courtyard to the upper story rooms.

Kulien hid in the shadows where she could hear Jiang's excuses. "She—she suffers with pain today, most honorable. You know how it is with women?" The *amah*'s voice trembled with the spoken lie.

By now the two were in the center of the courtyard outlined by the orange glow of a nearby lantern. Kulien watched from the darkened window, straining to hear every word. Lufong clenched his jaw and pulled at his goatee, speaking quietly to Jiang, too softly for Kulien to hear.

Then Jiang's voice rang out, "The barbarian is a bad influence. She plants seed thoughts in Kulien's mind that grow and choke out the traditions of our ancestors. And that foreign devil's brother has captured my baby's heart. She talks about him day and night." Jiang began to cry. "Oh, whatever will we do? Please, sir, I am most worried."

Lufong patted Jiang's shoulder and nodded. "I appreciate your concern, Jiang. You are a faithful and loving *amah* to my child. But she will leave here in less than six months, and she is very fond of Miss Whitfield. The woman will no longer be allowed to come as often, but I can see no harm in her coming for an occasional visit. The brother, however, is forbidden to be in my daughter's presence again. He will not enter the walls of this compound unless I invite him—and that will not happen," he added.

Kuang Lufong glanced toward Kulien's rooms. "Let her have these last weeks in her home doing the things she enjoys. Miss Whitfield makes her laugh, and I won't deny her that small pleasure."

Kulien pressed a hand to her heart. Oh, joy. Elizabeth Whitfield would still be her teacher and friend, and perhaps Father could change his mind and invite Lord Whitfield for an audience. She would at least catch a glimpse of him again—if only from behind a curtain. *Oh, may it be so!*

FIVE

As one long day blended into another, Kulien's unhappiness became her constant companion. She spent long hours daydreaming of the Englishman who had thought she was beautiful, and long nights filled with horrifying dreams of the man she was destined to marry. She had always felt loved by her father and believed he had a good and prosperous plan for her future. The disappointment and grief in learning of the unchangeableness of a union with the Kong clan had erected a wall of bitterness between them. The only hope she had within the compound was that Sunfu, her step-brother, would soon return from wherever he had gone.

Although Sunfu was, in reality, her uncle they preferred to think of themselves as brother and sister. Sunfu was like her in many ways. He was untraditional in his thinking, often disappearing for weeks, only to return with new ideas from the south of China. She loved listening to his stories, and he enjoyed her companionship, too, for she was the only one in the compound with whom he could speak freely.

One afternoon when Miss Whitfield came to instruct Kulien in her English lessons, Kulien ventured to ask, "I thought my father would invite your brother to meet with him, but he hasn't come. Is there a problem?" She held her breath, waiting for the teacher's reply.

Elizabeth Whitfield smoothed the folds of her heavy gray skirt before folding her hands neatly in her lap. Her blue eyes fastened on Kulien and a crease appeared between her dark brows. "My brother received word that your father was often away on business and could not meet with him. He was disappointed, but hopeful. He thought Kuang Lufong was a most intelligent man who would grant him an audience."

Kulien rose from the stool where she sat at Elizabeth's feet and spread her hands encompassing the garden classroom. "Father was here for a short time though I was told that he recently left for Shantung Province. I don't know how long he'll be away this time. Perhaps when he returns from Shantung, he will summon your brother. He seemed pleased to hear about his travels."

Miss Whitfield rose to join her near a small pool where carp darted between black granite boulders. "I believe I know the answer, Kulien. Marshall was taken by your beauty, and I'm sure that both you and your father were aware of his interest in you. He doesn't hide his feelings well; perhaps because he's inexperienced in the ways of the Orient. I'm sure that your father's greatest desire is to protect you from harm. Besides, I have learned that you're to be married soon." Her voice was soothing and low. "It's for the best, you know."

For the remainder of the English lesson, Kulien fought to control her tears. It was not for *her* best! Did Miss Whitfield know that the marriage was arranged due to Lufong's disobedience, and had resulted in her grandfather's suicide? Would Miss Whitfield approve of a sham marriage in which her favored student would be no more than an unwanted concubine in far away Hangchow? Kulien's heritage was a product of both China and Great Britain! Dare she confess the secret to her teacher? She should have the privilege to choose her own husband as her father had chosen his own wife. It was wrong for him to insist that she follow the antiquated promise made so many moons ago—a promise that even he broke.

Weeks passed, and mid-summer heats began, one long, sultry day melting into the next. The large Kuang compound seemed to grow with inhabitants as Kuang Lufong's brother's wives and concubines bore more children. Mahwu, the matriarch, held the primary role inside the compound and each morning all the women and girls would gather in her spacious rooms to embroider and gossip. Other than the morning hours, the women seldom left their apartments until the sun had set. Kulien, of course, was excluded from most meetings, and was even more persecuted since the compound had learned of her mixed heritage and rapidly approaching marriage.

The men and boys of the family disappeared each morning only to appear as if by magic when the delectable aromas of the evening meal wafted from the kitchen and it was time for everyone within the compound to gather in the main dining hall.

Kulien's loneliness grew with each passing day. Her father's stay at his Shantung post seemed longer than usual, increasing her sense of isolation. Even her *amah*, Jiang, wore a cloak of detachment that excluded Kulien. Her only comfort was the rumor that her father had promised Miss Whitfield that she could occasionally visit Kulien until the time of her arranged marriage.

Life as Kulien had known it was over. She was a prisoner in her own compound, and would soon be a prisoner in Kong Litang's clan.

Flowers faded and dropped their petals while smoke trees at the far corner of the estate flamed with an early autumnal glow. The late humid summer cast its brilliance over the trees as blossoms from once-colorful roses fell to the ground. With her father gone and Miss Whitfield's limited visits, Kulien spent most of the time in her rooms, continuing to practice English and dreaming of a life where she could make her own choices. Her dreams of freedom were only that, however. In less than two moons, about six weeks, she was destined to leave her family compound for Hangchow—and slow death.

Jiang could see Kulien's unhappiness and regretted her attitude of distance. She stepped into the room one evening with an announcement, "I know what will bring the blush of the lotus back to your pale cheeks. Look what I have here."

Kulien paid little attention to the *amah's* words and continued to pluck the strings of her musical instrument while musky vapors of incense filled the room. As a favored female in a wealthy family she had learned to play the *ching,* to excel in chess, and to master calligraphy and painting. But now, she had no one to challenge her in chess, and didn't feel up to painting. For days she had found some relief and serenity of spirit through her music.

"Come, child," Jiang pleaded after several moments, "please eat something. You invite the gods to take away your spirit before it is time." Jiang rested a plump hand on Kulien's arm. "Please?"

"I'm not hungry. And my spirit has no reason to stay. My father no longer loves me, and is sending me away to be a slave to a strange, and probably cruel man!"

Kulien's shoulders began to shake as springs of bitterness broke through the shell she had formed around her heart. She threw herself into Jiang's open arms and sobbed.

"There, there, my baby. Let the waters of the soul purge the poison that has gathered. You'll feel better."

Jiang held Kulien in her arms rocking her back and forth as she had many years ago. When there were no more tears, Kulien rested her head on Jiang's bosom, exhausted. She sniffed and spoke in a muffled voice, "I'm so unhappy. So alone." She looked into Jiang's eyes and touched the soft cheek with her fingertips. "I thought that you, too, had forsaken me."

"I have been a bad *amah*! I have treated you cruelly when you needed someone to love and listen to you. Please forgive me. I felt so helpless, and didn't know how to comfort you. I promise to be here as long as you need me. But look," she said releasing Kulien's hold, "see what I've brought."

Jiang lifted the lid from an iron kettle, and Kulien stared at the green seeds floating on the surface of steaming water. "What is it?"

"This is a very special fresh lotus seed soup that is good for old people. But it also gives new life to a young person whose spirit is weak."

Jiang dipped chopsticks into the hot water to extract one of the seeds, and began to roll it between her palms. When the skin fell away, she pricked at the seed with an embroidery needle until she removed the embryo. "The sprout is bitter," she said, "but the meat of the seed is sweet."

"It looks like so much work." Kulien watched in silence as Jiang removed several sprouts.

After she added the seeds back to the hot water, she ladled out a bowlful for each of them. They sat on low stools sipping the soup until it was gone. "I do feel stronger, Jiang. I truly do! And I don't feel so sad anymore. You must be a priestess or a doctor!"

Jiang returned her smile, "Oh, no child. Lotus seed soup is an old remedy. When I was a little girl, my mother's servant would take me to the charcoal stove, give me lotus seed soup and tell wonderful stories about the Monkey King! That was before my brother was born—before I was cast out of the house as a despised female." Jiang's smile became a scowl as she remembered her fractured childhood. Kulien's heart ached for her *amah* and the hard life she must have had.

"But now," Jiang said, dismissing the shame of her youth, "you must feel better, so I want you to put away your disappointments and fears and remember your Chinese heritage. Forget what you learned about your mother. You are not a foreign devil, but a child of the Middle Kingdom."

"You're wrong, Jiang. I am as much British as I am Chinese. I won't forget the heritage of my father *or* my mother. She died giving me life. How could you ask me to forget her?"

Jiang's eyes hardened and her voice was sharp. "The seasons are ordered by destiny. There is a time for good and a time for evil. It's true, I don't have your education, but the little learning I have enables me to accept life as it comes. You must learn the same—or you will have nothing but sorrow as your life companion."

"I cannot. I will not accept the future my father has chosen for me. I must have some rights as a citizen of two worlds."

"No child. You are of China—and that cannot be changed regardless of your stubbornness! You must accept the course of events as it unfolds. Do not practice the impatience and dissatisfaction of the Western world. Let go of the evil brought here by that Whitfield woman! Let go of your foolish dreams of escaping the plans of the gods!"

Kulien said nothing as Jiang led her to the bed and folded the silk sheet under her chin. "When your father returns from Shantung, you will go to him as in the past—with respect and honor. Besides," she said, patting Kulien's cheeks, "once you are in Hangchow, you will find happiness. I hear it is a beautiful city situated on a lovely lake."

But Kulien, though silent with her thoughts, had not given up. Before that late autumn day arrived, she would find a way to keep from going to Hangchow and the impending marriage to Kong Litang.

SIX

Safely protected behind the walls of the Kuang clan, Kulien knew little of the rebellion carried on by the Taipings, a dissenting group of peasants set to overthrow the Manchu Empire. She had learned from her teacher, Miss Whitfield, that the founder of the movement, Hung Hsiu-chuan, in order to deceive, had used Christian catchwords in propagating destruction and cruelty upon those who opposed them. In the wake of their advancing horde, they had murdered innocent people, and destroyed temples, works of art, bronzes, paintings and books. Only this past spring had they overcome the high-walled city of Nanking, making it their capital.

From earlier conversations overheard between her father and Ohchin, Kulien feared that Sunfu, her favorite step-brother, who always seemed to look for trouble, was involved. What would happen to him? Why had he turned away from the beliefs and customs of his own heritage? Were they so alike, this young man and herself?

Kulien pondered these questions as she continued to pray for a way out of the impending marriage to Kong Litang. She prayed to Kuanyin, Goddess of Mercy; but without an answer to her prayers, the future looked bleak and unbearable.

To occupy herself and hoping to forget her troubles, she continued to read poetry by the Tang dynasty poet, Li Po, and practiced her calligraphy with a passion. This evening she had been at her desk for two hours. She rubbed the ebony-colored ink stick against a flat oval stone, and then mixed ground powder of pine soot and glue with water until the substance was thick, the texture of fine oil. Careful to hold the fox hair brush at just the right angle, Kulien copied an ancient poem about a fair-haired lover who could not be forgotten.

Tears formed in the corners of her eyes and spilled over her cheeks and onto the parchment as she worked. Would she ever see the tall Englishman again? Would Marshall Whitfield find a way to regain her father's confidence? Perhaps it was foolish to think of him, but his eyes had touched hers with a promise. She looked up from her work. Why did she allow her imagination to soar like this? Was it as Jiang had said, "You are influenced by Western teaching…and it is eating your spirit"? Kulien's cousins were content to obey their elders, and all the aunts made obeisance to the grandmother every morning—with sweet smiles pasted on their faces. Was she so different because her mother had been British? Or was it because her father had raised her to think for herself? Surely he must understand why she could not accept the marriage he planned for her!

Kulien wiped the tears from her eyes and prepared to make the last downward stroke when the brush slipped, dragging a long black smudge across the translucent paper. *"Aiyah!"* She cried, and flung the brush across the room, spattering ink on the silk carpet. With the other hand, she snatched up the ink stone and hurled it through the open window where it clattered onto the flagstones below.

Patience was for turtles! She was tired, too tired to practice any longer. Her painstaking work had been destroyed with one missed stroke, and besides it was long past her bedtime.

She blew out the candle before leaning over the window ledge to look for the ink stone in the darkened courtyard. It was no doubt shattered in many pieces, but morning would be soon enough to gather up the fragments—before a family member could chide her for a bad disposition. She started to turn from the window when she heard a sound near the wall. Curious, she fixed her eyes on the movement of a shadowy bush. Something or someone was in the courtyard. "Sapphire," she called softly. She waited for the familiar, *"meow,"* but there was only silence, no sign of her cat. Suddenly, although there was not the slightest breeze, leaves of a bamboo bush quivered in the moonlight.

"Who's there?" she called again, this time a little louder. Still no answer. Who could be in the garden this time of night? Jiang had retired to her quarters hours ago; her rhythmic snores penetrated the quietness. Ohchin had not yet returned from the examination halls—thank the gods! And she knew her father was still at his post in Shantung Province. Could Sunfu possibly have come back to the compound? Oh, how she longed to see him. He had been gone for months and she missed him more than she could say.

With questions still rambling through her mind, Kulien undressed and climbed into bed. Perhaps it was all in her imagination after all. It must have been only a breeze blowing through the empty patio. Kulien closed her eyes, settled herself, and pulled the silk quilt over her head. In the morning when she swept up her broken ink stone, she would also search for signs of an intruder in the garden, be it cat or human. She fell asleep with romantic thoughts of the tall Englishman sneaking into her garden to take her away to foreign lands where he would love and care for her.

"Here is your ink stone, little sister." He held out both hands with broken pieces of stone before setting them on the floor. "Were you trying to kill your favorite brother?"

Kulien's heart pounded as she rubbed her eyes and stared into the semi-darkness. Sunfu knelt beside her bed, the corner of the quilt in his hand. She could barely see his silhouette outlined by the moon's rays filtering through the latticework of her window.

"Sunfu!" Kulien's voice caught in her throat as she recognized her midnight caller. He placed his fingers over her lips, and whispered, "Shh, don't speak, my lovely little sister. You are the only one who knows I've returned, and I know I can trust you to keep my secret."

Kulien reached out to touch Sunfu's arm and spoke softly, "I'm so happy to see you. Where have you been? Quick! Light a candle so I can see you better." She sniffed the air and shivered. "What is that unpleasant odor on you?" An acrid, coppery smell emanated from Sunfu's clothing as he left her bedside and moved toward the table. She watched his form cross the room, then the soft glow from the candle's flame revealed his face—a face she no longer recognized.

Kulien stared at his hair and gasped. "Your queue is gone! What have you done? Your hair hangs loose to your shoulders." Fear of his answer stopped her questions, and she covered her mouth with cold fingertips.

"I'll tell you later. I've been waiting in the courtyard for hours." A smile barely touched his eyes. "You almost hit me with your ink stone." Creases marred his forehead. "The compound is quiet for everyone sleeps soundly now. You must come with me while it is safe."

"Come with you? I don't understand. Where do you want me to go? I'm afraid, Sunfu."

"Please trust me, Kulien. You know I would never harm you. You are the only one in our family I can trust. Although I have a twin brother, we are as far apart as east and west—or as north is from south." Sunfu turned his back and stood at the doorway of her room. "Please, dress quickly and come with me."

Against her doubts and better judgment, Kulien slipped back into the cotton tunic and trousers she had left beside her bed, shoved her feet into cotton felt-soled shoes, and blew out the candle. She let Sunfu take her hand and lead her down the stairway, through the moon gate and over the winding pathway to the main courtyard. Whatever was in her brother's mind? Why had she relented and come with him? He turned to look at her and his warm grasp of her hand and soft brown eyes assured her that his purpose had to be a good one or he would never have involved her.

They stopped at the ebony spirit screen, painted with red dragons that guarded the outer gate. A large white cat, chained to the screen to frighten away evil spirits, blinked his eyes, stretched, meowed weakly, and then curled up into a ball evidently unconcerned with invisible devils.

"Come, quickly now," Sunfu urged, stepping around the screen.

"But I could never go outside the walls without a special prayer from the priest." Stories remembered from childhood flooded her thoughts. "*Kuei,* evil spirits, wait outside. No, Sunfu, I won't go with you. I can't!" She suddenly felt cold and began to shiver, the goose flesh rising on her arms.

"I thought you wanted to live—to know what goes on outside our compound walls."

"I do, Brother, but…."

"Don't be afraid. Come along now. I need your help. Someone, a—a friend, is injured. He needs your help, too. Please Kulien, trust me."

She held her breath while uttering a prayer to whatever god was awake this time of night, and edged around the screen, following close behind him. Sunfu pushed open the heavy wooden gate, cursing under his breath at the squeaky iron hinges. He moved along the stone wall with Kulien still clutching his hand. She dared not look up, for the trees in the woods nearby reached out spindly branches to snatch her away. What evil spirits hid in the woods that separated their compound from the family graveyard? Kulien could hardly breathe for the fear that encompassed her.

Minutes later when they reached the far corner of the north wall, Sunfu spoke in a low and commanding voice. "Don't ask any questions. Just do as I say."

Kulien clenched her teeth together and took a deep breath as she rounded the corner of the wall. She let out a gasp when Sunfu pointed to something wrapped in a dark blanket that had been hidden under a large bush. Drawing closer, she heard a groan and whoever was concealed moved slightly. Once again that distasteful coppery odor rose to assail Kulien's senses. Now she recognized the familiar smell known to women—blood.

Sunfu knelt beside the figure and tried to lift it to a sitting position. Kulien dropped to her knees next to him, but the moon had disappeared behind a cloud and it was too dark to make out the features of what appeared to be a large man.

"Who is this?" she demanded. "And why is he bleeding? Oh, what have you done? What trouble have you brought to our family?"

Sunfu sighed and bowed his head. "I only ask you to be patient, my sister. I'll give you the answers to all your questions soon. But first we must get this man to a place where we can dress his wound. He has lost much blood, and I fear for his life—and for mine if he dies."

Kulien felt anger boil within her heart in spite of her love for Sunfu. "You had no right to bring this man here! If he is one of your *secret society* members, you should have taken him to a doctor."

"You leave me no choice but to tell you the truth. I stabbed this man. It was a mistake, and if I'm found out I'll lose my head! Do you want that?"

Kulien, still angry, answered, "Let me think about it."

Sunfu's patience began to fade as his voice rose, "He's not a member of the Taipings; and we must hide him until he's strong enough..."

"Strong enough for what? To pillage another city like Nanking?"

"Kulien. Stop it. Listen to me. This man is from the British Consulate."

"The British...?" Kulien's hand flew to her breast. Could it be? No, she would not allow her imagination such an idea.

Sunfu interrupted her thoughts, "I know your secret hiding place is in the summerhouse—right behind this wall. If we work together we can get him in there where he won't be discovered. And we won't have to go through the compound."

"No. We can't do this. You must get him back to his own people. You put our entire family in danger."

Sunfu straightened and put both hands on Kulien's shoulders. "It is no use to argue with me. We can't take any more time. We must move him. I promise I'll explain all the details to you soon. You'll understand and support me, I know."

Kulien felt her resolve slip away. "But how can we lift a man over that high wall? It's impossible. Besides," she said, thinking over his last remarks, "how did you know about the summerhouse? It's been neglected and abandoned for years!"

Before answering, Sunfu busied himself, pulling away long grasses at the base of the wall, and then rolled aside several large stones. He glanced up at her over his shoulder, "Do you think you're the only one to seek privacy from the prying eyes of aunts and uncles and more cousins that I can count?"

While Sunfu spoke, he continued to pull and pry at the stones, finally removing enough to reveal a wide opening. "Now," he said, breathing heavily from the strain, "I'll crawl through first and pull. You push as hard as you can, and together we'll get the barbarian through."

Kulien doubted that it could be done, but he was so determined that she remained silent and did as she was told. It took all her strength working with Sunfu to get the man through the wall to the other side. His moans unnerved her, but she had gone too far to turn back now. After she crawled through the hole, the two of them managed to drag the man up the darkened steps and through the arched portico of the summerhouse. They laid him out on the mat she had so often rested upon as she read the forbidden book of Elizabeth's foreign religion.

Before she was able to rise to her feet, the man spoke, "Kulien, I thank you. I had hoped to see you again, but not this way."

Kulien felt the blood rush from her head as she heard the familiar voice that had echoed through her heart these many moons. She steadied herself to keep from falling, or from saying something that would cause her to lose face.

Sunfu lit a lantern before he removed the watch cap that had been pulled down low over the eyebrows of Elizabeth Whitfield's brother. Blond hair fell in limp strands on the high forehead; lips moved under the dark moustache as if to speak again; blue eyes searched Kulien's face before Lord Marshall Whitfield grimaced in pain and slipped into unconsciousness.

Kulien stared in horror, first at the Englishman, then at Sunfu. "What have you done? Why did you bring him here instead of to the Consulate? You could have taken him to the mission in Shanghai where his sister could get help!" Her eyes turned back to the man lying so still. Would he die? Her heart swelled within her breast as she took in his features. His wavy blond hair was matted with dust and sweat; scratches covered his forehead and nose. The dark moustache and beard were overgrown and untrimmed. Where had he been to have arrived here in such an appalling condition?

"Sunfu…?"

"Please, no questions now," Sunfu said, holding the lantern over the prone figure. "Open his shirt. He bleeds from a wound put there by my knife. I need for you to dress it."

"Me? I know nothing about wounds!"

With a mixture of dread and hope, Kulien took the blood-stained shirt in her hand and carefully unbuttoned the cotton fabric before pushing it aside until his chest and shoulder were exposed. She forced herself to look beyond the muscled chest to the deep wound in his left shoulder.

"Here, you hold the lantern," Sunfu said, bending over to examine the injury. The concern showed on his line-etched face when he lifted his head. "I went on a raid tonight with the Short Swords. Imperial soldiers guarded the docks while a cargo of opium was being unloaded. Our plan was to set fire to the ship, but first we had to kill the guards...."

"What? Have I lost my dearest friend who always made me laugh when Ohchin made me cry?"

Ignoring her words, Sunfu went on, "It was dark, and I thought the man standing nearby was one of the Emperor's men."

"This is the brother of my beloved teacher. He has even shared a meal with our father here in your home," she said, glancing anxiously at Marshall Whitfield.

Sunfu shook his head, the shoulder-length hair grazing his shoulders. "When I realized who he was, I was afraid I would be executed by the barbarians, and chastised by members of my own society."

Kulien stared down at the injured man. Here he was, helpless and possibly at the point of death.

"What do we know about medicine?" she asked, pressing fingers to her temples. "How are we to take care of him—and get him back to Shanghai?"

"I only know we have to stop the bleeding, and find something to fight infection." Sunfu's eyes widened. "He'll have to stay here for a few days until he regains his strength. You must get medicine, perhaps the same potion used to keep the bound feet of the girls from decay."

Kulien said nothing, touching Marshall Whitfield's face. His skin was cold and clammy and she drew back in alarm. "He might die before we can help him." As she spoke, her fear disappeared, and concern for this man she had secretly loved swept over her.

"How did you get him here all the way from the docks?" As she spoke, she knew she must find a way to bind the wound—and quickly.

"A friend helped me put him on my horse. I didn't know where else to go." Sunfu raked fingers through his hair and sighed. "Marshall Whitfield recognized me. We had met before and talked through an interpreter. Like me, he's opposed to the way the British treat our people—the way they have complete immunity from our laws. That's a crime. Even your teacher's brother believes as we do."

A moan brought Kulien to her senses. Why were they wasting time haggling over minor details? Lord Whitfield's life was slowly ebbing away; and she must keep him alive.

SEVEN

"Kulien, do something. Say something! Will you help me save this man's life? And mine?" he added. His short hair brushed his shoulders as he shifted his head in the direction of the prone figure at the far side of the summerhouse.

"Of course I'll help!" Kulien raced to the small stream that rippled nearby. Aloe plants grew in bright green clumps, and she quickly picked some of the tender shoots. Tearing at the sleeve of her cotton shirt, she pulled it from its seams and doused it in the cool water before running back up the steps and across the tiled floor. She knelt beside the man, a prayer rising from her heart.

"Get more water," she demanded, pointing to a cracked bowl that sat empty near the entrance. Sunfu obeyed, his eyebrows raised at her sudden strength. From the corner of her eyes, she watched him go, a slight smile on her lips as she took command of the situation. With the water-soaked fabric, she washed the wound, then took the fresh bowl of water and poured it over the gaping hole and his chest. Marshall Whitfield let out an involuntary gasp as cold water spilled across his fevered skin.

She pulled at the other sleeve of her tunic until it came apart, and then tore it into long strips. Kulien pinched the torn flesh together and carefully placed the leaves over the laceration before pressing a small square of fabric against the wound. A quick glance at the man's face told her he was unconscious. Without wasting a moment, she bandaged the shoulder and chest tightly so the pressure on the wound would be secure.

Sunfu dropped to his knees beside her. "You are a doctor, for certain," he said with pride. "I knew I could depend on you."

Kulien's expression betrayed her displeasure, but she attempted to assure him. "The aloe leaves have medicinal qualities. They will have to do until I can bring ointments from the house."

Together Sunfu and Kulien sighed as they silently walked to the two narrow steps at the entrance to the pavilion. When they were seated, Kulien searched his face, wanting some answers. "Now, my brother, talk!" Her tone was sharp and clear.

"The sun will soon light the rooftops, and I must be in my room before Jiang wakes up. How did you get yourself into such a situation? Have you become an outlaw?" In spite of herself, Kulien's voice rose with each word.

"I'll tell you what I can before daylight arrives." Sunfu combed long well-formed fingers through his short hair before beginning his story. "For many months, I've been a member of a secret organization, the *San Ho Hui,* the Triad Society. A chapter known as the 'Short Swords' only recently formed here in central China. Most of the members come from the south. Our motto is 'Oppose the alien Manchus and restore the Chinese Ming Dynasty.' It's not a new slogan, but one that was proclaimed as long as a century ago." He paused, seeing that Kulien waited patiently for him to continue. "That's why I cut off the Manchu queue. I want everyone to know that I am a free Chinese. I refuse to serve the Manchu pigs who rule our country!"

Kulien tried to understand Sunfu's motives. She too, longed for freedom, but was this rebellion the answer? "You know Father would not approve of your actions. You're the elder brother, born a few minutes before Ohchin." She paused, glancing up at the branches that draped the pathway. "You were chosen as the firstborn to inherit his legacy, but Ohchin is the one following in his footsteps. Why risk such a change of your destiny?"

Sunfu didn't answer, but only shrugged and lowered his eyes. "Your father, and the man I *consider* my father also, is a high official, a mandarin in the corrupt Ching Dynasty. Of course, he would not approve, therefore I shall continue to stay away from home. I strongly suspect he is aware of my allegiance to the Triads."

Kulien couldn't take her eyes off Sunfu's face. The gentleness she had loved and admired had completely vanished. He looked at her through Ohchin's stony eyes. She had lost her beloved step-brother to a fanatical group who hated all they had known as children—all that her father stood for as the honorable way of life.

A low groan from the shadowy darkness drew their attention toward the Englishman. "And what does Miss

Whitfield's brother have to do with your secret society? Kulien asked. "Is he also a member?"

Sunfu raised a fist into the air. "Of course not! Only our true Chinese brothers and sisters are members. Most of those who belong to the society are unemployed workers or poor farmers—peasants. All of our personal goods are of common ownership; there is also equal distribution of the land. The people live pure lives. In fact chastity is demanded of both men and women. No concubines or second and third wives among our members! I think you would support our doctrine if you'd give us a chance."

"Let me ask another question," Kulien interrupted, tilting her head. "If the members are poor, how can you, a step-son of a wealthy landowner, be one of them?"

Sunfu sighed before folding his fingers together. He closed his eyes a moment before answering. "You don't understand at all, do you? This movement grows, and as I said, it has spread from south to north. Leaders with education and influence are needed. Our founder seeks to bring in a peaceful kingdom. He calls our rebellion, "Taiping"—great peace. We will bring a vast and enduring change to China."

"Forgive me, but I think you're making a big mistake! You are too intelligent and well bred to be involved in such an uprising. You should prepare yourself to take the civil service examinations and be ready to rule this clan. As an official, you would be in a position to make changes the people would hear and respect."

"I can't believe you would suggest such a thing. I thought I knew you well, but it seems I've misjudged you. You led me to believe that you reject our antiquated customs as much as I do."

Kulien had no answer for Sunfu, for what he said was true about her basic beliefs. She did reject many of the customs, especially the bound feet and subservience of women. She wanted all the girls and women of the compound to know how to read and write. She decried the opulence and decadence of the Manchu Emperor and his court. Yes, Sunfu was right; she was more like him than she cared to admit.

Kulien lowered her eyes and studied the fingers entwined in her lap. After a moment, she glanced over her shoulder to take in the quiet form of Marshall Whitfield, then touched Sunfu's arm. "But you skip around my question. What has my teacher's brother to do with your secret society?"

Sunfu's voice dropped to a whisper, "Nothing. Except that he was in the wrong place at the wrong time. He's like many of the Europeans who oppose the Imperial government. Surprisingly some, like *your* Englishman, see the oppression of the poor Chinese while the wealthy live in luxury. They don't belong here!"

Kulien bristled at Sunfu's words. "He is not MY Englishman. He is the brother of my friend and teacher, Elizabeth Whitfield. I'm quite fond of her as she has opened the world to me. I care for him only because he's her brother." Kulien felt heat of the lie rise to her cheeks, and was glad for the dark shadows.

"You may say what you will," Sunfu added, "but I think the Englishman has more than a passing interest in you. I don't begrudge him because I've learned that he has an unusual sympathy toward our cause. However," Sunfu stood and gazed down at Kulien, "he had better watch himself. A passing interest I can accept, but you are Chinese—of my ancestors' blood—and no Englishman will touch you!"

Kulien's temper rose to the surface, "Then it seems you have not heard of my heritage. Father recently informed me that my mother was British, so I am only half Chinese!" She stood with hands on her hips. "You would do well to attend to your own rebellion and leave me to decide what direction my life will take." She paused and sat down as tears spilled over her smooth cheeks. "I'm a fraud, Sunfu! It seems I'm not free to decide the direction of my life after all."

Sunfu frowned and wiped at her tears with the back of his fingers. "What is it? Something has happened to change your destiny, hasn't it?"

Kulien gathered her emotions and told Sunfu about her father's contract with the Kong clan and the sham wedding ceremony soon to take place. She choked out the words, "I'm consigned *not* to be the wife of an honorable man, but a concubine in the house of a clan who was betrayed by my own father!"

"Kulien" he said, lifting her chin with a forefinger, "you should come with me, and escape this marriage. I know you would make a good Taiping! If only you could see what I've seen in my travels to the south of China. Our family lives in wealth and luxury while those people struggle to make a living." He sighed as if in great pain. "It's because of the ruling government. The Manchus are not true men of Han; they care nothing for the common man." Sunfu lifted his eyes to the graying dawn, "The Ching Dynasty must go!" He paused, waiting for her response. "I could help you, my sister," he added, his voice tender with concern.

Through the trees, a glint of light reflected off the tiled roof of the main house, and Kulien jumped to her feet. "You're a good brother, but your rebellion doesn't suit me; and I must go before Jiang discovers I'm gone." She frowned and glanced toward the still form of Marshall Whitfield. "Now we must decide what to do about the Englishman. You can't leave him here. You must take him to the Christian mission in Shanghai. Elizabeth Whitfield is there, and she'll find the medical help her brother needs."

Sunfu stood up and placed his hands on Kulien's shoulders, looking directly into her eyes. "I can't take him there. Don't you see? Not only would I be questioned and perhaps imprisoned, the other members of the society would suffer from my error in judgment. Lord Whitfield had no business being on the docks tonight. I had even warned him...." Sunfu stopped mid-sentence. "He will stay here, and you will aid him. When he awakes, you must tell him what happened and that he will be safe at our compound until he is able to return to the consulate."

Kulien's heart sank deeper with each of Sunfu's words. "It's *not* safe. He'll be discovered by someone. Then not only will he be judged, but I, too, will suffer banishment, maybe even death from our family. Please, Sunfu, be reasonable. Can't you see the danger to me? And you say you love me."

Sunfu wrapped his arms around Kulien and drew her close. "I do love you, my 'little sister.' I love you for the woman you have become. I love and trust you for your courage and determination." He stepped back and held her at arms' length. "I even love you for being a foreign devil!" A slight chuckle rose from his throat. "It's because of this that I trust you. You must hide the Englishman and keep him safe for a few days. No one will discover our secret."

She pulled away and her voice quavered. "I'm not so sure. You knew about my hiding place in the summerhouse, and I have no doubt that Ohchin does too. And as you very well know, he hates me and will do all in his power to discredit me even more before my honorable father!"

"Don't worry about that jackal. He'll be in Peking in the examination halls for another week."

"How do you know that?"

"I make it my business to know what goes on with my brother. He and I are opposites. You're the one most like me. We both rebel against a society that fears change. And we're both willing to risk ourselves for freedom, and to make changes for the better. Right?"

In spite of herself, Kulien smiled at Sunfu. He had always been able to persuade her to do his will, even when, as children, it meant punishment or isolation from other family members.

"Please watch over the foreigner for two or three days at the most. I promise to come back then with clean clothes and help him get back to his place of duty." He lifted his shoulders and winked. "Please?"

Kulien let her eyes rest on the wounded man who was now more visible in the emerging light of dawn. Her heart ached for him in spite of knowing that only trouble lay ahead. "I can't keep such a secret for long. You know how nosey Jiang is. She reads my mind and watches me like a bird of prey."

"This is one secret she cannot discover. You'll have to be as devious as you know how."

Kulien had no more arguments. Her better judgment cried out against the attraction she felt for Marshall Whitfield. But he was injured. He was helpless. He was here!

"I'll do as you say." Her voice was merely a whisper. "But you had better keep your word and return no later than three days from now." Sunfu placed his hands on Kulien's waist and lifted her feet off the ground, a broad smile on his handsome face. "What a good friend you are. Come; let's take another look at the Englishman."

They stood over Marshall Whitfield a moment before Sunfu knelt beside the still form. "Tell him he is safe here, and that you will bring food and medicine. Tell him, also, that it was a mistake that I stabbed him. I'm sorry for his pain, and I hope he will continue to be sympathetic to our cause."

Marshall Whitfield's eyes fluttered open for only an instant before he moaned and again fell into a deep sleep.

Kulien pressed a hand against her heart. "Suppose he dies?" The thought of the Englishman departing beyond the Yellow Springs swamped her with sadness. "What then?"

"He won't die. Not with your help and his own determination. I can tell this is a man who wants to live. And I'm certain his wound is not as serious as it appears."

Kulien's face paled in the early morning light, and her eyes burned from lack of sleep. "I pray that you're right," she said.

But as she gazed at the face of the sleeping man, her concern went beyond his recovery and healing. The tall foreigner with eyes the color of the sky and hair that shone like the sun had stirred within her a strange awakening she hoped would change her destiny.

EIGHT

Kulien stared at her reflection in the oval mirror of her cosmetic case. It was an unfamiliar face of a tired and anxious woman instead of the clear brow of a sixteen year old girl. Her eyes held a faraway glaze as if she could see beyond her own compound, her own province, even beyond her own country and culture. Thin rays of early autumn sunlight streaked through the latticed window, playing across the room like chords of a minor key.

What had she done? She had passed beyond the spirit screen that kept evil spirits from entering the compound. Very possibly an evil spirit had slipped in as she left with Sunfu. It was not as though the Kuang clan had remained one of harmony; all her relatives showed open opposition to Kulien and her father's favoritism. Kuang Lufong, a Scholar of the first class of China's social structure, constantly worked toward establishing a peaceful and prosperous home after the manner of *feng shui*, including the ever present spirit screen and all the rooms facing south.

Kulien shook the thoughts from her head and set her mind on what had followed that formidable trespass. After leaving the summerhouse with Sunfu still ministering to Lord Marshall Whitfield, she had returned to her quarters. She stopped first near the servants' gate where she hid the blood-stained cloths in the rag basket that would be picked up today. Now as she waited for Jiang's morning appearance, her spirits rose at the thought of the Englishman who lay nearby, no more than a *li*, a third mile, away. A flush rose to her cheeks as she recalled touching the foreigner, kneeling close beside him, and feeling the rapid beat of her heart as she looked upon his face. Lord Whitfield. Marshall. Did she love this strange man from a foreign land—the land of her mother's birth? Would the restless spirit of her grandfather rise up and claim him in the summerhouse as a sacrifice for his own suicide?

Kulien closed her eyes and pressed cold hands against her cheeks. She must not entertain such worrisome thoughts. Not now anyway. There were important duties to perform—and quickly. She had to get food and water to the Englishman, and also medicine.

"And what are you daydreaming about this time?" Jiang hobbled into the room, a brush in one hand, a comb in the other. "With those droopy eyelids, I think you might be repenting of your bad behavior toward your father." With her last words, she grasped a long strand of Kulien's hair and began to braid it while mumbling under her breath.

Searching for a way to divert Jiang's attention, Kulien smiled at the woman's reflection in the small mirror. "You're right. I was wondering if Father had returned yet. I've thought it over, and decided to forgive him." As Jiang finished braiding Kulien's hair, her thin painted eyebrows rose at the first words Kulien had spoken about her father in many days.

She nodded her head thoughtfully, watching Kulien as she arose from the low stool and crossed the room to stand at the window overlooking the courtyard.

After returning to her room from the midnight excursion, Kulien had dressed in a long lavender tunic and narrow black trousers. Her eyes, as well as her thoughts, cleared as she gazed out at birds wheeling freely through the morning sky before alighting in trees, brilliant with red and golden leaves. As a leaf drifted aimlessly to the flagstones, she turned to face Jiang, forcing an innocent smile. She needed to find medicine without arousing either Jiang's or her father's suspicions. Perhaps only her father would know where the strongest antiseptics were kept; but she knew where to find food—in the family temple.

"Before I go search for Father, I think I should make prayers to the gods," she said, pressing her palms together under her chin. "If I look with favor on the ancestor tablets, the spirits might have mercy on me, and grant a reprieve from the arranged marriage to Kong Litang!" She shrugged her shoulders and smiled weakly at Jiang.

"Well, this is a new day. First, I learn you've taken my advice to make peace with your honorable father who, by the way, arrived very early this morning. He left word that he will meet you in the usual place for your morning meditation." The woman wrung her plump hands. "And now you tell me you're going to the family temple?" Her round cheeks dimpled. "I'm sure the gods will fall from their platforms when they see you. You've not worshipped before the ancestor tablets for many seasons. And I blame that 'big-nose' Englishwoman who comes to teach you. She also brings her English god with her, I think."

Kulien stepped away from the window with hands on her hips. "Think what you will." Her tone was sharp. "Elizabeth's God makes more sense to me than all those old wooden planks painted with our ancestors' names!"

At Jiang's shocked expression, Kulien lowered her voice and reached out to touch Jiang's shoulder. "Forgive me, I'm tired today, and I just want to see my grandfather's tablet. Who knows? I might even light a candle for him."

Jiang's mood changed and dimples again appeared in her rosy cheeks. Kulien sighed with relief. The *amah* had evidently accepted her surprising and uncharacteristic announcement to visit the family altar. She had to admit to herself that she was also surprised by the clever scheme.

Jiang smoothed the silk dress over her wide hips, but before she stepped over the threshold to leave the room, she patted Kulien's shoulder. "When you bow before your ancestors in the family temple, be sure to bring an offering of food. The gods will be pleased that you remembered those who have passed beyond the Yellow Springs."

Kulien's heart seemed to leap in her chest. "Oh, Jiang, thank you for reminding me. That's an excellent idea." Of course, the idea had already begun to form as she remembered the bowls of food family members brought to comfort the spirits who roamed the earth. Fresh food was set before the ancestor tablets every morning. She would return later in the day when she was certain not to be seen, and hide some of it in her sleeves. She knew just where it would do the most good.

She also needed medicine—strong medicine. Perhaps the 'Goddess of Mercy,' *Kuanyin*, or Elizabeth's Western God would shine upon her and grant wisdom to find medicine without betraying her purpose.

It had been many seasons since Kulien had visited the family temple, the Hall of Ancestors, located at the far northwestern corner of the large Kuang compound. As she strode along the stone pathway, her eyes tinged with green highlights, danced with anticipation. But when she reached the family worship center nestled among thick pines, she began to shiver. The small building with red pillars and up-turned eaves contained ancestral tablets and row upon row of gilded idols. She remembered also seeing a life-sized painting of a red-faced god, and an altar laden with bowls of food and innumerable red wax candles. When she was a small child, she had been frightened of the gods' anger. Even now she dreaded entering the room to bow before them.

After a few moments and several deep breaths, she pressed her palms together and bowed from the waist before stepping over the threshold into the darkened room. The heavy air scented with the smoke of musky incense caused her to cough. Quickly she covered her mouth and prayed that the coughing would subside. As she neared the front, she noticed someone else at the altar. It was Mahwu leaning on the arm of a servant, her other hand grasping a gnarled cane.

If she had known her grandmother would be here, she would never have come at this time of day. There was no way to escape as Mahwu turned her head and glared at Kulien. "So, even wild rice knows where to find nourishment." Mahwu narrowed her eyes and her words hissed through tight lips like steam escaping from a kettle. "The daughter of the foreign devil who trapped my son and killed my husband has come to make obeisance to those far superior to her and her mother!"

"You speak well, Grandmother," Kulien said, attempting a tone of humility. "May the gods be kind to the father of Kuang Lufong, and may his journey in the depths of the earth be pleasant."

"Away with you, foreign child! Bitter Seed!" Complete your business and leave!"

Mahwu's remarks never failed to pierce Kulien's heart, but she forced a smile and bowed low before her grandmother before picking up a burning taper. Without another word, she lit both a candle and a stick of incense in front of her grandfather's wooden tablet. She would have to come back for the food later, perhaps at dusk when there would be no danger of meeting another family member.

No one ever questioned what happened to the food offerings. Each worshipper knew that the dead did not return to eat, but the food was always gone by the next morning—perhaps by the hand of a servant or a visiting priest—no questions asked. However, this food would not go into a servant's mouth. The meat and vegetables offered to the gods would renew the strength and life of Lord Marshall Whitfield.

Kulien's mind was still on the Englishman as she walked back down the pathway to the central garden. "Do not let your spirit pull so at your mouth," Lufong called as he waved for Kulien to join him. "We are father and daughter, and so we shall ever be." His voice held a hint of kindness, but his eyes were as hard as the black pebble-eyes of a nearby stone dragon.

Kulien quickened her steps and felt a trace of joy in his acceptance. "I'm glad you've returned from your duties in good health, Father." She fought back tears of relief. He seemed to have forgiven her for refusing to see him. She would also do her best to forgive him for promising her to Kong Litang. She would find a way to escape such an imprisonment, and it would have to be soon.

Kulien took her position beside Lufong and exhaled forcefully, expelling the unpleasant feelings she had harbored against him for so many days. Without another word, they began the *taichichuan* movements that had become such an integral part of their lives together. The steady breathing and slow, deliberate motions released the tension that had been growing even more pronounced after Sunfu's surprise visit and her encounter with the Englishman. Serenity prevailed. Kulien's spirit soared on the soft morning breezes that would soon be replaced by a humid fall afternoon.

After completing the final movement, father and daughter stood without moving or speaking, their heads bowed and arms at their sides.

"Kulien." Lufong spoke tenderly and stepped closer to her. "I want to speak to you about the contents of the bag you received on your birthday." He motioned toward a stone bench near an overhanging willow tree. "I have held those items in trust for you until you were of marriageable age." He paused as if needing strength to continue. "The bag belonged to your mother's family. It bears their crest."

Kulien nodded but said nothing.

"The contents are gifts from your mother: a small portrait of Marguerite when she was your age; a brooch given to her on her thirteenth birthday; and a parchment written by her own hand shortly before your birth. The jade ring—I gave to her on our wedding day. My father presented it to me before I left for Great Britain. It was the most valued item I owned at that time, and knew it belonged on Marguerite's finger. This is all that I have to give you, my daughter." His voice cracked with emotion. "I know that you will soon leave this compound to be joined to Kong Litang, and although you do not know him or his family, I believe he will show you kindness. At least, that is my prayer."

"Father, please...." Kulien lifted her eyes and rested a hand on his arm. "Please, don't send me away."

"As I said before, there is nothing I can do about the pledge that has been made. You will leave here, and as promised by the Kong patriarch, you will have a wedding ceremony befitting a first wife. It's true that Kong Litang is older than I am, and he already has a first wife, but," he rested a hand on her arm, "perhaps when his wife passes beyond the Yellow Springs, he will make you his first wife. You are from a noble family and deserve a high position."

"I'm afraid, Father. I have no experience outside this clan, and I can't go live with a family who feels betrayed by you."

Lufong's eyes narrowed and he stood up glaring down at Kulien. "It isn't your place to condemn me. I've done all I could do for you. You will have to trust the gods for good fortune. Your future is out of my hands."

Now. Kulien thought. *Now I must make my move.* Without warning, Kulien suddenly rose from the bench and ran across the flagstones to the goldfish pond. Purposely stubbing her toe, she stumbled, throwing herself against a granite boulder. She caught the edge with the palm of her hand, scraping it across the sharp stone.

"Oh, Father, I've cut my hand," she cried. Her tears were genuine as pain seared her hand and blood began to drip from the open wound, staining the pink flagstones of the pavement.

Lufong stared in amazement at Kulien's impulsive movement and injury. "My child, come here; let me see." He pursed his lips and clucked his tongue as he examined the deep scratch. With his arm around her shoulder, he drew her close. "What were you thinking, daughter? I know you are troubled, but it's not like you to be so careless!" He paused and held her at arm's length as tears coursed down her cheeks. "Oh, I'm sorry, my Lotus Blossom. I can see that you're in pain. I cannot bear to see you suffer, my favored daughter. Come, we'll go immediately to the kitchen to acquire proper medicine for such a wound."

Kulien knew his words went beyond the cut hand, and she leaned against him. "I believe you care for me, Father. And I also know that as broken skin heals with the proper ointment and the passage of time, so will all other hurts." She managed to smile at him as he released his hold and led her to the cook house.

Her smile was more for the possibility of fulfilling her plan to obtain medicine for Marshall Whitfield's wound than for her father's concern.

Kulien seldom had opportunity or reason to go into the kitchen, and she followed several feet behind her father as he made his way from the central courtyard down the path past the dining hall to the large cooking area. Cooks moved quickly as they prepared the noonday meal. One had just chopped off the head of a chicken, and the bird raced around in circles until it dropped dead. Another servant, with knife in hand, opened a large cage and tugged at a squealing pig. Steam rose from giant vats where rice for the large family boiled. A dog chased a cat behind a wooden tub filled with soiled cleaning rags. Kulien was so entranced by the scene that she almost forgot her purpose in visiting the busy room.

"Here, Daughter." Lufong removed a small brown bottle from a high shelf. He blew the dust from its sides and pulled out the cork. "This is a potent medicine that will fight infection," he said, while pouring a few drops of the sticky substance over the scratches on her open hand.

Tears rose in Kulien's eyes and she caught her breath. "Ow! If the sharpness means it is good medicine, then I'm sure it will help."

"It is a very strong balm with excellent healing properties." He pushed the cork back into the mouth of the bottle and handed it to her. "Take this to your rooms and apply the ointment in the morning and also in the evening. When the time comes for you to cease the application, you'll know, for only then will the stinging abate."

"Father, I know you care for me even though you're sending me away." She folded her fingers around the bottle. "This medicine is a gift from the Goddess of Mercy." Kulien struggled with the dishonesty of her words as she had never used deceit with her father—until recently. But she lifted her heart in thanksgiving to whatever god had presented her with the medicine she needed for the Englishman. Now she had to return to the temple to steal the food. She only hoped Marshall Whitfield was still alive.

NINE

The hot afternoon sun blazed endlessly overhead as Kulien waited for darkness to envelop the compound. Would she find Marshall Whitfield awake? Would he still be alive? Would he even remember her presence last night in the summerhouse? What would she say to him? And what would he say to her? So many questions.

At last the bright autumn orb slipped slowly behind the western wall shrouding the compound in shadows with the promise of night. Kulien's heart beat rapidly as she contemplated her visit to the summerhouse and the forbidden rendezvous with the foreigner. Marshall Whitfield was lying in pain from a dagger wielded by her brother.

She thought about the unusual occurrences since her sixteenth birthday: First, she had learned that her birth mother had been British and had died giving her life; then, she heard from her father's lips that she had been promised as a wife to the Kong family as a recompense for his own broken promise.

Kulien shuddered at the thought of a strange man touching her. Jiang had explained, much to the embarrassment of them both, the physical meeting of a husband and wife in the marriage bed. Kulien felt only disgust and revulsion at such a thought, and to imagine such an intrusion of her person by Kong Litang filled her mind with images too sickening to consider.

She could not marry the man her father chose for her. She would rather die than be sent away like a piece of meat to market. But ever since meeting the Englishman on her birthday, and then touching him last night, she sensed her own femininity stir, drawing her to him. Marshall Whitfield's words to Sunfu brought a sense of hope. There might be a future with him. Perhaps he would marry her and take her away from here and the vow Lufong had made to the Kong clan.

Kulien shook her head to clear away the images of marriage to the Englishman—of living in Great Britain in his palatial home. Dreams, that's all they were. Impossible dreams of a Chinese girl married to an aristocratic British lord. Or was the image too far removed from possibility? Her mother was British, and she herself, though retaining most of her Chinese heritage, did slightly resemble the Caucasian race. Her eyes, oval-shaped like her father's, were tinted with a touch of green; and her ivory skin accentuated full lips and high cheekbones. She was taller than most of her cousins, and quite slender with small breasts and a narrow waistline. Would Marshall Whitfield find her attractive? He had told his sister that he thought she was beautiful. Were his words sincere? Would he ever speak such bold words to her personally?

Now that the compound was dark except for the sliver of a moon that occasionally slipped behind passing clouds, and hopeful that everyone was asleep, Kulien crept as quietly as possible down the stairs, through her private courtyard and over the winding pathways until she reached the temple. She gathered up the items of food left for departed spirits and wrapped them in a clean white cloth. She had dropped the small brown bottle of strong medicine her father had given her into a pocket of her tunic. Then she raced over the arched bridge toward the summerhouse.

As tree branches cleared above her, a faint glow of the crescent moon shone on the pavilion; roof tiles glistened with evening dew and a breeze loosened drying leaves that drifted to the ground at her feet. Kulien paused, and holding her breath, listened for an indication that anyone could be watching. She never felt completely safe knowing how much Ohchin hated her and would delight in causing her to lose face.

Cautiously making her way up the steps to the floor of the summerhouse, she strained her eyes to see where they had left Marshall Whitfield. "Lord Whitfield, are you awake? I've brought food and medicine." Her voice was so soft, she barely heard herself speak the words. When no sound came from the dark recesses, she called again, this time a little louder. "Lord Whitfield. It is I, Kulien. I've come to help you."

Still there was no sign of life. Padding across the expanse and spying the still form, she inhaled deeply, and dropped to her knees beside him. His back was to her, and she could only make out the form of his motionless body lying under the quilts she and Sunfu had laid over him.

Kulien set down the parcel of food and reached into her tunic for the medicine. Dare she touch him? She must, if only to discover whether he were dead or alive. With her heart pounding in her ears, she rested cool fingers on his forehead. It burned with fever. Her breath caught in her throat as she allowed the back of her fingers to trace the bristles on his cheeks. He was still alive.

At her touch, Marshall Whitfield turned his head toward her and opened his eyes in a glassy stare. "The dreams. So frightening. They play over and over in my head." He groaned and placed a warm hand over Kulien's. "You came. You're really here, aren't you?"

Startled at his voice and the touch of his hand, she drew back and stood up. "You are burning with fever, Sir. I must cool you with water from the brook." She untied the bundle of food, leaving it beside him, and took the cloth to soak in the stream flowing beside the summerhouse. Her mind whirled with unbidden emotions. His voice—the touch of his hand—the sense of his manliness stirred her in ways she had never known. She forced her mind to think only of what she needed to do, and hurried back with the cold wet cloth.

With care, she gently lifted his head to dab his mouth, forehead and throat with the cool liquid. Repeatedly, she returned to the stream to fill the cloth with fresh water to soothe the raging fever of this foreigner who, she feared, had already stolen her heart.

Trying hard not to gaze upon the man's sculptured muscles, she opened his shirt and sponged his broad chest until his moans became sighs of contentment. "Thank you, Kulien. You are truly a gift from Heaven! I feel better already."

Kulien smiled as she reached for a bottle of stolen plum wine and lifted his head. "You must drink some of this. It will revive your spirits." His lips opened and she strained her eyes to see his every movement as she directed the liquid into his mouth.

"I can't see you. It's so dark."

Kulien rose from her knees and went to a pillow near the back corner of the summerhouse where she removed a hidden candle and a small stick of pinewood impregnated with sulfur. Scratching it against the rough tile floor, she held it to the wick and watched the flame shine in a glowing circle before setting it in a lantern.

Quickly returning to Marshall Whitfield, she held the lantern between them. "I've brought a strong ointment," she said, her words faltering as she looked into his eyes. "I must remove the bandage and dress your wound so there won't be infection."

Marshall reached up to touch her face. "You are so kind to help me. I know that you're taking a great risk."

"The greater risk would be if you should die. My brother would be executed, and my family would suffer great shame!"

"Is that the only reason you're helping me, Kulien? You know that I've wanted to see you again, but I've not been able to receive permission to visit your compound. I'm afraid I insulted your father when I came with my sister. I'm sorry to have caused you any grief."

"I, too, am sorry that you couldn't return. Elizabeth doesn't come as often as in the past. My father has restricted her visits." *Until I am sent away,* she said to herself. Turning her attention from her dreaded future, she began to remove the bandage from Marshall's shoulder. "But we must only think about your getting well and back to your post."

As the bandage and aloe leaves fell aside, Kulien gasped. The wound was oozing blood and pus. Infection had begun. Her heart fell at the sight, and her stomach turned. She was unaccustomed to such things. The only blood she had ever seen had been at her time of women, and then Jiang had disposed of the cloths.

She put aside her revulsion and reached for the bottle of medicine her father had given her. She warned, "This is a very powerful medicine and it will cause pain as I pour it into your wound. But it could very well save your life. Please try not to cry out. There might be a beggar passing by and he would hear and report it to my father."

"I won't make a sound," he promised. But when Kulien poured the ointment in the wound, he groaned through clenched teeth. When he was able to speak, he said, "You were serious, weren't you? I don't think your brother's knife was as painful." He waited until she applied clean strips of cloth to the wound before touching her face again. "How can I ever thank you enough, Kulien? I know I will recover, and then I will find a way to repay you."

Kulien's face warmed where his fingers rested on her cheek. "It is my honor to aid my teacher's brother. Truly, Elizabeth is not only my teacher; she's my dearest, my only friend. She tells me of your world outside the Middle Kingdom. She has spoken to me of your God, the one you call Jesus. I've learned that he even cares for females...so it is I who am grateful, Lord Whitfield."

Too weak to hold his hand to her face any longer, he let it drop to the pallet and sighed. His eyelids fluttered before closing. His last words before falling asleep were, "My friends call me Marshall. I hope you'll be my friend."

Kulien knew that she should not stay much longer or her absence might be discovered. But Lord Whitfield needed food and was unable to feed himself. She would have to wait until he woke up, so she sat beside him, unmoving, taking in his every feature, his every sound. He was so unlike her father and brothers. His shoulders were broad and there was much hair on his face and arms. What was it about him that caused her heart to swell so she that could scarcely breathe? Was this the love women have for men—this man whose ways were so unlike hers? Would it be forbidden by the gods and his God for them to love one another?

No, it could not be wrong. Her own father had loved Marguerite Howard, and Kulien had been the result of their love. Although they were not accepted by their cultures or families, she had been born. Her love for the Englishman would be like her father's love for her mother. As Kulien waited for Marshall Whitfield to wake, her eyelids drooped. Every bone in her body ached. Weary from not having slept the night before, and from carrying the burden of her duty to Marshall Whitfield—and Sunfu, she eased herself onto the floor beside the mat and closed her eyes.

An hour had passed before a cool breeze passed through the latticework of the summerhouse tinkling wind chimes that hung at the entrance. Kulien awoke confused and disoriented. Where was she? What time could it be?

When she turned, her eyes widened in surprise and fear. Marshall's face was just inches from hers. The candle had burned out and only the thin rays of moonlight shone upon his face. His deep blue eyes, no longer glazed with pain and fever, studied her. A smile creased his cheeks and his eyes shone with interest.

"Kulien, you are truly beautiful! I can't believe that you're here beside me. I've thought only of you since the night of your birthday. I should not have such feelings for you because you are only sixteen, and I am twenty-five, three years older than my sister."

Kulien found it hard to speak, but rose up on one elbow to look down at him. She had never been so near any male other than her father and step-brothers, and the thought of lying next to the *fankuei* thrilled her while also sending shivers of fear through her body. "I'm sorry to tell you that as the Westerner counts years, I am only fifteen. We are considered one year old on the day of our birth."

Marshall groaned and glanced away. "Oh, it is even worse than I thought. You are but a child."

"No, I'm not a child. I am to be married soon." At his questioning look, Kulien went on. "My father contracted a marriage for me with a man I have never seen. Kong Litang is older than my father!" A heavy sigh escaped her lips. "My wedding is to take place at the Moon Festival." She couldn't tell him that she would be a concubine.

"But that's only weeks away!" Marshall's eyes swept over her face and rested on her parted lips. "That's horrible! I can't believe he'd treat you like that! Kulien, you deserve so much better. I don't know what to say or do!"

"Thank you. Your kind words mean more than I can express." Kulien rose to her knees and began to apply more medicine to the wound, a sense of inner joy calming her spirit.

She carefully replaced a fresh bandage on the gash, and when she saw that he was more comfortable, reached for the chopsticks and began to place small bits of meat and vegetables in his mouth. It was obvious that the effort tired him as he could barely hold up his head. She moved closer and lifted his head to rest upon her knee. His nearness unnerved her and she began to tremble. "I must go now," she said, setting the chopsticks next to the food.

"You're trembling. Are you cold?" Will you return?" As she moved away and placed his head back on the folded blanket, he asked again, "When will you return? Will Sunfu come to take me back to Shanghai?"

Kulien stood and, with a faltering voice, answered, "I will be back tomorrow night with more food. Perhaps you will be well enough to return to your post by then."

Marshall managed a smile. "No, I think I'll need for you to come to me for many nights. After all, I've waited more than four months just to set my eyes on you." He reached out to touch her arm. "Kulien, please come back as often as you can. I don't want to cause you trouble, but I must see you."

Without speaking Kulien disappeared into the shadows and returned with another quilt. She leaned over Marshall Whitfield and tucked the edges around the mat. "You'll be warm until morning. There's enough food to last until I return. If you're able, you should apply more medicine to your injury. But, whatever you do, you must not leave this place. If you're discovered, it will mean death, not only to you, but also to Sunfu and me."

As Kulien bent over to secure the blanket, Marshall put his right hand on the back of her neck and drew her face close to his. "It's true that I'm twenty-five, ten years older than you, and if we were in my country I would look upon you as a child. But, as you say, you're not a child." His words wavered as he chose his next words carefully. "Here, with the fragrance of the pine trees and the scent of jasmine in your hair, I see a most beautiful woman. No, Kulien, you are not a child."

"I must go now," she said quickly, glad for the darkness that concealed her burning face. "I'll be back tomorrow night when the moon is high in the sky."

Kulien wrapped her tunic tightly around her shivering form as she raced back over the pathway to her quarters. The man...Marshall...his words, his touch; everything about him thrilled her spirit beyond understanding, beyond control. There had to be a way to escape the planned marriage to Kong Litang! She knew now that she loved Lord Marshall Whitfield and wanted to spend her life with him. Were her thoughts foolish? Were they only dreams of an unhappy girl?

Perhaps the God of the Bible had thoughts about her that she didn't know yet. She remembered a portion of Elizabeth's holy book that she had recited to Kulien. She had made a point to commit it to memory. "I know the thoughts that I think toward you,' saith the LORD, "thoughts of peace, and not of evil, to give you an expected end."

Could it be true that this strange, invisible God would bring her peace and a good future?

TEN

"Kulien, I've been watching for you."

Kulien's heart seemed to stop as she heard the foreigner's voice coming from the dark side of the pavilion. Throughout the long, wearisome day, she had thought of no one but Lord Marshall Whitfield. Knowing that he lay such a short distance away kept her moving about in a trance, waiting for the moment when she could steal some food, break away from the family compound and run to the summerhouse.

That morning as she practiced her embroidery, seated with the other girls of the compound, each delicate stitch seemed to spell out *his* name—Lord Marshall Whitfield—Lord Marshall Whitfield. What a strong name for a man. The gods had blessed her teacher, Elizabeth, to have grown up with such a fine older brother!

Kulien had glanced from time to time over her shoulder to see if her cousins or grandmother noticed the flush on her cheeks. As usual, she sat apart from the chattering gossip, excluded from their friendship and acceptance. She would always be hated by Mahwu as the child who brought death to the family—and as the favored daughter of the patriarch of the Kuang clan. No one paid attention to her, and she often wondered why her grandmother demanded that she attend some of the women's classes. Perhaps it was simply to bring more shame upon her. She knew her present misery would soon be multiplied if she became a concubine in the hated Kong clan. She must find a way to escape. The thought of disobeying her father caused her heart to beat so rapidly within her breast she felt certain others could hear. But what choice did she have?

Lord Marshall Whitfield could be her only way out of the debt owed by her esteemed father. Kuang Lufong would no doubt lose face over her actions, but he was already separated from her, and would be forever once she departed for the distant city of Hangchow.

If only she could see Elizabeth Whitfield soon and ask her advice. Would she be willing to help? Was she truly the friend Kulien had come to trust? Perhaps the God Elizabeth called, "Lord," could give her the answer she sought.

Lord Marshall Whitfield. There was his name again. He had said she was beautiful, and now he depended on her help to stay alive and safe in the summerhouse. Could she persuade him to help her escape her despicable destiny?

As her mind wandered, she noticed the stitches of her embroidery had become as tangled as her emotions. Would the handsome foreigner still be waiting in the summerhouse for her aid, or would Sunfu have rescued him and returned him to his company along the Shanghai waterfront? He seemed to be much better last night; she could only hope that his wound would continue to heal.

Finally when the long day had passed and darkness crept over the compound, Kulien slipped from her rooms, clad in pants, a light tunic and cotton slippers. Once again she visited the temple, and now held the wrapped bundle of stolen food close to her body as she entered the summerhouse.

Her heartbeat quickened as Marshall's voice reached her ears. "You've been watching for me?" She knelt beside him and laid the bundle of food on the floor. "Is it because you are hungry or because you are in pain and need my medications?"

"That's true, Kulien. But my reasons for wanting to see you again far outweigh my own discomfort."

Kulien lit the candle in the lantern before touching the bandaged shoulder. "Are you truly better? Is your pain less than it was last night?"

"I am better—much better--and truth be known, I'm starving. What have you hidden in your parcel tonight?"

As she carefully opened the cloth, rich aromas of food surrounded them. "I have chicken and pork tonight. There is also rice from the south and apples and plums." Her eyes twinkled in the soft glow of the warm light. "Our gods eat quite well, you know."

She glanced up to see the man's deep blue eyes resting, not on the food, but on her face. Her heart skipped a beat and she set her attention on the task at hand, still unsure of the strange new emotions that swept throughout her being.

Beside the mat she placed a bowl decorated with the red figure of a dragon. Taking chopsticks, she dropped small pieces of food into the bowl before handing the ivory implements to him. Marshall Whitfield leaned forward on one elbow, his eyes still on Kulien. "I fear that you must help me. I never could handle these things very well, and with this shoulder...well...." His dark eyebrows raised in a question.

Kulien remembered the birthday meal in her father's dining room and how she had to restrain a smile at the Englishman's struggle with chopsticks. She picked up a piece of meat and watched his face as he opened his mouth to receive the offering. After several bites, Kulien allowed her eyes to meet his for only a moment before picking up another morsel.

"Kulien," Marshall said softly, touching her hand. "Why are you afraid to look at me? Am I a frightful *fankuei*, a foreign devil? I would never hurt you. I only admire you and know you are taking a great risk in coming here."

"Did you use the ointment today?" Kulien asked.

"Yes, I did. But you didn't answer my question. Are you afraid of me?"

Kulien inhaled deeply before answering. "I'm not afraid of you. It is my own self I fear."

"But why? I can see that you're troubled, even more so than last night. Has something happened to cause you grief? If you would rather not bring me food and medicine, I will understand. It's too much for Sunfu to expect of you. What is it that you fear for yourself?"

How could she explain the unfamiliar emotions she had for this man? Would he understand the turmoil that had disturbed her spirit over the past weeks?

"It is not *for* me that I fear coming here, Lord Whitfield. It is *about* my feelings for you. I have never been alone in the presence of a man apart from my own family. And you," she paused before going on, "you are not at all like them."

"Is it because I'm British? I know my sister has been coming to teach you for a few years, and she said you are accustomed to our ways."

"I'm accustomed to Elizabeth's ways, but you are a man...a very beautiful man...and I...I...am drawn to you like a moth to a candle flame! I have no strength when I'm in your presence." There. She had said it. She had no doubt lost face, and Lord Marshall Whitfield would no longer want to see her. He might even tell Sunfu what she had said, and then he, too, would be shamed.

Several silent moments stretched between them before he spoke, "Oh, Kulien, I am both humbled and proud that you would consider me worthy of your admiration." Marshall slowly lifted her fingers to his lips and held them there.

Oh, by the gods! Would she faint from pure desire? His lips soft and warm against her cool fingertips sent waves of longing through her body like the rollers of the sea pounding against the shore. The moustache and short beard felt strange and foreign, and as she looked down at him, his deep blue eyes held hers in a grip that she could not, did not, want to loosen. She inhaled deeply to quiet the storm raging through her mind and body. Could she reveal her deepest fear to this man she barely knew?

Drawing her hand away and clasping her fingers together in her lap, she made her decision. "Lord Whitfield, I...."

"Please, Kulien, call me Marshall. We are friends. Remember?" He stroked her smooth cheek with the back of his fingers as he waited for her reply.

"All right, then, Marshall. I told you before that I am contracted to marry an old man that I've never seen, but I didn't tell you why." She sighed before going on. "The Kong family was dishonored by my father when he didn't keep the promise to marry a daughter of their clan. Not only did his actions shame the Kong patriarch, my grandfather committed suicide...." She paused and glanced around at the dark corners of the summerhouse. "...here in this very place. Because of my grandfather's death, this place is forbidden to all members of the family. I know my father has suffered much for his crime against both our family and the Kong clan; now I must suffer because I am the cause of the distress brought upon so many."

"But..., I don't understand." Marshall's brows drew together and he leaned so close to her, she could feel his warm breath on her face. "How could you be at fault? Why must you suffer for something your father did?"

Kulien's voice was calm now as a plan unfolded in her thoughts. "It is our way. You see, I was born to a British woman my father secretly married when he went to the university in Great Britain. She died soon after giving me birth; and although my honorable father has given me more opportunities than most girls, he feels it is his duty to surrender his firstborn daughter in marriage to the son of the man who would have been his father-in-law." It was hard to breathe, and she hesitated before continuing. "Although I have been promised a regal wedding ceremony to honor my father's pledge and position of wealth, I will be no more than one of many concubines to that old man. I will be used at his will, and can never have a life of my own...unless..."

When Kulien looked at Marshall's face, she noticed the creases of concern forming on his brow. "I can't let that happen!" he blurted. "There has to be a way for you to escape such a future! What can I do? Is there someone at the British Embassy I could contact? After all, you said your mother was British!"

"You're so kind, so like Elizabeth." Her heart began to pound. "There is only one thing you could do to help me."

"What? Anything. Tell me. When I get out of here, I'll talk to the authorities. I don't care what your culture demands. How could a loving father send his daughter away like that? And it is said that the *British* are cold and insensitive!"

Kulien lowered her eyes to her hands, and then fastened her attention on Marshall. "You could marry me, and take me with you to your country."

Marshall drew in his breath. "Marry you? Do you realize what you're saying? We would both be going against the laws of our countries...and our families. Oh, dear girl, I am so much older than you. I'm afraid I've been too forward and have given you a false hope. More than anything I want to help you, but..."

Kulien covered her face with both hands and fought the hurt rising from the depths of her soul. She felt as if her heart would break, and she could barely move as weakness overcame her. "Please forgive me; I'm so ashamed for suggesting such a thing. You have your life—your very important position—and it has nothing to do with me." She turned aside and started to stand. All she wanted was to run away, and return to her rooms. She must be brave and find another way to escape the miserable future that lay ahead.

Marshall's hand reached out and held her arm. "I'm sorry. You don't need to be ashamed. Please, don't turn away from me. It's just that you're so young, and I'm afraid that I would only bring you more unhappiness."

With her eyes still lowered, she spoke softly, "Yes, I suppose you do think that I'm too young for you—but you could never bring me unhappiness." Her arm warmed where Marshall's hand remained, and she relaxed, thinking of a way to change the subject so she could stay longer.

"Before I leave, may we talk of other things? I was at fault to speak to you of my concerns. You must get well, and return to your post...and I...well, I will manage though I have seldom left this compound."

Marshall seemed to sense her change of attitude and her discomfort, and leaned back with a sigh. "All right then, if you insist. We will talk of other things, as you said. I want to know more about you, Kulien, and don't think I'm not concerned about your future." With his eyes fastened on the ceiling, he urged, "Please, tell me, have you been to the docks of Shanghai where I spend so much of my time? Are you aware of the problems we have there with the import of opium?" His voice took on an impersonal tone.

Kulien closed her eyes for a moment to regain her composure, glad that Marshall was willing to forgive her impetuous words. "I confess that I know very little about the problems of our people or what goes on around the port. I did go to Shanghai once with my father and brothers when I was twelve years old. Sunfu and I managed to elude our father and ran away to look in the shops." She smiled to herself. "That was one of the rare times when my father punished me."

Marshall turned his head to look up at her. His eyes widened in surprise. "But the city walls are only about five miles from here. I would have thought you had been to the city many times, and that your father, who is so concerned about your education, would inform you of the conditions."

Slowly shaking her head, she said, "No, my father tries to protect me from the world, but I want very much to learn about life beyond these walls. You are a fortunate man to have traveled far and experienced so much."

She touched the bandage on his shoulder, longing to trace the muscles of his chest. "Why were you at the docks when Sunfu arrived with his secret society? Was it because of this opium trade you mentioned? You must know that my brother does not follow the customs of our family. Jiang, my *amah*, calls him a renegade; and his brother Ohchin calls him a 'dog-turd,' whatever that is. He calls me names, too, but I would be ashamed to speak of them."

Marshall couldn't repress a smile at Kulien's innocence. "To tell you what I was doing there would take longer than the time we have. But I suppose I, too, could be considered a renegade...or whatever...." His lips curled up in a smile. "I think Ohchin is a very crude man, and could learn much from you and Sunfu."

Kulien nibbled at the edge of her lip. "I know Sunfu has traveled far from here, but he shields me from his escapades. I always enjoy it when Elizabeth tells me of far-away places—and of the large estate where you both grew up. Now that she seldom comes to see me, I miss hearing about those regions beyond the Middle Kingdom."

Marshall fell back on the pallet, tired from the exertion. "I'm sorry that Elizabeth isn't permitted to come as often." He sighed before going on. "She's told me how much she enjoys your company, and how quickly you learned our language. I've been very busy, and haven't seen much of her myself. But I have a question. Isn't it unusual for a man of your father's position to give you lessons from an English teacher?"

Kulien stretched out her legs and leaned back on both hands. She wiggled her toes in the soft slippers. "As you've noticed, my father didn't have my feet bound. He's allowed me privileges unknown to girls of my class. So it isn't my fault that I have a restless spirit and an inquisitive mind." She glanced down at Marshall. "I suppose that he limits Elizabeth's visits because he fears I'll be drawn further away from the beliefs of my ancestors. He was very unhappy when he saw my interest in you." She shivered and wrapped her arms about herself as she imagined her father's ire if he knew of her nightly meetings with Miss Whitfield's brother.

"Are you cold, Kulien?"

"No. I'm very warm here beside you, but now, it's your turn. Will you please tell me about Shanghai and what you do there? As you can see, the moon begins its descent into the western sky, and dawn will soon arrive. I shouldn't stay much longer; but if you're not too tired, would you tell me about some of your adventures?" She turned toward Marshall and lay down beside him, resting her head on her arm. "I'll close my eyes and imagine life outside these walls."

Although Marshall's voice was weak, and he stopped often to rest, he told stories that thrilled her. She learned about the thirty-seven mile waterfront along the Huangpu River and the many boats, ships and junks that passed through those waters. He spoke about his meeting with Sunfu at the Yu Yuan Garden where old men carried their teacups to the teahouse and children dropped rice into the goldfish ponds.

Kulien tried to hold back her surprise when she heard that Marshall Whitfield had conducted business with her brother and asked, "Was that the only time you met with Sunfu?"

"Oh, you are curious, aren't you? I'm not sure I should let you in on my secrets; but no, I met him on another occasion." Lord Whitfield related how frightened he had been when Sunfu and his companion from the Short Sword society led him through an opium den. "I thought we'd never get out of there," he said, the weariness creeping into his voice. "It was so dark and evil-smelling. The men were lined up on shelves, like the dead— opium pipes dangling from their lips. It was horrible!"

Even though Marshall's stories were frightening and she felt for his safety, she marveled at it all, taking in every word, delighting in his closeness.

By now, the moon barely shone through the lattice work, dappling the tiled floor with silvery shadows. Kulien, her eyes open now on the changing shadows, continued to revel in the stories of the bustling port city with its many shops and tall buildings. *What a noble, strong man,* she thought. *If only he could love me as I love him.*

Marshall's voice was soft and calm, and without realizing how weary she was, Kulien drifted into a deep sleep.

When she awoke, she discovered that she had moved closer to the foreigner and his right arm was around her shoulders. She made no attempt to move, but lay still, enjoying the pleasure of his closeness and the steady breathing of his restful sleep. Carefully, so she wouldn't wake him, she reached over to touch his face. It was cool, and soon he'd be well enough to leave. Like his sister, Marshall Whitfield would disappear from her life, and her future would be doomed to a hopeless existence in a city far away from her home.

As she moved away from him, she watched his face for several moments. He had said words that led her to believe he cared for her and he had pressed his lips on her fingers, sending shivers of pleasure throughout her body. Yet he balked at the thought of marriage.

With an aching heart, Kulien scrambled to her feet, gathered up the leftover food, and wrapped it in a bundle. She positioned both the food and the bottle of medicine close enough for him to reach. Without looking back she darted through the pavilion entrance and over the pathway leading back to her rooms.

It was a night she would never forget, whatever the gods had decreed for her. She had felt strong pulls of love, and for a moment, held the hope that she was loved in return. However many days or weeks she had left in the Kuang household, her search for a way to escape the marriage bed of Kong Litang would continue regardless of the consequences.

ELEVEN

"Why do you lie about the rooms half asleep?" Jiang pinched Kulien's shoulder hard enough to make her wince. "There is no time to daydream away the hours. You must tend to your duties; go to the embroidery class; practice your *ching.* Just do something. You must be prepared to take your wedding trip to Hangchow soon. There is much to be done to make you ready! You have to be fitted for your wedding attire as well as traveling clothes." Jiang paused, a frown wrinkling her brow. "Of course, you will be allowed to wear the crimson brocade even though you will not be accepted as the primary wife. It is too bad; you deserve more." She patted Kulien's shoulder where she had pinched it. "The physician will examine you to be sure of your chastity. Oh, dear, oh, dear, there is so much to do!"

Jiang scurried across the room on tiny feet and pointed out the window. "I suppose you could go outside and get some fresh air before the preparations begin. I see nothing here but a pale face and a lazy girl!"

"You don't own me, Jiang! I'll do as I please until that horrible day that is supposedly a wedding. And no physician or priest will examine me!" Kulien's voice was sharper than Jiang had ever heard, and she raised her thin eyebrows in surprise.

"I may not own you, but you own me and I will be with you for the rest of your life! You don't need to be afraid, for I'm going to Hangchow with you. I'll always take good care of you."

Kulien stretched her arms overhead and sat up before moving across the room in a languorous fashion. She sat in front of her mirror and fingered the lotus box with the ivory comb she had received for her birthday from Elizabeth and Marshall Whitfield. She ignored Jiang's reflected frown as she combed her bangs over her forehead and brushed her long tresses until they shimmered like black satin. She smiled at her reflection, and fastened the beautifully carved comb behind her ear.

Jiang was beside her in a moment and snatched the comb away, hiding it in her tunic. She lifted her chin in defiance, her eyes daring Kulien to object.

"How could you!" Kulien snapped at her *amah*. "That is my property, and you have no right to take it away!"

Jiang folded her arms in front of her and lifted her rounded chin. "You think I don't have the right? Your father gave me the right the day you came to me as a suckling infant. It is my duty to watch after you, and all I see today is a naughty child who wants her own way."

"I'm not a child," Kulien muttered. "I'm a woman who is to be married. I'm old enough to bear children, so I'm old enough to choose what I want to wear. And I want to wear that comb today."

"That will not happen." Jiang started toward the doorway. "Because I know why you want this comb—you are smitten with that foreign woman's brother. It's a good thing your father has denied him admittance to this compound. You have too many romantic ideas in that head of yours. Face up to the truth, young lady; in only a few weeks you'll be the wife of a respected man, and your father will have repaid his debt."

Kulien whirled around and blocked Jiang's exit. She glared down at her, speaking in a strong, but modulated tone, "I will not be that man's *wife*! And you know it. My fate is to be one of his many concubines. My father didn't train and educate me for such a degrading position. My birth-mother would be ashamed to know that I had been sent away to be used as a *whore* because Kuang Lufong chose to marry her instead of the woman chosen for him."

Jiang responded with a hard slap on Kulien's cheek, the first time she had ever resorted to such an action. Kulien backed up in surprise, pressing her fingers against the sting. "Why did you do that?"

"You should be ashamed for using such language, and you know that you have no choice." Jiang inhaled deeply and her voice softened. "It isn't that I don't care; you know I do." She reached out to touch Kulien's cheek. "I love you as my own child, and I would much prefer that you have a fine young husband who would treasure you as I do. But it is from the gods. Your destiny is settled. There is no way out."

Her shoulders stooped, Jiang with the comb in her tunic pocket, hobbled from the room and hid herself away in her own quarters.

The words, "No way out...no way out!" echoed in Kulien's mind. There had to be a way out. She had read stories in Elizabeth's book about the power the "Most High God" had to change circumstances. She had read about three young men who survived a fire, and of their friend who lived through the night in a lion's den. She must pray that Elizabeth's God would save her, too. Elizabeth had told her about many answers to her prayers—how she had prayed to come to China as a missionary, and God had supplied the way and the finances. She said she often prayed for Kulien that she would come to understand and know the one true God. *I wonder if she would pray that I can escape the marriage contract with Kong Litang.*

Before Kulien had time to think any longer about prayer or her dire circumstances, a servant stood in the doorway, a sneer twisting his mouth. "I've been instructed to tell you that the foreign devil has arrived, and is in your courtyard."

Elizabeth! Oh, before she had even asked, her prayer was answered. She must talk with her teacher and maybe even confide to her about Marshall Whitfield's presence in the summerhouse.

Kulien glanced in the mirror and smoothed her hair again before dashing from the room and down the short stairway that led to her personal courtyard. If only she had been wearing the ivory comb. She slowed her pace before stepping out onto the flagstone area where Miss Whitfield sat quietly listening to the gurgling waterfall at the edge of the garden. Several leaves loosened from an overhanging birch tree and drifted down to the pool where they floated on the surface like golden coins.

Elizabeth turned when she heard Kulien's footsteps. "Oh, my dear child, it seems like such a long time since we've been together." She held out both hands to enfold Kulien's fingers in a warm grasp. "I hope you've been told that my visits with you will be limited, and that there will be no more lessons."

Kulien pulled her hands away to wipe at a tear forming in her eye. "I am most saddened that my father has taken away my privilege of learning more of the English language." Kulien focused eyes on her own satin shoes before glancing up at the teacher.

Shyly, she lifted her eyes to Elizabeth's face. "You have heard about my impending marriage, but did you know that I'm actually being sent away to Hangchow to become an old man's concubine?"

The teacher's face paled, and she covered her mouth with her hand. "Oh, no, Kulien—that's horrible! I did know that you were to be married soon, but I had no knowledge about this terrible news! I just assumed that some young man had made arrangements with your father."

She drew Kulien to the bench where she had been sitting, holding both her hands. "Do you know why your father has made this decision? I can't tell you how saddened I am."

Kulien let Elizabeth hold her hands for several moments, drawing strength from her teacher's touch. Should she tell her about her grandfather's suicide and how her own father had defied his ancestors? Would that cause her father to lose face with the English woman?

She lifted her chin and withdrew her hands, and lightly clasped her fingers on her lap. It wouldn't be wise to speak of the past to this one who had become her friend; but she could reveal what future had been planned for her.

"You remember the night you and your brother came to honor me on my birthday?"

"Of course. It was a lovely occasion, but I must apologize again for my brother's behavior. He spoke out of turn. You heard and understood him, and I'm very thankful your father didn't understand his words." Miss Whitfield lowered her eyelids and smoothed the folds in her long brown skirt.

Oh, but he did, Kulien thought. *He understood every word and although his anger was controlled, he was more determined than ever to send me away.*

Drawing in a deep breath, Kulien explained, "Do not be concerned. The fault was not yours or you brother's. That was the night I learned of my heritage—and my future. Many years ago my father had promised me in marriage to the son of an old acquaintance, Kong Litang …. Now that I'm of age, I'm to travel to Hangchow to go through a pretense of a wedding, only to become a concubine."

She forced herself to continue, "I will leave in only a few short weeks. The preparations for my journey have begun." She lifted her head and squared her shoulders as her decision to tell Miss Whitfield about the past rose to the surface of her uneasiness. "There is more about my life that I want you to know."

Elizabeth's eyes were wide and she leaned forward, encouraging her to go on.

"My father also told me that my mother was British."

"What?" Elizabeth gasped, her eyes searching Kulien's face. "I—I don't know what to say. I always wondered why you looked so different from other Chinese girls—your eyes—your skin tone—but I would never have guessed that your mother is British. Do you know what has become of her? What is her name? How…?"

Kulien wondered if she had revealed too much, but the words were already out. She may as well continue. "My father attended Oxford University in Great Britain. While there he met and fell in love with Marguerite Howard, an educated upper class woman, the daughter of a professor. They married secretly, breaking the rules of their families."

Kulien's hand went to her throat where she fingered the silk loops at the neckline of her gown. "My mother died shortly after giving me life."

Elizabeth opened her mouth as if to speak, but no words came. A strand of long blonde hair had slipped out of her bun, and she absentmindedly swiped at it as she waited for Kulien to go on.

Kulien inhaled deeply as her eyes swept over the birds that soared freely to the tops of the tall pines that edged the compound. "He promised my mother that he would teach me the ways of her world as well as his. That's why my feet aren't bound, and why he wanted me to learn English."

"But why then would he send you away as if you were an ordinary Chinese woman?" Elizabeth's words came out in breathless spurts. "How do you feel about it? Are you happy, Kulien?"

If only I could tell her how I truly feel...that I love her brother...that he is only a li (a third mile) *away from where we now sit!*

"Of course, I am not happy. I want to stay here with my father. The only comfort I have is that Jiang will go with me, so I won't be completely without a friend in that faraway place!"

Kulien's heart seemed to swell within her as she thought about Marshall. He had said that he was her friend; and she knew she would see him tonight when the moon was high. She would touch him and look into his intensely blue eyes. *Can I convince him to change his mind and rescue me from the impending marriage?*

Elizabeth's voice broke into her thoughts. "Would it help if I spoke to your father, Kulien? Would he listen to reason?"

Before Elizabeth could say another word, Kulien stood. "No, please don't try to dissuade him. His mind is made up. I must go, my friend. But I will always remember you."

As she turned to leave, Elizabeth put a hand on her shoulder. "Kulien, I want you to know that I too, have a concern—yesterday the British Consulate advised me that my brother is missing. It's believed that he's either been kidnapped by bandits or possibly killed." She closed her eyes as if in silent prayer, and then put her arms around Kulien and hugged her. Although Kulien wasn't accustomed to such affection, she returned the hug.

"Fankuei! Foreign devil!" Mahwu stood in the opening of the moon gate, leaning on two canes. She hobbled closer, her eyes glittering with hatred, her mouth twisted in scorn. "Your kind has brought nothing but misery and death to this clan—and this daughter of a demon-whore is soon to leave us in peace!" She raised a cane and struck Kulien across the back causing her to gasp with pain.

Elizabeth Whitfield started to reach out, but Kulien stopped her. "No, she is right. My grandmother speaks only what she believes is the truth, though I'm sorry that you understand her language. Please go, my friend. As I said, I'll never forget you." She forced a weak smile, "And who knows? Perhaps we shall meet again someday."

Kulien turned and strode past her grandmother without giving her a glance. Her broken heart hurt much more than the welt forming on her back. As she raced up the stairs to her rooms, her decision to escape with Marshall Whitfield's help calmed her spirit and energized her resolve.

The rest of the day, Kulien avoided other family members by hiding away in her rooms. She answered Jiang with short, curt replies, but the *amah* was not easily discouraged. "I don't know what ails you, but I think you need a tonic. Your cheeks are flushed and you're as jumpy as a tree frog."

Kulien tried to appease Jiang so she wouldn't be too suspicious. She knelt on a satin pillow before her cosmetic case and stared into the oval mirror while dusting rice powder on her face. "Please don't worry about me. I have determined to behave from now on. Both you and my father have your desires regarding Miss Whitfield. She won't be coming back. I will submit to my father's decree."

Kulien rose from the pillow and pretending to be interested in the overcast sky, stared out the window that overlooked the compound. *He's out there waiting for me.* The very thought of his touch brought a flush to her powdered face, and her heart begin to beat wildly. She pressed a hand to her chest and breathed deeply. Jiang was at her side in a moment.

"What is it, my pet? Oh, my spirit longs to take away your fear and sadness." She placed a plump hand on Kulien's shoulder. "I am no more pleased about this marriage than you are, but the contract cannot be changed."

Kulien took Jiang's hand in her own. "If only I could talk Father into letting me stay here, but I know I cannot. There is only one thing I can do—and I will do it."

A smile creased Jiang's face, and her small ebony eyes glistened. "There now, my child, I know it won't be easy for you, but you are making the right decision to submit to your father. Your life will be much more difficult if you fight against the will of the gods."

The Planting Season

*"He, who goes out weeping, bearing the seed for sowing, shall
come home with shouts of joy, bringing his sheaves with him."*
~~~~Psalm 126:6~~~~

TWELVE

A blanket of darkness shrouded the compound as only the
sound of crickets echoed through the night. Kulien inhaled
deeply, believing that, at last, all the members of the household
had settled down and were sleeping. Mahwu had been more
obstinate than usual—demanding that Jiang, instead of her own
servant, increase her opium allowance. Her cries for Jiang to
come to her aid kept the *amah* scurrying from one apartment to
another trying to soothe the old lady, and at the same time,
comfort Kulien in her unhappy state.

Kulien was actually relieved to have Jiang not constantly
hovering over her, but she would never understand her
grandmother! Was she trying to keep Jiang from her duties to
Kulien? And how did she become so dependent upon the strong
drug? Peace finally reigned over the compound once the
matriarch had fallen into a stupor.

Jiang stopped by Kulien's rooms before retiring to her
own just a short distance away. "Sleep well tonight, my child,"
she said in a soft voice. "If you have trouble, let me know, and
I'll give you a little of Mahwu's potion."

Kulien pretended to be asleep and listened as her *amah*
hobbled down the hallway on her bound feet to a much needed
rest.

After waiting for what seemed hours, Kulien combed out
her hair in long raven sheets that flowed over her shoulders
almost reaching her waist. She brushed at the bangs worn by
virgin girls, knowing that soon the bangs would be allowed to
grow out. Although it was too dark to see well, she felt through

the wardrobe for a favorite satin gown and dropped it over her head. Her hands smoothed over the crimson fabric embroidered with white lilies, and she fastened the knotted frogs into their loops. Behind her clothes, she had hidden a basket of food stolen earlier from the gods of the temple. Not only had she invaded the temple, but she also had breached her father's rooms, and had taken one of his ankle-length robes, a pair of scissors, and a razor. Her heart pounded as she remembered the unforgivable deeds she had committed that afternoon. She would never have undertaken such actions, but for the love she felt for the Englishman. She would change his bandages, trim his moustache, and shave his face; and then she'd help him dress in clean clothes. Perhaps they would touch again, yet she must be very careful not to frighten him away with her words of marriage. She had lost face with him the last time they spoke, and to win his love, she must be careful how she presented herself.

Cautiously and quietly, she crept down the stairs, across the inner courtyard and over the crescent bridge. A sliver of the moon, partially hidden by clouds, was the only light on her pathway, but she had been to the summerhouse so many times, she had no need of light.

The eaves of the pavilion's tiled roof stood out against the dark sky like fingers pointing upward and far away from this place. Kulien approached the steps holding the basket and the clothes against her pounding heart. Would Marshall Whitfield be happy to see her again, or was he only concerned about the food and drink she brought?

As she stepped onto the stone floor, the quietness of the room sent a shiver of fear through her body. There were no sounds coming from the corner where the man lay. Had he died during the day? Was she too late? Or perhaps Sunfu had returned, and taken Lord Whitfield back to his post in Shanghai.

She set the basket down and reached for the lantern where she had left it the night before. Her hands trembled as she lit the wick of the candle and held it overhead. As the rosy glow of the light shone across the mat, Kulien fell to her knees and leaned over the prostrate figure. Marshall Whitfield lay on his back, his eyes closed, and his face pale. She touched his forehead; it was cold and damp. Had her only hope, her love, departed beyond the Yellow Springs?

A groan startled her. "Kulien," he spoke so softly she could barely hear him. "There's pain...so much pain."

She pressed a hand against her heart and breathed a sigh of relief. "Oh, Lord Whitfield, I feared that you had died!"

"Perhaps death would be a release from this pain. I don't know if I can bear it much longer."

Kulien touched the bandaged wound, and began to remove the cloths. There was not only blood, but the bandages were soaked with infection. Without flinching she set her mind to unwinding the cloths and held the light closer to examine the deep laceration.

"Oh, it is very red and swollen. I've seen this kind of infection before...on my cat."

Marshall couldn't repress a smile. "Your cat? Don't tell me you will treat me as you would your cat."

"Oh, but I love Sapphire with all my heart. The doctor came to our compound and lanced the wound. When it ran clean, he applied a medicine, the same that I have here, and Sapphire recovered!" Her enthusiasm eased the tension between them, and their eyes met in understanding and trust.

"Then you must think of me as your cat and do what needs to be done."

"I'm afraid it will hurt very much, but I have some strong wine to dull the pain." She lifted his head and held the bottle of rice wine to his lips, and watched him swallow, grimacing with each sip. When she lowered him back onto the mat, she warned, "Now this will sting, but I must cleanse your wound thoroughly."

Kulien held the sharpest edge of the scissors near the light and poured part of the wine over the blade to disinfect it, and the rest over the gash. Marshall Whitfield moaned and braced himself for the expected lancing. Kulien gathered the strength she had left and pressed the sharp point of the scissors against the swollen and seeping wound. Pus streaked with blood drained from the injury for several moments. When it looked clean and the swelling had somewhat subsided, Kulien administered the medication she had left and then wrapped the injury with clean bandages she had torn from an old tunic. She smiled down at him, proud of his courage. "It will heal now," she said. She gathered up the bloody rags and buried them behind the summerhouse under some dead leaves. She returned with a bowl of cool water from the stream and knelt beside him.

Marshall took a deep breath and relaxed after drinking some of the water. "I am sorry to be so much trouble for you. Sunfu should never have brought me here. I have put you in danger."

"Oh," Kulien sighed, gazing down upon Marshall's face, "it is I who am sorry for your pain. How could he have done such a cruel act? He shames our family." Her last words were barely audible. "But now, brother of my esteemed teacher, the blood has stopped seeping, and I think the infection is well drained and properly dressed. I can only hope you will soon be well." She touched Marshall's face, gently stroking the broad forehead as his eyes closed and he rested peacefully.

Kulien sat for many minutes watching the face of this man who had captured her heart. Impulsively she leaned over him and whispered, "You can't die, Marshall Whitfield. I love you, and I always will."

It seemed that hours passed before Marshall opened his eyes, and with effort spoke softly, "Kulien, I dreamed that you said you loved me. Could one as pure and untouched as you possibly love a man like me?" His voice cracked with emotion.

Kulien pressed her fingers over her lips. "Forgive me...you did not dream my words. I spoke without caution." In the faint light of the moon's rays, her tears sparkled like jewels before streaming down her cheeks. "I have lost face once again, and have disgraced myself before you."

With his hand held out to her, Marshall took her cool fingers in his and urged her closer. His bandaged shoulder lay on a small satin pillow, but his free hand slipped under her hair and rested on her neck. Tenderly, he drew her face to his and kissed away the tears.

Kulien's heart thrilled as his lips caressed her eyelids and cheeks. She caught her breath and pulled away.

"Now I need your forgiveness," he said. "I have no right to touch you like that. You belong to another man."

Kulien leaned closer; her perfumed hair brushing Marshall's cheek. "My marriage is not until the Moon Festival. It is not a marriage of my choice as I have explained to you." She sighed deeply. "I am yours, Lord Whitfield—if you'll have me." *Oh, by the gods, I've done it again,* she thought. *Whatever must he think of me?*

Marshall's voice broke with huskiness. "This must be a dream. I cannot believe that you, a pure young virgin, would offer yourself to me."

He sighed before continuing, "I am a man of breeding, Kulien. I cannot take advantage of you as you suggest." His eyes searched hers, and then rested on her parted lips. His voice lowered to a whisper, "But I am a man, after all, and you are the loveliest creature…."

Kulien pressed a finger on his lips to stop his words. "I do not know much about love, but I have been given instruction about marriage…how a man and woman seal their wedding vows." She felt her face warm as she spoke, remembering the words of Jiang regarding her duties as a wife. "If we—if we should 'marry ourselves' to each other, my father would have to release me from the contract with Kong Litang. Then later we could have a formal ceremony and I could be with you forever!"

Had she said too much? Had she brought more shame to herself and put this honorable English gentleman under obligation to her pleas?

Marshall waited several moments before responding. His voice faltered, "You would be disgraced if you gave yourself to me, Kulien! Your father would disown you. I find it most difficult to reject your proposal, but I cannot allow you to dishonor yourself."

Kulien closed her eyes, imagining her future with Kong Litang…or with Marshall Whitfield. "I have already been disgraced and disowned. My father has consigned me to a form of death. If there is disgrace or dishonor, it would not come from you. I make my own choice. As I said before, if you will have me, I am yours."

Marshall's eyes met Kulien's again, "Can there possibly be a future for us?"

Kulien stretched out beside him careful not to brush against his injury. Marshall pulled her closer with his right arm and heard her say, "There is now—this present moment. I don't want to think beyond this moment."

They lay side by side not speaking, but watching the shadows cast on the ceiling by the flickering candle. Kulien snuggled closer. "Tonight I can lie here beside you and imagine that you might love me."

Marshall's voice trembled with emotion, "There is a story in the Bible about an ancient Eastern king by the name of David. In his old age, he often lay shivering in his bed, unable to keep warm."

He stopped talking long enough to brush the top of Kulien's head with his lips. "A young virgin by the name of Abishag ministered to her king by lying beside him to warm his body." Marshall's arm tightened around her shoulders. "You are my Abishag, Kulien. You warm my body and my heart. In spite of all that is right or wrong, I want you for my own!"

Kulien's heart soared with joy. "Oh, Marshall, after we say our vows to each other here, I will go with you to the British Consulate. They will permit us to marry because my mother was British."

Marshall sighed. "I can't promise you that we can legally marry. We will have to be content with the present, but we must both think seriously about what you've suggested."

Kulien, discouraged by Marshall's words, rose to her knees and glanced toward the eastern sky. "The hour grows late, and I must return to my rooms before I am missed. Perhaps Sunfu will come for you before night falls again."

"Sunfu! Oh, I forgot to tell you. He came here early this morning. I didn't fully understand him, but he left a message." Marshall felt under the mat. "I put it beside the Bible I found hidden under here." He smiled and handed her a scroll. "I can only read a few Chinese characters. Will you read it to me?"

With her head bent over the scroll, Kulien said, "My step-brother sent a friend who understands English to the consulate. He heard, and so did your sister, that you were kidnapped or killed by a band of thieves. Everyone looks for you. Sunfu says for his safety, it would be wise for you to stay here for two more days. He will come back with English clothes and take you to the Bund when the moon does not shine."

Kulien's heart filled with gratitude. There was still time for Marshall to make a decision about her proposal for them to marry. "This means I can come back to see you…if you want me to?" Her words ended in a question.

Marshall lifted both arms to her, flinching in pain. "I do want you as long as possible. But I don't trust myself. I would rather die than hurt you."

Kulien lay back down and rested her head on his chest. "Do not speak of death or hurt. We are alive now, and even though there is the possibility that we may not legally marry, we have more time together before fate separates us. Please consider my plan. I have not changed my mind about what I want."

She rose to a sitting position and nodded toward the graying sky, "It grows light in the east, so I must leave before Jiang discovers my empty bed. Do not concern yourself about human laws, or about my age and my father's determination to send me away to Hangchow. I know it's possible for us to change destiny, but only if you are willing to take the risk."

THIRTEEN

Kulien spent most of the next day in her rooms, her mind and heart battling over her desires and the plans of her father. She knew in the depths of her spirit that she belonged to Lord Marshall Whitfield, and that his love for her was just as strong. She would not marry Kong Litang even if it meant her death. The plan forming in her soul was the only answer…if only she could convince Marshall that there was a way for them to be married.

Jiang seemed agitated and looked in on her more than usual, a frown crinkling her smooth brow. "Why do I have to keep nagging at you? You spend too much time idling about the house."

"I don't feel well," Kulien answered. "It is time for crimson snows, and there's pain in my body." She surprised herself at how easily the lie came.

Jiang stood in front of her and shook a finger in her face. "The visitation was upon you two weeks ago! I washed the cloths myself. You don't fool me, my pet. You know better than to lie to me."

Kulien had forgotten that Jiang knew everything about her. *Actually, you don't know everything!* "I'm sorry," she said. "It's just that I'm tired and want to stay in my rooms today." She lifted her shoulders in a shrug.

"You've been behaving strangely for days. Do you tell the truth now? If you do, swear upon the graves of your ancestors."

Kulien put her hands over her face and pretended to cry. "You're so mean, Jiang. Why can't you leave me alone? You know how sick I am about leaving home and going so far away. If you had to marry an ugly old frog, you would be miserable, too."

Jiang patted Kulien's bowed head. "I know, child. I'm not happy about the arrangement either. I have to leave this place, too, you know." Jiang turned to leave the room, her shoulders stooped, and her steps slower than usual.

Kulien had not even considered Jiang's future. Even though she would continue to be Kulien's *amah* in Hangchow, she would be leaving the only security she had ever known. And perhaps the old Kong patriarch would forbid her to wait on Kulien any longer. *None* of this could happen. It simply could not!

She glanced out the window toward the northeastern trees where the summerhouse was secluded, and where the man she loved waited. Only the gods knew what the future held. She closed her eyes, imagining the future.

After several quiet moments, she opened her eyes and went to the window overlooking her private patio. There beyond the woods in the summerhouse was the only man she could ever love. He was older and wiser than she, but she believed that he truly loved her. He had held her close and gazed into her eyes, and then he kissed away the tears from her cheeks. The very thought of his closeness sent a shiver up her spine. If they should…if they should come together as husband and wife, the marriage contract with Kong Litang would be broken. The man was expecting a virgin daughter from the House of Kuang, and Kulien's father could not keep the bargain if his daughter had lain with a man.

She wrapped her arms around herself as she contemplated her father's response when he learned that she had willingly given her maidenhood to the Englishman. He would be furious, but surely he would forgive her and allow her to leave China with Marshall Whitfield. He himself had broken the marriage contract to take an English bride.

She began to relax as she imagined first Lufong's anger, then his remorse. He had always loved and spoiled her, and would understand the passion that drove her into the Englishman's arms. There was no other way. She and Marshall Whitfield would pronounce their own marriage vows to their gods and, then at a later date, marry under the law of the land. They would be heard for their sincerity and love for each other. Although Kulien could not be certain that Lord Whitfield would agree with her plan, she would prepare herself for a private wedding ceremony to take place tonight in the summerhouse.

She trembled at the thought of an intimate union with this man who had won her heart, and quickly dismissed the idea that it might possibly be an immoral act in the sight of the gods.

Even though chastity for Chinese girls was demanded, the gods of her ancestors might look the other way as they did when young girls were sold into slavery or offered as concubines to rich old men.

Kulien lifted her head as a smile crinkled the corners of her eyes. She had made the decision. Her fate, from this day forward would be forever changed.

Once again, Kulien waited until it was nearing midnight and there were no sounds from any part of the compound. She removed all her clothes and dressed only in a gold silk gown with an opening from collar to hemline. Over the gown, she wore a long black cloak. Inside the pocket, she tucked a square of white cloth and the jade ring that had been her mother's. She brushed her long flowing hair, and lifted it to drape over her shoulders before dabbing a fragrance of jasmine behind each ear. It was too dark to see her reflection, but she knew her eyes sparkled with excitement and her cheeks flushed with anticipation. She glided down the stairs from her rooms, careful to avoid the one that squeaked. She edged her way in the shadows through her courtyard, and trying to quiet her racing heart, headed down the pathway through the woods to the summerhouse.

When she stepped into the opening that led to the summerhouse, her breath caught in her throat. Marshall, with a trimmed moustache and shaved face, stood in the entrance dressed in Lufong's robe. Holding the lantern in his hand, he set it down when he saw her, and held out an arm, inviting her close. She had to repress a smile at his hairy legs showing below the hem of the gown, but she rushed up the steps to him.

"You—you look so much better. Your wound must be almost healed!" She paused to stare. "And you're dressed and look so very handsome! I must confess I am surprised."

Marshall laughed aloud as he encircled her with his good arm. "My Abishag, my nurse, took good care of me. She tended my wound; she fed me; and…," he brushed his lips over her forehead, "…and she won my heart."

Kulien was unsure of his meaning, but as he lowered his face to hers she knew he declared his love. His lips whispered softly over her forehead, her eyes, and her nose, and with gentle, yet eager persuasion, he led her to the mat, holding her close beside him. "This has been the longest day of my life," he said. "I thought you would never arrive. I've thought of nothing, of no one but you."

His nearness was overwhelming, and Kulien caught her breath as she sat beside him on the mat. She took his hand and held it to her face, her eyes not leaving his. "This has been a day for me to make final arrangements. I hope you will agree with them."

Before the last word was spoken, Marshall placed his hand on the back of her neck; his fingers entwined in her hair and drew her face to him, capturing her lips with his. His passion unnerved her and she could barely speak when he released his hold.

She covered his lips with her fingertips. "You must let me speak before I lose my courage. I have given it great thought and have implored the gods and your God also, for wisdom. You said our laws forbid us to marry, yet is there a higher law than the law of Heaven?" She didn't wait for an answer, but went on. "And when we arrive at the embassy, could we not make our spoken vows legal?"

Marshall kissed her fingers before responding, "All right, then. I give up; you have my complete attention...and my love."

Now, she thought, *I must prove to him that we can and must marry ourselves tonight.*

Kulien inhaled deeply, overcome by the moment and the words she wanted to say. "We will marry ourselves before my gods and your God. Elizabeth once told me that your God is always present, and that it is He who joins a man and woman in marriage." She smiled at his surprised expression. "You see, although Elizabeth thought I didn't understand what she said about her God, I listened and have given it much thought."

Without another word, Kulien rose from the mat and slipped off the heavy woolen robe. She stood before him with only the flicker of the candle illuminating her long golden gown and flowing black hair. "We will promise to love each other for as long as we live; then we will go to my father. When he learns that we have made vows of marriage, he will set me free from the marriage contract to Kong Litang. We can be together always as husband and wife."

She fingered the fastenings at the neck of her gown before going on. "Your country will make an allowance for you because you are a British noble." She unbuttoned the first two frogs of the high collar. "If you truly love me as you say, let us marry…tonight." Her last words were an anxious whisper.

Marshall looked up at her, his eyes wide and his mouth partially open. "Are you saying that we should…? That is, do you want us to consummate our wedding vows? Here? Tonight?" He raked long fingers through his hair and continued to gaze at her, his eyes sweeping from the top of her head to her silk-clad feet. "Kulien, as I said last night, I am moved and honored by what you suggest, but have you seriously considered the consequences? Are you certain this is what you want?"

She bent to trace the side of his smooth face with her hand. "I am willing to accept whatever awaits me. I am choosing my destiny. I love you and want to give myself to you…if you will have me." She closed her eyes, her heart pounding as she waited.

Quiet reigned throughout the forbidden pavilion for several moments. Marshall stared at her showing his concern about the possibilities and the problems ahead. A cold breeze wafted through the room scattering dry leaves that lay on the floor. As the wind rose in intensity, a cloud covered the moon and the candle sputtered and died. Neither of them spoke or moved. Then as suddenly as it had begun the wind ceased and faint rays of moonlight shone through the latticed windows illuminating Kulien's delicate form.

Marshall was on his feet and gathered her in his arms, ignoring the pain. His kisses were the answer she hungered for and she surrendered herself to his passion. When he loosened his hold, he stepped back. "I've lost my senses and feel like a crazy man. I can't go on without you, yet what you suggest is more than I can expect of you."

Kulien lifted the cloak off the floor and reached into the pocket to take out the jade ring. She held it in an open hand in the ray of the moon. "See, I have a token of my love to give you as we are wed. This was my Mother's wedding ring given to her by my Father. It has passed from generation to generation. It will be yours now."

Marshall touched the ring, then Kulien's face. "This ring is too valuable. You are too valuable. I cannot take it—or you," he said, his voice breaking with emotion.

Kulien's voice was firm, but soft, "My ring is but a symbol of something more precious…and you do not take it…I give it. I give you not only my treasured ring, but also my marriage vows…and my virginity."

She held out the ring before placing it in his hand. "May this remind you of me always because jade possesses five virtues: love, goodness, wisdom, justice and courage."

Marshall glanced from the ring in his open hand to her face. "You are all that and much more. What can I give you as a token of my love?" He frowned as if thinking before his teeth shone in a smile. "I know. This, then, is yours." He twisted the gold circle off the little finger of his left hand, and held it so the rays of moonlight would shine upon the engraving. "This is my family crest—all that I have to give you. Its value is that only those born to the noble House of Whitfield are entitled to it. It is my signature on legal documents." He paused and placed it in her hand. "In giving you my signet ring, I entrust to you my rights as the only son of Lord George Whitfield, Baron of Whitfield Manor."

Neither spoke for several moments as each held the treasured objects. Finally Marshall, with her ring on his little finger, took her hand in his. "Do you think your gods consider us married now?"

"It is for you to decide." Kulien's voice trembled as tears rose to her eyes. "But let us bow our heads and pray to our own gods, then regardless of laws and cultures we will consider ourselves wed."

Marshall bit the edge of his lower lip. "Kulien, I must confess to you that I am not a religious man. My beliefs are not strong like my sister's. I'm not sure that God will hear my prayers."

"But surely you believe in the same God. I thought all Europeans believed in the God of your Holy Bible. Won't you vow before him to love me and take me for your wife?"

"All Europeans are not Christians, Kulien." He lowered his head. "I am called a Christian simply because I'm British, but I don't believe the way Elizabeth does. I do love you, but I can't promise that God will hear, or that our marriage vows will be acceptable to Heaven."

"I don't care about that," she said firmly. "I only care about you." She paused as her feelings for him intensified. "If you do not take me as your wife tonight, I have no future but to be sent away to Hangchow. It has been decided that I leave in only a few short weeks. Do you want me to be a slave to an old man whose only desire is to own me?"

Marshall took her in his arms again and whispered in her hair. "I won't allow that to happen to you! We'll do as you say, and your father will have to release you from that contract." His voice broke with huskiness.

Kulien's heart beat faster. "I confess that I'm afraid—not of you or of what will happen between us, but of my father. He has always forgiven my deeds in the past, and my hope is that he will do so again—that he will acknowledge my love for you and let me return with you to Great Britain."

Marshall held her at arm's length and spoke slowly. "My dearest love, more than anything I want you to be with me forever, but it will take time and the bending of some rules. However, I'll do all I can for us to be legally married so we can return to England together."

"Are you certain that you love me as a husband loves a wife?" Kulien folded her arms tightly against her waist as she waited for his answer.

"I do. I love you with all my heart." His voice smoldered with passion.

"Then let us say our vows to each other and whatever gods hear us, they will bless us with favor."

"Do you realize what it will mean for us to come together as a man and woman—to make love?"

Kulien lifted her head and put both hands on either side of Marshall's face. "I know. I have been given instructions, and although the thought of such actions with Kong Litang sickened me, when I am in your arms, I only long to be totally yours."

Marshall drew her close and she clung to him with the rising wind as the only sound echoing through the small building. Kulien shivered as a cloud passed over the moon and an image of her grandfather's restless spirit swept over her. She felt the struggle between what might be right and wrong in the eyes of the gods—and of her father. But her love for Marshall won over her indecision. She stepped back, and with her eyes lowered, she began to open the fastenings of her gown until it fell at her feet like a pool of molten gold.

She heard Marshall gasp, and wondered if he found her unattractive. Standing still and straight, but with her head bowed, she asked, "Marshall, have I shamed myself before you? Am I too thin and immature for you?"

Marshall's voice was husky and barely audible. "Oh, Kulien, you are so beautiful, so young and pure. I 'm not worthy of your love."

Kulien's strength returned, and she lifted her head, her eyes searching his face. "It is I who am unworthy, Lord Whitfield. You are a man of power and wealth; I am but a young woman who has been bargained away for my father's crime."

She turned to reach for the woolen robe that lay nearby. Removing the white cloth from an inside pocket, she dropped to her knees and spread it over the mat. "This is the customary cloth of the wedding night," she said, "so that you will be assured that I am a virgin bride." She glanced at Marshall as he knelt beside her on the mat, and took her hand in his.

His touch sent a tingle of pleasure through her body, and his voice was as gentle as an early spring breeze. "You are my only love, Kulien—you are my wife."

Kulien felt her cheeks color under his ardent gaze. "And I am yours—forever," she said. Whispered words of surrender and love were barely heard as the wind again rose and began to blow violently through the pavilion.

FOURTEEN

"Kulien, by the blood of our ancestors, what have you done?" Sunfu's voice raged above the sound of the continuing storm. A burning torch held between Kulien and the voice lit up Sunfu's face, twisted in anger and surprise. He held a dagger in his other hand and stood over Marshall Whitfield. "I should have killed you at the docks, *fankuei*. I wanted to, but my companions stopped me."

Marshall and Kulien were now wide awake, and sat up covering themselves with the quilt. Marshall's eyes widened in fear and his skin glistened with perspiration. "Put away your knife, Sunfu. Your sister's not at fault. I took advantage of her innocence. And you wouldn't dare kill me."

Kulien reached for her gown and covered herself as she stood. She shook uncontrollably, but forced herself to address her step-brother. "You cannot fault either of us. We have married ourselves in the eyes of our gods, and we have sealed our vows by coming together as husband and wife." As she spoke the words, her eyes rested on Marshall's upturned face, and her heart fluttered with the remembrance of their wedding night. "There is nothing you can do now. If you kill the foreigner, you'll be found out and your rebel band will be disgraced."

"You talk of disgrace? I thought you were my pure little sister. Now I know that you are no more than a prostitute to a foreign devil! Get away from here! Go to your rooms...now. I'll deal with this pox ridden son of a turtle!"

Kulien stared at Marshall, her eyes pleading, her mouth open in distress. Marshall rose to stand beside her, wrapping the quilt around himself. "Your sister has done nothing wrong. As I said, I forced myself on her."

Kulien gasped and looked up at him. "No, I won't let you say that. I gave myself freely and completely to you." She reached out for him, but Sunfu pushed her aside so hard, she almost fell. "Go put on your clothes." He reached down and picked up the soiled wedding cloth with the point of his dagger and shoved it at her. "Take this with you. I don't ever want to see or speak to you again."

Kulien ran to the corner of the room where she slipped the gown on and wrapped the cape over her shoulders. She folded the cloth and put it in her pocket. Tears stung her eyes as she strained to see Marshall's response. His gaze caught hers, and he lifted his shoulders and nodded for her to leave. Before she turned to go down the steps, she saw him hold up a finger where her jade ring shone in the early dawn light. She responded by raising her hand to show him that she wore his ring on her thumb.

As Kulien ran down the pathway leading to her quarters, her torn emotions replayed the hours she had spent in the arms of Marshall Whitfield. She would never forget his words of love and comfort as they came together. They had whispered endearments, laughed about the awkwardness of their movements, and even wept together as Kulien surrendered herself to him. Whatever Kuang Lufong or the gods prepared for her future, she would always have this one night of love to remember. But she knew it was only the beginning of a wonderful journey as Marshall's wife.

The sun appeared over the wall when she reached her rooms, expecting to be alone. She stopped mid-stride because Jiang stood in the center of the room, wringing her hands. "Where have you been? You were not in your rooms all night, neither were you in the gardens. Your bed hasn't been slept in." She hobbled closer to Kulien. "Your father came home last night and has been searching for you, so don't pretend to be innocent with me. I know you've been up to no good, and I can see that you swallow much bitterness. Tell me, and tell me now! Where have you been?"

"Oh, Jiang, please don't ask. I'm so tired. And why is Father here? I didn't expect him for days."

"I'm sure you didn't. Now answer me. I do not ask. I demand that you tell me where you were."

Jiang turned away from Kulien as if she could not bear to look at her. While her back was turned, Kulien rushed to the laundry basket and hid the soiled cloth under some other clothes. Jiang had been watching Kulien from the corner of her eyes, "What have you there? Don't try to hide from me."

Kulien put her hands on her hips and shouted back, "It's nothing. Leave me alone! Am I a baby that I must still nurse at my *amah*'s breast? I needed some privacy, that's all. I spent the night in the summerhouse…reading." Kulien's voice rose higher with each word, and beads of perspiration dotted her forehead.

Jiang came closer, and fastened her eyes on the basket. "You spin a web of words to veil the truth. I've suspected for some time that you sneak away to the summerhouse; but your face tells me you did not read last night." Before Kulien could stop her, Jiang pulled the lid off the basket and removed the white cloth smeared with blood.

Tears glistened in the older woman's eyes. "Have you been violated? Who did this? I'll kill him!" Her words ended in a sob.

Kulien, weak from the emotions of the night, crumpled at Jiang's feet. "I cannot speak of it yet. Please, Jiang let me gather the strands of my thoughts. I will not lie to you again, but I must be alone now. Please?"

Jiang's shoulders slumped in defeat. "It is worse than I thought, isn't it? Very well," she said, after reaching the doorway. "I'll go to my room, but first I'll put some warm water in your tub so you can cleanse yourself. I should insist on a scalding bath before you take a tonic to kill the man-seed. Unfortunately," she said, wringing her hands again, "the visitation of women passed two weeks ago, the worse time for a woman. Will there ever be anything but disaster in the House of Kuang?"

After mincing in and out of the room several times, Jiang finally produced a bottle of dark syrupy substance. "This is a potion of green ginger, orange peel and ginseng, blended with other secret ingredients. It will cleanse you and bring a flow of blood." Her eyes bored into Kulien's as she forced the bottle into her hand. "My spirit tells me I should stand here to see that you drink every drop! But we are both tired, so I leave you alone." She started down the hallway, her voice a shrill cry, "Oh, by the mercy of the gods, whatever are we going to do?"

"Whatever are we going to do? Whatever are we going to do?" Jiang's words echoed in Kulien's mind as she eased her aching body into the porcelain tub only partially filled with warm water. As she relived the events of the night, her heart pounded at the remembrance of the union that had brought happiness beyond her greatest fantasies. She had known the completeness of her womanhood and the joyous freedom of surrender and release in giving her body and soul to the man she considered her husband.

After Kulien dried herself and dressed for the day, she picked up the bottle that Jiang had left, and smiled within herself. Jiang could be right. Since the crimson snows had passed, perhaps Marshall's seed would grow, and she would have visible affirmation of their love. She stared at the bottle for only a moment before pulling out the cork and pouring the pungent solution into the bucket used for night soil.

The late afternoon sun was directly overhead when Jiang came back into the room. Kulien took the *amah*'s hands in hers and led her to a carved mahogany bench beside the window. "I have decided to tell you the truth, and then you will go with me to my father." She sighed. "I'm glad he is home. I want to speak with him before the day is over. He will be angry, but I am sure he'll forgive me as he has in the past."

Kulien pointed beyond the trees to the far northeastern corner of the compound as she related the events of the past week. She paused often to wipe away both her own and Jiang's tears as she told of the wedding ceremony and her great joy when she and Marshall consummated their love. After she finished speaking, they sat quietly looking over the trees, each enveloped in her own private thoughts. "Will you go with me to my Father?"

Jiang's face drained of color. "He will be furious! Suppose he does away with himself as his father did."

Kulien laced and unlaced her fingers. "Kuang Lufong is against such a practice. He is too wise. I know he'll be angry, and perhaps lose face with the Kong clan, but he loves me as he loved his chosen wife. I hope very soon, if not today, he will understand and forgive me."

"I'm not so sure," Jiang said, reaching for Kulien's hands. "This is different. You are a female, and *that* man is a foreign devil who has invaded our land...and you." She closed her eyes, "*Aiyah*! It is too much. Kuang would forever lose face if he forgave you. He will have to bring the foreigner to justice. But," she added, "he brought this grief on himself. If your feet had been wrapped as your grandmother and I wished, you would not have been able to run into such mischief."

It was after the evening meal that Kulien, dressed in a new turquoise gown embroidered with silver cranes that she prepared for an audience with her father. She surrendered to Jiang's ministrations as she braided Kulien's long hair and coiled it around her head like a crown. The *amah* continued to fuss like a mother hen while she dusted Kulien's face with rice powder to disguise her flushed cheeks.

With a somber face Kulien walked through the gardens, Jiang following close behind. When they reached the library, Jiang clapped her hands to alert the patriarch of their arrival. Kuang Lufong sat on a high-backed chair, arms folded against his chest, dark eyes piercing the faint light shed by the lantern on his desk. He sat stiff and erect, wearing the full regalia of a third degree mandarin.

Kulien pulled aside the drapery, stepped over the high sill and entered the doorway, but instead of running to him as in the past, she waited for his invitation. Her knees trembled as she laced cold fingers together at her waist. Jiang stood aside, holding her breath.

"You may approach, *Bitter Seed*." Lufong's voice was as cold as a winter stream and his expression was filled with contempt. "I am told that you were not in your rooms last night. Is that so?"

Kulien searched her father's face for any sign of compassion before answering. "That is true, honorable Father. I have come to confess my disobedience." She averted her eyes, staring instead at the intricate tapestry on the wall behind him. Her breath was labored as she took a step closer and pressed a cool hand to her warm cheek. "My Father, I pray that, as a most merciful man, you will forgive me; however, I must be honest and confess that I have no shame for my behavior."

"That is most unfortunate," he said, grimacing as if he were in great pain. Muttering to himself, he glanced from Kulien to Jiang who stood near her charge. "And why is it that you are not shamed for leaving your rooms in the middle of the night?" he roared. "Have you no concern for propriety? Where did you go, and what were you doing?"

Kulien felt in the depths of her heart that Lufong knew the answers to his questions, but had put her on trial. "I—I went to the summerhouse, Father. I spent the night with Miss Whitfield's brother. I lay with him as a wife with her husband."

Lufong's face paled as he listened, weighing the consequences of her actions. "No! You lie! You are contracted to marry Kong Litang. It is he who was promised a virgin bride." He clenched his jaws so tightly that his chin jutted forward as if pointing a finger of accusation at her.

Kulien fell to her knees at Lufong's feet touching her head to the floor three times. Tears poured from her eyes and she made no effort to stop them. "No, my Father, no, please hear me." She lifted her head. "I love Lord Marshall Whitfield, and he loves me. We have repeated vows of marriage before our gods. I cannot marry Kong Litang!"

Lufong leaned forward in his chair, his voice like sharpened iron. "You have no need to kowtow to me. Regardless of what you say, the matter is settled and cannot be changed."

Jiang edged forward, her eyelids fluttering, and her breathing heavy. "Master, may I speak?" She bowed from the waist, her fingers entwined so tightly her knuckles were white.

"Jiang, I entrusted my daughter to your keeping. What could you have to say that I don't already know?"

Jiang gathered up all the strength she had left. She reached out a hand to touch Kulien's shoulder, urging her to stand. "I would only ask that you allow your daughter to explain, though I do agree that she has behaved badly by disobeying you and *loving a foreigner*." She emphasized the last words with the hope that Kuang Lufong would remember his own past and show mercy.

"Very well, Bitter Seed, you may speak, though your words are as empty as a dry well and totally meaningless to me." His words continued to cut away at her courage.

Kulien could not bring herself to look at her father, but kept her head down as she related the past days' events to him.

"Your step-son, Sunfu, injured Miss Whitfield's brother with his knife. He brought the foreigner to the summerhouse and begged me to minister food and medicine to him. If the Englishman had died, Sunfu would have had to pay with his life." She peeked up through her bangs to see if her father's expression had changed, but he continued to glare, clenching his teeth, and breathing heavily.

Kulien inhaled deeply before continuing, "Lord Marshall Whitfield's condition was serious for as many as four days. I went to him every night and took food and medicine. I do love this man, Father, and he loves me." She lowered her eyes, imagining Marshall riding back to Shanghai with Sunfu's dagger at his back. "As I said, we vowed before the gods to love each other forever—much like you and my mother did; then we sealed our vows by joining our bodies...."

"Silence!" he shouted, holding up a hand. "Do not compare this unlawful whoring with the marriage that took place between Marguerite Howard and me. You are but a child, and that foreigner invaded not only my home, but even worse, my betrothed daughter. There is no comparison." Lufong looked past Kulien to Jiang while stroking his goatee, "Prepare Bitter Seed for her wedding to Kong Litang. She will be kept in isolation for the four weeks preceding her journey to Hangchow for the wedding."

"But Father, you must forgive me. I told you..."

"Jiang," he said, deliberately turning his eyes away from Kulien, "I will not listen nor speak with this young woman again. I rely upon your discretion to keep secret what you have heard in this room tonight. The marriage, though postponed to a later date, will proceed as planned. My father must find rest for his spirit—now more than ever. This woman," he gestured toward Kulien who stared in disbelief, "this woman has defiled even the place of my father's death." He continued to speak to Jiang as if Kulien were invisible. "Go with your charge to Hangchow. At the risk of losing *your* life, carry out this deception—and find a way to prove that Bitter Seed is a virgin bride. Convince the groom and his mother. Appropriate gifts will be sent."

Without another word or glance in Kulien's direction, Lufong, patriarch of the Kuang clan rose from his seat, walked past Kulien and Jiang, and disappeared through a sliding panel.

Kulien couldn't believe that he would use the painful birth-name with such a tone of dismissal and even hatred! He had always been her champion even when other family members mocked and cursed her. Had she lost him forever?

She fell in a heap at Jiang's feet and wept. Although she loved Marshall Whitfield with all her heart, and knew that he loved her, would their love replace the devotion and respect her father now denied her? The cruelty in Lufong's eyes and his total disregard for her would remain as a heavy stone in her heart for the rest of her life.

FIFTEEN

That night when Kulien returned to her rooms, she considered her father's words to Jiang, "Prepare Bitter Seed for her wedding to Kong Litang. She will be kept in isolation for the *four weeks* preceding her journey to Hangchow for the wedding."

Four weeks? That meant she would stay in her home beyond the celebration of Moon Festival late in September, which had been the scheduled wedding date. Her heart thrilled to know she would not leave as soon as she had dreaded. Four more weeks would be after the Chrysanthemum Festival. She would have two or three more weeks to make plans, and perhaps her father, though angry, would change his mind and allow her to be with Marshall Whitfield.

"Jiang," Kulien asked the next morning, "was I wrong in believing the marriage ceremony to Kong Litang was to be at the time of the Moon Festival?"

Jiang's round face creased in a slight smile. "You were not wrong, child. Your esteemed father told me the Kong clan has agreed to a later date." She patted Kulien's shoulder before she sat on a low stool. "But you must not deceive yourself by thinking that your father has reversed his decision. The change was made because Moon Festival is one rich in poetic significance when the moon is perfectly round." She hobbled to a bench facing Kulien, and folded her hands in her lap. "Because it is a happy celebration, your father does not want to associate it with your marriage."

"Is it because he regrets that he promised me to Kong Litang?" Kulien knew the answer before Jiang spoke.

"The reason your father changed the wedding ceremony is because of your wicked behavior with the foreigner. He gives you time to repent of your actions." Jiang tilted her head to one side and lifted her shoulders. "You do repent, don't you?"

Kulien stood up and placed her hands on her hips. "Never! I will never be sorry that I gave myself to Lord Marshall Whitfield. I will love him always. My body and soul are dead to Kong Litang!"

The following weeks passed slowly for Kulien as she was confined to her rooms with Jiang as her only companion. Her mind and heart yearned to know of Marshall and where he had been taken. Was he at the British Consulate? Would Sunfu forgive her and bring news of Marshall? Sadness and a sense of despair washed over her spirit, as day after day she brooded about her future. Only the remembrance of Marshall's touch and his words of love enabled her to face each new day.

"I heard the family celebrating yesterday," she said one evening as she sat eating rice with Jiang. "From my windows I could see that the tubs of flowers had been set out for the Chrysanthemum Festival. The gaiety seemed much greater than in past years."

"It's true," Jiang replied. "Your brother, Ohchin, passed the second of the official examinations." She paused, her brow furrowed. "He completed the test of fine handwriting and expressed knowledge of the classical texts. He has only to write prose and poetry that contain elegant echoes of the past." She smiled broadly as she rehearsed some of the parts of the civil service examinations. "The family, particularly your father, finds hope in his step-son's great accomplishment. He will be fully prepared to rule this clan as a wise patriarch when the master passes beyond the Yellow Springs."

Kulien threw down her chopsticks. "A wise patriarch indeed! He is cruel and vicious. The family will suffer under his leadership. I should be glad that I'll be far away from here when that day arrives."

"You are not the only one who will be glad to have you away from this compound...foreign devil...whore!" Ohchin stood in the entrance to her quarters, his unattractive face marred even further by a sneering mouth and glinting slits for eyes. He was dressed in full mandarin regalia and fingered the amber beads that hung around his thick neck.

Both Kulien and Jiang gasped at his appearance because the men of the compound never entered the residences of unmarried females. "What right do you have to come here?" Kulien shouted, stepping close enough for his garlic breath to assail her senses. "Leave at once."

"I have every right to enter this room," he said, still squinting at her. "You are neither an unmarried female, nor are you even a member of this clan anymore. You are an outcast, a half-breed who fornicated with a 'big nose' *fankuei!*" He turned to leave, but stopped before crossing the threshold. "I wish I could see what happens to you when the Kong patriarch discovers his 'virgin bride' has been bedded by a foreigner! Ha! I hope he beats you to death!"

Kulien paled at Ohchin's words. How could he be so cruel? Would his wish be fulfilled? She turned to Jiang's open arms as Ohchin disappeared from sight. "Oh, Jiang, what is to become of me? Can you help me escape?"

Jiang's face showed her concern. "There is nothing an old *amah* can do to save you. You must pray to Kuanyin, Goddess of Mercy. She cares for all females and perhaps she will show you how to bear whatever destiny has planned for you."

"But Jiang, I can't pray to a statue anymore. I need someone strong to help me!" Her thoughts turned to Sunfu. He had always been the strong one on her side, at least until he discovered her with Lord Whitfield. "Do you know where Sunfu is? Is there gossip among the clan members? Has he completely abandoned me, too?"

Wrinkles creased Jiang's brow. "It is said that your brother has forsaken his ancestors to join the bandits from the south."

"Then he's gone from my life. I have no one now."

"The rumor is that he travels with the Taipings who set up a kingdom in the walled city of Nanking." Jiang shook her head and sighed. "Your brother follows a man who is Chinese yet practices the Western religion. Disgraceful!"

Jiang had told her nothing new except that Sunfu had left the province and that it was unlikely he would return. Was there any way for her to reach Marshall?

"I must know what has happened to Lord Whitfield. Has my father ordered him to be executed? Oh, Jiang," Kulien begged, "will you try to learn what's become of him?" She blinked her eyes to keep the tears from escaping.

With effort, Jiang lifted herself from the low stool and rose from the table. "I don't know what you think I can do. I cannot learn anything about this man; nor do I want to. He has defiled you, a young girl. I'm ashamed even to think of him."

Kulien gripped both Jiang's hands in hers. "But I love him! You could go to Shanghai to see my teacher. She lives in a place called, 'Orphanage of Shang Ti.' She might know where her brother is."

"No, I will not do that!"

"But I have to know if he's still alive. I must know if he's in China. If you don't do this for me, I'll die, I know I will." As she spoke, she felt the bile rise to her throat and raced for the night soil bucket.

Jiang followed Kulien and wiped her mouth with a clean cloth she had tucked into her sleeve. "Why are you sick? I know you haven't eaten a rotten egg, yet I hear you vomit every morning." Jiang paused, her dark eyes narrowed. "I remember I had that sickness when I was expecting a child." She arched her thin eyebrows. "You didn't drink the tonic, did you? That foreign devil planted his seed in you, and you did nothing to kill it."

Kulien pressed her fingers to her lips and closed her eyes. *Could she be right? Am I carrying Marshall's child?*

Jiang didn't miss Kulien's hidden smile. "Then it's true, isn't it? You carry the demon seed in your belly."

Kulien flushed with pleasure. "Are you saying that I am 'with happiness'?"

The older woman grasped Kulien's arm, digging her fingernails into the skin. "Not if I have anything to say about it. I've failed enough by not keeping a closer eye on you. I'll not let you marry Kong Litang with a baby growing inside you." She loosened her grasp. "I know a woman who is expert at such things. She will remove the devil seed before it grows any larger. I will send a messenger for her tomorrow."

Kulien pulled away to gaze out the window. Although the sun had set, it was still light enough for her to see the changing colors encompassing the compound. The leaves had turned to gold and with every gust of wind a few loosed their hold and drifted to the ground. Although the sap had ceased its flow to the branches and sure death and decay lay ahead for the abundant foliage of the surrounding woods, life grew within her body. A beautiful child, a lasting token of Marshall's love would be her companion, her joy, and her purpose for living. She faced Jiang with a radiant smile, and rested both hands on her abdomen. "This is all I have of the man who loves me. The only way anyone can take away this life," she said, "is to take mine as well. We are one!"

The next two weeks were filled with preparation for the long journey to Hangchow, and Kulien centered her thoughts on Marshall and dreamed of ways to reach him—the only way she could exist or survive. As the wedding date drew near, she spent hours standing by the window caressing Marshall's ring that she now wore on a silk rope around her neck. She stared at the family crest, Marshall's own signet ring, and comforted herself that one day the noble clan of Whitfield would welcome their heir.

Her thoughts went from Marshall's heritage to her own. What should she do about her mother's letter, the diamond-studded brooch, and the miniature portrait? At present, there seemed to be no way out of her marriage and move to Hangchow, and she couldn't take those valuable mementos with her. Marshall, of course, now owned the jade wedding ring, but she needed to find a way to conceal these other precious objects.

While deep in thought, Jiang entered the room and began to put Kulien's personal items into a large silk bag. "You can't sit around daydreaming any longer. Tomorrow is the day we leave here forever. You must pack all your clothes and belongings in those chests brought by the servant boys," she said, pointing to the corner. "Lay out some travel clothes, too. You will leave the compound in your wedding attire so the family can celebrate, but you can't wear those heavy clothes for long."

Kulien reached under the padded mattress of her bed and withdrew the red silk bag that held her mother's gifts to her. "I must also find a place to hide these things. It has to be a location where no one will ever find them. Where could that be?" Kulien rushed to the window again and her eyes traced every stone of her private patio. Jiang could help her hide them, but it would have to be near her rooms.

"Why do you ask me such things? How can I know what to do with your foreign belongings? I don't want to touch them!" She shuddered and lifted her nose in the air.

"But Jiang, you're my only hope. My history, and possibly my future, is contained in this small bag. I hope to return to this compound some day, and I'll need these items to prove my heritage to both Kuang Lufong and Marguerite Howard." She glanced out the window again, recalling a loose flagstone at the far edge of the courtyard. Long branches of flowering bushes draped over the stone, concealing it from exposure.

"There!" Kulien whispered. "There, under that stone. Jiang, I can dig a deep hole and place the bag in it, then cover it with the stone. No one will find it. But you must help me by keeping watch." She put her hands on Jiang's shoulders and tilted her head. "Won't you please do this...for me?"

"The bag will rot under the earth," Jiang said. "All the contents will be lost anyway."

"No they won't," Kulien said, reaching for a blue and white Ming ginger jar on her cosmetic table. "I'll put the bag in here and with the lid on tight, no moisture can get in." She smiled, the dimple in her right cheek accentuating her moment of joy. "We can do it tonight after dark. It will be our secret!"

Jiang's mouth turned down in a scowl, but she responded, "I'll help you. I don't think you will ever return to this compound, but if it gives you comfort, we can do it tonight when the rest of the family sleeps."

Soon after midnight, Kulien and Jiang crept down the stairs to the edge of the patio. Kulien used an abalone shell to scoop out the soft soil under the paved flagstone. She made it deep and long enough to completely hide the Ming jar. No one would ever find it here, and one day she would return and claim the heritage that was hers as the daughter of Kuang Lufong and Marguerite Howard.

An artificial show of jubilation greeted Kulien the morning of her departure to Hangchow. An entourage of sedan chairs decorated with red tassels and beads, mule carts loaded down with trunks of clothing and gifts, and sedan bearers and servants lined the road outside the heavy gate. This was the last time any member of the Kuang family would see Kulien. Neither would the servants or bearers be allowed to look on her face until after the marriage ceremony was completed.

Jiang and three servant girls prepared Kulien for the arduous journey to the south—a journey of five days. She sat through the long ritualistic preparations, only half listening to the excited chatter. After several minutes of fictitious information, she snapped, "The Grand Canal was *not* the result of a dragon's journey!" Her voice was sharp and a frown creased her brow. *How did such myths get started?* "The digging was begun many centuries ago and was completed by the Mongol, Kublai Khan."

Jiang patted her shoulder. "You must be calm, child. Do not flaunt your knowledge."

The servant girls continued their preparation by polishing her face with a hot damp cloth. Jiang stretched two fine silken cords between her fingers and rubbed it over Kulien's face to remove any stray facial hairs. After she finished, the girls dusted a fine coat of white powder on her face, added carmine to her cheeks, and painted a small red circle on her lower lip.

Jiang gave final orders to the servants who braided and coiled Kulien's long hair before they helped her into the red bridal dress. As the final piece of clothing, the servants placed a pearl-encrusted headdress with a thick veil of golden beads on her head. Kulien almost toppled over from the weight.

"Do I have to wear this for the next five days?" Her eyes brimmed with tears.

"You'll wear traveling clothes on the journey. You will change into them when we reach an inn a *li* away from here. It is the custom," Jiang said.

Kulien noticed that her *amah* seldom smiled, and her shoulders seemed more stooped than usual. Her heart was as heavy for herself as it was for Kulien. Both of them were being sent away to live in a compound where they were not wanted. They were nothing more than a bargain price for a long overdue debt.

As the wedding procession began, Jiang walked behind Kulien down the stairs and through the courtyards to the outer gate. Family members lined the paths waving red and green streamers and shouting false wishes of happiness. Kulien kept her eyes lowered even though she had to hold her head erect in order to balance the heavy headdress. Through the beaded veil, Kulien caught sight of Mahwu and Ohchin, but where was her father? Was it not his responsibility to present her to Kong Litang?

She was close to tears as she left her home for the last time, but restrained her emotions by taking deep breaths. Kulien stepped around the spirit screen and through the heavy red gate that opened onto the road...and there he was! Lufong stood at the door of the bridal sedan and held out his hands. Kulien's heart skipped a beat when she placed her hands in his for the last time.

"My little Lotus Seed," he said softly so only she could hear. "You have brought sadness and grief to yourself and you will live with your rebellious spirit for the rest of your life. I know—I am living witness to the suffering of a disobedient son. But," he said, lifting a hand to move away the beads so he could look into her eyes, "wherever the gods lead you, remember the joys of your youth and that your father loved you. Your mother would have loved you, too," he said, with a sad smile on his face.

"I have one last thing to say to you; do not forget your past. Bring it to the surface of your memory often, for the fragments of the past remind us of our birthright. You are both Chinese and British, but because I nurtured and trained you, your Chinese heritage remains stronger. Remember that! No matter how you may try to erase your mixed Chinese ancestry, you are—and always will be—*my* daughter and the only child of Marguerite Howard." He looked deeply into her eyes one last time, his own eyes strangely moist.

Tears stung Kulien's eyelids as she watched her father turn and walk back through the gate. He would not be going to Hangchow, but his words would be with her forever. Kuang Lufong loved her! He would never forget her.

SIXTEEN

The sedan had not traveled far when the coolies stopped, setting the carriage down with a bump. Kulien lifted her hands to hold the heavy headdress in place and cast a worried glance at Jiang who sat opposite her.

Jiang's smile reassured her that it was a scheduled stop, the one where she would be allowed to shed the wedding garb for travel clothing. The guards turned their faces away as they helped Kulien and Jiang step down onto the hard-packed earth. A tall man led them to a small cottage where he opened the door, then strode back to join the other men.

The room was dark except for a dim light shining through one shuttered window. Kulien sat wearily upon a bench in the narrow, unadorned room while Jiang lifted off the headdress and veil and set them on the floor beside her. Kulien twisted her head this way and that to relieve the cramps in her neck.

"Dear child," Jiang said softly, "your face is flushed with the heat, and I can see that you're in pain."

"I have felt sick all morning," Kulien replied, pressing her fingers against her forehead. "The shame of being sent away along with the bumpy ride causes my stomach to rumble like thunder on a spring day."

Jiang's narrowed eyes traced Kulien's delicate features. "It's the sickness that comes with the growing seed. My heart grieves for you; this is far too much for you to bear at your young age."

"No more than you did. Father told me you were sent away from your home, too. He said you were misused by a man you didn't know...and your baby died at birth." Kulien's eyes welled with tears. "Please tell me that I won't lose my baby."

Jiang stepped behind Kulien and began to massage her shoulders. "It was a sad day when you allowed yourself to be bedded by a foreigner, but I know from your words and your face that you love him." She lifted her eyes to the ceiling as if beseeching the gods. "You can be sure that when you bear this child you will have more grief and heartache than you could ever imagine."

She moved around to look into Kulien's eyes. "Although I am against this, I love you and will do all I can to help you keep the baby that grows inside. We all need something or someone of our very own. The foreigner is gone, and you will never see him again; and who knows what will happen in the Kong compound!" Jiang turned away to hide her tears, but her voice was husky with emotion. "I've had you since you were but an infant. To me, you are the child I lost." She faced Kulien and straightened her shoulders. "I will stand beside you as long as I am able."

She withdrew a dagger from her tunic and handed it to Kulien. "You must have this with you when you sleep tonight. Put it under your mattress to keep the evil spirits away from the growing baby."

In only a short time, Kulien had changed from the wedding attire into a padded jacket and loose-fitting trousers, and returned to the sedan with Jiang close beside her. After they had settled themselves back on the hard seats, they opened their noon meal of dried figs, toasted rice cakes, and tepid water. They spoke little that first day of travel, each wrapped in her own thoughts. Finally as the sun set, the long parade of sedans, mules and carts loaded with baggage and an entourage of guards, stopped under a grove of trees. Kulien and Jiang followed the same tall guard to a clean room in a large wayside inn where a warm dinner of roast pork and steamed vegetables awaited them.

Kulien barely tasted the food though her stomach growled with hunger. As she traveled farther and farther from her childhood home, her spirit grew weaker. How would she survive the future? She had no desire to talk with Jiang of her concerns. There was nothing a servant could do to help her. There was no one.

While she picked at her food she tried to recall some of the words she had read in Elizabeth's book. She remembered reading of the God, they called Lord, being faithful, and caring for his people. But she knew that she did not belong to the foreign religion, so why should she expect this strange invisible One to notice her?

When they had finished their meal in silence, and Kulien had changed into her sleeping garments, she peeked through the window at the knife-armed guards who stood watch outside the door. She wondered if they had been stationed nearby to keep intruders out or to keep her from running away. They seemed always to be awake no matter how early or how late. Too tired to keep her eyes open any longer, Kulien lay down on the thin pad that covered the raised mud bed called a *kang*. It had a small fire inside that kept her warm throughout the night. As a member of a wealthy family, she had never seen such a bed. Jiang explained that the *kang* could serve as a table, heater, bench or a bed; and that as a young woman she had always slept on one until she was brought into the Kuang compound where there were beds with soft down mattresses.

Each succeeding autumn day was an endless series of bouncing and jolting inside the darkened, stuffy sedan. One afternoon while Jiang slept, Kulien removed the dagger from her tunic and with the sharp point she pricked a tiny hole in the opaque paper curtain. If she could see something of the countryside to take her mind off her discomfort she might endure the journey. Pressing an eye over the hole, she spied a neglected altar badly in need of paint and tended only with smoking incense to bulge-eyed gods. She amused herself for hours by looking at the passing scenery and imagining herself free from the restraint of the sedan. What would it be like to mingle among crowds of people traveling to sell their wares? She saw laborers who carried poles over their shoulders with heavy loads balanced at each end. One day she watched a funeral party dressed in white, all wailing to the gods of earth, water and wind.

So fascinated by the new surroundings of an unknown world, Kulien could sometimes forget the purpose of her southward journey. On the fourth day of travel the caravan reached the muddy banks of the Grand Canal, China's only north-south water route where the sedan bearers set down their burdens. She watched through the small hole as half-naked coolies with queues twisted around their heads loaded the carts, trunks, furniture, and even the mules onto large boats that bobbed restlessly on the choppy water. After lifting the sedan carrying Kulien and Jiang and placing it on the deck, the men dropped to their knees and kowtowed to the First Guard, a regally-dressed old man. An exchange of bags of coins and beads of opium passed between the coolies and the guard. No wonder the coolies were so gaunt and yellow, she thought. They were addicted to the poppy-weed.

When they began the passage downriver with coolies straining on the shore and tugging the boats with long ropes, Jiang and Kulien were allowed to leave the sedan. They lifted their heads to breathe in the fresh air before looking down into the murky water. Kulien's secret plan of escape vanished. The canal was too deep to wade and she had never learned to swim. Even if she had been able to keep afloat she couldn't bear the thought of touching that filthy water. Dead fish, rotting food, and human feces floated by, a reminder that the waterway was more than a passage for boats. "If I should fall overboard," Jiang uttered after several minutes, "don't bother to save me. I wouldn't want to live after coming in contact with that water!"

After a long day of boating down the Grand Canal, the bridal procession reached Hangchow, the ancient residence of twelfth century Southern Song emperors. Kulien had often heard the quotation, "Above there is Heaven, below there is Suchow and Hangchow." Riches, loaded on carts from the House of Kuang, were removed from the houseboats, and with a heavy heart Kulien climbed back into the sedan chair. This would be the final leg of her journey—to the home of the Kong clan at the northern shore of beautiful West Lake, a large freshwater lake surrounded by wooded hills, pagodas, temples, gardens, and several sizeable family compounds.

The arrival was well-timed, for a large gathering of merrymakers waited outside the walls of the Kong compound shouting and setting off strings of red firecrackers. The sultry heat of the enclosure and the barrage of noise intensified the pain in Kulien's throbbing head. She had bathed at the village inn that morning and had submitted for the last time to the heavy crimson gown, necklaces, the beaded veil and towering headdress. Even at the last stop Kulien tried to envision a way to escape, but she finally accepted that she had no control over her destiny. There was nothing to do but submit to Jiang's instructions and go through the sham of a marriage ceremony.

The sedan came to a standstill and Kulien's eyes widened in fear. "Jiang, listen!"

The caravan had stopped before the main gate, flanked on either side by immense stone dragons. There was the crash of cymbals and shouts of "The bride is here! The bride is here!" Jiang reached over to touch Kulien's cold hand. "Don't be afraid. At least, don't show your fear."

The vermilion and gold bridal sedan swayed into the courtyard, and Kulien's emotions lurched with each movement as she imagined the ceremony that lay ahead. She silently offered a prayer to Kuanyin, Goddess of Mercy, as she waited for the guard to open the door. The musicians continued to play, and as was the custom, the bride was left to wait inside the dark, humid interior of the sedan chair in order to test her patience. When at last the music stopped, the bridal chair was set down at the entrance of the reception hall, and the door of the sedan opened for the last time. Kulien inhaled deeply of the late afternoon breeze blowing across West Lake and through the courtyard, and tried to close off the terrifying thoughts of what lay ahead.

Jiang and another servant helped her alight from the sedan, and as she stepped out, gasps and whispers undulated through the crowd, "Look at those feet! The old Kong patriarch gets a big-footed slave for a bride." Men laughed aloud and women tittered behind colorful fans.

Kulien stiffened, but Jiang squeezed her arm. "Be still. You are not to speak or show any sign of emotion. You must do this or both our lives are as nothing."

Kulien lowered her eyelids and focused on the red carpets covering the walkways. With Jiang close behind, she followed a servant along with the cacophony of drums and flutes until she passed through a doorway and across an expansive wood floor. At last the procession stopped and the heavy headdress was removed, leaving only the beaded veil. From under the folds of the beads, Kulien glimpsed a man's white-soled slippers and the hem of his blue gown. His labored breathing was evidence of his excess girth. Her heart froze and she felt herself begin to tremble. Was this Kong Litang? Her stomach churned, and her knees turned to water while vivid colors and sounds crashed upon her senses. Was she going to faint right here? Jiang gripped her elbow and whispered. "Be calm. I'm with you."

Kulien blinked back tears and fastened her gaze on the floor, but she willed her mind to see only the clear blue eyes of Marshall Whitfield. Her heart recalled his words of comfort and love; and she imagined that she could feel his touch...his lips upon hers. He was with her even here. His child, the expression of his love, had been planted in her body. She knew that in this moment of anguish, she must guard her thoughts because it was believed that everything she did and saw would influence her unborn child. She had once read that, according to tradition, a pregnant woman should read good poetry; she shouldn't gossip, laugh loudly, or lose her temper. How would she be able to keep all these traditions in the House of Kong?

After long, stifling hours of blindly kowtowing first to ancestor tablets, then to line after line of relatives, Kulien was finally led down a flower-strewn pathway. She was certain she would die from exhaustion and despair if she had to drop to her knees and touch her head to the floor one more time.

A door opened and a servant took her arm to lead her into a large room where she was told to sit in a satin-covered chair. Then she heard the soft footsteps walk away leaving her with a sense of aloneness. She listened for a sound, but it was as quiet as a place of death. Was the wedding completed? Was Kong Litang in the room, or was she alone? With the marriage ceremony completed, she knew she was not a legal wife, but another of the old man's concubines. What would he to do her? How could she avoid his advances?

Kulien groaned in desperation at what would happen in the next hours. Fearfully and with care, she reached up to draw aside the beaded veil to see if anyone else occupied the room.

SEVENTEEN

Her mouth dry with fear, Kulien let her eyes scan the spacious room. Although it was dark, except for a lantern on the table near her, she glanced from one corner of the room to the other. Silk paintings of birds with brilliant-colored plumage, as well as jagged mountains and waterfalls, had been painted with care and skill. Elaborate mother-of-pearl screens stood in various parts of the room separating it into sections for reading and music. Thick carpets of carved flowers softened the dark wood floors. Then she saw it—a large sandalwood bed partially concealed by red silk curtains and covered with embroidered quilts dominated the room. It had carved panels that reached to the floor and a low pedestal used as steps into the high bed. The pedestal extended the length of the bed and was beautifully decorated with peaches, storks, and doves. She remembered reading a saying that went, "In bed a man can behave like an ordinary creature, but out of bed he must be a gentleman." Was she to occupy that bed with Kong Litang?

Kulien felt the bile rise to her throat and swallowed deeply. As she did, she spied Jiang in a far corner, almost hidden from view. Her hands were folded at her waist and she cast a worried glance at Kulien before lowering her head.

Sounds from the outer hallway signaled that many people were about to invade the room. Kulien held her breath as the man with the blue silk robe entered alone. She closed her eyes, but heard him cross to stand before her. "You may remain here with your mistress," he said to Jiang in a raspy voice.

The *amah's* words sounded like a rush of wind, "Thank you, Honorable. That would make me most happy."

Kulien relaxed, thinking, *if Jiang stays here with me, the man won't touch me. He will behave like a gentleman.* She clasped her hands in her lap and waited as Kong Litang sat in the chair opposite her.

"Remove her veil," he ordered Jiang.

She hobbled to Kulien's side and lifted the beaded veil. Several moments passed before Kulien raised her eyes to see Kong Litang for the first time. She held her chin high and her back straight; she didn't blink or flinch. She wouldn't allow this man to frighten her, and she wouldn't show him respect.

Kong Litang stared back at her, his mouth partially opened, his eyes piercing like daggers. "Your face is bold for a woman who is no more than a slave to me!" He twisted his moustache with a long curved fingernail. "You have the eyes of a foreign devil." His mouth twisted in disdain. "Never mind that," he said. "Do you find me to your liking?"

The man was even older than she had expected. His thick lips, partially concealed by a gray moustache, revealed missing teeth when he spoke. Fat cheeks squeezed his eyes to narrow slits, and the same yellow pallor she had noticed on the river coolies colored his face. He was a replica of the statue of Buddha in her family temple—but without the smile. Kulien gathered up her nerve and answered, "You are what I expected."

"But you are not. I think our family has been deceived again by the Kuang clan!"

"I disappoint you then," she said, hope rising in her breast.

Litang's fleshy lips quivered. "I am neither disappointed nor pleased. It was not my idea to take on another concubine. I have more than enough women to satisfy my needs. You are but one more mouth to feed!' He rested plump hands on his equally plump belly. "It was only because of our family's long history with your clan that I agreed to this mock wedding ceremony." Spittle ran from the corner of his mouth and he wiped it away with the back of his hand.

It couldn't be true! He was lying! Her father said he *had no recourse* but to give her to the Kong clan. Kulien gripped the arms of the chair and leaned forward. "You lie! Your family *demanded* a Kuang bride because my father dishonored Meilu when he married another woman."

Litang's eyes glittered. "You've been misinformed. This so-called marriage only eases the Kuang conscience. Our clan is no longer concerned about the broken contract between Kuang Lufong and Kong Meilu." He pulled off his skull cap and stroked his oiled crown with fat stubby fingers. "I am moved neither to the left nor to the right over this matter. Our family regained face many years ago when Meilu married an even more respectable and wealthy man than your father." His sneer became an evil laugh. "I think your father only wanted to get rid of you so the spirit of his father could find rest. I know what a dishonorable act Kuang Lufong did in bringing a half-breed into his family!" He leaned closer, his sour breath assailing Kulien's senses. "But I've never bedded a Chinese woman with foreign eyes—so I am eager to learn what you have to offer!"

Kulien was out of her chair, glaring down on the man. "I don't believe you. My father loved me as he loved his British wife. He would never have sent me here willingly!"

Jiang touched Kulien's shoulder, urging her to sit down. She spoke close to Kulien's ear, "You speak out of turn, my child." Louder, and for the benefit of Kong Litang, she added, "Let your words be rare as pearls and sweet as honey."

"Listen to your *amah*, young woman. I don't appreciate being called a liar by a discarded half-breed! From now on, you're my property, and you must do as I say! Do you understand?" His voice grew louder with each word. "No one else would have you with those big feet and green eyes." His eyes swept slowly over her. "I'm sure that I will discover some finer qualities as we get to know each other better." His eyes shifted from her to the bed, then back to her small form.

Kulien nodded, outwardly agreeable to calm Jiang; but inside she seethed with an unfamiliar hatred.

Kong Litang leaned back in his chair. "You deserve a beating for your behavior, but I'm a generous man, and I must say that I do admire your courage and your fire. I look forward to tasting that hot blood for myself." Kong raised a hand toward the doorway. "As is the custom, it's time for the wedding guests to examine you. They know nothing of your history, and have been told that I'm taking you as a primary wife because my first wife died three moons ago. She had long ago stopped bringing me pleasure, and I no longer care for the burden of a wife whose only interest is to bear children and wag her tongue. My clan is aware of my other concubines, but I thought it would give them pleasure to experience a lavish wedding ceremony, even though it is not truly a marriage!"

He stepped to the door and before drawing aside the heavy drapery, said, "I demand that you remain quiet as my family inspects you. Whether they accept you or not, you will soon be forgotten when you take a room at the far side of the compound."

Kong adjusted the skull cap on his smooth crown and beckoned toward the outer chamber. "There are more than three hundred members of this clan, and I, as the patriarch, am respected more for my age than for my appearance at family gatherings. After you settle into your role, you may become invisible except to attend the most important of the festivals and, as a concubine, to come to my bedchamber at my request."

Before Kulien could gather her thoughts, the drapery was drawn aside and a houseboy tied it back with a thick silk cord. A stream of well-wishers, critics, and pranksters marched into the room carrying lanterns.

After what seemed hours of long looks and whispered observations, some of the men drew Kong Litang aside to voice their opinions. "She has a good face, but strange eyes. And look at those feet! You won't get much pleasure from those."

"Still" added another, "she does have a dimple in her cheek. That's a sign that she has other fine features—ones we can't see!"

One man taunted, "Her face is passable, but those big feet, laughable!"

The women had words as well. "Grandfather was cheated. This woman is no more than a large-footed demon—a foreign one at that."

"Too thin."

"I think she's ugly. Those twin boats are a disgrace. She is nothing to be desired."

The hours, under the tedious gaze of the Kong family, drug on like days. Kulien sat without expression as she was poked and prodded, complimented and criticized. Would the day never end? Yet she feared what would happen when she was alone with the old Kong man. Her head swam with anxiety and her stomach convulsed, churning bile into her throat.

She lowered her eyes as the remaining guests withdrew, laughing and talking with Litang. Exhausted from the long journey to Hangchow and the emotional strain of the past month,

Kulien watched Kong Litang follow the others from the room. Another trial had passed, but the next would be the worst yet.

"My baby, what an ordeal for you." Jiang smoothed Kulien's glossy hair and caressed her smooth cheeks. "I think the man will be back soon. Stay in your chair until he tells you what to do."

Before Jiang had finished speaking, Kong Litang stepped over the doorsill and strode across the room. "It's time for you to go," he said to Jiang. A houseboy appeared and led Jiang from the room, but before she disappeared, she glanced over her shoulder at Kulien, her mouth drawn down with gloom.

"Now," he said, when they were alone, "we will have privacy for the next three days. Perhaps you can produce a male child for me. There can never be too many sons in a large house!"

Kulien covered her mouth with her fingers and swallowed deeply. What could she say? What could she do? She was at the mercy of this man!

He lowered his voice and sat back in the chair he had vacated. "You don't need to be afraid of me. As I said before, I have plenty of women in my harem—women with fragrant lotuses." He paused to study his fingers before leaning over the small chest beside him. "I'm sure you will bring me pleasure, but I find my greatest joy in this." He opened a drawer and removed a long stemmed pipe and a pungent-smelling brown ball. "The opium is my most faithful friend. It doesn't require anything of me, and gives me only happiness. But," he said, bringing the opium ball to his flaring nostrils, "before I indulge myself and feel too sleepy, we will consummate this union."

Litang held the sticky bead in the palm of his hand and eyed it hungrily. "Take off your clothes," he said suddenly. "Let me see what that miserable Kuang clan has sent my way."

Kulien's mind whirled and she felt the blood drain from her face. "But you said I didn't need to be afraid of you—that you have other women to serve your needs."

"That is true, and unless you greatly please me, I won't call for you often. I only want to be assured that I received what I was promised—an untouched, pure maiden." His laugh chilled her to the bone.

Kulien began to tremble and wrapped her arms tightly about herself. "I think you would have more enjoyment if you smoked first."

"It's not your duty to think!" he shouted. He lifted the brown ball to his face again and flicked his tongue over it. "Obey me. Take off your clothes. You belong to me and I'm getting impatient. The family waits outside to learn of our consummation, and to see the soiled wedding cloth."

Kulien could see the veins throbbing at his throat and perspiration began to appear on his fleshy face. She picked at the buttons of her bridal dress. "I need my *amah* to help me," she said, after fumbling for several moments. "I can't undress myself. What kind of poor house is this that a woman must do such menial work?"

Litang lunged from the chair and snatched Kulien up in his arms. Her struggles only fueled his strength as he carried her to the bed and threw her across the thick quilts. As his eyes glistened with lust, he began to rip and tear away the brocaded silk gown. "You are my property, Kuang Kulien—a Bitter Seed that I will plant in my own garden of pleasures."

She pushed against him, and jumped from the bed to run across the room and hide behind a chair. "Please don't touch me," she pleaded. "I'm only sixteen, and I've had no instruction in the art of love. I'll disappoint you. I know I will." Her hands clutched the collar of her dress. "Be merciful, Sir. Let me spend the first night alone in the wedding bed. Please?"

Kong Litang was in front of her in a moment. "I'm too old for all this strife. But you've aroused my appetite for a sweet young morsel. I like inexperienced girls, and I will make a good instructor!"

Litang took off his robe and began to remove his undergarments. "No more of your whining. Take off your clothes, or I'll rip them off one piece at a time."

Kulien rose from the floor and forced herself to think of Marshall Whitfield and the beautiful night of love they had shared. What would happen with this disgusting man had nothing to do with love and marriage. She silently besought the gods of strength to endure the bitter trial that lay ahead.

As the red gown fell to the floor, Litang's eyes widened, and his breath came in uneven gasps. Kulien stepped out of the layers of heavy attire, wearing only the sheer silk underclothes.

"I like what I see so far," the voice rasped. "I have seen many women in my seasons, but this blending of East and West has created the most beautiful creature of all."

Litang grabbed for Kulien and pressed her against his flabby, obese body. She clenched her teeth to stifle a scream as his wet mouth trailed over her neck and shoulders. She couldn't stand it a moment longer. With all the strength she had left, she tried to push him away. But they fell to the floor, his arms still holding her tight. "I like your fire," he groaned in her ear.

Kong Litang's bulk lay heavily across her chest and he laughed. "You make me feel like a young man," he said, lifting himself to his elbows.

With every ounce of power she could gather, Kulien twisted and turned, thrashing her arms and kicking her legs. Litang was caught off guard, and stared in amazement as she jumped to her feet and screamed, "Touch me and you die! I am not your pure, chaste virgin!"

Before the man could reply, the words were out of her mouth in a joyous shout, "I've been with a foreign devil and I carry his pox-ridden seed in my belly!"

EIGHTEEN

Kulien's confession stunned Kong Litang for only a moment before he was on his feet and raised his hand to strike her. As she turned away to cover her face, his long nails ripped across her back like stinging serpents. His voice hissed, "The blood of your virginity was not mine, but you'll go through life with the scars of my disfavor, *fankuei!*"

Still shaking with rage, Litang dropped heavily onto a nearby couch and reached for his opium pipe, a long reed about an inch in diameter. His eyes glittered with hatred as he looked from Kulien to the ball of opium. She knew her grandmother used the drug, but had never seen anyone smoke it, and from the corner of the room, she watched Kong Litang with disgust. The bowl of the pipe was small, and, with a trembling hand, he placed a minute particle of the drug in it and lit it with a candle from the lantern. He stretched his perspiring, flaccid body out on the couch and rested his head on the padded arm before inhaling. She watched with revulsion as the drug took effect and he mumbled in a low voice, "I'll stay here tonight to ease the concerns of the family, and deal with you tomorrow. For now I'll find a satisfying lover in this." After only a few puffs, an idiotic smile came over his face, but instead of fear and hatred, Kulien felt pity for the old man.

When his eyes closed in a deep stupor, Kulien pulled two quilts from the bed, and threw one over Kong Litang before wrapping herself in the other one. She found a washstand near the bed and carefully sponged the scratches, wincing as cold water ran over the burning welts. After drying herself, she crept to her wardrobe chest for a change of clothes. Without fear of disturbing the drugged man, she dressed for travel in cotton pants and a brown padded jacket. Litang had said he would deal with her tomorrow, and perhaps if he sent her away, she would not be allowed to take her clothes or the gifts she had brought from home. At least she would have some warm garments for the cold autumn nights. She had also found Marshall Whitfield's gold signet ring hidden in a secret pocket of her padded jacket. She looped the silk cord over her head, and pressed her lips on the carved crest, an engraved "*W*" on a field of wheat. Marshall had worn the ring on the little finger of his left hand before he removed it and slipped it onto her thumb. *Oh, Marshall, Jiang believes you are forever gone from me, but I know you love me and will find a way for us to legally marry someday.* With those words of assurance filling her mind, she climbed into the enormous bed and buried herself under the silk sheets. In spite of her fears of the future and the pain throbbing across her back, she fell into a deep sleep.

Kulien had no idea what time it was when she opened her eyes to the gray light of a melancholy day. What would this day hold? Was she to be punished? And what would happen to Jiang because she concealed the truth about Kulien's relationship with Marshall Whitfield?

She pushed aside the heavy bed-curtains to glance around the empty room. She wondered when Kong Litang had awakened and left. Her heart fluttered with gratitude that he hadn't come to her bed. Although still weary from the events of the last day and night, she went to the washstand to discard the soiled sponge and pink-tinged water into an empty wooden bucket; then she poured fresh water into the basin and washed her face.

Jiang was nowhere to be seen, and neither were any other servants in the room. She would just have to be brave and wait to see what the day would bring forth.

She remembered the shocked expression on Litang's face when she shouted that she had been with a foreign devil and carried his child. *Marshall, you are not a foreign devil to me. To me you are a god, so kind and gentle.*

Lord Marshall Whitfield had not only surrendered his valuable ring, but he had given her his noble name in their private wedding vows. Beyond even that, he had awakened her femininity, a gift she would always treasure.

As the hours passed, a cold wind swept down from the north draping dark clouds over the compound like a shroud. Kulien imagined that the Hour of the Horse, midday, had arrived, and that perhaps Kong Litang would send for her soon. Anxiety grew as time inched by, minute by minute. Kulien set her mind on Marshall and the child they were to have together. She waited in a straight-backed chair, not moving a muscle and scarcely blinking an eye.

She waited until the sky began to grow darker with heavy rain clouds.

No one appeared. There were no sounds outside the room or in the courtyard. It seemed that her world had vanished and she alone was left. She wondered what had happened to Jiang. Would she be allowed to return? How could she exist without Jiang in her life?

Her back throbbed with pain and her head ached. Still she didn't move, but sat with her eyes straight ahead and her hands folded in her lap. Why was she being kept in such suspense? When would she be summoned? Twilight brought more chill into the room, and Kulien finally rose from the chair to close the fleece-lined winter curtains. A white marble fireplace stared back at her with its cold, dark eye, the brazier empty of coals.

A deep grumbling came from the pit of her stomach and a wave of sickness spread throughout her body. Kulien ran to the basin and leaned over, retching. But there was nothing as she hadn't eaten for almost two days. Knife-sharp pains continued to rip her body, and she ran to the basin only to clutch her stomach and double over in distress.

Tales of *kuei* came to mind. Had demons come to destroy the baby-seed? Was her body to be turned inside out in order for others to see her spirit? Words from the writings of Buddha came to mind, "…foolishness is the greatest of poisons." Would she die of this poison before the day ended?

After the illness passed, Kulien dropped back down in the chair to wait for Kong Litang to call for her. All night she sat, her eyelids drooping, her head falling forward. Her legs cramped and her shoulders ached, but she didn't move. She knew she had to stay alert and have her wits about her when she was called to answer for her crimes.

It was the next morning before a servant scratched on the door jamb and drew aside the curtain. "The master, Kong Litang, requests your presence in the Hall of Audience," he said in a somber voice. "He waits now. Come!"

Slowly, Kulien lifted herself from the chair and rubbed her neck and shoulders. At last the man was ready to make his decision known. But was she ready? She had no acceptable defense to offer the Kong clan. She had denied the Confucian ethic and had chosen to give herself to a *barbarian* instead of obediently following the traditions of her heritage. Although she felt no shame in her love for Marshall, she was confused by her feelings toward her father. Before she left her home, he had expressed his love for her; but it seemed that he had only used her to satisfy the roaming spirit of her grandfather.

Kulien ask the servant for permission to cover her travel clothes with a dark blue robe while he waited at the doorway, his arms crossed over his chest and a frown on his high forehead. When they reached the Audience Hall, Kulien drew in a deep breath and walked into the room where only hours before she had been honored as a virgin bride.

Kong Litang stood in the center of the room holding the priceless Tang Dynasty porcelain, her father's wedding gift, over his head. He shouted words she had never heard before he threw the vase at her feet, shattering it into a pile of colorful fragments.

Kulien winced inwardly at the rage she saw and felt, careful to remain unmoving and silent, her head bowed in submission.

"Get over here!" the man demanded, motioning her to step forward. A row of stony-faced men sat at a long mahogany table, their hands folded in front of them. She glanced at each man, their sharp eyes boring into her. Kong Litang took a long white banner, emblazoned with the red ideogram, "Justice," and placed it over the front of the table. He stepped to the side where he put on a black, long-sleeved robe, and set a bowl-shaped hat upright on his head. Then, with purpose, he took his position at the center chair behind the table, and without speaking raised his hand to direct Kulien to move to the middle of the room. Kulien stepped to the appointed spot and held her breath.

All eyes turned away from her to watch the entrance as the matriarch of the Kong family hobbled into the room with servants supporting her on either side. They helped her sit down beside Kong Litang, where she joined in the icy stares.

Kulien was amazed at the age of the shriveled woman; she must be even older than her own grandmother. All she knew to do now was to kowtow to the austere group. She fell to her knees and pressed her forehead three times against the silk rug. It was for her father's sake that she bowed before this new family. She must show *hsiao,* filial piety, so the disgrace of the Kuang clan would fall only on her. She hoped to persuade her judges that neither her father nor her *amah* knew of her relationship with the Englishman.

"Rise," Kong Litang said, striking a small brass gong with a mallet.

Kulien did as she was told, and forced her legs to hold her up in a steady position. Not only did she feel weak from the lack of food, but she was terrified. Would they sentence her to death? What would happen to her unborn baby?

As she stood before those who were now her family and her judges, she dared not raise her head, but fastened her gaze on the intricate pattern of the carpet. The room seemed to vibrate with hatred and violence. Finally, the thick voice of Kong Litang echoed through the wide Audience Hall, "The family is the most important social group in China. For one member to lose face is for all to lose face. The shame of one is the shame of all."

Kulien swallowed the lump in her throat as she heard the shuffling of feet and mumbled voices of the men at the table.

"Our philosophy," Litang continued, "teaches us to maintain harmony, and because of *you,* that balance has been broken. The teachings of Confucianism, Taoism and Buddhism are accepted and practiced in the House of Kong because all three schools lead toward one goal—a moral life and right conduct on earth.

"This woman," he paused and pointed a finger, "is guilty of immorality. She has committed an unforgivable crime by fornicating with a barbarian. She has shown an even greater guilt by her disregard for our family when she took vows of marriage with deceit and disloyalty to our ancestors." He struck the gong again, louder this time. "Approach, woman!"

Kulien took one step forward and looked at the man she had shamed. His squinty eyes glared at her, his thick lips turned downward. His face showed no compassion, no recognition, only extreme hatred.

"You, who were formerly known as Kuang Kulien, have broken the marriage contract even though you knew you were not to be a true wife. By allowing a foreign devil to bed you, I have been shamed before my family." He glanced away from Kulien and waved an arm over the gathered group at the table. "The greater abomination is that you bear the filthy seed of a barbarian. You have knowingly brought death and disease to this house!"

He turned to address the others. "Because this woman is guilty of fornication, the contract between the House of Kong and the Kuang clan is forever broken! Before you, honorable members of an honorable family, I divorce this woman for her immorality. The House of Kong is absolved from its duty and honor to the House of Kuang. May the Kuang clan lose eternal face for sending a whore to shame us!"

Low whispers passed back and forth between family members before he went on. "Because the 'marriage contract' was a settlement for a previous debt to the Kong family, and an appeasement for the Kuang clan because the spirit of Kuang Linho cannot rest, there is only one way for this crime to be settled."

He raised the mallet to strike the gong once more, and the air crackled with suspense as each person waited for the verdict.

NINETEEN

"Death!"

The word hung in the air like a vulture scanning the earth to satisfy its hunger.

The only response from the rows of men was a sucking sound. At last, the matriarch nodded her nearly bald head and lifted one of her canes to tap the wooden floor. "So be it," she said. "So be it!"

As the matriarch spoke, Kulien fastened her eyes on the old woman, "Please, Great Mother, I ask permission to speak—to confess my crime." She inhaled deeply and her voice trembled with emotion. No one spoke, but all appeared dumbfounded to hear Kulien's voice. "I am without defense," she said. Her shoulders drooped and she folded her hands in front of her to express humility. "It is true that I have been with an Englishman, but he is a clean man—without disease. We did not exchange marriage vows lightly. We performed a wedding ceremony before the gods, the gods of our fathers as well as the invisible European God." She waited a moment for a response, but when there was none, she went on. "You also tell the truth when you say I am with child. *Yuejing,* 'the flow of the moon' has not passed through my body for as many as two times."

` The air was so heavy, Kulien could scarcely breathe, but she gained more courage in the silence. "Your judgment of me is just. I do deserve to die for my unfilial actions and my deception before you and my father."

She raised her eyes to see Kong Litang's questioning glance. "Yes, my father was as deceived as you. He had no knowledge of my wicked behavior. I was able to fool him as well as my *amah*. No one but the barbarian and I are aware of my foolishness." Kulien clenched her teeth before going on. She had never felt so alone and afraid. She lowered her eyelids and dropped to her knees. "I beg your mercy, most honorable House of Kong, not for me, but for my former family. They do not share my guilt. Please clear them from your judgment. It was with pure motives that my father, Kuang Lufong presented me to your clan." The lie to protect her family came without hesitation.

Kong Litang turned to the rows of men, whispered a few words to his mother, and answered, "We will accept the defense for your family because you show *hsiao,* honor, by pleading for them."

"And most honorable sir," Kulien interrupted, "may I also beg for mercy upon the poor, miserable child I carry? As you know, the foreigners are so inferior to the Chinese that my child deserves to live only because the blood of a superior race fills its veins. Would you be kind enough to grant me permission to live until the child is weaned? Then my life is as nothing anyway."

Kong Litang glanced in the direction of the expressionless men, waved a hand of dismissal, and bowed to his mother before she was escorted from the room. Moments passed before he turned to face Kulien with a sneer on his ugly face. "You are a half-breed yourself! Your child will have very little noble blood in its useless veins. You mean nothing to me, and neither does your bastard offspring!" He stroked his fleshy chin with stubby fingers. "Perhaps your judgment *would* be greater if you were to suffer the pains of childbirth. Then the child would be taken from you and destroyed before your eyes!" He smiled as if the image gave him pleasure. "Yes, I think I have a better plan for you. I could either return you in disgrace to your family, and they would cast you out, or I could ...."

The man picked at his yellowed teeth with a long fingernail, examined the piece of food he had extracted, then nodded his head. "I've reached a decision."

Kulien relaxed as hope began to rise. Perhaps she would not only be allowed to give birth to her baby, she would continually search for a way to reach Marshall Whitfield. She waited for the man to speak.

"Chiu," Litang called to the houseboy who stood in the hallway. "Take the whore to the Beggar's Gate. I'll have a cart pick her up there."

"But—but where are you sending me?" Kulien cried. "What about my *amah*? May I take Jiang with me?"

Kong Litang's derisive laughter filled the room. For several minutes, his flabby cheeks shook with glee before he wiped tears from his eyes. "I think that fat old woman would be out of place where you're going."

Kulien rose from the floor and searched the man's face. "I don't understand; where are you sending me? Why must Jiang and I be separated? She's been with me since I was a baby."

A movement at the doorway drew Kulien's attention. She gasped and covered her mouth with a hand as Jiang was violently shoved into the room by a burly servant. Kulien rushed to keep her from falling, and with an arm around Jiang's shoulders, she shouted, "You don't have to treat her like this! She's done nothing to deserve your wrath."

Kong Litang folded thick arms over his protruding belly and beckoned them to come closer. "Your crime, Jiang, is to have associated yourself with this half-breed whore."

Jiang turned her head to look into Kulien's eyes. "Have they hurt you, my pet? What will happen now?"

"Shut up, old woman," Litang ordered. "I don't believe for an instant that you're ignorant of the crime perpetrated by this female dog. I hold you equally responsible for the shame brought on me and my clan. However," the man's lips curled back in a sneer, "you would be of little use in a joy house! Men prefer young blood and smooth bodies."

Kulien stepped away from Jiang as if to protect her from contamination. A joy house! "Surely you wouldn't send me away to such a place."

"You're going to die one way or another. Many of the sing-song girls don't last long after they contract a disease." He stepped closer to Jiang. "Yes, your *pet* will serve both foreigners and Chinese in a way appropriate for a woman who has had experience in the ways of love. I've decided to sell Bitter Seed to a well known prostitute shop in Shanghai. She can make some money for the proprietor for a few months before she becomes fat and useless. After the baby is born, she can resume her new career!"

"No! No!" Jiang screamed. She reached into her tunic and drew out the small silver dagger she had retrieved from Kulien before the wedding ceremony. "I won't let you do that!" She lunged at Kong Litang with the knife pointed at his throat.

"Jiang! No!" Kulien grabbed for Jiang's sleeve to stop her, but the woman hobbled out of her reach, and with surprising speed was only inches away from Litang's face. The man straightened his arm to keep her at a distance, and stomped on her tiny feet. Jiang screamed with pain and fell to her knees, stabbing wildly at the air. "You will never put my baby in that place," she sobbed. "I'll kill you…" The *amah's* words ended in a low gurgling yelp.

Kulien stared in horror as Kong Litang wrested the knife from Jiang's hand, and in one smooth movement plunged it into her neck, slitting her throat. Jiang toppled over onto her face, a pool of blood widening around her and soaking into the carpet.

Kulien dropped down beside her and lifted her head, gazing into the sightless eyes. "Oh, Jiang! Jiang don't die— please don't die!" Bile rose into Kulien's throat as she watched the life ebb out of Jiang, staining her own blue robe and hands. Jiang was like the mother she'd never known. She had loved her and taught her about life…but she had never taught her about death. Kulien looked up from the dead woman to Kong Litang who stood over her, a smirk on his face.

"You beast! I hate you! Wherever you send me will be better than here with you!"

Litang shouted for the houseboys, "Come get this corpse out of here." He pointed at Kulien, "And while you're at it take the half-breed out of my sight."

Before Kulien could resist, a tall, husky servant seized her. She flailed her arms and kicked her feet, but she was no match for the man. He hefted her over his shoulder, and as he carried her from the room she saw another man drag Jiang's limp body through a back exit to be thrown into an unmarked grave.

The following days and nights Kulien was barely aware of the long, miserable trip from Hangchow to Shanghai. She knew from the jolting of the boat that they were in rough seas. Some days, the rain pounded endlessly on the skin tarp covering the deck, other days there was only the biting cold that penetrated her padded cotton jacket. She had one blanket to keep her warm, and once a day, a bowl of lukewarm rice gruel was set beside her. She was bruised and sick, and slept restlessly as images of the past returned to her troubled mind like vivid paintings.

> *"Come here, my lovely Lotus Blossom," Lufong called to the little girl with long braids tied in red bows. "Come to Baba. You are my precious daughter, more precious to me than the most priceless jade!"*
>
> *Kulien crawled into her father's lap and listened to his low voice as he told tales of the "Monkey King" and other ancient stories. She nestled close within his arms, feeling his steady heartbeat against her ear. How could one little girl be so happy? So loved and protected?*
>
> *"Baba, I love you and will always live here with you!"*
> *"Of course, you will, my child. I'll never let you go."*

Kulien wiped the warm tears from her chilled cheeks as she remembered his loving words; but he had forced her to leave him. As she turned over on the hard mat trying to find a comfortable position, her mind turned to Elizabeth Whitfield and the words she had spoken.

"Kulien, I know that you do not believe in the one true God, but I want to read you some words from the Bible." Kulien's curiosity about other cultures and gods had opened her mind to the words Elizabeth read. "It says here about God, 'I will never leave you nor forsake you.' Do you understand what that means, Kulien?"

Kulien had glanced around the garden to see the stone gods who never moved. "I know that our gods have made no such promises," she answered.

"That's why I want you to understand and believe in the God of the Bible, and his Son, Jesus." Elizabeth had closed the book and reached over to touch Kulien's hand. "There might come a day when you are alone and need someone to comfort you. The Lord God of Heaven and Earth has made this promise to you. If you believe in him, he will be with you."

Kulien wanted to believe, but she was afraid. She had been taught that the God the foreigners brought with them was only interested in Europeans, so she had only smiled and nodded her head. Miss Whitfield returned her smile, and continued throughout their years of study to speak of her God. She had also given Kulien the Bible that she kept hidden in the summerhouse.

The boat rocked and lurched over the waves of the eastern coastline of the Yellow Sea. Kulien's head, pounding with pain and nausea, was almost more than she could endure, but she knew she must be strong for her baby. If only Jiang were with her. Jiang, dear Jiang. Murdered and dragged away like a sack of rice. Everyone she loved had disappeared from her life; all that was left were the sailors on this wretched boat who kicked at her when they passed and thrust the bowl of food down as if she were no more than a dog.

She had decided the only way to survive was to remember the past, and try not to fear what the near future held. Kong Litang had said she was being sold to a house of prostitution in Shanghai. The thought of what must lie ahead was so fearful, that she must not think about it. She was certain to be rescued by Marshall Whitfield. Surely he would learn of her fate and find a way to reach her. She moved her hand to touch the slight bulge of the ring hidden under her jacket. Marshall's signet ring. He said he signed documents with it. Perhaps she could use his name to find release from Kong Litang's judgment! *Marshall. Marshall.*

Kulien, weakened from the abuse and lack of food, slipped into unconsciousness—a release from the pain and fear that had almost overwhelmed her. Another day and night on the rough seas passed without Kulien regaining consciousness. She wasn't aware of the small ship docking in Shanghai, or of being dropped into a wooden cart and wheeled down a cobblestone street to a building painted bright blue with large yellow letters, "The Blue Chambers."

TWENTY

"What's this?" Sharp fingernails pinched Kulien's upper arms and poked at her thighs. "Does Kong Litang take me for turtle dung, selling me a good-for-nothing half dead child? I pay for girls with flesh. This is no more than a bone. She has nothing to please a man—not even golden lilies!"

Kulien opened her eyes and groaned. She had no idea where she was, nor did she care. Jiang was dead. Murdered.

The last few days' rising and setting of the sun had blurred into an eternity of twilights. She had been only half-conscious when men carried her from the shed near the Beggar's Gate and dropped her, first into a cart, then later onto the rotting deck of a boat. She felt bruised and beaten, and so very tired. And what had they done with Jiang's body? Jiang. Beyond the Yellow Springs now.

Kulien remembered only a few details of the trip up the coastline. She had rallied enough to eat a little thin rice soup and drink some tepid water, but for most of the journey, she slept, trying to forget the events of the past week.

"So you are alive, after all," the woman said, leaning over her. "Well, she does have a good face," she remarked to a man who stood nearby. I suppose I can fatten her up. Since, as your master says, she has already shared the 'rains and dew' of a foreigner, she could be useful to me."

The woman took Kulien's hands and raised her to a sitting position. "How long has it been since you've eaten?"

"I—I. . .." Kulien's lips cracked and she tried to moisten them with her tongue, but it, too, was dry and swollen.

The woman turned to the man as he walked away. "I should demand my money back! This poor wretch might not live through the night."

"Take it up with Kong. Or sell her as meat. I've done my job."

Kulien watched the dark figure disappear through a heavy curtain. Her head swam and objects of the room floated by on waves of nausea. She closed her eyes, and then opened them again when the woman tucked a quilt around her. The sweet scent of rose oil lingered between them.

"I will bring soup before you take a bath," she said. "My name is Swan. I'm the procuress here. My establishment is called, 'The Blue Chambers.'" She shook Kulien's shoulder to wake her more fully.

"Listen to me. I can see that you are ill, and I've been told of your past. But now you are my property, and you must obey me. Do you remember why you were sent here? Do you realize that if I hadn't purchased you, you would be dead?"

Kulien nodded, but at this moment, she wished for death. Her head throbbed with pain, and sharp pangs of hunger tore through her stomach. A prostitute shop! This was better than dying? She watched through swollen eyelids as the woman laced and unlaced her fingers. What kind of woman would deal in human flesh?

Swan wore a heavy coat of rice powder on her face, and though in the dim light of the lantern she appeared to be young, there was an old woman looking through the obsidian eyes. "Well, what are you gaping at, Imbecile? Have you no tongue? Speak to me!"

"I—I feel like vomiting, but there is nothing in my stomach. I would be very grateful for a bit of food."

A sigh of exasperation escaped Swan's carmine lips when she turned to walk away. Long strands of beads tinkled as she swayed out of the room on tiny feet. Again, Kulien drifted into a soft dark slumber, but was suddenly pulled back by a voice, "Come now, you stupid girl, eat this!"

On a small table were a bowl of rice, dishes of fruit and a cup of clear soup. Kulien, with effort, lifted herself to one elbow and stared. "I've seen this soup before. It's made of lotus seeds." Her heart stirred with longing for Jiang's scolding voice.

"Yes, it's an old remedy. Big trouble to prepare, but good for many ailments. Consider yourself privileged. For this one time only!"

Kulien managed to sit up before she dipped chopsticks into the liquid, careful to take only one of the seeds at a time. She remembered Jiang's words about the embryo, or sprout, of the lotus seed. "Bitter," she had said. "The embryo must be removed or it will be a bitter seed."

Bitter Seed. Had the name given by her grandmother been prophetic? Kulien's other hand went instinctively to her stomach. Swan would want to remove Marshall's seed, but she would die first.

"You like it?" Swan asked. "It's good for the heart as well as other problems. Diarrhea and . . . ," she laughed. "It even cures nightmares."

"Hurry it up, little snail," she said, after several minutes. "I want to see what I've purchased under all that filth." She pressed a handkerchief to her nose, "And you smell like the fish boat that brought you here."

Kulien finished the light meal, and on wobbly legs followed Swan up a dark stairway to the second floor. She stopped often to catch her breath and take in her new surroundings. One side of the long passageway, which seemed to stretch the length of the building, was lined with closed doors, while on the other side folding doors with transparent panes partially concealed a wide veranda. Tables and chairs had been stacked and covered for the winter.

"Do people sit outside to eat when the weather is warm?" Kulien asked.

The woman stepped aside, and with hands on her hips, she turned to survey Kulien from head to toe. "The girls sometimes walk on the veranda—as a preview of what one will find behind those doors." She tipped her head. "I can see you're not a city girl, but you don't talk like a farm girl, either." She pointed at Kulien's canvas-clad feet. "My Chinese customers prefer women with lotus feet, but some foreigners find them distasteful. You will service them."

Kulien shuddered and folded her arms around her waist. No man would touch her. She would think of a way to protect herself. Hadn't she frightened Kong Litang away? "I'm *not* a prostitute," she said, lifting her chin and straightening her aching back.

"You are now."

"I cannot be with a man. Surely Kong Litang told you that I carry the seed of a barbarian. And," she lied, "the Englishman was infected with the pox."

"That makes no difference to me or to my customers. This isn't an entirely clean shop. Some of my girls are high class and entertain only the wealthy, but there are others, like you who, because of disease, haven't many years left."

Swan smoothed her red silk gown over curvaceous hips and sniffed the air. "Some men, who frequent my establishment, want only a little time for a few string of cash. The girls who service them make enough money to pay for a room and meals. No more." She pushed aside a filmy curtain. "This is where the girls bathe and receive instructions. You have the stink of fish and night soil on you, so first you must bathe."

The thought of a bath calmed Kulien's spirit, and she looked forward to a private time of sinking into warm, fragrant water. She followed Swan into the room that was empty except for a bench and several beds. A large metal tub in a far corner was attended by a young child no more than five or six years old. "Well," Swan shouted, "don't just stand there. Take off your clothes and get in." Swan nudged Kulien nearer to the tub.

"Do you have to watch me? I'd like to have some privacy when I bathe."

Swan threw back her head and laughed until tears ran down her cheeks, smudging the heavily powdered face. "You think you're quite a princess, don't you? You'll have no privacy since you belong to me. You do what I say—when I say it. Take off your clothes—now!"

Kulien turned her back to remove the satin rope from around her neck.

"What's that?" Swan shrieked.

Kulien's fingers tightened around the ring. "What? What are you talking about?"

"Those scratches! They're oozing with pus! Did Kong do that to you?"

Kulien nodded, thankful that Swan hadn't noticed Marshall's ring.

"Well, never mind. Get into the tub. After you dry, I'll have someone put ointment on those scratches. I don't like for my girls to have scars!"

Kulien let the traveling clothes drop to the floor and quickly stepped into the tub with the ring held tightly in one hand. As she sank into the scented water, she sighed with pleasure. The warm liquid soothed her spirit as well as her body. How long had it been since she'd bathed? Days? Weeks? No wonder she smelled like a beggar.

She leaned her head back on the rim of the tub and glanced around the room. Paintings of nude men and women covered the walls and decorated the folding screens. The display sickened her, and she closed her eyes and sank deeper under the water until it covered her head. If only the water could cleanse her mind of the shame and fear as it did her body.

When she sat up she kept her eyes lowered but felt refreshed. Her hair streamed down her back and flowed over her shoulders like a sheet of black satin. When she heard a movement she looked up to see Swan standing beside the tub, the little girl close behind her. "Do you have to watch me? Will I never have any privacy again?"

"You need to shut up! You not only have big feet, you have a big mouth. But I am here to teach you manners." Swan's voice was no longer melodic, nor pleasant. She stopped speaking long enough to hand Kulien a large towel. Your body is too thin and your hips too narrow, but your skin is light and nice to look at. You also have eyes that have a nice shape, but the color is dark green. You are a strange one!"

The child, her eyes brimming with tears, helped Kulien dry herself. She seemed to sense Kulien's discomfort and Kulien wondered if she, too, was a prostitute. Or perhaps Swan was her mother.

Swan ordered the girl to leave before she sat on a peach-wood bench and beckoned for Kulien to come near. "Let me see your legs and thighs," she demanded, jerking the towel away. "I want to see if you have open sores." She poked Kulien's hips and upper thighs with a long painted fingernail.

"Stop that!" Kulien grabbed the towel from the woman and held it against herself. "You say that I'm your property, but you won't touch me in my private places." The woman seemed not to hear. "How many times did you share the 'rains and dew' of foreigners?"

Kulien felt the blood drain from her face, and her knees grew weaker. "What are you asking? You think I'm accustomed to being with men?"

"This is what I've been told, and I want to know how much experience you've had so I'll know how much training you'll need to satisfy my customers. You won't be allowed to entertain my most wealthy patrons, but you must work for repeat clients. Most foreigners come from the ships; some from the consulates; and there are those who live on the Bund with their families."

Swan tilted her smoothly coifed head and her painted lips turned up at the corners. "The Westerner believes the anatomy of a Chinese woman is different from the barbarian. Many pay just for a look." Swan seemed amused as she watched Kulien's horrified expression. "So, tell me, how much experience you have had—and with how many men?"

Kulien's voice was so low, Swan could barely hear, "One time—one man."

Swan was still smiling when she brought Kulien clean clothes—a cheaply made gown of inferior pink silk and cotton undergarments. The young child returned at Swan's call and dabbed Kulien's scratches with ointment. Then she helped her dress before Swan sent her away. She ushered Kulien back down the hallway and opened a door to a narrow cubicle. Inside was a bed, a small table with a candle, and two chairs. "Sleep now," she said, pointing to a bed with several pillows and draped with blue silk. "I'll wake you when I think you've had enough rest."

It was dark when Kulien awoke, and for several moments, she was confused about her surroundings. She lifted herself to one elbow and glanced around the room lit only by a candle that glowed on the bedside table. She dropped back onto the bed, sighing as she remembered where she was--and why.

From somewhere in the distance came high-pitched singing along with light laughter and the strumming of lutes. Kulien held Marshall's ring to her lips and kissed it. She was far away from home and from anyone who had ever loved her. She was in a prostitute shop, "The Blue Chambers." She belonged to Swan.

What would become of her? She must escape, but how? Even if she and her unborn child were killed, it would be better than submitting to the advances of a strange man. She absolutely would not allow it!

She slipped the signet ring onto her finger and watched the candlelight glisten off the engraved crest. Marshall. Where had Sunfu taken him? Could he still be in Shanghai, possibly nearby? Had his superiors learned of his involvement with Sunfu's renegade band and sent him back to England? There had to be a way for her to find answers to her questions.

Suddenly voices, as clear as if in her room, broke her reverie. "I don't have time to listen to your music." A man spoke Chinese in a throaty whisper. "I've had ginseng, and I can't wait much longer."

A soft voice answered, "Why didn't you tell me, Sir? I would have given you white chrysanthemum tea to relax you."

"There's no time for that! Now come on, let me see your crimson shoes. Those tiny feet stir my spirit."

Kulien shuddered with disgust, and sat up to look around the sparsely-furnished room. Only a thin partition divided her quarters from those on either side. She would be forced to listen to the light laughter and squeals of delight coming from the room on one side, while groans and sighs invaded her privacy on the other. Kulien covered both ears with her hands and buried her head under the quilt. The words faded, but she still heard the music, the voices, and the cries. Her stomach churned with revulsion, and her determination to escape grew with each revolting sound.

Unbidden and the almost-forgotten words of Elizabeth Whitfield entered the half-open door of her mind. "The Invisible God has promised in the Bible that when trouble comes, He will make a way for you to escape." Kulien shook her head and rubbed her tired eyes. Could it be true? Elizabeth had certainly spoken the words with conviction. If only there were such a being who knew of her plight and cared.

A glimmer of hope began to shine in her darkened spirit as she recalled the times Elizabeth had tutored her in English, and in the ways of the foreign God. She had never told her father what she had learned in the black book with words about a man named Jesus who cared about helpless women. The book was hidden in the summerhouse. The summerhouse…

She allowed her mind to carry her back to those nights when she ministered to Marshall Whitfield's wound. She had loved him from the moment he first entered the audience hall on her birthday—and then he had loved her, loved her with his heart and soul. They had married themselves to one another. She was the wife of a British noble, and the daughter of a British woman and an honorable Chinese mandarin. Regardless of what Swan had planned for her future, she would hold onto those truths. "One day," she said in a whisper only she could hear, "one day, by the promise of the Most High, I will escape this place and be reunited with my husband. We *will* raise our child together."

With such hopes painted on her mind with strokes of an imaginary brush, she closed her eyes—and her ears to the sights and sounds of "The Blue Chambers."

TWENTY-ONE

After a miserably sleepless night, morning finally arrived and Kulien was bidden to the instruction room. Swan, dressed in an orchid robe, stood in front of twelve girls in loose-fitting gowns. "This is Bitter Seed," she announced. "She is a new girl—experienced with foreigners." She glanced at Kulien, then back to the others. 'You have the rest of the day to teach her the ways of an enlightened joy girl. In today's class I want you to tutor her to be sensuous and erotic. Show her how to satisfy a variety of tastes." Swan's words were as cold and academic as if she had been speaking of the civil service examinations.

"Melody, teach her some ballads and the strings of the lute. Sweet Fruit, show her a few tricks of magic." She turned to Kulien. "There are men who enjoy a little appetizer before the main course."

Kulien closed her eyes and inhaled deeply. The act of love with one man—her beloved Marshall—was her only crime. And now she was expected to submit herself to strangers!

"No! I can't do it! I won't!" A surge of energy filled Kulien's veins and she ran from the room and up the stairs. After several minutes, Swan hobbled into her cubicle and screeched, "What do you mean, you won't. You will!"

"I can't. I can't lie with another man. I won't. I'm married, I tell you. I'm married, and I'm with happiness!"

"Silence, Bitter Seed!" Swan grasped Kulien's shoulders and shook her. "I know what you are and where you came from. If the barbarian seed is your problem, we can take care of that immediately." Swan's long fingernails jabbed at the air.

"Don't pretend to be superior to the rest of us. You're not. My girls didn't have your opportunities. Some of them were beggars; others unwanted daughters, cast out on dung heaps. None could boast of their ancestors serving as magistrates. Not one had the privilege of private tutors or loving fathers. What sensible woman would throw away the privilege to be the wife (or even a concubine) of a wealthy man like Kong Litang? You're not only ungrateful, you're stupid!" Swan grabbed Kulien's shoulders again and shook her even harder. "You will do as you're told."

She stepped back and glared into Kulien's tear-filled eyes. "I could have extracted the foreign seed while you slept, but decided to let you keep the devil-baby as long as you can. You will work for me until you're too far along to do your job. Then," she added with a sneer, "I will have another slave, whether boy or girl, to bargain with."

Kulien covered her face with both hands and sobbed. "My baby? You even own my baby?"

"Of course. All you have is mine. That includes the ring you're trying to hide under your dress," she said in a low voice.

Kulien pressed her hand over Marshall's signet ring and wiped her eyes with her other hand. There was no point in arguing with Swan. She would have to do as she was told.

"You may keep your little treasure for the present. Wash your face and apply some powder. You've caused a scene, and will have to make an effort to gain the respect of the other girls."

Kulien spent the rest of the day in, what seemed to her, the lower parts of the earth. One girl instructed her in the art of pouring tea while another showed her how to strum a lute and sing. An older woman explained how she could make small talk, "...if the gentleman is in no hurry."

"Now," said a young woman, who had remained aloof most of the day, "Swan tells us you have slept with only one man, a barbarian. Well," she said, hands on her wide, soft hips, "you have much to learn if you want to succeed in this business, and make a little extra money for yourself.

"A little song, a little magic, and much sweet fruit!" The woman smiled and introduced herself as Ping, a citizen of Soochow. "The women from our city are the most desired of all joy girls," she said, "because we can satisfy a man as no other women, whether he is from China, Japan or across the Peaceful Sea."

Ping removed her gown, and clad only in silk undergarments, began to arrange pillows on a bed that was situated in the center of the room. Kulien didn't see or hear what came next. She managed to block out Ping's performance of contortions while the other girls "oohed and aahed" in appreciation.

"I prefer my own countrymen," said a bored young woman sitting next to Kulien. "But some of the foreigners pay better and find Chinese women extremely delightful. And of course they would. Have you seen those fat she-dogs they have as wives?"

All the girls began to laugh and talk at once. "The foreign woman is cold and she has a big nose and boat feet," said one. "Like your feet!" added another. "But all men, Chinese or foreign, like thin waists and strong thighs, and you do seem to excel there."

Kulien didn't want to hear another word of their disgusting and degrading conversations. If only she could escape and hide under the quilts as she had the night before; but Swan stood at the doorway, her intense dark eyes boring into her. She would have to observe the instructions today, but before she had to "service" a man, she would run away.

She turned these thoughts over in her mind as one after another of the girls gave instructions. "Never bruise the customer's heart," one said. "He must believe he is the most wonderful man you have ever been with. If you convince him, he will give you jewelry and money. And he will ask for you again and again."

"Never become involved with a patron outside 'The Blue Chambers,'" said the older woman. "It was different back in the days when we served only Chinese. In those days, a girl could become the concubine of some official. But the invading foreigners come here against orders of their superiors."

"And their superiors come later!" There was a burst of laughter.

By the end of the day Kulien's head throbbed, and pain from standing with the group of prostitutes gripped her back and legs. She dropped onto a low couch beside the youngest girl in the room—the girl who had filled her tub and put ointment on her back. "How old are you?" she asked, desperately wishing for some relief of the day's instructions.

"I'm ten on my next birthday," she said. "I'm small for my age, and Swan says I won't be ready for work for another year. How old are you?"

"I'm sixteen," Kulien answered, as she studied the girl's face. "How did you happen to come here so young?"

The small girl, whose face was much older than her body, lowered her head. "Swan rescued me when I was five and brought me here. I owe her my life." She stretched out crooked legs. "I was cast away to die because my legs were broken when I was beaten by my father. I'm crippled, but with Swan as my caretaker I can make a living without having to beg."

Kulien could scarcely believe what she heard. "But what you will have to do here is much worse than begging."

"Oh, no," the girl exclaimed, "It is a great honor to work for Swan. She is famous for her house, and for the excellent work her girls do for the customers."

Honor? Kulien's mind whirled. This poor child felt it would be an honor to be used as a prostitute. *One's shame is another's honor*, she thought. *It is all dependent on fate.*

She touched the slight bulge of the ring hidden under her sheath and marveled that only a few moons had passed since she lived as an innocent girl behind the high walls of her ancestral home. There, a life of honor was her heritage as the daughter of Kuang Lufong. Now, because she had given her heart to Lord Marshall Whitfield, she was the property of the procuress, Swan, and the newest prostitute in "The Blue Chambers" joy house.

Kulien sat in front of a mirror appraising her painted and powdered face. "You see, now you look like one of us." Golden Bell stood behind her balancing her delicate form on tiny shoes that tinkled when she walked. "Except for your feet, of course."

The young woman patted Kulien's shoulder. "Forgive me, sister. It is unkind to draw attention to your feet. How thoughtless of your mother not to bind them!"

Kulien stared at her reflection. Was she the same girl who a short time ago practiced *taichichuan* in the garden with her beloved father? Golden Bell had applied dark paint around the rims of Kulien's green eyes, and had transformed her full lips into shiny carmine bows. Pink circles graced her sculptured cheekbones, and her long silken hair had been piled high on her head and decorated with jeweled combs and brilliant peacock feathers. The borrowed gown was as rich and elegant as any she had left behind in the Kong compound. It was made of deep emerald silk with metallic golden embroidery at the throat and hems of the full sleeves. Its smooth silkiness stretched across her firm breasts that seemed to grow fuller each day. The dress was form-fitting and hugged her tiny waist and cupped her rounded hips. She turned sideways to look at her full view. Was that a slight bulge of her abdomen that had always been so flat? Could Marshall's seed already be growing? She spread her fingers and rested hands on her narrow waist. What would happen to her unborn child if she couldn't escape?

Seven days had passed since she had arrived at the prostitute shop, and she had been allowed to eat whenever she felt hungry, and sleep at any time of the day or night. Because she could read, Swan commanded her to study, *Memoirs of the Plum Blossom Cottage,* an instruction book for prostitutes. Each evening Swan tested her on what she had read. "You've become a good student, Bitter Seed," she had remarked that morning. "Tonight you will have you first customer."

"But I'm not ready." She paled and bit her lower lip.

"You know the words. You know the movements. You only need practice. You're still slim, and practically a virgin, so...." Swan had taken out the green gown. "So, now it's time for your debut." I will personally introduce you to the patrons as they partake of their evening tea. Then I will choose the right man for you. A barbarian will find you to be a delightful partner, and I expect you to please him in whatever way he asks."

Kulien's voice trembled. "May I just sing him a song this time? Please?"

"Don't be ridiculous. The foreigner is not civilized like our people. He comes to 'The Blue Chambers' for only one purpose. He expects you to entertain him with only a song or two, and then satisfy his desires. We want our patrons to return; so I will give you only one man on your first night. After tonight, though, you will service more than one customer a night."

Swan paused a moment to study Kulien's face. "Don't be afraid. If the man is rough or cruel, I want to know—after he has left."

Now the time had arrived. She was dressed, her toilette completed, her hair braided, her bed perfumed and ready. All was ready, except for her own heart. *Oh, Marshall, where are you? Where is the God Elizabeth said would show me a way of escape?*

TWENTY-TWO

The musicians, with pipes and stringed instruments, filled the night air with lilting melodies. Kulien, her heart pounding in her ears, joined with the other girls as they stood at the top of the stairs singing in thin, reedy voices. At the foot of the stairway men gathered at round tables, some drinking tea, others imbibing strong liquor. They stopped talking to listen and watch as the girls walked slowly down, balancing their lavishly dressed bodies on tiny feet. Each girl wore an expensive silk gown and ornate jewelry. All, except Kulien, wore small satin slippers decorated with jewels and ribbons. Two girls strummed lutes as the others sang love songs written centuries before by famous Chinese poets.

Kulien struggled to force the words out of a throat that felt choked with fear and anxiety. How had she come to this? A prostitute! With her head bowed low, she lifted her eyelids to see the room full of men, young and old, ogling each girl as she stepped onto the floor and was escorted to a table by Swan. Some of the girls were immediately hired, while others were taken from one table to the next until a man held out his hand to show his acceptance.

As Kulien reached the bottom of the stairs, she suddenly felt sick and leaned against one of the girls for support. "Are you ill?" asked Jade Treasure, a frown on her high forehead.

"Yes. I must return to my room." Kulien spoke in whispered words.

Swan stepped to her side and grasped her wrist. "You are not sick. You will put a smile on that sad face and do as I say! I've already warned you. If you don't obey me, I'll have that seed, you so desperately want, plucked out of your body!"

Kulien drew in her breath, knowing that Swan didn't make idle threats. The day before, she had seen her beat one of the older women until she was unconscious, then had told a servant to dispose of her as he saw fit. Swan tightened her grasp and Kulien winced. "I'll do as you say. Please give me another chance."

Swan seemed to relax her fingers and muttered, "I know this is your first time. I will see that you get someone as inexperienced as you are." Her laugh was soft and hidden behind long fingers. "That should be quite a sight! I might just have to come and watch."

Kulien wanted to curl up in a ball and disappear. How degrading to imagine herself with a strange man, and even more so with an audience.

It was ten o'clock, the Hour of the Pig, and the teahouse had been vibrating with loud words, laughing and music as the girls descended. But now, as each girl was presented, all eyes were upon Swan and the young women who were offered for the best price. They minced in and out among the tables, stopping often while Swan pointed out the good features of each girl.

"This one is robust and strong and will last most of the night," she said of Golden Pearl.

"This girl is very young, but adept. Fresh Blossom will do anything you ask of her."

"This is one of the favorites," she said of Ping. "She's from Soochow, and you know of their specialty!"

Finally, it was Kulien's turn. Swan led her to a table where a tall, thin foreigner sat with a boy no older than Kulien. Swan spoke to the older man. "Virgin for you," she said in broken English. "Only slightly used," she said under her breath to Kulien. She turned back to the man. "She sing and speak English much good." Swan leaned forward, her long gold chains jangling. "Much good, many ways."

The man motioned toward the boy beside him. He spoke pidgin, "Not for me, never mind. Son ready learn man-woman play. Clean girl. No pox!"

Kulien turned her head, trying to avoid the exchange of words and looks that passed between the man and his son. "She's good looking," he said to the boy with a pimple-marked face. "What do you say? You want her?"

The boy stammered, "I don't know, Father. She looks kind of frightened."

"Well," laughed the man, "then that makes two of you." He held out a stack of foreign bills, and speaking with a British accent, added, "We'll take her—at least William will. I'm still looking for someone more to my liking. How about that girl from Soochow?"

Swan tucked the money into her flowing sleeve and pointed toward the stairs. "You know what to do, Bitter Seed. Take the 'spring chicken' to your room." She pulled Kulien aside. "This boy is inexperienced, so you will have to be patient with him. Put him at ease first, and give him some tea and cookies. Then," she said with a smile, "let nature take its course."

Hot tears burned Kulien's eyelids and her mouth was dry as dust. Her knees shook and her hands trembled as she led the boy up the stairs and down the long hallway to her room. As she stepped into the narrow cubicle, fragrant with burning incense, an unexpected prayer arose in her heart. "O, Most High, God of Elizabeth Whitfield, hear my cry. Please show me the way to escape this wicked trial!"

Kulien gestured toward a chair and watched the boy sit, perspiration running down his ruddy cheeks. She sat opposite him and reached for the blue and white teapot on the table beside her chair. As she began to pour the pale amber liquid, the young man spoke louder than necessary, enunciating each English word. "Is your name really Bitter Seed? That's an ugly name!"

Kulien kept her eyelids lowered and handed him a tiny cup balanced on a matching saucer. Did he think she was deaf? Why did he speak so loudly?

"My name is Kulien, Bitter Seed."

They boy's eyes widened and his mouth dropped open. "You speak English with a British accent. Now that is a surprise!" When she didn't respond, he went on. "My name is William Walker. I did not choose to come here, and my mother would be appalled if she had any indication of my father's intent." He sat stiffly on a high-backed chair and studied his folded hands. Under his breath, he added, "I had no idea that Father would also hire a prostitute for himself."

"I understand your unhappiness," Kulien said, leaning toward the boy. "I don't want to be here, either." She watched him sip the hot, fragrant tea. "How old are you, William?"

"Fifteen," he answered, lifting his eyes to hers.

"As the Westerner counts years, I, too, am fifteen, though I feel much older." She poured herself a cup of tea and left it on the table. "Would you like for me to sing for you?"

"If you wish." He sipped the hot liquid, watching her over the rim of the cup.

As Kulien sang, the fear and dread of the ordeal ahead dissipated. Words about soft winds and fragrant blossoms comforted her, and as her sweet voice filled the room William closed his eyes and rested his head against the back of the chair.

"You look very tired." Kulien felt a strange sense of pity for the boy who had been brought to a prostitute shop against his wishes. "I can rub your shoulders for you."

William lifted his head and stared at Kulien with red-rimmed eyes. "Thank you," he said. "I've been traveling for many days. My family—father, mother, and my little sister—arrived in Shanghai yesterday. Father is with Her Majesty's Service in Peking, so we will only be in here for two days before continuing our trip."

William Walker rose slowly from the chair, and walked to the bed that had been arranged with soft pillows and sprinkled with rose petals. He brushed aside the petals and sat down before looking up at Kulien who stood beside the bed. As he lay back, he smiled at her. "You said you don't want to be here, either. Then why are you employed as one of the prostitutes? My father said that many of the women who work here were discarded from their families as 'unwanted females.' Is that what happened to you?"

As Kulien watched the young man settle against the pillows, she thought of Marshall. William had the same blond hair and blue eyes, but there was hardness around his mouth that revealed a selfish spirit. Could she trust this English boy with her secret? Would he be willing to spend the night sleeping on her bed—alone?

"My story is different from most of the girls here," she said tentatively. "I come from a noble family. My father is a high-ranking mandarin who presides over an extensive compound not far from here."

William's expression showed his interest as he leaned up on one elbow and stared at Kulien. "So then what happened? Why aren't you living with your father?"

Kulien sat on the bed next to William, confident that she could share some of her problems with him. He was British after all, and perhaps he could persuade his father to help her to find Marshall.

"I was sent from my home because I married one of your countrymen, a member of the British Consulate here in Shanghai." She paused, wondering if she should go on. William's expression didn't change, so she continued, "I believe my husband is still here in the city. Do you think your father could help me find him?"

William sat up straight, his eyes narrowed, his mouth in a sneer before he shouted, "I cannot believe that! You lie. An Englishman would never stoop to marry a Chinese! A prostitute at that!" His watery eyes roamed over her face and down her body, taking in every curve. "You're no more than a dirty Chink liar!"

Kulien drew back in alarm. The viciousness of the young man shocked her. He had seemed so calm and kind. She felt warmth spread over her face and pressed her hands over her flushed cheeks. "You're wrong. I don't lie."

William grabbed at Kulien, pulling her closer. "You're good for only one thing, as my father says." Holding down her arms with surprising strength, he pressed a wet mouth on hers. She struggled, turning her head away, pushing against him as he pulled at her clothes. "My father paid a lot of money for you, so I want what is coming to me!"

As Kulien rolled out from under him, she shouted, "I'm not a liar! Swan is the one who lied. I'm married, and I'm expecting a child."

The young man's face contorted in anger and disbelief. "Wait until my father hears about this. You will be in great trouble because you didn't submit to me!"

William Walker flung himself from the bed, almost knocking Kulien down. He ran from the room and down the passageway, calling for his father.

Kulien could hardly move she was so startled by his actions. Then she realized there was not a moment to lose. She reached under the bed and pulled out a wooden box supplied by Swan. With one quick movement, she reached for Marshall's ring and looped the satin rope over her neck. Grasping the ring in her hand, she darted for the door. Her feet seemed to have wings as she fled down the back stairway to the door opening into a vermin-infested alleyway. She threw open the door, and disappeared into the darkness.

Clinging to the side of the building, she heard voices shouting from the top of the stairs, and, with a racing heart, she began to edge her way along the alley, not knowing or caring where it might lead.

TWENTY-THREE

"Get that girl! She belongs to me!" Swan's high-pitched voice ripped through the night air. Kulien dashed behind a huge crate, flattening herself against the wall of the building. Pungent odors of decaying garbage and rotting filth stung her eyes and nose, and she covered her face with both hands.

"She must have gone that way!"

"No, she went over there."

Swan shouted instructions from the doorway as several men ran past the crate into the street. They strode back and forth, straining to see a young woman running away. When they saw only beggars and shopkeepers, they returned to Swan shaking their heads.

Kulien peered around the edge of the crate to see Swan silhouetted against the dim light of the interior. "That Bitter Seed won't get far," she said. "I wager she'll return before morning and beg me to take her in. Her kind won't last long on this street."

Several of the girls stood around Swan, some stepping out into the alleyway. "She doesn't deserve your kindness," said the small girl clinging to Swan's gown. "She never could be one of us," said another. "She's too high and mighty! Let her die— or worse, I say."

"Yes, let her try to find help from those beggars who lurk outside the shops."

"I hope some men will find her and have their way with her, and she won't even be paid!" Laughter erupted among all the girls before the door slammed shut and darkness covered the alley like an old blanket.

Kulien ventured away from the wall and stepped on something soft that seemed to melt under her foot. A thin ray of light filtered into the alley, and she gasped in horror. At her feet lay a bloody mass—a barely formed baby. Bile rose to her throat and her head began to swim. She reached out to steady herself against the wall, hoping against hope that she wouldn't faint. *Get away from here! But where? How?* She was alone in a strange city—an outcast from both her birth family and the prostitutes that had pretended to accept her as one of them.

Kulien eased her way around the crate and crept along the wall of the blue-painted building. She must think. *Elizabeth Whitfield! She is here—somewhere in Shanghai.* Kulien searched her mind. Elizabeth had told her where she lived. *Think! Think!*

Like a veiled mist, a conversation between Kulien and Miss Whitfield began to materialize. They had been sitting beside the miniature waterfall outside Kulien's rooms. "I've often wondered where you live," she had said. "Do you stay with the other Westerners on the Bund? Are you able to live close to your brother?"

Elizabeth Whitfield had smiled, her blue eyes sparkling, her dark eyebrows lifting in a question. "I think you are curious about me, aren't you Kulien? We've been meeting for almost three years, and this is the first time you've asked about my private life."

Kulien had lowered her eyes in shame. "Forgive me, Teacher, if I have offended you. I meant no harm."

"Of course, you didn't offend me! I'm pleased that you want to know. After all, I know quite a bit about you, and I consider us to be more than teacher and pupil. I like to think that we are also friends."

The conversation on that spring day continued to play in Kulien's mind as she ventured out onto the dark street. "I reside in a British mission house. Actually, it's an orphanage where young girls live and are cared for with love. The mission is several miles from the British Consulate where Marshall is stationed. We're situated in a place where the poor can be reached—on Nanking Lu—Nanking Road, near Jiangning Road."

It all came back to Kulien as she hurried away from the alley. "Our building is decorated with a gold cross on a red door. There is a sign with large Chinese characters that announce, 'The Orphanage of Shang Ti.'"

Kulien remembered how they had then discussed Shang Ti, which means "Highest Lord." She had learned about Shang Ti in her studies of Chinese Literature in the Five Classics. This name was given to the Supreme God of the Han Chinese people from the second millennium B.C. He was a God so great that no images were to be made to represent him. Miss Whitfield told her that the name was adopted by Protestant missionaries in China to refer to the Christian God.

Kulien turned her attention back to how she might reach the orphanage on Nanking Road. As she ran along the street, staying close to the buildings, her heart fluttered in her chest like a trapped bird. She stopped occasionally to read placards on the face of the buildings, hoping to find a familiar landmark. She had visited the city many years before, and although she was only a child, perhaps a memory of that long ago trip would remind her of where she was. She heard a scuffling sound from behind, and felt a hand grasp at her gown. A man shouted, "Come here, singsong girl. I don't want to go home to my fat wife!" Kulien pulled away and ran across the dirt road, avoiding the eyes of people who strolled on the streets so late at night.

She walked until she felt she would drop from exhaustion, but knew she had to keep going. Finally, she came upon a stall where an old woman sat weaving shoes from long grasses. "Do you know of an English mission—an orphanage named after Shang Ti?" The wrinkled face thrust out her chin and scowled.

"Please, can you tell me how to find Nanking Lu?"

Ignoring her question, the woman began to chant her wares until a late-night customer stopped to bargain. Kulien forced herself to walk on, shoved and pushed by a growing noisy, restless crowd. Beggars sat against the walls holding out claw-like hands, screaming threats, "Give me a copper or the gods will strike you with the pox!"

Even though it was well past midnight, the Hour of the Rat, an endless stream of people rolled by in waves: crying children, men with baskets of fish dangling at the ends of poles balanced on their shoulders, vendors pushing and shoving their produce in the faces of those who scurried along the roadway.

To avoid the crowd, Kulien turned onto a narrow street and nearly bumped into a scampering coolie balancing two open buckets of night soil. She stopped to catch her breath and leaned against a dilapidated building. She heard voices coming from inside that rose in volume. They were talking about an uprising, a rebellion. They began to shout over and over, "Kill the foreigners. Redeem Shanghai!" A chill ran up her spine. Was this the group Sunfu had joined?

Afraid to linger any longer, she ran up and down dark, winding roads, her eyes darting around like a frightened animal. Where was the orphanage? Where was Elizabeth Whitfield? She had left the area of known prostitute houses and was now entering the section where foreigners made their homes. She stopped to ask an old Chinese man for directions to the orphanage. He smiled pleasantly, showing the absence of teeth. "Ah, yes, I know of that place," he said, circling his finger in the air. "The big noses there talk about a foreign god. They take in worthless females."

At her insistence, the man pointed up the road. "Go north to the creek. Turn east and go two streets more. Nanking Lu. Red door. Gilt cross." He shook his finger in her face. "You're stupid to go there. Foreign devils eat little girls, you know!"

Kulien turned away and began to run again. At least now she had some directions. She raced up one narrow street, and down the next, trying to remember when to turn east. Through dark allies, past makeshift huts, around muddy puddles. On and on she ran until she had no more strength. Down one more street; her eyes strained for some evidence of Nanking Lu—of a building with a red door and gold cross. When she was about to give up, she saw it—"The Orphanage of Shang Ti." Lanterns on each side of the door lit up the bold characters.

With a surge of strength Kulien threw herself against the door, and beat on it with both fists. "Let me in! Please, let me in!"

The door swung open, and Kulien fell to her knees into the room. The first things she saw were black shoes and the hem of a brown woolen dress. Before lifting her head, she reached out to touch the toes of the shoes. She had found her teacher and friend. She was safe at last.

A hand rested on her head. "Get up, child. You're welcome here."

Kulien rose to her feet, but kept her head bowed, too ashamed for her teacher to see her like this.

"Don't be afraid. We'll take care of you."

When Kulien lifted her head, Miss Whitfield's mouth fell open, her eyes wide with surprise. She didn't speak, but put a hand on Kulien's shoulder. Finally, she seemed able to form words, "Kulien? Is it really you? I don't understand. Why is your face painted like that? And those clothes? Where have you been?"

Before Kulien could answer, Elizabeth moved quickly to the door and slammed it shut, bolting it. She held a lantern closer to Kulien's face. "I can't believe it's you. My dear girl, I'm so glad to see you." She set the lantern on a nearby table and put her arms around Kulien and drew her close. "It's all right, child. It doesn't matter where you've been, or what you've done. You're here now and you're safe. This is where you belong."

Kulien let Miss Whitfield hold her. She felt secure and loved in the arms of this woman who had been her friend and teacher for so many years. When she pulled away, she lowered her head and focused her eyes on the floor. How could she tell Elizabeth Whitfield that she had been sold into prostitution? How would she explain about her relationship with Marshall and the baby she was now expecting? She touched the ring hidden under her close-fitting dress. "I should not have come," she said at last.

Elizabeth placed cool fingers on Kulien's chin and lifted her face. The clear blue eyes shone in the semi-darkness with tears, and her pink lips curved slightly upward. "I'm glad you came, Kulien. There are no secrets in China. Word came to us that you had been sent away from Hangchow in disgrace. We weren't told the details, except that your dear *amah,* Jiang, was dead. You don't need to tell me anything you don't want to. If and when the time comes and you want to talk about it, you may. There is no judgment here, only love."

She stroked Kulien's hair that had come loose from the braids, and now lay tangled about her shoulders. "What you need now is a warm bath and some food." Elizabeth took one of Kulien's hands and began to lead her from the reception room and down a long hallway. "I'll fill a tub and find you some comfortable clothes. Her eyebrows drew together as her eyes traveled over Kulien's form-fitting gown. "What we have here is simple, but clean."

After Kulien had bathed in a small wooden tub, she crumpled the tight "joy" dress into a ball and stuffed it into a dark corner. The blue cotton pants and shirt, left on a stool by Miss Whitfield, smelled of soap and felt clean and soft against her freshly scrubbed skin. She had tried to wash away the filth and sordidness of the past weeks, but had only succeeded in bringing a warm pink glow to her skin. Could she ever rid herself of the memory of Jiang's murder? How would she be able to forget the degradation she had seen and felt as a "joy" girl in "The Blue Chambers?"

"Do you feel better now?" Elizabeth asked, as Kulien entered a kitchen lit with several lanterns. The teacher sat on a bench at a long table in the center of a spacious room.

"Come, have something to eat." She motioned to the place set with chopsticks and a tea cup. "Then you can sleep as long as you wish." She rose from the bench and went to the black iron stove at the far end of the kitchen. She set a bowl of rice in front of Kulien, and then from a large pot, she ladled fish soup into another bowl. Kulien's stomach rumbled with hunger, and for the first time in many days her appetite returned.

She ate slowly, relishing each delicious morsel. Tentatively, she sneaked glances at Miss Whitfield. Here she was with Marshall's sister—her sister now. Would she know of Marshall's whereabouts? Her heart raced with the thought that perhaps she would be with him before another day had passed. Her greatest concern was how to tell her teacher of her secret marriage to Marshall Whitfield. And she would have to tell her about the baby growing inside. She was beginning to show, and even with loose-fitting clothes, she couldn't hide the truth much longer.

When Kulien finished her meal, Elizabeth stood, and beckoned Kulien to follow her. "As I've told you, our place is primarily a refuge for abandoned girls, but we also treat some medical problems here as well. We have a physician, Dr. Gordon, and his wife, Hope, who is a nurse. Our pastor and head of the mission is Reverend Mortensen. His wife, Julia, is my closest friend. You will love her as I do."

Elizabeth held a lantern overhead and led the way into another large room where beds were lined up against three walls. "We are a little crowded now, but there's plenty of room for you, Kulien." They stopped at the far corner of the room, and Elizabeth waved her arm encircling the sleeping girls. "They've been asleep for many hours so you won't be disturbed by curious, chatting little ones."

Kulien stretched out on the cotton-filled mat and relaxed as Miss Whitfield tucked a fragrant-smelling quilt around her small form. "Sleep well, child," she whispered. "I know God brought you here. You have nothing to worry about anymore."

As Kulien closed her eyes, her body yearning for rest, she continued to wonder how and when she would tell Miss Whitfield about all that had happened in the summerhouse. She had betrayed her father and her heritage; but she had married the man she loved with all her heart. And now she carried his baby.

Perhaps Shang Ti, the Most High God, *had* brought her here. At last, with a growing sense of peace, she drifted into a dreamless sleep.

TWENTY-FOUR

When Kulien opened her eyes to the bright autumn morning, she was surrounded by a wall of inquisitive faces. Towering over the heads of black hair was Elizabeth, her blue eyes dancing with humor. "This is your welcoming party, Kulien. I want you to meet your little sisters—and your big sisters," she said, placing an arm over the shoulders of a large, husky girl.

Kulien rose to a sitting position and smiled. "Thank you" she said, looking from one child to the next. "Thank you for sharing your room with me."

The girls whispered among themselves before one spoke, "Teacher said you were her student, and that you speak English. She said you might help us pronounce the foreign words better." The girl paused, then tried her English, "We bery glad you here where we find kindness."

Elizabeth Whitfield nodded. "That was well spoken Chengli," she said in Mandarin. "Chengli's family was salt smugglers, and she was wounded by a stray bullet. By the time she was brought here, her arm was too infected to save." Chengli smiled and held up a short stub as if it were a symbol of heroism.

"Tell about me, Teacher. Oh, please, tell about me!" A tiny girl, no more than three or four years old, tugged at Miss Whitfield's long black skirt.

Elizabeth picked up the child, whose shoes were on backwards, and wiped a strand of hair from the little girl's dark, glowing eyes. "This is Pau, which means Precious. When she was two years old, her mother left her on a grave mound to die."

She kissed the rounded cheek before removing the backward shoes to reveal toeless stumps. "Pau's feet had been mangled and were hanging by shreds. Dr. Gordon thought she would die of infection, but...," she hugged her closely, "but...well, she fooled us all!"

Precious kicked her legs and laughed.

"She has no toes, but this little one gets around quite well." Elizabeth sat on the bed next to Kulien's and held Pau on her lap. She smiled from the little girl to Kulien as she replaced the shoes with the heels where the toes should be. "We're never quite sure, though, if Pau is coming or going."

All the girls laughed and reached out to pat the happy child on her head. "As you can see," added Miss Whitfield, "through the love of these children, she has gained much more than she lost."

As their teacher introduced each girl, Kulien's heart ached with a newfound love for them. Some of the girls clamped their lips shut, and wouldn't speak; others smiled broadly and waved; still others drew closer to Kulien and put their arms around her neck.

"All right, children, it's time for breakfast. Come along and show our newest guest her place at the table."

Kulien could hardly move through the room and down the hallway as each girl tried to hold her hands and be as near to her as possible. This was an entirely new experience for Kulien. She had been despised and ridiculed by her own family, yet these unwanted and abandoned children reached out to her in love and acceptance. For the first time in many months, she felt laughter begin to bubble up from her spirit and float through the bustling, happy crowd of girls. Elizabeth turned to watch Kulien as she was pulled this way and that, each girl wanting to sit beside her. Finally, Miss Whitfield clapped her hands and spoke, a smile on her face, "I know you already love the newest member of our family, and you will each get a turn to sit next to her at a meal."

Elizabeth put an arm around Kulien and motioned her toward the head of the table. "For this meal, I think we'll put her at the head of the table so all of you can see her."

After they had found their places, Miss Whitfield said, "Let us thank the Lord for our food." The room became quiet as the girls folded their hands in front of them on the table and closed their eyes. "Thank you Father, in Jesus' Name, for this new day. Thank you for each lovely girl you have brought into this house of love and forgiveness. Thank you for showing Kulien how to reach our home and find safety."

Kulien's heart fluttered when she heard her name associated with Elizabeth's God.

"And thank you for the abundance of food that arrives each day." She paused, glancing up at the children. "Amen."

Kulien watched as the children lifted their heads and quietly waited as older girls began to fill bowls with gruel from the stove. Before many minutes passed, each person had been served and began to eat with relish. Kulien sat as still as a statue, taking in every movement, every word spoken.

Elizabeth Whitfield touched Kulien's arm. "Are you all right, my dear? I know how you must grieve the loss of your family, but we're your family now. I hope one day you will feel a part of us. I'd be so happy if you would stay here and become a member of our staff."

Kulien fastened her eyes on her teacher. "I'm honored, Miss Whitfield, that you should ask me to stay, and to help with the children. But," she paused, glancing down at her bowl of food, "as you know, I have dishonored my family. I'm not qualified to work with you." Tears formed in the corners of her eyes, and she brushed them away with her fingertips.

Elizabeth's eyes crinkled as her lips turned up in a smile. "You are more than qualified, Kulien. I know you've been deeply hurt and embarrassed. I don't know why Kong Litang forced you to leave Hangchow, nor do I understand why your family would not receive you back into their protection. There are many customs that I do not understand." She glanced around at the girls who had finished their meals and were waiting for Miss Whitfield to excuse them. She nodded, and as one, they rose from the benches and left the room. "Perhaps, someday you'll meet a fine Chinese gentleman who will take you as his wife. I do pray for your happiness, Kulien."

"Oh, but Miss Whitfield, I already have a husband."

"Well, dear, Kong Litang has divorced you. Now you're free from him."

Kulien inhaled deeply, wondering if this was the time or place to tell her about Marshall Whitfield and their marriage in the summerhouse. Would the prim British teacher accept the marriage? Would she love the baby that she carried near her heart? Could Kulien ever tell her about the degrading things she had seen and heard in the prostitute shop?

Elizabeth turned away from Kulien as a tall, white-haired man walked into the room carrying a large black book. "Kulien, this is Reverend Mortensen. He's the director of our orphanage. You can trust him."

The man smiled down at her, warming her with his gray eyes. "I've heard many fine things about you, Kulien. You may stay here as long as you wish. God has provided these quarters and plenty of food for the discarded girls of Shanghai."

"I...I.... Thank you, sir." Kulien's voice cracked with emotion. "I have no home or family."

"You do now," he said, softly. He crossed the kitchen and called down the hallway. "Come children! It's time for chapel. After the Bible lesson and prayers, you may return to the kitchen to finish your morning chores."

Two weeks passed quickly as Kulien adapted to the schedule and strange customs of the British. She liked the women who lived in the mission. Julia Mortensen, wife of the minister, spent most of her time outside the orphanage visiting the sick, and trying to convince them to come into the mission hospital for Western medicine. Julia was younger than her husband, and her quick, bustling ways had earned her the nickname, *Tai Foong,* Great Wind.

Hope Gordon, the doctor's wife, assisted in surgery and in caring for the patients. She spoke of little else than the sick and Kulien found her more reserved than either Elizabeth or Julia.

One evening, after the other girls had retired, Elizabeth stopped Kulien on the way to the sleeping quarters. "Kulien, may we talk privately?"

Kulien's heart skipped a beat. This was the first time Miss Whitfield had asked to meet with her. "Oh, yes. Have I done something wrong? Did I clean the kitchen well enough?"

"Of course. You've been a great help, and as usual, whatever you set your hand to, you do it with care." She motioned toward her room at the far end of the kitchen. "Please join me for a cup of tea. There's something I must say to you."

Kulien laced her fingers in front of her as she followed the teacher to her private quarters. What could she want to say? Would this be a good time to tell her about Marshall? About the baby?

"Sit down, dear," Elizabeth said, as she closed the door.

Kulien glanced around the room at the sparse furnishings: a narrow bed covered with a blue and yellow quilt, a dressing table with only a comb, brush, mirror, and a bottle of some white liquid. Next to the bed was a table with a framed picture. Kulien leaned forward to see, and gasped. Marshall! Marshall dressed in his finest clothing. He stood beside a large chair, his hand resting on the carved back. She hardly recognized him as his face was grim and his eyes straight forward without the slightest hint of a smile.

"Oh, Kulien! You remember my brother, don't you? It seems so long ago now that he came with me to greet you on your sixteenth birthday." She paused, a crease in her forehead. "That must have been about seven or eight months ago."

Kulien felt so weak, that if she hadn't been sitting, she would have collapsed. A warm blush spread over her face and body, and she closed her eyes—remembering.

"Are you all right? You suddenly look quite ill. Oh, I hope this evening's dinner didn't upset you."

"No," Kulien managed to answer, "I'm not ill. And the meal was very good. I don't know what came over me." Kulien kept her eyes averted from the picture, and avoided answering Miss Whitfield's question. How could she ever forget that first meeting in the Audience Hall of her home? Her heart was filled with memories of their closeness, the wedding vows, and the marriage bed.

Elizabeth interrupted her thoughts, "Your face is flushed!" She pressed a cool hand against Kulien's forehead. "I do believe you have a fever. Perhaps I should have Hope take a look at you."

Kulien lifted her chin. "Don't worry about me, please. I'm not ill, just a little tired, that's all."

Elizabeth pulled up another chair, facing Kulien. "Then, I'll get right to the point. But first," she lifted a teapot decorated with roses and began to pour the amber liquid into a small cup, before placing it on a saucer, "we need some tea." She smiled as she handed the cup and saucer to Kulien.

"Do you consider us to be friends, Kulien?"

"Oh, yes, you came to my home for more than three years and you taught me so much! And I do thank you, Miss Whitfield." Kulien leaned forward as if beseeching her teacher. "Now here I am in your home seeking even more help."

"You're right that we've known each other for three years. I've learned as many things about your culture as you have of mine. But we seldom spoke of personal concerns."

Kulien lifted the cup to her lips, watching Miss Whitfield over the rim. "Personal concerns? What do you mean?"

"I knew you were unhappy about having to go through a contracted marriage. But even now, though you are free from those marriage vows, you seem to strain against some invisible bonds. Would you trust me enough to say what troubles you?" She glanced down at her white apron, and tugged at a long thread. "I think there's more troubling you than the divorce by Kong Litang. I recently heard that he sold you to 'The Blue Chambers.' Is that what worries you?"

Before she could form an answer, Elizabeth absentmindedly picked up the picture of Marshall. Kulien's hand began to tremble, and she dropped the cup which shattered on the brick floor. She gasped and jumped to her feet. "Oh, forgive me! I'm so sorry. I should never have come here!"

She ran from the room and down the hallway, leaving Elizabeth Whitfield standing at the door, calling Kulien to come back.

Days at the orphanage dissolved into weeks. Kulien had managed to calm herself, and without anywhere to go, she settled into the life at the orphanage. Autumn's Tiger would soon return to the west and Winter's Tortoise would bring cold winds and snow from the north. Elizabeth didn't press Kulien for more information, but treated her kindly, encouraging her as she helped the younger girls with their English lessons.

The girls were responsible to keep the rooms clean; and they scrubbed floors and walls every day, and then after completing their jobs, they started over again. They also washed the eating utensils, boiled the drinking water and laundered the clothes. Such duties were unfamiliar to Kulien, having grown up in a wealthy home with servants, but she was careful not to complain as she was grateful for a clean place to eat and sleep. Her loose tunic covered her growing abdomen, and no one seemed to notice or ask questions. All the people, both adults and children were kind and generous, and she felt a sense of love and acceptance that was foreign to her.

One night, after Reverend Mortensen had preached a sermon about Jesus, a man he said had died for the sins of the whole world, his eyes suddenly flashed and his tone changed. "You girls may remember that about three or four months ago, the Short Swords waged a battle here in South City and seized it from the government." He glanced over at Dr. Gordon who stood near the entrance to the hallway. "That secret society perpetuated that offense in the name of the Taipings, who call themselves, 'the Worshipers of Shang Ti.' I want you to know the truth. The god they worship is not the God of this Book, the true Shang Ti of ancient China. The true God loves you, and would not murder innocent women and children." He held the black book close to his chest and let his eyes wander over the unturned faces of each girl. "We love you, too, and have come to your land to help you and give you hope for your future."

Elizabeth turned in her seat to glance back at Kulien. Did Miss Whitfield know that Sunfu was a member of the Short Swords? Had her step-brother been part of that raid? Her mind skipped backward, and she lowered her eyes to her hands folded in her lap.

Three or four months ago? That was about the time Sunfu had brought Marshall Whitfield to the summerhouse. Had there been a battle raging in the streets of Shanghai that night? Was Marshall aiding the Short Swords or fighting against them when Sunfu wounded him?

Kulien's mind whirled with new thoughts and old memories. The past months had flown by as swiftly as birds soaring over her family compound. Yet so much had happened in that short time span.

After Reverend Mortensen concluded the evening chapel hour with prayer, the girls started for their rooms to retire for the night. Kulien had turned toward the door when she heard angry shouts and screams coming from the street.

"Quick, get the children into the back of the building!" Reverend Mortensen shouted as he lifted the heavy night curtain to peer outside. "There's trouble! I see 'Red Turbans' in the street. Hurry, douse the lanterns!" he shouted. "We can only pray they march by and leave us alone!"

Kulien reached for Precious and held her in her arms. She had turned to run out of the room when there was a pounding on the door. Loud voices shouted, *Ta kuan! Ta kuan!* Smash the officials!" There was a clank of swords, a piercing scream, and more banging against the heavy red door. "Let us in foreign devils! We have something for you!"

Kulien darted around the corner, but stopped to see what Reverend Mortensen would do.

He stood close to the door and called out, "We are friends in here. We have come only to help your people. Our interest is not in the government."

"Down with the Manchus! Bring back the Ming Dynasty!" Many voices blended together as one, shouting out in frenzied tones.

The minister turned to see Kulien standing in the doorway to the hall. He motioned her to run to safety, but she didn't move. There was a voice she heard above all the others. A familiar voice crying out, "Whitfield! Whitfield! Open the door!"

Kulien set Precious down and ran to Reverend Mortensen's side. She tugged at his sleeve. "Oh, sir, please open the door! I recognize that voice! It's Sunfu—my brother!"

TWENTY-FIVE

Kulien cupped her hands around her mouth and shouted through the thick door, "Sunfu? Is that Kuang Sunfu?"

"Yes—yes! Who's speaking? Help me, please."

The voice on the other side of the door grew weaker with each word.

"Sunfu—it's Kulien—your sister."

"Help—please—help."

The clanging and shouting had stopped. The only voice remaining was Sunfu's. Why? Where had the others gone?

Reverend Mortensen lifted his thick white eyebrows. "Kulien, do you believe the man out there *is* your brother?"

"Oh, yes, I'd know his voice anywhere. Please let him in. He must be in great trouble."

The tall man lifted a heavy wooden beam from its fastenings and slowly pulled open the door. Sunfu lay unmoving in the doorway. His red turban was twisted around his neck and, in his back the hilt of a short sword was all that was visible among the folds of his cloak. Blood soaked the dark blue cloth and pooled around Sunfu's still form.
Kulien gasped and dropped to her knees.

"Sunfu! Oh, what have they done to you?"

Reverend Mortensen nudged her aside, and before kneeling over Sunfu, he called to Dr. Gordon who stood in the hall, ushering the children out, "Dr. Gordon! Come here, quickly!"

They lifted the unconscious young man and carried him to the small operating room where there was a long table and cabinets filled with surgical instruments and bottles of all sizes and shapes. Kulien walked along beside them, holding Sunfu's limp hand. "Oh, please," she pleaded, looking up into Dr. Gordon's concerned face, "please save his life."

Reverend Mortensen held Kulien back after Sunfu had been laid on the operating table. "You must stay in the hall, my child. You can pray for your brother. Dr. Gordon and his wife will do all they can, but as you can see, his wound is very severe."

Elizabeth Whitfield waited with Kulien until surgery was over and the men carried Sunfu to a room that held only four narrow beds. The room was whitewashed and smelled of antiseptic. They placed him on one of the beds and covered him with a clean white sheet.

"We've done all we can," said Dr. Gordon. "The rest is up to God."

Kulien's eyes were on Sunfu's still form. "May I stay with him? I want to talk to him when he wakes up."

The men exchanged glances, before nodding in unison. "Of course. You should be with your brother," Reverend Mortensen said.

"Yes," added Dr. Gordon, "it will give him comfort to see you, and your presence could be what he needs to fight for his life. I must warn you, though; I can't give you much hope. His injury is very serious, and he continues to bleed on the inside."

Through the long night, Kulien sat at Sunfu's side, bathing his burning forehead with cold cloths. Dr. Gordon had extracted the sword from Sunfu's back, poured medicine in the wound, and had stitched the gaping hole. Through the entire procedure, Sunfu had remained unconscious, and was now beginning to stir and moan in pain.

Kulien had heard the doctor's words, but she continued to bend over the prostrate form, speaking words of comfort. "You must live, Sunfu. You are the elder son and have a responsibility to the Kuang clan. Our father needs you now more than ever. To him, I am already dead, and Ohchin will only bring pain and suffering to our family."

The pale sunlight moved slowly across a gray and threatening sky. It was the Hour of the Monkey, about four o'clock in the afternoon, when Sunfu finally opened his eyes. They shone with fever, but he focused on Kulien. He tried to speak, but his mouth was dry, and Kulien soaked a cloth in a bowl of water and moistened his lips and tongue.

"I...I realized the Short Swords didn't really fight for peace. They weren't true Taipings. I tried to break away from them, but...."

Kulien continued to dab at his mouth and forehead with the damp cloth. "Don't try to speak. I know that you meant well."

Sunfu reached for her hand and though he was weak, his grip was strong. "I shamed my father, but my motives were pure." His voice rattled in his throat.

"I fought for my country, for Hung Hsiu Chuan, but the Triads were cruel." He stopped talking and coughed violently. "I couldn't bear the torture they inflicted upon women and children." His words trailed off, and his eyes closed.

"You did what you thought was right." She leaned close to his face. "Will you tell me what happened to Lord Whitfield? Where did you take him?" Tears filled her eyes and ran down her cheeks. "He is my husband! I know that our actions shamed you, but we, too, did what we thought was right." Kulien whispered in Sunfu's ear so that no one else could hear, "I am with happiness. I carry his seed, and will give birth to his child."

Sunfu forced his eyes open, and his words came with great effort. "So that's why Kong Litang…"

"Please, tell me where you took Lord Whitfield. Where is he? I must find him."

Sunfu coughed again, this time harder than before. A spray of blood spattered Kulien's blouse, and she stared helplessly as her brother struggled for breath, gasping, gurgling. His eyes bulged in terror as he tried to speak, but when he opened his mouth, it filled with blood and streamed down the side of his face, soaking the bedclothes.

Unknown to Kulien, Dr. Gordon had been standing nearby. He stepped to the side of the bed and gently closed Sunfu's eyelids. He leaned over the young man and rested an ear on his chest. Several moments passed before he lifted his head. "I'm sorry, Kulien. Your brother is gone."

Kulien stared at Sunfu's face, unable to speak. *Sunfu, where did you go? Have you left to travel beyond the Yellow Springs? Why did you leave without answering my question?* She raised herself slowly from the edge of the bed and closed her eyes. Sunfu—her once playful step-brother, who was more of a true brother than any she could imagine. Sunfu—the only friend and ally she had in her family compound. Of course, her father had once loved her; and Jiang had cared for her as well as any mother would have. Now, both were dead—dead. What did that mean? And where did their spirits go?

She fought back the impulse to cry out, to screech her objection, and her rage to the Heavens. But she remained silent, unmoving. She must show the foreigners that a woman of mixed race could be serene and strong in the face of death.

When Kulien opened her eyes, Dr. Gordon had covered Sunfu's face with a cloth. Only the black strands of his blunt-cut hair showed around the edges. Even in death, Sunfu had refused to bow to Manchu rule by wearing the queue. She sighed. She and Sunfu were alike in many ways. Perhaps she would come to a similar end.

Reverend Mortensen and Elizabeth Whitfield stood on either side of her, offering condolences and encouragement. "Come, Kulien," said Miss Whitfield. "You're tired and need to rest. We'll take care of everything. Sunfu will get a decent burial."

"No!" Her voice was louder than she meant it to be. Her mind returned to the funeral of an old uncle. She had been a young child at the time and was not allowed to participate, but as was her practice, she sneaked about the compound, hiding first behind a screen and then under a table. The ancestral hall had been hung with white lanterns and ashes of paper money were scattered over the floor. Old Uncle's body had been washed and a piece of silver placed under his tongue so he would have money to spend in the after-world. Hired mourners along with white-robed priests chanted prayers for the soul's safe deliverance beyond the Yellow Springs.

The minister's soothing voice interrupted her thoughts. "Then what is it you want us to do? Although he was not of the Christian faith, we will give him a Christian burial if you wish."

Kulien lifted her face to the tall man with the thick white hair. "No, that is very kind of you to offer, but there is nothing for you to do. It is the family's duty to prepare the body. Sunfu is the first-born of twin sons, and the ceremony will be long and elaborate." She paused to think what must be done. "However," she added, "if I may be permitted, I should like to honor my father in this one last deed."

Now, not only were Elizabeth Whitfield, Dr. Gordon and Reverend Mortensen in the room, Julia Mortensen and Hope Gordon stood in the doorway. All eyes were upon her, waiting to hear what she would say.

"My brother wears the shoulder-length hair of a rebel, and he died grieving that he had shamed his father. I would desire that Sunfu's crown be shaved in the manner of his filial duty, and that his hair be braided. When my father looks on his son, who defied the customs by cutting off his queue, he will find comfort. It will also be my way of showing *hsiao* to my honorable father." Kulien paused, thinking about what to say next. "If you will permit me, I would like to travel with you to my father's house." Although she didn't utter the words, she thought, *I might see my father this one last time when he comes outside the gate to receive Sunfu's body.*

Seven o'clock, the Hour of the Dog, had arrived by the time Sunfu's body was ready to be transported to the Kuang compound on the outskirts of the city of Shanghai. A cold wind blew from the north, pelting sheets of bone-chilling rain on the cortege of closed sedans as they wound their way through the dark, muddy lanes of the countryside. Dr. Gordon and Reverend Mortensen's sedans flanked the one carrying the pine box where Sunfu lay, dressed in the finest clothing Reverend Mortensen could obtain. Following them were sedans bearing Mrs. Mortensen, Mrs. Gordon and Elizabeth Whitfield. In the last sedan, Kulien sat alone in her grief. Only the men would be allowed to alight from the chairs at the compound gate to relate the news of Kuang Sunfu's death. Because the women had to remain in the sedans, Kulien would have to view her father from a distance. But the thought of seeing him, even from afar, strengthened her heart. Just to catch a glance of him tonight, though it was a time of sorrow, would be a cherished memory.

She sat stiffly in the jostling, lurching chair with arms folded across her waist. Even through the padded jacket and trousers, she felt the chill and shivered. How would her father receive the information? Would he show his grief to foreigners who brought the sad news? If only she could leave the sedan chair and run to her father and comfort him. But she could not.

For Kuang Lufong to see his disobedient, discarded daughter at the same moment he saw his murdered step-son, would be most unkind. She would have to be content to view him through the curtains—this one last time.

But it was not to be. She watched, and listened through a partially opened door as the guard at the main gate heard Dr. Gordon's words. The guard nodded in understanding before he disappeared behind the high walls, leaving Dr. Gordon and Reverend Mortensen standing in the rain. After a long wait, the guard reappeared and announced that servants would bring Sunfu's casket into the compound. He said that none of the barbarians would be allowed to accompany the body. "Kuang Lufong thanks you for bringing his son to him, but he is unable to greet or thank you personally."

Both Dr. Gordon and Reverend Mortensen offered words of condolence. Before returning to their sedans, they glanced in Kulien's direction, aware that she had wanted to glimpse her father.

As the sedan-bearers headed back toward the city, Kulien's body shook with sobs. If only she could have seen her father—just to know that he was well. Had he remained inside the compound because of grief, or was he ill? Oh, how she missed him. After passing the boundary of the Kuang compound, Kulien wiped away her tears, and settled into an unknown future. Where would she go from here? When would she be reunited with Lord Marshall Whitfield? As these questions tugged at her mind, she felt a slight movement under her folded arms. Like the wings of a butterfly, ripples of the life growing inside, lifted her spirits. She did have a future, after all. She had a husband waiting for her somewhere, and his child grew steadily day by day.

Death—life. Somehow there was a pattern. She would persevere day by day; and she would find a way to once again belong to a family—a new family—her own family.

TWENTY-SIX

Another week passed with Kulien scarcely speaking for the grief she carried in her heart at Sunfu's violent death. Although she knew that her step-brother had been angry and shocked when he discovered her in Marshall Whitfield's arms, she had hoped that one day he would forgive and understand. But now he was forever gone.

Tears stung Kulien's eyes as her mind turned to the disappointment she felt at not being able to see her father when Sunfu's body was taken to the compound. His last words to her before she left for Hangchow had been kind; but she knew she had hurt and disgraced him.

She rested a hand on her abdomen when she felt a slight flutter coming from deep within. She still had her baby! There was hope for the future.

After she had washed her face and helped the girls with chores, she started toward the sleeping quarters, hoping to lie down and rest for awhile before the afternoon classes began. Elizabeth Whitfield called from the kitchen, "Kulien, I know that you're tired this morning, but could you spare me a few minutes before you go to the English class?"

Kulien turned and smiled at the teacher. "Of course. I'm not so tired today. The girls did most of the work while I did the supervising!"

Miss Whitfield didn't return her smile, but beckoned Kulien toward her own room. As Kulien walked beside her, Elizabeth whispered, "It's imperative that we talk."

Imperative? Kulien turned the unfamiliar word over in her mind.

Elizabeth seemed to understand Kulien's questioning expression, and added with clipped words, "I have something important that we need to discuss today."

When Kulien entered the teacher's bedroom, she noticed that Marshall's picture was not on the table. She sat in the same chair as she had before and watched Miss Whitfield reach into the deep pocket of her apron. She drew out the silver frame and stared at it for a moment before fastening her eyes on Kulien.

"I don't know exactly where to begin," she said, a frown creasing her forehead, "but I received a letter from my brother that you must hear." She held out the picture, and Kulien took it with trembling hands.

"Before I read what he has written, I want to say that I've watched you closely the weeks you have lived here. You've performed your duties well, and the children love you." She sat in the chair across from Kulien, and folded her hands under her chin and closed her eyes as if in prayer.

Kulien waited, wondering what Miss Whitfield was about to say. What could Marshall have written to her that would cause her to behave in such a serious manner?

Elizabeth opened her eyes, the frown even more pronounced. "I know you have suffered many losses in the past months—your family home, your *amah*, and now your favorite brother. You showed great strength when your brother died. It was obvious that you loved him. I'm not sure I could be so strong if Marshall died in such a way."

Kulien felt her cheeks warm at the sound of Marshall's name and wondered if Miss Whitfield noticed.

She turned from Kulien to the small desk nearby and opened a drawer. She took out a folded parchment with a broken wax seal. "I want to be your friend, Kulien as you have no other family. I hope that you will feel free to confide in me after you hear what Marshall has written from Hong Kong."

Hong Kong. So that's where he is. Oh, at least he hasn't returned to Great Britain.

Elizabeth held the letter in both hands and began to read aloud: "Greetings from Hong Kong, Sister. I trust this correspondence finds you well and prospering there in Shanghai. You may have wondered where I am as I was not permitted to bid you farewell. The British Consulate wanted me as far away as possible from my post there before sending me back to England. I have much the same duties at this port as I did in Shanghai. Why, you might ask, was I sent away under such undisclosed circumstances?

"I hope that you are seated, because what I am about to reveal will no doubt shock and disappoint you."

Elizabeth glanced up from the letter. Kulien's face showed no expression; her hands were clasped so tightly in her lap, her knuckles looked like white stones. She inhaled deeply and lowered her eyes to her hands.

"Do you want me to go on?" Elizabeth's voice was as cold as a winter stream.

Kulien could not speak, but nodded her reply.

"About three or four months ago, I'm not sure because time seems so unreal to me these days, I was at the docks aiding some of the Chinese men who had begun an uprising. I know it was none of my business, but I've seen how we foreigners have come here and disrupted their lives. I was mistaken for an enemy when a young man, stabbed me in the shoulder. The pain was more than I had ever known and, to my shame, I lost consciousness. When I revived, I found myself in the Kuang compound summerhouse. The young man who had injured me was Sunfu, Kulien's brother and an heir to the Kuang fortune."

Elizabeth stopped to watch Kulien as she leaned closer, not wanting to miss a word.

"Kulien was brought to the summerhouse where Sunfu ordered her to care for my wound. I could not return to my post in that condition, so I depended on that beautiful young woman to care for me. She brought me medicine and food—at her own risk.

"There is no painless way to reveal this, so I will be as forthright and honest as possible. Kulien and I fell in love!"

Kulien gasped and covered her mouth with her fingertips. Oh, was he going to tell her all that happened between them?

"I know that I am much older than she is, but I could not deny my attraction for her. She clearly returned my devotion. She was also most distressed about being sent away to Hangchow to marry an old man who had been betrayed by her father. Now comes the part where you need to be sitting. Kulien and I performed our own marriage ceremony! It was not something that either of us entered into lightly. We said our vows, I to the God of Heaven, the Christian God…and she, to whatever gods she believes in. I'm sure you can imagine what happened next. However, early that morning, Sunfu showed up unexpectedly and was furious. He struck Kulien, and intended to kill me; but instead, he put me on his horse and brought me back to the Consulate. He said I was never to tell anyone what had happened. He believed I had raped Kulien, and that she was an innocent victim, although she told him she had not only consented, but had deliberately chosen to be my wife—with all that entails."

Elizabeth's face hardened as she laid aside the letter; but when she looked up at Kulien, there were tears in her eyes. "Kulien," she said finally, "I am *so ashamed* of my brother. He has defiled you; and now I understand why Kong Litang divorced you. Did your father know about this…this so-called *marriage?*"

Kulien lifted her chin. The truth was out, and she felt relieved. "Yes, my father knew, but was determined to hide the truth from Kong Litang. I confessed to Litang that I had been with a 'barbarian.' And I told him more…."

"More? What more could there be? Marshall ruined your life! I don't think I can ever face him again!"

Kulien reached for the letter with one hand, and rested her other over Elizabeth's. "Your brother didn't ruin my life. He gave me life! I'm *with happiness.*"

"You're what?"

"I am going to have Marshall's baby." A smile crinkled Kulien's eyes and her straight white teeth sparkled in the light of the candle. "Don't blame Marshall for what I wanted. If there is blame, it is mine. I loved your brother the first time I saw him. He is a kind and respectable man. It was never his intention to bring shame upon you or your family."

Kulien tugged at the silk cord, and withdrew the signet ring with the Whitfield crest. "Marshall gave me this ring as a symbol of our marriage; I gave him the jade ring that my father had given to my mother as a wedding present. He told me he would love and care for me either here in China or in your country." Kulien placed a hand on her abdomen, "And when he learns that he is going to be a father, he will find a way for us to be together!"

Elizabeth groaned and covered her face with her hands. When she looked up, she said, "Surely you realize that a few words and a ring are not enough to constitute a marriage." She took Kulien's hands in hers. "You are not *legally* wed. And Marshall knows that it is against the laws of both our countries for its citizens to intermarry!"

"Are the laws of men more powerful than the laws of the gods? Of your God?"

Elizabeth let go of Kulien's hands and folded hers into a tight ball and pressed them under her chin. She walked to her bed, and dropped to her knees. After several minutes, she rose. "There is nothing we can do at present. As soon as possible, Reverend Mortensen and I will go to the British Consulate to learn what has become of Marshall since his transfer to the British Colony. We can only hope that in the time it has taken his letter to reach us that he hasn't been sent back to England. If he's still in China, we will exert all the power we have. And we'll pray that God's perfect will be done!"

She paused before standing and raised Kulien to her feet. "What's done is done. We have now only to think about the future and how to accomplish a reunion. I don't know how our governments will react to the request for a legal marriage, but somehow, someway, we'll find a solution."

In the days that followed, it was as cold inside the mission as out. December had brought freezing rain and snow from the north; and Elizabeth Whitfield had distanced herself from Kulien as if she carried an infectious disease. Only when necessary did she stop to greet Kulien, and even at those rare times did she attempt to smile or acknowledge the secret they shared. Reverend Mortensen, on the other hand, seemed more cordial than usual, and Kulien's spirit lifted when he held her hand and spoke a kind word, the tiny wrinkles burrowing into the folds around his pale eyes.

Had Miss Whitfield been able to contact the British Consulate? Was she trying, as she had said, to find a way for her to be with Marshall? Kulien wished Elizabeth would tell her what she had learned, but not wanting to ask, she clenched her teeth and bowed humbly when they met in the hallways.

As days passed, the orphanage took on a festive air. Flowers made of red paper graced the doorways, and red and green streamers stretched across the front of the chapel. Then some unusual objects appeared in the corner of the large room. Pieces of straw had been laid out upon a table, and a group of clay figures sat in the center. Kulien was drawn with curiosity to the scene which included a woman kneeling beside a crib that held a baby. Reverend Mortensen explained the figures and their meaning night after night in the chapel service. He told the story of a baby, a King, who came to earth through humble circumstances. He said the child was the Son of God. He pointed out the figures of shepherds, sheep, camels and wise men that came to a stable to worship the King. Kulien listened attentively, strangely drawn to the virgin mother who gave birth far from her own home.

She tried to understand and reflect the happiness she saw in the foreigners' faces, but her heart was too troubled. Would Marshall return to Shanghai to claim her as his legal wife, or would she and her child be trapped forever behind the walls of the Westerners' orphanage?

One night after finally falling asleep, Kulien was awakened by a hand on her arm. "Please, come with me."

She rubbed her eyes, draped the quilt around her shoulders, and followed Elizabeth through the rows of sleeping children and into the kitchen. "Let's go to my room," Miss Whitfield whispered.

Kulien shivered in the pale moonlight streaming through the small kitchen window. "I—I will do as you say," she stammered, her eyes fastened on the tall woman. "What is it? Do you have news of Marshall?"

"Shh. We'll talk where we won't be heard."

The teacher's slim form glided through the darkness with Kulien close behind. When they reached Elizabeth's bedroom, she lit a candle, and Kulien could see, for the first time, her teacher's long blonde hair flowing over her shoulders and down her back. Elizabeth reached into the desk drawer and took out another folded sheet of paper. She held it to the light before handing it to Kulien.

"My dear sister," it began. Kulien's heart skipped when she realized it was the long-awaited letter from Marshall.

"I received the letter by special post three days ago," Elizabeth said, "but Reverend Mortensen and I needed to make arrangements before I could tell you about it. Kulien," she said, motioning for her to sit down, "*you* read the letter. Aloud, please."

TWENTY-SEVEN

Kulien's heart pounded so hard, her hand went instinctively to her chest. She sat near the orange flicker of the candle, her face warmed from the flame, and her body from the desire burning in her heart. She held the letter written by the man she loved, her hands trembling with emotion, and her eyes blurred with tears.

"My dear sister," she read slowly, "It is with relief and gratitude that your dispatch reached me here in Hong Kong. I have been most concerned about Kulien. I assure you that I am not proud of my actions. I have brought disgrace to Kulien and her family as well as to my post at the British Consulate. My superiors have ordered me back to Great Britain."

"Oh, no!" Kulien closed her eyes and lowered her hands, feeling all hope dissolve.

Elizabeth touched Kulien's hand. "Go on, dear. There's more."

Kulien lifted the letter from her lap and strained her eyes to read the beautifully scrolled words on the parchment paper. "When I received your letter, that arrived by no less than by the Queen's courier, I felt extreme gratitude to learn that Kulien is safe—and there with you. At once, I requested permission to return to Shanghai, but was denied.

"Forgive me for the shame you expressed because of my ungentlemanly behavior; but I must assure you that my affection for Kulien is genuine. I want to do what is right regarding her."

Kulien gasped and held the parchment to her breast before continuing. *He does love me,* she thought, *and he wants me to be with him.* She began to read again, "If someone will accompany her, she could sail to Hong Kong on the ship, *Houqua.* Although British officials have denied my request to return to Shanghai, they cannot stop Kulien from coming here."

Kulien glanced up at Elizabeth Whitfield, hoping to learn from her expression what her thoughts might be, but her eyes were lowered and she said nothing. So Kulien continued to read aloud. "The ship, an American Clipper, leaves Shanghai for Hong Kong on December 21. It docks at this British-owned port to take on contract laborers for the gold mines of California. You can book passage for two people with the enclosed notes.

"It is imperative that she sail on the *Houqua,* for that is the only ship arriving in this island port before I am scheduled to depart for Great Britain. I have made arrangements with a British cleric to perform a legal marriage ceremony. I ask for your prayers and perhaps a letter to our family informing them of this change of plans. I can only hope they will learn to regard and respect this young woman as I do. Unless I hear otherwise, I will be at the docks awaiting the arrival of the *Houqua* in the port of Hong Kong.

"Your humble brother, Marshall."

Kulien's spirits rose and her eyes sparkled with excitement when she handed the letter back to Elizabeth. "But," she glanced at the calendar hanging on the wall beside a chest of drawers, "December 21 is tomorrow. It will be impossible for me to leave so soon. Won't it?" Kulien steepled her fingers under her chin. "How can we be ready to leave so quickly?" A frown creased her brow and she leaned toward Elizabeth. "Marshall didn't mention the baby! Did you tell him that I am with happiness?"

Elizabeth folded the letter and slipped it into the pocket of her robe. Her lips formed a thin line and her words were strained. "No, Kulien. I didn't tell him. That information would have to come from *you.* I thought it was enough to let him know you were here. I didn't want to pressure him if he were not inclined to see you again. My brother has many duties as the son of a British noble. A marriage outside our family's choosing will be a great burden to him and others who are involved. I wanted him to tell me his desire, and if he truly loved you enough to face the family and their possible rejection of you both."

Kulien's heart froze at Elizabeth's pronouncement. She would not want to be the cause of pain or disrespect from Marshall's family. But—he had said he wanted her to be with him. She stood and faced Miss Whitfield, her head held high. "You have read his decision. He wants our marriage to be legalized. You must admit, then, that he has made his choice. How can we be ready to leave on the ship tomorrow?"

Elizabeth's expression softened and she rested a hand on Kulien's shoulder. "You're right, Kulien, though I fear there will be suffering ahead for both of you." She went on, "There is a problem, but," she said, searching Kulien's face, "I'm certain that with expedient planning, you can be on that ship when it departs in the morning. Please, sit down, and I'll tell you what we must do.

"Reverend Mortensen and I went to the British Consulate when I received Marshall's letter. I had hoped to travel with you and also see my brother before he leaves for Great Britain. However," she paused, searching for the right words, "I was denied passage on the *Houqua*. It seems that this sailing ship has been contracted by the Americans to take Chinese laborers across the Pacific Ocean to work in the gold fields of California. Westerners are not permitted to sail as passengers."

Kulien inhaled deeply before asking the dreaded question. "Are you saying that because I am a young woman of mixed heritage, they will not allow me to travel on that ship?"

"That's only part of the problem." Elizabeth folded her hands and closed her eyes as if in prayer. "Reverend Mortensen and I have been praying about this predicament, and we've talked to the other members of our staff. We think we have a solution—but only if you're willing."

"I'll do anything you say. I only want to be with Marshall!"

"You could possibly be in great danger, Kulien, and I fear what might happen to you if you board this ship with all those men! I can't—I won't take the responsibility!"

"You are free from any responsibility. As you know, I took that onto myself when I defied my father's rules. My life is nothing if I can't be with Marshall. He is your brother...and my husband." She spread her fingers over her waist. "And the heir of the noble House of Whitfield grows under my heart." A smile crinkled her eyes and the dimple in her right cheek appeared. "What is your solution?"

Tears suddenly welled up in the large blue eyes of the usually sedate Englishwoman, and she reached out her arms to gather Kulien to herself. Kulien wrapped her arms around her teacher's waist, and for several minutes they stood, drawing strength from each other. "Oh, my dear Kulien, I pray that the life you carry will not be a fulfillment of your name, Bitter Seed. I wish for you and your child that you will find acceptance and understanding from your people and from mine." She stepped back and placed her hand on Kulien's head as if pronouncing a benediction.

"May this life, which shares my very own blood, somehow bridge the gap between East and West. May the God of Heaven be with you and bless you with His love and grace."

Kulien stood quietly with her eyes closed. She felt a sense of peace and joy at Elizabeth's words, and a slim light of understanding began to penetrate her soul. She could not perceive this invisible God that Elizabeth and all the people in the mission seemed to revere, but she wasn't afraid of him as she had been. Her curiosity had been aroused in the many weeks she had spent in the mission. She would have to give it more thought at a later time. For now, her primary concern was to board that ship by whatever means Elizabeth and Reverend Mortensen had decided.

She lifted her eyes to Elizabeth's. "Tell me now, aunt of my unborn baby, what must I do to board the *Houqua?*"

Before sunrise touched the shores of the Middle Kingdom, Kulien was being prepared for the journey to Hong Kong. Her clothes of soft, clean cotton had been exchanged for the rough rags of a coolie. Where Miss Whitfield found such clothes was a mystery to Kulien, but she asked no questions; she simply surrendered herself to her teacher. Next to her body, she still wore the silk cord with the gold signet ring and the fine undergarments brought from Hangchow. Outwardly she had taken on the appearance of a low class boy—a laborer seeking fortune across the sea in the Land of the Golden Mountain.

Elizabeth explained the plan, "You will board the *Houqua* with a large group of men leaving Shanghai to sail south before crossing the ocean; however, the majority of Chinese contracted for the gold fields of America come from the southern delta plains. Floods and famine force those men to leave their families for years as they try to find sustenance to send home."

Kulien, having lived her youth in a sheltered environment, had only learned a few details from Sunfu about the deprivation suffered by her people. She inwardly sorrowed for the wives and children who had to be separated from their men for—who knew how many years?

"My child," Reverend Mortensen said, coming into the room after Miss Whitfield had dressed Kulien in the tattered trousers, shirt, and thick padded shoes, "you must be careful to keep to yourself. The fact that you are a young woman *cannot* be discovered!" He shook his head of white hair and his mouth turned down, revealing his anxiety. "I know I should not worry about you, but I cannot help it. If only…well," he added, "we will have to trust the Almighty to watch over you."

Kulien felt compassion for the old man. "I understand what to do," she said. "I'll separate myself from the other passengers as much as possible. After all, it will only be a few days, or perhaps a week at the most before the ship arrives in Hong Kong."

Elizabeth Whitfield sighed. "Those days may seem like months to you." She turned to the tall man with the pink face and snow white hair. "This is a most unchristian thought; but if she is found out, should she carry a weapon—perhaps a dagger—to protect herself?" The woman shuddered.

An unbidden image of Kong Litang with Jiang's knife slicing across the *amah*'s throat flashed through Kulien's memory. "No! I won't need a knife. Please, don't be anxious. I'll be safe."

Reverend Mortensen paced the kitchen floor, stopping now and then to straighten a stack of dishes or refold a dishtowel. He turned and bent his head to Kulien. The odor of stale tea on his breath came with his rush of words, "Are you certain this is what you want to do? I simply don't feel right about it!"

He turned to Miss Whitfield. "I've always known I was doing the right thing when I felt peace. This time, I feel only a deepening sense of trouble." He glanced back and forth between Elizabeth and Kulien. "Perhaps she should stay here where she's safe and the baby is old enough to travel. By then we could try to obtain the proper travel papers for you to accompany her to England."

"That's true, Kulien. Will you reconsider? There's only a vague hope, at best, that you can accompany Marshall back to England. We have no idea what kind of documents you would need to go with him!" Elizabeth clasped and unclasped her hands, then gently placed them on Kulien's shoulders. "Please reconsider. Stay here."

A mask of determination hid Kulien's fears. "I have decided to go. I'm going today. There is nothing either of you can say to change my mind. Please forgive me if I appear to be ungrateful. I thank you both for your concern, but I must leave. You may continue to prepare me for the journey."

"Oh, there's another thing we must do. You may have forgotten, Kulien, but for you to pass as a man, the crown of your head will have to be shaved." Elizabeth sighed as she glanced at the straight-edged razor that lay on the nearby table. "I don't know if I can cut off your beautiful hair!"

"Then I'll do it," Kulien said. She picked up the razor, and with clenched teeth and eyes squeezed tightly shut, she hacked her bangs off close to the scalp. Then she lifted the long strands of hair up from her crown, and with another pass, she cut off more of the jet-black tresses. "Now," she said, handing Elizabeth the razor, "it will be less painful for you to shave the top of my head. She smiled at her teacher's open mouth. "See, I'm practically a boy already!"

No words passed between the three as Elizabeth Whitfield carefully shaved Kulien's crown. When she had finished, she combed the long hair that flowed down her back and began to twist it into one braid that hung to her waist like a shiny black rope. Reverend Mortensen watched in silence as Elizabeth wrapped the queue around Kulien's head in the typical work-fashion. After she finished, she handed Kulien a looking glass.

"I don't believe that I am a girl! Will Marshall want to be married to such a one as I?" She held the mirror in her hand and studied her face. "My skin is too pale for a worker, isn't it?"

Miss Whitfield reached into a drawer for a jar of yellow loess, the dust that blows over the northern plains of China. "We have used this to stain the walls," she said. "It should do."

Kulien took the jar and began to rub the dust over her face, neck, arms and hands to darken them. When she had finished, she rubbed the rest on her clothes. She hunched her back and shuffled across the room with her head down. "Now I am only one of the hundreds of young men and boys on the way to make my fortune." She lifted her head and forced a smile. "Do you think I will pass as a boy now?"

In spite of her concern, Elizabeth laughed. "You certainly don't look like that high-class girl I taught in the Kuang compound."

Kulien caught her breath at Miss Whitfield's words, and the teacher added quickly, "I'm sorry, Kulien. I shouldn't have reminded you of the past."

"Oh, I will never forget my past, because it is what has formed my future. Thank you for remembering the girl I once was." Kulien clapped her hands as if to change the somber mood. "Now, what must I do to complete my outfit?"

"We have an old well-padded jacket to keep you warm. The boy who delivers vegetables from the countryside sold it to us," Elizabeth said, as she helped Kulien slide her arms into the long, thick sleeves.

"And you will need this—the most important item of all." Reverend Mortensen held out an official-looking document stamped with several red seals.

Kulien took it and began to read. "What is it?"

The kindly minister blinked his pale gray eyes and his face became even more pink than usual. "It's a contract that guarantees your passage on the *Houqua*." He pointed to a blank corner of the page. "All that is left is for you to sign it with your thumbprint. It promises you a job when you arrive in America, and..." deep creases marred his brow, "you will have a year to repay the agent, a Jack Burton, who arranged the transaction— for a young *boy*."

"I don't understand. I am going only as far as Hong Kong."

"Yes, that's true, Kulien. And we're embarrassed to admit that you hold a forged contract in your hands. The only way we could get you on that ship was to prepare false papers." Elizabeth lowered her eyelids.

"May God forgive us if we have sinned!" Reverend Mortensen exclaimed.

"Oh, my dear friends do not be concerned. You have given me the greatest gift—a passage to meet Lord Marshall Whitfield, the father of my child—the man I love." Kulien held the document to her lips before adding, "I will soon be with the only family I have left. I don't know how to thank you."

She dropped to her knees and kowtowed before Reverend Mortensen. "Oh, no, child. Please don't bow to me!" He took her hands and lifted her to her feet before touching the top of her head with his lips. "We consider you to be part of our family here at the mission."

She smiled up at him, and then reached for Elizabeth's hand. "And I thank you, most honorable teacher for all you have done for me! If it were not for you, I would not be able to speak the English language; nor would I have met your brother."

Elizabeth held Kulien's hand, but nodded without smiling.

"I will see you again—in England," Kulien said, stepping back. "I shall be there with Lord Marshall Whitfield as his wife. Together, with the rest of your family, we shall greet you when you return to your home."

Kulien stared at the document that guaranteed her passage to Hong Kong; then after Reverend Mortensen brushed her thumb with ink, she sealed her fate by making her mark on the top of the page.

TWENTY-EIGHT

After tearful "goodbyes," and prayers for safety, Reverend Mortensen and Elizabeth Whitfield watched Kulien leave the building through the back door and walk cautiously down the narrow alleyway leading to Nanking Road. Directions to the docks were engraved on her mind, and papers of false identification, with the promise to repay the borrowed passage, were hidden inside her clothing. She touched the hidden parcel and felt renewed strength knowing Marshall's signet ring also was hidden under the layers of her padded jacket.

Moments of fear caused her heart to race as she walked on, head bowed, shoulders bent. The sights and sounds of the streets at dawn were new to her because she had been secluded behind the mission's wall of safety for the past two months. Now as she walked along the road, her vision cleared and her senses reeled with awareness of growing activity. Men in long gowns, black boots, and freshly oiled queues hanging down their backs scurried past; some disappeared through painted doorways, others into narrow alleys. The markets' colorful banners bounced in the wind and sprang to life as the pale winter sun filtered through storm-laden clouds.

Kulien wore the conical straw hat of the Chinese laborer, thankful for the narrow chin strap that kept it from slipping. On her shoulder she carried a small bundle of food and a few items of clothing. Like many other men on the street, she shuffled through the crowd with her eyes lowered. However, her attention was drawn to the new things to see and hear. Sidewalk vendors bartered their wares with prospective customers. Oblivious to their words, she heard only the shrill staccato monosyllables of her native tongue with its constantly changing pitch. A rich old man sat in a *minjiao,* a private sedan such as used by the landed gentry or urban rich. The man drew aside the curtain and glanced in her direction, only to drop it back in place. Kulien's heart leapt within her breast as she recalled how similar the carved wooden sedan was to her father's.

As minutes passed Kulien felt herself caught up in the excitement of the street. She turned down a side road where men played mahjong and women fried fish in street kitchens. She stopped to watch barbers shave heads in their sidewalk shops. She heard the cries of peddlers who sold crickets in bamboo cages, the creak of wooden cart wheels bouncing along the rutted road, and the sizzle and crackling of pork, the "Great Meat," as it roasted on charcoal stoves. She inhaled aromas new to her senses: garlic and onions sitting in baskets at her feet; and unfamiliar fragrances of incense that drifted from a religious store where paper money was sold for honored ancestors who had gone beyond the Yellow Springs.

As the cloud-covered sun reached its zenith and began its downward journey, Kulien removed a piece of bread from her small bundle and began to gnaw on it, her stomach sending out grateful sounds. Still captured by the unfolding scenes on the busy Shanghai streets, she stopped to watch a cook prepare a duck for market. First he placed the fowl on top of a stove under a huge iron basin; then he added a small amount of red vegetable dye to sesame oil and carefully smeared it over the skin. By the time it was brought to the display window, the coating had hardened to a glossy reddish-brown, the texture of varnish. The turned-back neck formed a loop which the cook fastened to a bamboo rod. Kulien licked her lips wishing for just a taste. *To think I have eaten that meat without the slightest concern of how it was prepared!*

She walked on, and as she neared the Huangpu River, the inland access to oceangoing vessels, she saw boats of every size and shape bounding over the waves, gliding up to the docks, and sailing downriver toward the sea. Her heart skipped a beat when she spotted the word, *Houqua,* painted on the side of a monstrous ship that bore many high masts with giant sails yet unfurled. Flying high in the brisk wind were not only unfamiliar flags, but also the yellow dragon flag of China. The banner representing her own country seemed to wave her on, to calm her fears, and to encourage her to get aboard. After all, she was on her way to meet Marshall Whitfield—and to spend the rest of her life with him as his legal wife.

She edged her way closer to the crowd and mixed among the coolies waiting at the dock. "It's unfortunate our wives can't go with us," she heard one man say to another, "but no respectable woman would want to leave home."

"You're right about that! Our women would not be safe in such a wild country. I hear that in America there are men from all nations of the world! I couldn't protect my beautiful wife from their advances." He smiled, showing only a few blackened teeth. "We'll make a fortune in the gold mines. I have a friend who returned from 'Ka-la-fo-ne-a', and he said there are gold nuggets scattered over the hillsides!"

"That's what I heard. My wife tried to keep me from leaving the farm, but when I return as a rich man, she'll welcome me gladly!"

Kulien turned from the men to glance around at the people waiting to board the ship. There were no women; only hard-working men, farmers, burden-bearers, and beggars. Some carried one or two bundles on their shoulders. Others, like her, wore the wide-brimmed hats of split bamboo. She had never seen such a varied group of individuals—not even at "The Blue Chambers."

She imagined that some of them were lawbreakers, glad for the opportunity to leave their native soil. However, she supposed most were simply overworked men who hoped to make a fortune across the sea. She wrapped her arms about herself, feeling a strange kinship to those who were leaving family.

The great dividing line between us, she thought, *is that I'm going only as far as Hong Kong; I won't be leaving my family, but will be joining the man I love—the father of my child.*

Hope filled her spirit as a light snow began to fall. In spite of the cold, she was warmed by the sure knowledge that she was going to a new life—a life of freedom and joy.

"Get over there, boy!" A man dressed in merchant's clothing nudged Kulien out of her pleasant thoughts. "Get in line if you want to board this ship. We leave before the sun sets."

The labor agent, satisfied that she obeyed, continued to march back and forth beating a drum and waving a banner that proclaimed, "Be rich! Go to the Land of the Golden Mountain!"

Kulien shuffled to the end of the line to await her turn. Would the man who examined her papers question her? Would he realize she was a woman and turn her away; or would she be shoved along with the others onto the ship?

She held her breath until she reached the top of the gangplank, then turned to glance over her shoulder. She lifted her eyes to the distant hills where she and her family had lived in safety behind high walls: Kuang Lufong, her dear father, was the only one she truly cared for, and Sunfu had gone beyond the Yellow Springs. She would never see either of them again. Even the thought of leaving Ohchin and Mahwu sent an unwelcome pang of regret through her heart. She was leaving Shanghai—leaving forever.

She turned to see the city and its docks for the last time. Steamers, tugs, and junks painted with huge round eyes to watch for river demons, bobbed up and down on the choppy water. Sampans, protected only by a low-arched covering of bamboo mats, lined the shore and extended into the river. Families lived on the little boats as happily as she had in the Kuang compound. It seemed to matter little where one lived if there was love and harmony.

On deck officials checked papers and pointed the men toward a narrow door. When Kulien arrived at the table where an ugly foreigner sat, she reached into her jacket and pulled out the forged document. He glanced up at her. "Ah, you be the young boy sponsored by those religious folks. I be Jack Burton. You kin thank me fer yur passage!" Without another word, he stamped the paper with another red seal, and barked, "Go through that hatch and down the steps!" Then in one movement he stood and waved his arms; a dusting of snow on his sleeves drifted away in the rising wind. "This be the last of the dirty yella Chinee! Let's get underway!"

This was not what she had expected, but she followed the line of men down a ladder into the dimly-lit hold where swaying, pitching lanterns moved in rhythm with her churning stomach. She was pushed through the press of unwashed, stinking bodies until she found an empty shelf with a thin pad for a mattress. Like the other men, she laid down her bundle to claim a space before stretching out to rest. Would she be able to sleep with all the strange men and odors that surrounded her? She would try to keep her mind occupied with other matters so she wouldn't feel frightened by the course talk and actions of her companions. She pulled a thin woolen blanket up to her chin and strained her eyes through the dim light, trying to make out the ship's hold where she would spend the week's journey to the southern island of Hong Kong. She must remember the purpose of this trial—she would soon be with Marshall as his wife. They would sail to Great Britain where she would meet his family and live in their fine mansion. It would be the ideal place to raise their child.

She could make out shelves where hundreds of men would be stacked like logs along the walls. There were still empty beds, but she felt certain that after they took on more laborers in Hong Kong, every narrow shelf would be filled. She sighed with anticipation. *But this one will be free because I'm getting off!*

When the ship finally reached the open sea, it was obvious that a storm had arisen. The men were tossed back and forth, up and down, and Kulien had to hold onto the edge of the bunk to keep from being thrown onto the filthy floor. Some of the men began to retch and vomit, and it was all Kulien could do to keep from losing the small lunch she had eaten before boarding. She turned her face to the rough wall. It smelled old and musty, and she wondered if she could stand the stale, fetid air for the days it would take to reach her destination.

She had almost fallen asleep when the man on the shelf above hers asked another, "How long will we be in Hong Kong?"

"Only long enough to take on more passengers. I hear that most of the men come from the river region near Canton."'

"I hope we dock long enough so that I have time to visit an uncle who lives in Hong Kong," said another across the aisle from Kulien. "Even if I don't see him, I'd like to get some fresh air and take in a few sights."

"My family came from Canton, but I already know we won't be making a trip up the Pearl River." A man on the shelf above Kulien joined the conversation. "Too bad. I've heard that until one has seen Canton, he has not seen China!"

"Well, you can forget your dreams—both of you," said the first man. "No one can leave the ship at Hong Kong, or at any of the ports along the way. I've been to America once before, and we were allowed on deck for a few hours every day, but never long enough to leave. We're on our way to the Land of the Golden Mountain. Stop thinking about getting off!"

Kulien couldn't keep quiet a minute longer. She tried to lower her voice to sound more like a man. "But I might change my mind about going to America. I think I would like to stay in Hong Kong." Her heart seemed to stop as she heard the men laugh. Finally, one spoke up, "You can forget that, too, young man. There's nothing on that island but the stinking British. You have passage to America. There's no turning back now!"

TWENTY-NINE

Kulien refused to believe the words of these uncivilized, uneducated men. She must find a way to leave the ship. Marshall would be there waiting for her; he had promised, and she was determined to meet him whatever the cost. She turned her head to the planked wall, and drew out the long silk cord that held Marshall's ring—her wedding ring. As she gripped the gold circle, even though she was chilled through and through, the ring warmed in her hand. She lifted it to her lips, remembering the night of love and commitment. The summerhouse. Oh, it all seemed so long ago, yet the memories of their words and the full expression of love filled her heart and mind with ecstasy and hope. Marshall had held her as gently as he would a small child. His lips had covered her face and neck as he spoke words of endearment. They had come together in a union that both surprised and satisfied her longing. He had told her that she was the only woman he would ever love—and she believed him.

Sharp pricks of pain, from the hard surface of the bunk, stabbed at her hipbones, her shoulders, and her head; and she longed for the soft mattress and quilt of her childhood home. She had never taken thought of how privileged she had been: loved and nurtured by her father; coddled and preened by her *amah;* and instructed and encouraged by her teacher. In less than a year, she had been disgraced by Kong Litang, sold as a prostitute to "The Blue Chambers," and now consigned to a dark galley as a laborer for the gold fields of America. But she must not forget the good that had come to her as well: the love of a British noble; a child of that love growing inside; and the hope of a future with Marshall Whitfield in the land of her mother's birth.

Days of sailing through the storms along the eastern coast of China passed slowly, and nights were even longer. Once a day, the hatch above them was thrown open and the voice of Jack Burton, the labor-master shouted, "Out on the deck! Ya need food and fresh air. I don't wanna deliver a shipload a dead Chinee ta yur new owners!"

Thankful for the escape from the dark prison of the ship's hold, Kulien inhaled deeply of the cold, mist before separating herself from the rest of the men. It was at that time they not only received their day's ration of food, but they were each given a bucket in which to relieve themselves. Kulien had to scramble to find a private place behind a stack of cargo where she wouldn't be seen by the others. When she reappeared to return into the hold, some of the men drew circles around their heads and cried out, "Hey, crazy boy, how come you hide your private parts? You got the pox?"

Kulien had no idea how many days had passed before the word came, "We approach the port of Hong Kong." The men all began to shout and chatter among themselves, "At least we'll get a glimpse of land before beginning across the Peaceful Sea."

Kulien wanted more than a glimpse. She wanted off the ship. As usual, she followed impatiently at the end of the line, up the ladder and onto the deck. At last, she was here in the growing city of Hong Kong, also known as the "Fragrant Harbor." Kulien had read about the first opium war between the British and China; in 1842, the island was ceded to Britain by the Treaty of Nanking. Today many ships filled the harbor; some proudly flying the Union Jack of Great Britain; on others, flags of many nations, including China, blew in the strong winter breeze. There were armed clippers, and merchant ships, some no doubt bearing either a load of opium or possibly tea.

Kulien pushed and shoved her way to the railing as the ship glided to the dock and dropped anchor. Hundreds, perhaps thousands of men, women and children swarmed like a colony of ants alongside the approaching ship. "There she is!" they shouted from shore. "The *Houqua* has arrived!"

Lines of men wearing heavily padded clothing, with bundles on their backs, crowded near the edge of the pier waiting to board. Wives and children stood aside, some crying, others stoic, knowing they had no choice but to let their husbands sail away in search of gold.

Kulien's heart pounded and her eyes strained to see a tall blond Englishman. There seemed to be many English scattered throughout the throng, but they all looked the same to her. "Marshall!" she cried out above the raised voices surrounding her. "Marshall!"

Then she saw him! He worked his way through the teeming crowd, his hat in his hand, his eyes searching the lines of men on deck. His voice called out, "Kulien! Kulien! Where are you? If you can hear me, you must come down while you are able to get through the crowd!"

Kulien struggled to attract his attention by waving her arms overhead, but she knew he wouldn't recognize her in the padded clothes of a coolie—with a long queue hanging down her back and her crown shaved! No matter. She cried back, "Marshall. Lord Marshall Whitfield!" No longer caring about her disguise as a boy, she pulled off her skull cap and threw it in the air. Marshall turned his head toward her, his eyes wide with surprise. "Kulien, hurry!"

Kulien used all the strength she could muster to push her way through the mass of men and boys who were beginning to ascend the gangplank. She could see Marshall's blond hair as he stood tall in the crowd of black-haired men. He edged closer to the end of the gangplank, urging her on. When she finally broke through and stepped onto the dock, Marshall held out a gloved hand, his eyes bright with excitement.

"Kulien! My darling girl. You're here at last."

As his fingers wrapped around her small hand, she felt her heart would burst with joy. "Yes, I'm here! I'm free!"

He drew her close to his side and began to move away from the ship. "You're safe now! You don't ever need to be afraid again."

As she looked up into his clear blue eyes, she barely heard the clamor of shouting voices and the stomping of many feet on the gangplank. It no longer mattered what anyone else did, she had escaped the walls of confinement. She was now free to fulfill her destiny.

Suddenly, before Kulien could respond, she found herself surrounded by a crowd of Chinese men who forcefully pulled her away from Marshall Whitfield. "Help! What are you doing? Let me go! Marshall! Marshall!"

She heard his voice above the din, "Kulien, I cannot reach you!"

The men, some of those who had traveled with her from Shanghai, and others, who appeared to be workers from the

Houqua, closed around her forming a stronghold of humanity. They moved as one, drawing her back to the gangplank and up to the deck where Jack Burton stood, his arms crossed over his chest, and his feet spread apart.

"So that Engishman thought he could steal my property, did he?"

"No! You don't understand. I'm his..."

"Shut up, and get below with the others," he yelled. "No one gits off 'til we reach San Francisco! He shook the forged contract under Kulien's nose, "Yur not gittin' off that easy, boy! I dinna know who ya think ya be—but it's obvious yur no more than an underfed weakling. I'm gonna be surprised if ya last the months at sea." He gave her a shove. "Now get below!"

The man turned away before she could answer his accusations; but lacking the strength to scream or fight back, Kulien, along with many of the laborers, stumbled down the steps into the hold of the ship. Her chest heaved with fear and loss as tears filled her eyes and ran down her cheeks.

It was over—her life was over; her hopes dashed to pieces like priceless porcelain cast to the earth. She had met and joined Lord Marshall Whitfield as he waited for her to be his bride. They had actually touched, and looked into each other's eyes. Why hadn't he been able to save her? The men who came after her were strong and refused to listen to her cries. What would happen now? Surely Marshall would find a way to rescue her and make her his wife.

With a heavy heart, Kulien returned to her bunk, thankful that none of the new passengers had taken it from her. Crawling onto the narrow shelf, she pulled the light blanket over her head and let the tears flow. Her sobs came freely, but no one heard or cared. The noise and confusion of hundreds of men settling in was a constant roar throughout most of the day.

As the days passed into weeks, Kulien forced herself to eat for the sake of her baby. The tight binding Miss Whitfield had made to hide Kulien's breasts became tighter by the day. Her abdomen rounded as the baby grew and her only joy on the long journey was the occasional movement of the tiny child growing inside.

The American clipper, *Houqua*, named after the Canton hong merchant, a well known warehouse agent, raced against time and violet storms. Days passed with the cargo of humanity experiencing only a brief hour of daylight and fresh air, and that only once a day. Most days all deckhands worked feverishly, sometimes having to lash themselves to the masts to keep from being washed overboard by the cold winter winds and driving rain. Below deck many of the passengers died of fever and dysentery. Their bodies were wrapped in heavy burlap soaked in briny water and stored in a compartment at the rear of the ship. The bones of the deceased would be returned to China for burial in family graveyards.

As Kulien's body changed, the men laughed and pointed at her. "Stay away from that son of a turtle. He's got the worms. Look how he bloats!"

Glad that they believed she was infected with pox and worms, she was able to avoid mingling with them. She ate her bowl of rice in solitude; when weather permitted, she walked around the deck alone, but was always observed by Jack Burton, who showed more interest in her than the others. One day, after two months at sea, as she sat behind a barrel eating a chunk of dried-out bread, Jack Burton came up behind her and yanked at the queue hanging down her back. He lifted her up by her hair and glared at her with one blue eye. The other side of his face was marred with an ugly purple scar that ran from his ear to his eyebrow.

"What's this boy?" Before she could stop him, the man reached inside her jacket and grabbed at the tight bands around her chest. "Whatcha hidin' here, *boy*?" He ran his hands over her abdomen. "I think ya need some special doctorin' seein' ya might just be expectin' a youngun." He pressed his mouth against her ear, and she recoiled from his strong breath of stale cigars and whiskey. "Maybe I kin be that doctor."

Kulien pulled away, but he grabbed her face between his thick fingers and squeezed. "Smooth skin, eh, boy? Soft. Not like these here coolie boys—more like a woman, I say."

She pushed at him with both hands and backed away. "So sorry," she said, lowering her head. "No talk English."

She turned to run toward the hole that led into the depths of the ship. Before starting down the ladder, she heard him shout, "Well, boy, in case ya do understand a little—ya best be careful. Yur slant-eyed companions are gettin' restless for a woman. They might even be satisfied with a soft boy!" His laughter followed her all the way to the bottom of the steps. She ran between the rows of bunks and crawled into her small space. Curling up in the corner, she pulled the blanket over her head and waited for the worst to happen

"Not much longer now!" As the days passed an educated man, who had traveled to America on several other occasions, marked the hull near his shelf with numbers. He knew the approximate amount of time it would take to arrive in the Land of the Golden Mountain. His announcement brought a cheer from all who heard him. Kulien's emotions raced from gratitude in leaving the ship and the stale, stinking air of the crowded hold, to the apprehension of what her future in a strange land might be without friends or family.

The voyage turned out to be longer than anticipated because of storms and dense fog; and another week passed with Kulien trying to avoid any further advances from Jack Burton. Even though he hadn't approached her, she knew he watched and waited for an opportunity to trap her alone; so she began to join the outer circle of men when they gathered on deck to eat. She did notice, however, how some of the men ogled her and whispered among themselves. Was it true what Jack Burton had said—that the men attack her if they discovered she was a woman?

"So—here ya be!" One week before the clipper sailed into San Francisco Bay, the man stopped her from hiding behind a stack of barrels. "Ya kinna fool Jack Burton. I knowed lots a women—and I know ya understand English. I been watchin' ya." He pinched her side and pulled her closer when she struggled against him. He pressed his wet lips on hers before she could turn away.

"Don't! Please don't!" Kulien's heart raced with fear. What was he going to do to her?

"Don't cha worry that pretty head of yurs, *girly!* His hot breath, laced with alcohol, turned her stomach. "Ya kin thank me later fer savin' ya from them coolie-boys. I heard 'em talkin'. Stupid fools finally figured ya was a woman. They got plans fer ya soon as ya git down in the hold tonight!" The man chuckled and blinked his one good eye. "I kin see yur in a family way."

Kulien froze, unable to move. She stammered, "What—what are you—going to do?"

"Well, little lady, I been thinkin' bout that. Here's what I decided. I'm gonna keep ya in my cabin till we reach Frisco. I got a chest of clothes in there I picked up at one a them 'fragrant ladies' houses. Ya know what I mean. I figure ya can dress yurself up reel purdy fer when we anchor."

"I don't understand," Kulien said, unsure of what Jack Burton intended for her.

"Here's the way I see it. There's a real good-lookin' Chinee, Ahtoy, by name. She's a first-class lady of the night. She don't run one of them stinkin' cages fer slave girls." He nodded and showed his yellowed, crooked teeth. "She'll give me a mighty good price fer a little girl like you!" He poked at Kulien's stomach. "It'll be a fine arrangement for Ahtoy—she gets two bodies fer the price of one."

PART TWO

AMERICA 1854-1863

Most Chinese immigrants were men who came to America seeking a good life for their families still living in China. They first came during the California Gold Rush, arriving in San Francisco, known as Gum Saan—"Gold Mountain''—a place where they hoped to find freedom and prosperity. About 322,000 Chinese came to the United States between 1850 and 1882.

However, because the majority of immigrants were peasants and gained passage funds through the "Coolie Trade," they had to repay their passage by signing term contracts for service. This Credit Ticket system involved Chinese brokers who advanced passage money. Instead of a good life and freedom, these hopeful people found themselves enslaved: hard labor for the men and prostitution for the few women.

The Growing Season

"If seed in the earth can turn into such beautiful roses, what might not the heart of man become in its long journey to the stars?"
~~~~G.K. Chesterton~~~~

THIRTY

So near, yet so far. Kulien's hopes to be with Marshall Whitfield for the rest of her life had been dashed by Jack Burton's words, "…two bodies for the price of one." The odious man intended to sell her to yet another house of prostitution. Her heart seemed to stop, her ears roared, and her vision blurred as Jack Burton put a beefy arm around her shoulders and led her to a small compartment.

The cabin was narrow, with two bunks on one side and a trunk at the end of the room. A stained wash basin and cracked pitcher sat on the chest as well as a smoke-smudged lantern. Streams of light from a square window exposed the empty whisky bottles scattered over the floor—but, she thought, at least there was some light in the room. The cluttered cabin was a mansion compared to her former living quarters in the dark hold of the ship.

She managed a weak smile at the man who led her to the center of the room, then stood before her with arms folded over his bulging belly. "Thank you," she said, forcing the words from her lips. "Thank you for protecting me."

Burton walked over to the window, and with little effort raised it to let in the cold, damp sea air. Kulien inhaled deeply, relishing the fresh air, before he shut and latched the window.

"Don't cha be thinkin' about tryin' to git away. I'm not gonna hurt cha, and I ain't got no hankerin' to take ya for my woman. Just stay in here till we reach America. I want Ahtoy to pay well fer a healthy lookin' girl, even if ya are damaged goods!" He poked a pudgy finger at her abdomen again, and motioned to the wooden chest. "They's clothes in there. Git cleaned up, and I'll bring ya some supper."

The *Houqua*, with sails waving, lurched over the violent waves and through the Golden Gate entrance of the bay named for St. Francis of Assisi. Giant winds roared a welcome to the many foreign ships entering the new world. A blanket of misty fog obscured all sights except the crashing surf against the rocky headlands.

On the chill, windswept deck, Kulien stood beside Jack Burton shivering in the dismal gray light of dawn. At Burton's order, the hatch was flung open, and hundreds of men staggered out of the hold to gaze upon their first view of land in months. The gaunt figures crowded close together until every space of the deck was occupied. Some coughed uncontrollably from the unaccustomed fresh air, while others leaned over the rail, retching with never-ending seasickness.

"There, but for the mercy of Jack Burton, goes you, missy." The man put a possessive arm around Kulien's shoulders and drew her closer. "Yep, we lost almost a hundred of the 'monkey-boys,' but they gits fed better on this ship than most."

For several minutes, Kulien watched the men dressed in identical course blue clothing before she turned away with a sigh. What would become of these lonely men in a strange country? How would they communicate, and where would they live? Then the questions became more personal. *What will become of me? How will I fare in this foreign land as the property of a so-called, "high-class lady of the night"?*

Once again she forced the uncertain future from her mind by directing her attention to sea gulls that soared and screeched overhead. The memory of birds dipping and gliding over her father's garden replaced her sense of isolation with continuity. The New World. Was it really new? New to her of course, but the same world. Customs would be different, as well as the food, clothing and language. It was likely that even the trees and flowers would differ from those in her homeland, but it was the same sky—the same sun and moon, which rose each morning and evening on Kuang Lufong—and on Lord Marshall Whitfield.

Kulien inhaled deeply of the salty sea air, gaining new strength and fresh resolve. She had survived yet another hardship. She had yearned to experience life outside her compound walls, hadn't she? Her youthful daydreams had often taken her across the oceans. How many girls of her class and culture would ever journey to the outskirts of the known world? She had. She was in America! Elizabeth Whitfield had told her about the discovery of gold in California. Now she would see for herself. Firsthand.

Rough fingers grasped her chin and turned her head. "Like what cha see, missy? Fog's liftin' now. Kinda hazy-like today. Yep," he said, sweeping a hand to encompass the unfolding panorama. "It's good joss for a little Chinee girl to enter the bay with spring not so far away."

Kulien tilted her head to stare at her protector. The man expressed an artistic side to his nature that came as a surprise. She said nothing, but waited for him to continue.

"I come into the bay at all times a the year, but this here's the best time a all after the bitter winds and rains of winter. See! Look over there!"

Kulien watched the islands and hills of the shoreline come and go as the clipper continued to glide over the rolling waves to its final destination. She pointed at the many deserted ships rotting with disrepair. "Why have those ships been forsaken? They have broken masts and holes in their sides. Many are sinking."

"Gold fever, missy. Soon's those vessels reach San Francisco harbor, the crews take off fer the hills hopin' to make their fortunes!"

Kulien nodded, but her concern was not for the deserted ships or their crews; her eyes searched the shoreline to see where the *Houqua* might anchor. Would Marshall be there to meet her? He saw how Jack Burton and those other men surrounded her, pushing and shoving her up the gangplank and onto the ship bound for America. Was it possible that another ship had been ready for him to board? Oh, if only he had arrived in America before her. A sigh escaped her lips. Another fantasy. He would not be here. She would never see him again.

The baby, growing larger and more active each day, moved under her blouse, and she smiled to herself. Lord Marshall Whitfield may be at the other side of the earth, but he was also here with her. She had his child growing close to her heart. She would not be alone in the New World.

"Well, little lady, yur gonna create quite a spectacle when ya git off the ship even if ya are a green-eyed half-breed. Of the thousands of China boys arrivin' every month, there's only a handful of women. Yur gonna make lots a money. You can thank old Jack Burton for the good fortune that's a comin' yur way. I'm a smart one to sell yur papers to Ahtoy instead a one of them Chinese coolie agents!"

"Yes...yes, you speak the truth." Kulien's voice trembled. Although her future *was* bleak, Jack Burton had possibly saved her life, and certainly the life of her child. He had been kind to take her out of the ship's hold, and he had never violated her person. She could only hope the woman he spoke of would be compassionate. She clamped her teeth to keep them from chattering. She must not allow this unwashed foreigner to know that she was frightened.

"Scared, are ya?" Jack Burton's voice softened. "I ain't no monster. I coulda made you my woman, or coulda thrown ya overboard. But I didn't, did I?" He continued to watch as men on shore tugged on ropes and cables until at last the ship scraped and bumped alongside the wharf. "Nope, I'm doin' ya a favor sellin' ya to Ahtoy. She's not a bad sort. She a real fine China lady who receives plenty a gold nuggets so's the miners can 'look on her countenance,' so she says." He snorted. "I don't owe ya nothin', but I'm a fair man so's afore we git off, I'll tell ya a little 'bout yur new owner."

He paused to shout at some men tugging at the rigging, then went on, "Ahtoy's been in America, hmm, maybe four or five years. She's a beauty, and bein' the first Chinese joy lady, she got herself quite a followin'." He laughed. "Yep, I seen the miners line up outside her place fer half a mile. Well," he lowered his voice and shifted his wad of tobacco from one cheek to the other, "I hear she done and got herself a rich white man to manage her business. Name's John Clark. You'll see him, sure."

He stopped talking long enough to spit a stream of brown fluid into the bay. They watched together as the crew lowered the gangplank and a mass of pigtailed men poured off the ship.

For almost an hour, the desolate cargo of cadaverous men spilled onto the docks. Chinese coolie agents walked among them, glancing at each face, listening to the differing dialects. With a gesture, the agents separated the men into groups of ten, twenty or thirty to await a customs officer who would check each man's papers.

Jack Burton tugged at her sleeve. "Time to go, missy. Ya look real nice in that getup."

Kulien brushed a hand over her hair which had grown long enough to comb into bangs; she smiled to acknowledge the compliment.

The man motioned her to follow him down the gangplank. Her joints and muscles throbbed as every step sent blood rushing through her body. Bending slightly at the waist to conceal the growing bulge under a knee-length yellow tunic she wore over green satin trousers, Kulien lifted her eyes to the crowds of white people who lined the wharf laughing and pointing.

What did they find so amusing? What could possibly provoke the raucous laughter and crude remarks? All she saw were groups of men squatting near their small bundles. The rapidly spoken English words assailed her ears and her heart, "Look at them! Monkeys with tails hanging down their backs! Listen to them jabber. Ching, chong, Chinamen! Ha! Ha!"

Kulien lowered her eyes, feeling shame both for her countrymen and for the barbarians. Without warning, a mud clod struck her cheek with a stinging thud. A boy laughed, and a man scolded, "Stop that Edward." The man turned to his companion, "Not that she deserves any better—the whore!"

The other man spoke loud enough for Kulien to hear, "That's a prostitute all right. The yellow heathen leave their families in China, and bring their diseased whores here! I heard just yesterday that almost thirty thousand of these dirty yellow bastards have come to California to take away our jobs!"

"String 'em up, I say."

Several men joined the laughter, and Kulien shivered. What manner of people were these Americans? And why were they so cruel? She touched the throbbing lump on her cheek, and searched the crowd for Jack Burton. He had led her onto the wharf, commanded her stay in one place, and then he vanished into the milling throng. Why had he abandoned her? Although surrounded by human faces of every color and culture, Kulien had never felt so alone. Fear clutched her throat as she peered through the swirling mist.

San Francisco's Long Wharf stretched almost a mile, and was congested, not only with yellow men clasping their few belongings to their chests, but also with brown-faced women in brightly-colored shawls, carrying baskets of fruit and vegetables on their heads. There were shabby, bearded miners loaded down with supplies; and working near the ships were black-skinned stevedores shouting and lifting giant crates. The odors of rotting vegetables, mingled with the sweat of men's bodies, drifted across the wharf on fishy breezes.

In spite of her fear, Kulien's curiosity drew her attention to the lively scene unfolding before her. Crates of produce, sacks of flour and beans, and stacks of barrels lined the wharf. Horses *clip-clopped* over the wooden planking and wagons creaked and rumbled by, loaded down with provisions to stock merchants' shelves. Customs inspectors and coolie agents stepped around horse droppings to check the papers of men waiting patiently to begin their adventure in the Gold Mountains. After they were motioned to form single-file lines, the tired, wasted men spoke excitedly to each other of the gold that would soon line their pockets.

After what seemed hours, Kulien spied Jack Burton walking toward her with a tall Chinese woman at his side. Ahtoy wore an American style dress of red silk, decorated with frills and bows. A ruffled bonnet partially covered her onyx hair, and she carried an unopened red parasol in her hand. All eyes turned toward the elegant woman as she made her way down the wharf on bound feet. Kulien, too, stared in amazement. A Chinese woman in Western clothes! She had never seen such a sight, and covered her mouth to keep from laughing aloud. When she realized she was staring, she lowered her head and clasped her hands at her waist.

"Here she is," Jack Burton announced. "This here little girl is a bargain, for sure. Only two gold nuggets." He tipped Kulien's chin with a forefinger. "No scars or blemishes. Perfect features. Even speaks English."

The woman said nothing, but walked slowly around Kulien, occasionally prodding her with the tip of the parasol. Suddenly she screeched. "What this? You no say China-girl full up with man-seed!" She tilted her head to glare at the sailor. "You do it?"

Jack Burton laughed and rubbed a hand across his one eye. "Nope. Savin' myself for a white woman. I like them French mademoiselles! This one got herself poked by some China boy, I s'pose. Sides, yur getting' two fur the price a one! I sell ya her papers and after she drops the kid and has time to git her figure back, she can be one a yur girls. And when the brat is older, ya got either a boy to work around the place or another female to please the stinkin' Chinee!"

"China boys not come my place—only 'mericans! I 'Queen of Celestials.' White miners pay big money to look on my countenance!"

"So we gotta deal?" The seaman shifted with impatience.

"Give one, not two." Ahtoy opened a satin bag and held out a small gold nugget. "Spoiled merchandise!" She lifted Kulien's chin with a gloved hand. "Half-breed!"

"Ya think I'm crazy? This is a high class lady worth two gold nuggets."

"Big feet! No high class."

"No deal then. I fed her and kept her alive. I gotta git my money's worth." Jack Burton grabbed Kulien's arm and started to walk away. She held her breath. What now? Would he sell her to the slave market? She loosed her arm from Burton's grasp and, setting aside her dignity, kneeled before Ahtoy.

"Most honorable 'Queen of Celestials,'" she said in faltering Cantonese, "it is true that I have big feet and I am with happiness, but I can work hard. I learned from foreigners to clean house and cook." Kulien searched her mind for what words to say, and then bowed again touching her forehead to the wooden planks. "I have been with barbarians at "The Blue Chambers" in Shanghai. I can please your customers."

For several moments, Ahtoy stared at the young woman with delicate features and aristocratic bearing. In one smooth movement, she reached into her bag and held out an open palm. Two gold nuggets glistened in the sun's rays now slanting through thin mist.

Jack Burton skimmed the nuggets into his pocket with a quick swipe. With the other hand, he held out the papers he had taken from Kulien. "Can't read this monkey-scratchin', but this was on her!"

"Papers for coolie," Ahtoy said after studying the document.

"So what? Ya got papers. Ya own her. Do what cha want." Jack Burton's words tumbled out, one on top of the other. He glanced at Kulien. "Yur a good lookin' girl and kin do well if ya play yur cards right." He blinked his pale blue eye, and patted the top of her head. "Bye, missy."

Kulien wondered at her strange sense of loss as she watched Jack Burton disappear among the motley throng. Overcome by the rapid changes and the swirl of activity around her, she was startled when Ahtoy touched her arm and motioned for Kulien to follow her down the wharf to a narrow, muddy street. "We go to *Tong Yen Fau,* 'Port of the People of Tang'," Ahtoy explained. "'Mericans call Chinese Quarter, 'Little China.'"

Kulien kept her head lowered to shield the color of her eyes and to avoid the blatant stares and crude remarks of the barbarians. She noticed that some coolies had been loaded into wagons along with large pieces of lumber. Ahtoy turned to see Kulien's curious glance. "That for 'China houses.' Not muchee wood for Chinese. China merchants help people. Give lumber...build shelters." The woman waved an arm toward the little shacks that had grown into communities surrounding Bartlett Alley. "*Tong Yen Fau* many big. You see."

Ahtoy stopped at the edge of a large plaza where the newly arrived men had been herded. "This Portsmouth Square," she said. "You listen to Chinaman. He dirty skunk, but you listen."

Kulien was interested to hear what the squatty, moon-faced man had to say. He wore the regal robes of a mandarin with a fur cape draped over his shoulders, and a huge pair of horn-rimmed spectacles balanced on his button nose. He introduced himself to the large crowd of coolies, and although it was difficult for her to understand his rapidly spoken dialect, she listened in rapt attention.

"I am Norman Ahsing," he said, his voice loud enough to reach every person. "I have been in this county four years. I speak the language of the land, and I am on good terms with the lawmakers. I own many businesses. You will find me to be your friend and advocate as you make your fortunes here."

A man standing nearby spoke to his friend in Mandarin, "I understand the Cantonese dialect and have heard about Ahsing from a cousin who returned to China. This man has power in San Francisco, and will see that we are treated well."

After Norman Ahsing concluded his remarks, three Americans welcomed the "citizens of the Middle Kingdom," and assured them that they would be glad they had crossed the Peaceful Sea to the Land of the Golden Mountains.

Ahtoy nudged Kulien, "You hear plenty much," she said in her Pidgin English. "Come."

The two women broke away from the crowd to climb a steep, muddy hill. Kulien drew her breath in sharply, and looked up and down the narrow road. Chinese men. Chinese shops. Familiar sights, sounds and smells wrapped around her, enclosing her in a warm cocoon. Although in a strange land, she was still among her own people. Somehow with the help of this kindly woman and the various gods she had learned to petition, she would find safety, perhaps even happiness in the Land of the Golden Mountain. She didn't know what lay ahead, but she believed not only that Heaven had ordered her state of affairs, but also that the Invisible God was somehow watching over her. She would wait patiently for the next event to take place.

THIRTY ONE

After Kulien arrived at Ahtoy's house on Clay Street, her curiosity about her new owner grew by the day. She learned from one of the women that Ahtoy had arrived in San Francisco from Hong Kong in 1849. Her husband had traveled with her, but died before reaching America. Ahtoy claimed to have been the mistress of the ship's captain, who rewarded her with gold. Tall and beautiful, Ahtoy attracted the men in her new home, and because they showed such an unusual interest in her, she began charging them for a closer look, and eventually opened a brothel.

She treated her call-girls with kindness—and assured customers that they were free of disease. Kulien was also the recipient of Ahtoy's beneficence, but only because she had paid two gold nuggets for her papers. Kulien and her child were property that could be used in the brothels she planned to open throughout the camps of gold seekers.

A month had passed since Kulien's arrival in the "Market of the Three Barbarian Tribes," as San Francisco was called by the Chinese. It was spring, and Kulien had reached the seventeenth anniversary of her birth. Every grassy hill in the rapidly growing city on the bay displayed a palette of spring blossoms: clusters of golden poppies, various shades sweet peas and blue lupine splashed color over an otherwise bleak environment.

Kulien, dressed as a common laborer in order to walk safely to the markets, watched with wonder as carts rumbled by carrying provisions for gold seekers who showed up daily from every part of the world to strike it rich. Men on horseback shouted gleefully as they took their gold dust to the banks rising up on busy streets. Gambling, rioting and disregard for the law became the norm with the arrival of ruffians and cut-throats from around the world.

The little city was a wild whirlpool of bellowing, rowdy men with only one thought in mind—gold. Fortunes were made in a week. Prices soared. And as men's dreams came true, more outcasts of humanity set their sails for California: convicts from England and Australia; exiles from India and the South Sea

Islands. There were also Mexicans from Sonora, Kanakas from the Sandwich Islands, Frenchmen, Italians, and Americans from the backwoods as well as the big cities.

Kulien knew of these people only through what she saw from a distance, and from what she heard as merchants conversed in the now familiar Cantonese dialect. Although she never left the safety of Little China, even in that congested place she had to keep her head down and her wits sharp if she wanted to survive.

As days and weeks stretched into another month, Kulien's body grew more cumbersome and awkward. Her back ached continually from scrubbing floors and washing clothes. Two other Chinese women lived in Ahtoy's house—women recruited from Norman Ahsing's bordello—and Kulien was expected to wash their clothes as well. But she never complained. What good would it do? At least she had a place to sleep. The food was good as well, prepared by an old cook who decided his fortune was in the city, not the hills.

One night, after an exceptionally wearisome day Kulien, groaning with fatigue, lowered her aching body onto the mat in the corner of the kitchen. The pain in her back persisted; cramps in her lower body grew stronger. She had worked too hard that day. There had been windows to wash in addition to her other household duties. The reaching and bending had deprived her of all strength. She sighed. *Tomorrow I'll ask Ahtoy to lighten my workload.*

Music from the upstairs rooms filtered down into the kitchen where Kulien attempted to recreate images that were becoming more obscure as the days passed. In her mind she saw her father's bright eyes shining with humor. She recalled their early morning exercise in the garden—his words of encouragement. And there was Jiang—murdered as she tried to protect her charge. The *amah* was assured a good journey beyond the Yellow Springs because she gave her life for another. Then she thought of Sunfu, her step-brother, who had died so violently. How she missed him. Ohchin would be next in line as patriarch of the Kuang clan. All she could recall of him were his outcries against her behavior. Perhaps Ohchin had been right after all. If she had not pursued the studies of English…if she had not met and loved Marshall Whitfield….and if she had not surrendered to her love for him, she would not be alone in a strange country. But she had chosen her destiny, and she would never regret the love shared with Marshall, nor their baby who would soon be born. She wiped away the tears that streamed down her cheeks, and with fresh resolve, dismissed the past.

After hours of tossing and turning, unable to find a comfortable position on the hard mat, Kulien finally drifted into a fitful sleep. Throughout the night, she awoke with low, wrenching cramps in her stomach. But she attributed the recurring pains to either her dinner of cabbage or a too heavy workload. When at last the sheen of dawn spread its rays across the darkened room, Kulien woke with a start. *Oh, by the mercy of the gods, what's happening to me?*

The cramps of deep, searing pains left her shivering with weakness. Each pain began in the small of her back, pressing, tightening, and twisting through her body until every fiber of her being cried for release. It was time for her baby to be born! There had been no instructions—no plan to call for help.

Kulien rolled to the side and rose to her hands, then to her knees. As she stood, an inward shift of movement sent a gush of warm liquid pouring down her legs. "Ahtoy!" she cried. "Gold Precious! Jade Precious! Help me!" Not a sound came from the second story rooms.

It was the custom for Ahtoy and the other women to sleep well past noon. The men who frequented the bordello had departed hours earlier; and the cook had returned to his small shack in one of the narrow alleys of the Chinese Quarter. Kulien's cries went unheard.

She caught her breath and bent over again, grimacing, waiting for the pain to recede. *I must wake Ahtoy. I need someone to help me. What am I to do?*

Another sharp pain ripped through Kulien's body and she dropped to her knees on the mat, and cried out, "If there is a God who hears, please help me!"

But the agony did not let up. Excruciating pain gripped her back, her midsection, her loins, with each pain lingering longer than the last. Still unable to attract attention with her cries, Kulien, drenched with perspiration and the waters of childbirth, struggled to her feet. She staggered from chair to table, from doorway to the stairs leading to the second floor. Grasping the handrail, she pulled herself up, step by step, stopping often to bend over in pain.

When she reached Ahtoy's room, she stopped to lean against the door. Dare she cross the threshold? She had been taught that it was a crime to enter another's room during the month preceding the birth of a child. Not only was the occupant's welfare in danger, but in her next life, Kulien would have to return to scrub the floor of the room she had entered.

Careful not to step over the threshold, Kulien fell against Ahtoy's door as another pain seized her. "Help! Please help me!" Perspiration began to run off her forehead into her eyes.

But Ahtoy, beautiful in her satin bedclothes, lay in an opium stupor. She lifted her eyelids slowly, and closed them against Kulien's pleas. The other rooms presented the same scene. The women slept heavily with the long pipes still at their sides.

Another white-hot pain gripped her and Kulien fell to her knees fighting against the screams rising in her throat.

Pain. Incredible pain. Steady now, it bore down with intense ceaselessness. The child would soon be here. The pressure forced the baby down, down. Kulien reeled to the staircase, clutching her swollen belly. *I have to find help. There must be someone.*

Through the suffering, a memory surfaced. An American woman near the border of the Chinese quarter had recently given birth. Men in the market place said the woman's husband was a doctor—one who had shown regard to the Chinese.

Kulien willed her feet to take her down the stairs, stopping repeatedly to sit on a step until the pain eased. But how could she reach the doctor? She opened the door and looked wildly up and down the busy street. *Help. Hurry!*

She stumbled out the door and onto the street. A man carrying vegetable baskets suspended on a long pole passed nearby. Kulien bumped against him, knocking some onions to the ground.

"What you do? Crazy boy! Get out of my way or the gods strike you dead!" The man stopped his tirade long enough to stare in amazement at Kulien's soaked trousers.

"Where does the white doctor live? I need help. My baby comes—now!"

The man shook his head, babbling in a dialect she didn't understand.

Kulien fell at his feet in the dusty road. Drenched now with perspiration, she placed hands over her bulging blouse and cried again, "Baby comes. I am a woman. I need help!"

A smile spread across the smooth face, and the man set down the pole and motioned for her to follow. She attempted to stand, but fell again. "It's too late!" she shrieked.

The next pain clutched and squeezed. The man's figure blurred into the background. Shanties, curious bystanders, carts—all faded into a swirl of brilliant color before darkness snuffed out the light.

THIRTY-TWO

A crowd of men gathered on the muddy road surrounding the dead-still woman. Instead of their usual high-pitched words, they spoke softly, if at all, while waiting for Dr. Benjamin O'Kelly, the foreign devil who worked his medicine among them. One old man removed his blue coat and draped it over Kulien; another carefully lifted her head and slipped a rolled-up blanket under it.

"He comes." The onlookers repeated the words over and over as a tall man with thick red hair ran toward them.

The doctor knelt beside the limp form, and with a thumb drew back an eyelid and peered into the unseeing eye. Kulien blinked, then saw the round hooded eyes and heard a soothing voice. "Don't be a fearing, lassie. I'm helping you."

Dr. O'Kelly scooped up the frail figure and spoke Cantonese to the men staring in amazement. "If a body is asking, I'm taking the lass to my home on Sacramento Street."

The man raced down the rocky path to a small house at the corner of Sacramento and Stockton Streets. "Quick, Lucy, *macushla*, my darling," he called as he pushed open the front door. "We're having trouble here!"

From the edges of consciousness, Kulien saw a thin, pale woman standing in the doorway holding a baby. "What is it, Ben? Has a China boy been injured?"

"No," he said, rushing past her into the house, "this girl's in labor. This could be the first Chinese born in America!" His voice rose with excitement. "I noticed that her eyes are green, which means she has either a Caucasian mother or father."

Although still weakened by her own recent delivery, Lucy O'Kelly quickly laid her tiny baby in a small crate lined with warm blankets. She ran to join her husband as he worked over the half-dead girl. They stripped back their bed, and covered it with newspapers before laying Kulien down. Lucy removed the soaked trousers and washed Kulien's legs and lower body while Benjamin pressed an ear on her chest.

"Her heartbeat is faint."

"Poor child," Lucy sighed. "She looks so young. Is she one of the prostitutes?"

The words and surroundings barely touched Kulien's awareness. She tried to speak, but the effort was too great—and she was cold, so very cold. Perhaps, at this very moment, she was standing on the banks of the Yellow Springs, the waves of the otherworld ready to pull her into its icy depths.

"She's having a hard time." The doctor shook his head. "She's in heavy labor, but the baby seems large. Too large for this small girl. I don't know if I can save her, or the baby."

"Oh, Ben, we must! Please try!"

Benjamin poured water into a basin on a corner table and scrubbed his hands with lye soap while Lucy tied a large apron around his waist. When he had finished washing, she also washed her hands and joined him beside the still form. "Tell me what to do, Ben! I'll be doing whatever you say!"

"Press down on her abdomen, Lucy. Firmly—steadily. She's not strong enough to do this herself, and I'm fearing the baby is in distress."

Kulien's eyelids fluttered open to see Lucy brush a golden strand of damp hair off her pale forehead. She felt cool fingers press down on her bare abdomen—hard. Then she let up. Again the woman pushed. And again. Kulien groaned with pain.

"Once more," the man ordered. "Push harder. I can see the head. With God's help we can do this!"

As Lucy applied more pressure with both hands, Kulien felt a ripping pain, and heard a low moan followed by a shriek. Was that her voice? Then another sound filled the room. A cry! A baby's cry!

Kulien used all the strength she could muster to open her eyes. A squirming wet body had been placed on her stomach. She lifted her head enough to see the baby covered with a white creamy substance. She let her eyes roam over the tiny form. A boy! She had a baby boy! Her head fell back on the pillow. The baby was alive—and so was she. Marshall's son was whole and crying lustily.

A woman's voice spoke close to Kulien's ear, "You have a healthy and quite lively boy. He is a very fine *baibin*."

Kulien's eyelids fluttered open again. "Thank you," she said in English before closing her eyes. She was warm now, and at peace. She was free from pain, and wanted to see her baby, but her body was exhausted. She drifted quietly into a deep sleep.

The next two days were a series of ripples on a quiet pond. Kulien slept more than she was awake. Both Benjamin and Lucy O'Kelly waited on her, bringing her food and drink. She luxuriated in the soft warmth of the feather bed, the caring hands that brought nourishment, and above all, she cherished the moments when her baby rested in her arms and hungrily rooted for nourishment at her breasts. On the third day, she felt the milk come in and the baby's satisfied sucking moved her heart with a love she had never known. Lucy watched with a slight smile, and helped Kulien to a sitting position where she leaned against soft pillows covered with cases decorated in fine embroidery stitches. She held her baby, delighting in his sweet fragrance and beautiful features. She stroked his fine black hair and stared in wonder at his eyes. They were more round than slanted, and she thought they had a bluish cast. Would his features be like his father's? That was her hope and prayer.

Kulien pulled her eyes away from his face and smiled up at the young couple who had cared for her so lovingly. "You have been most kind," she said, in precise English. "I am humbled by your generosity. I will do all in my power to repay you both for saving my life, and the life of my child."

Benjamin raked his fingers through thick red hair. "You surprise us, Colleen. You're very young. And you speak excellent English!"

Lucy leaned closer to Kulien and said, "We be sharing your gladness. Your baby is healthy—and so are you." She spoke slowly and enunciated each word. "As my husband says, we are surprised, and I might add, a little curious."

Kulien lowered her gaze once more to the baby—Marshall's baby. What should she name him? It must be a fine name; one to honor the Whitfield clan. She glanced up again.

"Forgive me," Lucy added, "if I caused you embarrassment." She frowned. "Although we admit we are curious, we do respect your privacy. You don't be needing to tell us anything. We are wanting to help."

"If you've run away from a bordello, we'll be doing what we can to protect you," the doctor said. "There's a Presbyterian mission nearby whose people regularly take in runaway girls."

Kulien inhaled deeply, drew the baby closer, then spoke softly, "I am not a prostitute, although my papers were purchased by Ahtoy. I came to America by mistake. I lived near Shanghai, and was to meet my husband in Hong Kong." She gathered strength to go on. "I was not permitted to leave the ship."

"Your husband? But I thought…."

"We thought," Benjamin continued Lucy's remarks, "that your child, who seems to bear European features, was perhaps the result of, well, how can I say it?" He stumbled around for the right words. "Well, you, too, appear to be Eurasian."

"I am not a joy girl. My husband is British, as was my mother. I, that is, we were married in China." She brushed the back of her fingers over the downy cheek resting against her breast. "Because Ahtoy owns me, she will force me to return to her house and fulfill my obligation to her."

"You mean you have to go back and become a prostitute? Lucy's fingers flew to her mouth.

Tears welled in Kulien's eyes and rolled down her cheeks. She wiped at them with the back of her hand. Her words were barely heard. "I must go. I have no choice!"

"No Ben—we simply can't allow it. We must protect her!" Lucy leaned forward to cover Kulien's hand with hers. "What is your name? And how old are you?"

"You called me by my name," she said to Benjamin. "I was surprised that you knew that I am called Kulien—Bitter Seed."

Benjamin and Lucy stared at each other a moment, then smiled. "I called you 'colleen,'" Ben said quickly. "That is Irish for 'girl.' It does sound like 'Kulien.' I am Dr. Benjamin O'Kelly, and this be Lucy, my wife. He draped an arm over the frail woman's shoulders. "We have a baby too—Kathleen. We call her Katie."

Kulien nodded and glanced over at the wooden crate where Katie lay barely whimpering. She set her baby on the blanket beside her and let her blouse fall back down to cover her breast. She pushed the quilt aside and tried to stand up. "I have taken too much of your time; and I've deprived you of your bed. I will take my son and return to Ahtoy."

"Oh, no, not yet, young lady." Dr. O'Kelly's voice was firm. "You had a difficult delivery and must regain your strength. Your wee one needs a strong mother with good milk."

Kulien allowed the doctor to lift her legs back onto the bed and tuck the blankets around her. Lucy carried the sleeping baby to another box she had lined with clean quilts. Kulien knew the doctor spoke the truth. She *was* weak, too weak to return to Ahtoy's house where she would get little, if any, care. She closed her eyes, thankful for each and every moment in the clean quiet home. The gods had favored her. They had not yet discovered that she had a baby boy, and she must be careful not to alert them or evil spirits would try to kill him. She would call him by a girl's name until the danger period had passed. Only in her own heart and mind would she know the name she had chosen for him.

Her thoughts returned to the first time she had heard Marshall speak of his father, George, Lord Whitfield. Yes, she would name their son George after his paternal grandfather. She smiled sleepily to herself. He would be a great man someday, a continuing bridge between East and West. Her son, Marshall's son, would bring together a people separated by much more than oceans.

As Kulien's daydreams swept her along, she was suddenly jolted back to reality by a harsh, steady knocking on the front door. Her eyes flew open when she heard a familiar voice.

"Want my slave! You give," the woman's voice shouted in Pidgin English.

"We have nothing that belongs to you." The doctor towered over the woman and his voice carried authority, but she repeated, "You give slave. See, I have papers."

Kulien raised herself to one elbow to peer through the opening of the bedroom into the small living area. Standing in a swirl of morning fog was the beautiful, well-dressed Ahtoy. She held out a document tightly clutched in one hand. "I own girl. Pay two gold nuggets! She my slave."

"Come in," Lucy said in her soft, gentle voice. "It is cold and damp outside and we have babies we must keep warm."

"Yes," the woman repeated in a harsh voice, "baby mine, too."

Lucy and Benjamin stared at each other with concern showing in their eyes. Finally, Benjamin spoke, "I be wanting to see that document."

"You see, but give back. Girl belong to Ahtoy."

As Kulien listened to the conversation, she struggled out of bed and wrapped a blanket around herself. She staggered across the sparsely furnished room to lean against the doorway. Ahtoy pointed in her direction, her voice grew louder. "There my slave! You give back!"

Lucy ran to stand beside Kulien and steadied her with an arm. She led her to a low couch and helped her ease onto it. Every bone and muscle in Kulien's body cried out in pain. The rigors of childbirth had left her battered and torn.

Benjamin O'Kelly bowed his large red head over the contract, reading softly in Cantonese. When he looked up, he said, "These papers belong to a boy. As you can see, this is a woman."

"That her mark!" Ahtoy jabbed at the paper with a long red fingernail. "She put left thumb print on paper when get on boat. She owe passage money. I pay. She mine. Baby, too!"

Benjamin O'Kelly knelt down beside Kulien, the contract still in his hand. "Is this yours? Did you steal these papers to come to America? Has this woman purchased you as she says?"

Kulien glanced from the man's concerned eyes to Ahtoy who now stood over her, hands on hips. "Yes," Kulien said. "What she says is true. I didn't steal the contract, though it was falsified by my friends in Shanghai. As I said before, my plan was to get off the ship in Hong Kong to be with my husband." Tears gathered in Kulien's eyes, and she quickly wiped them away. "I was not supposed to end up in San Francisco."

"Come, Bitter Seed. Come with me." Ahtoy spoke with tenderness now, her words slow and soft. She held out her hands. "I take care of you. When body well, you work for me."

"Ben!" Lucy clutched at her husband's arm. "We can't let her go. She's too weak; and the baby is too young! She's not a prostitute—I know it!"

The doctor patted his wife's hand while speaking to Ahtoy. "Let us make a bargain; leave the girl and her baby with us for two weeks. We will feed and care for her. Your people trust us. We have done many good works for our Chinese brothers. We are friends." He motioned toward Kulien. "Your slave, as you call her, needs medical aid. If you take her now, perhaps both she and her baby will die; then you will lose all you paid for. You come back in two weeks, and then you can take her. Agreed?"

The painted lips pouted for only an instant, then turned up in a smile. "White doctor help Chinese. Many talk of you. Girl stay two weeks. That all!"

With those words, Ahtoy reached for the papers, slipped them into a silk bag she carried over her arm, and walked toward the door. She opened it, stood a moment looking over her shoulder at Kulien, then, with a rustle of petticoats; she swept off the narrow planked porch and down the two wooden steps. Before the door slammed behind her, a blast of cold air blew off the bay, ruffling a small rag rug in the center of the room. Lucy put her arms around Kulien to ease the uncontrollable shivering that shook both of them.

Minutes passed after Ahtoy's departure, minutes of silence as if each were afraid that words would bring Ahtoy back. Finally, Benjamin walked to the couch to kneel beside Lucy and Kulien. "We have to think of something, Lucy." His voice was determined. "We can't let Colleen go into a bordello. We must find a way to help her..." He glanced toward the bedroom, "...and the wee laddie!"

THIRTY-THREE

The following days and nights were Kulien's happiest since leaving China. She wasn't plagued with fears or nightmares. She felt her strength returning; and she slept, ate, and slept again. Dr. Ben watched over both her and her baby as if they were his own family. Kulien spent every waking moment becoming acquainted with motherhood and the precious baby she called "Baby George." She was careful not to utter his English name aloud in case there were evil spirits in the room who would snatch away his life. For hours, she held the small bundle, studying the shape of his face, and delighting that his eyes were round and possibly blue like his father's.

Lucy O'Kelly also helped Kulien regain her strength—at the loss of her own. She spent hours washing the soiled diapers of both babies, and pinning them on a line to dry in the sunshine. She changed Kulien's bedding and helped her dress; she cooked the meals and, with Ben's help, cleaned up the dishes and pans. The heavy toil wore on the young American woman. Her skin took on a sallow tinge and dark circles ringed her droopy eyes. Her baby, Kathleen, cried day and night, always hungry, but never satisfied. One morning as Kulien and Lucy sat at the kitchen table sipping tea, Lucy voiced her concern. "My Katie is two weeks older than your baby, yet she doesn't seem to be growing. I worry about her." A tear escaped Lucy's eye, and she brushed it away with the back of her hand. I've never been around children, and if I didn't see how well Baby George is doing...."

"Shh," Kulien cautioned, putting a finger to her lips and glancing around the kitchen. "Please, when you talk about my baby, you must use a girl's name. When I speak about him, I call him Mary, a name I read in your Holy Book."

Lucy's lips turned up in a slight smile. Is that a Chinese custom—to call your child by another name?"

"No, it's not a custom, but it is a common practice." She looked over her shoulder again. "You see, it is the way we deceive the demons. Because a boy-child is most valuable, the demons will torment, even kill a baby boy! But a female, because she is considered inferior, is no threat. So it is also wise to dress boys in girl's clothing until the spirits give up and go away. That's why I've asked to use Katie's dresses and bonnets."

Lucy's smile broadened until she realized that Kulien was serious. But there are no such demons in America!"

"Oh, yes! *Kuei,* demons, have followed my people to this country. We must appease them."

"Well, I do understand your anxiety for your child because I am concerned for mine, too." Now Lucy's eyes filled with tears that she didn't bother to wipe away. "I don't know why, but Ben doesn't take my worries seriously."

"But your husband is a doctor, a good one. Surely he knows that Katie is doing fine."

Lucy pushed a strand of hair back from her forehead and wiped her hands on the starched, white apron she always wore. "He says I'm too anxious, yet," she looked toward the door to see if Ben had come into the house, "yet I *have* seen the concerned expression on his face. When he thinks I'm not looking, he gives Katie a tonic; and then he tells me to keep my faith in God."

"The gods determine our fate," Kulien said. "To fight against the decree of Heaven is useless." Her voice echoed lessons she had learned at her father's feet.

Although Lucy and Kulien held different beliefs, Lucy sat back, folded her hands in her lap and nodded. "Perhaps you're right in some ways. I do fight against my circumstances. I don't have the peace that God has promised in the Bible. I haven't trusted Him to order the direction of my life. I've been a Christian for many years, Kulien, but, I confess that sometimes I have my doubts."

Kulien had no answer for Lucy, but nodded her head and remembered how Elizabeth Whitfield and Reverend Mortensen had spoken about the Invisible God who was always faithful even when His people doubted.

Four days before Ahtoy's expected arrival Lucy and Kulien sat at the kitchen table, this time shelling peas. Both babies slept nearby, and as the green pearls slipped out of pods into a wooden bowl, Lucy stopped working and held out her hands. "Just look at my fingers! I'm only twenty-six years old, and they're already calloused and inflexible. Can they ever again dance over the strings of a violin?"

Kulien bit into a plump pea, savoring the tender sweetness on her tongue as she glanced up to see Lucy's outstretched fingers. She nodded, and waited for the woman to continue.

"I trained as a concert violinist, but here I am in the middle of nowhere without my beautiful instrument." Lucy stopped talking to dab at her eyes with an edge of the apron.

At that moment, Baby George began to whimper from his bed at the corner of the room. Kulien opened her blouse and tenderly lifted him to her breast. He rooted and fussed until his lips found the source of nourishment. As he sucked, Kulien sighed with pleasure, delighting in his warm softness, the sounds of his swallowing and her own femininity rising and falling from deep within. She pulled her eyes away from the baby long enough to respond to Lucy's grief. "Where is your violin? Why didn't you bring it on your trip west?

"Oh, I did! I would never have been without it. Music was my life." Lucy closed her eyes, but continued to speak. "When our covered wagon hurtled down the face of that mountain into a deep ravine, I. . .."

At the remembrance of the horrifying experience, Lucy's eyes flew open. "My violin was dashed to pieces along with many of our hopes and dreams. I thought, well, I was afraid Ben had given up, too."

"Do you feel that you can speak of your pain to me? I care for both you and Doctor Ben, and would like to know more about your past." Kulien spoke quickly, encouraging Lucy to voice her bitterness. Perhaps if she would let the hurt come out through her mouth, the weakness plaguing her body would be replaced with new strength.

"I don't know if I *can* tell you about it. I am trying to put that journey with all the death and disease behind me, but perhaps it *will* relieve me of some of my fears if I talk it over with you." Lucy sighed, gathering courage before she went on. "It had been a tortuous trip across the country with a long train of wagons. More families joined us as we passed through towns and villages. When we finally reached the High Sierra, we knew we were nearing the end of our ordeal. But the mountain facing us was so sheer, so steep, that we had to get out of the wagons and hoist them up the rocky incline with ropes and pulleys." She closed her eyes again before adding, "I should start at the beginning."

"Yes, please do." Kulien shifted the sleeping baby to her other breast and tickled his cheek until he continued his sucking.

With eyes focused on the window behind Kulien, Lucy went on with her monologue. "I'll tell you how we happened to come to San Francisco, then perhaps you will tell me a little of your past, and how you came to be here."

"Perhaps," Kulien said, as she touched the baby's silky black hair.

Lucy set aside her bowl of shelled peas, and then sat straighter in her chair. "Ben and his family came from Ireland to New York where we met through mutual friends of our parents." She smiled brightly. "Oh, Kulien, New York City is a wonderful location far from here. It is civilized, so unlike this godforsaken city. There is running water, shops with beautiful clothes, and, oh, the concert halls! Ben finished his university training there and, at only twenty-five, he became a doctor, his lifelong dream." Her smile disappeared as she returned to her story. "Ben and I married and planned to settle in New York near our families, but our plans changed drastically. We had been married for only a few months when one of Ben's friends returned from China. He had been living in the southern city of Canton working as a doctor."

At that moment, Katie began to cry and Lucy stopped talking to take up the frail child. She lifted the baby to her breast but she turned away, crying even harder. Finally, Lucy lifted Katie to her shoulder, patting and soothing the tiny girl until she quieted. "I don't know why she refuses my milk. I seem to have plenty."

While Kulien continued to hold and caress her boy, Lucy picked up the story. "Ben's friend told us of the great need in China, not only for Western medicine, but he also said there were people who wanted to learn English. So we decided to put our plans aside and go to the Orient while we were still young—in our twenties. Friends and colleagues sponsored us for a three year term."

"But you are here?" Kulien's voice held a question and a frown creased her brow. "Why have you not gone to China as you planned?"

Tense lines pulled at Lucy's mouth. "We not only lost my violin in that accident, we lost all of our belongings, including most of the money raised for our passage." She sighed and lifted heavy eyelids. "Fortunately Ben had several hundred dollars in a bag he wore around his waist, or there would have been nothing to live on. There is very little of that left now." Her words ended with a frown and turned down lips

The front door opened and Benjamin strode through the living room into the kitchen. He paused to look at George as Kulien tucked him into his makeshift crib, then he leaned over to kiss Lucy on the cheek. She turned away as if she had been bitten, and Katie began to cry again.

"I'll take her to our bedroom," she said, looking up into Ben's stricken face. "There's soup on the stove. You and Kulien have something to eat. I'll eat later."

Kulien noticed Lucy's unusual reaction to Ben's touch and wondered at the strangeness between them. Without speaking, she walked to the large black woodstove and began to dip up two bowls of thin soup. Careful not to spill any of the precious liquid, she set them on the table and sat across from the doctor. They ate without talking; the only sound was the clink of spoons on their tin bowls. When they had finished, Benjamin removed the bowls and poured himself a cup of coffee from a heavy iron pot that was always at the back of the stove. He looked at Kulien over the rim of the cup, his frown disappearing. "You look well. I'm pleased your strength has returned so quickly."

"I am indebted to you and Lucy for saving my life."

"Ah, Colleen, most of your people are too far gone before I arrive. They fear me more than their sickness. I have been able to save only three slave girls from the bagnios. But I fear they won't last long. The pox is. . .."

"Forgive me, Doctor Ben, I'm not familiar with the word, 'bagnio.' What kind of place is that?"

"No, I don't imagine you would know. A bagnio is a type of slave prison. Here in San Francisco, Chinese girls are put in cages in the dark alleyways and have to submit as prostitutes to anyone who is willing to pay the price to her master! It's a horrible practice, Colleen. I'm so thankful that we found you before you were sold as a slave!"

"I don't believe Ahtoy would do that. In her house, there were only two or three Chinese women, and they were treated well." She glanced up into the man's kind face. "You are a good doctor, and one day you will be trusted. My countrymen have known Westerners only as those who brought opium to our land; and many of the men who came here with hope were mistreated on the voyage across the Peaceful Sea."

A sense of weariness seemed to envelope Benjamin, and he leaned back in his chair and closed his eyes. Kulien took the opportunity to study his features. He was unlike Marshall Whitfield and Jack Burton. His body was strong and powerful, but his manner was gentle and thoughtful. He was older than Marshall, and younger than Burton. His hair was the color of burnished copper, his eyes green and turbulent as the ocean depths. She wondered at his age—perhaps thirty as the Westerner counts years.

"And what do you see, Colleen?" Ben's open eyes twinkled and his even white teeth shone under the full moustache.

Kulien felt the blood rise to her cheeks. "I—I have never seen a man with crimson hair. And there is not a man in my land with emerald eyes like my own."

Benjamin stood, motioning Kulien to follow him through the small house and out the front door. "The sun is bright today and the breeze is warm. Your doctor orders fresh air!"

Fragrant white lilies and yellow wildflowers bloomed along the planked walkway leading to the road. Ben picked a white blossom and handed it to Kulien, then walked to the splintery fence and opened the gate. "You're not strong enough yet to walk far, but I'd like you to see something."

"Is it safe? Ahtoy said a woman would be stolen and sold into slavery."

"You're safe with me. No one will bother you." He laughed. "They still fear this foreign devil."

"I must not go far. My son. . .." Her hand went to her heart. "He is everything to me."

"Do you trust me?" Benjamin stopped walking to look down on Kulien.

"Yes, Dr. Ben, you saved my life—and the life of my baby!"

"Then would you be willing to tell me about George's father?"

Kulien sighed. Could she review the past and remain serene? "Yes," she said after several moments, "but perhaps I will speak of him when Lucy is also present."

After walking a short distance, Kulien bent over and drew in a deep breath. She had been lying about in bed or sitting in the kitchen for so many weeks, every muscle ached, and she wanted only to sit in the thick grass at her feet.

Ben reached over to lift her to a standing position. "I'm sorry for walking so fast, Colleen. It is a shame for me to expect you to move along so soon after giving birth." With those words, he asked her permission before lifting her in his arms as he would his own child, and then he strolled up the hilly path as casually as before. He talked about his desire to go to China, and how the accident on the trail changed their plans.

Kulien was grateful for his concern, and although he seemed like an older brother, her face flushed and her heart beat rapidly at his closeness and the strength of his arms.

"I thought Lucy would die of grief," he said, his warm breath brushing her forehead. "We had almost reached our destination; we had covered two thousand miles in eight months on the Overland Trail. Twenty men and women, and fifteen children died along our way." His voice was tender, almost reverent as he spoke.

He reached the crest of the hill and set Kulien on her feet, then raked fingers through his thick red hair. "Lucy's faith brought her through that hard time. We've been here for six months, but our troubles aren't over yet. The wee lassie has taken most of Lucy's strength and," he added, "I can see that she is unhappy and depressed."

Kulien said nothing.

"I once had a strong faith." He paused to look at Kulien's confused expression. "I'm a Christian, Colleen. My faith is in Jesus Christ. At least it was." He clenched his teeth before going on. "There was so much death on the trail." His words faltered as if he were unsure of his thoughts. "I have a hard time reconciling a God of love with so much suffering and dashed hopes!"

Kulien weighed his words, so like Lucy's, yet as husband and wife, they seemed to be distant from one another.

"But enough of that. I brought you up here for another reason." He squared his chin and pointed toward the north. "Look! That's what I want you to see—the San Francisco Bay. It is a few miles away from here, but near enough to catch the sight and scent of the ocean. If I couldn't be near the sea, life away from New York and the east coast would be unbearable."

Kulien understood most of Dr. O'Kelly's discourse, and listened quietly, sensing his need to rid himself of private demons.

By now late-afternoon sunshine cast pink and purple shadows over the surrounding hills. Persistent northwesterly breezes cooled, flapping Kulien's borrowed skirt around her ankles and lifting her long hair from her shoulders like a cape. A sense of peace seemed to envelope them both as neither spoke. They breathed deeply of the tangy ocean air and watched the sun settle lower in the west.

Would Ahtoy allow her to walk on the hills to enjoy the beauty so forgotten in the Chinese Quarter? Would the gods, or the God of the Christians, allow her to live in freedom one day?

"I must return now," Kulien said, turning from the view. She folded her arms tightly over her full breasts. "It is time to feed my son."

For the next two days, fog hung over the city on the bay casting a gloom over Dr. O'Kelly's household. Both babies cried more than usual; Lucy was withdrawn and morose; and Ben's usual patience was displaced by abrupt answers and a scowling face. Even the two cats fought and howled throughout the night. When the morning of Kulien's departure arrived, Lucy took her hands and drew her near to the baby boy's makeshift bed. "Kulien, you must leave Baby George, I mean, Mary, here. We will tell Ahtoy the baby died. Ben is at the back of the house now digging a grave. Your child will be safe here with us." She held Kulien's hands tightly as they stared at the sleeping boy.

"No!" Kulien pulled away to lift George and held him so tightly he began to whimper. "He is all I have. I cannot part with him!"

Before she finished speaking, Ben walked into the room, perspiring and wiping his brow with a large white cloth. "And he always will be yours if you will part with him for just a few days. They would take him away from you, Colleen." He groaned and shifted his weight.

"I've hesitated telling you this, but we have learned that Ahtoy sold your contract to an 'Old Mother,' a creature who deals in human flesh. There's to be an auction tomorrow of slave girls who arrived this morning. That will include you as well." Ben sighed, his face grim. "I'm sorry you have to go through this, but it may be the one chance we have to save you."

Kulien paled and gasped, "Ahtoy sold my papers? I must go to the slave block?" She pressed her nose against the baby's face, inhaling deeply of his sweetness. Her full lips covered his eyelids and cheeks as she drank in the perfect features and eyes that now reflected a summer sky.

Outside, the gate creaked and footsteps sounded on the wooden walkway. Kulien and Lucy stared at each other, then at Ben. "Please, give him to me," Lucy said before holding out her arms. "You must trust us. It's the only way to save him!"

Knuckles rapped on the door, and Kulien thrust George into Lucy's outstretched arms. She pulled the silk rope with Marshall's ring from around her neck, and tucked it into the folds of the blanket. Lucy dashed from the room to the back of the house where she hid in a closet.

Before Benjamin opened the door, he whispered, "I have a plan to get you away from the 'Old Mother,' Colleen. You must be brave once more. I swear I will not allow you to be sold into slavery!"

THIRTY-FOUR

Dr. O'Kelly's final words along with a quick embrace imparted strength as Kulien stepped through the door into the possession of two hollow-eyed men whose yellowed skin betrayed their addiction to opium. *Where is Ahtoy? Has she truly forsaken me?* The men pushed her into a wheelbarrow, then each taking hold of a handle, they trotted over the bumpy roads to the crowded docks where an old hag waited with a group of women.

By the time they reached the docks, Kulien's body ached from the rough ride. "You cost me long string of 'cash' worth one gold nugget," the old woman screeched in a mixture of Cantonese and Pidgin English. "You bring good price. Here, tie scarf on head. Badge of honor!"

Kulien looked around at the long line of women and girls who had begun to walk down the wharf single-file. The "Daughters of Joy" all wore the same head-covering, a checkered cotton handkerchief. Some were dressed in cotton tunics and trousers, and others wore silk. Kulien's heart moved with pity to see so many who had been sold by their families to become slaves in the Land of the Golden Mountain. These girls were no doubt familiar with slavery because females in China were often born into humiliation and wretchedness. There was despair written on their faces, and in the way they walked, that spoke of utter hopelessness.

Kulien stepped beside a girl who appeared to be her age. "How did you happen to come here?" she asked in faltering Cantonese.

"I came to marry a rich merchant," she said. "I am not like these other girls. I was not a prostitute. My parents came on hard times with the floods, and a rich merchant here in San Francisco paid my passage."

The old hag sidled up to Kulien and struck her across the head with a stick. "Get back in line, dog dung. No talking on way to 'Queen's Room.'"

Kulien's heart sank even lower for she had heard of the "Queen's Room" an underground barracoon, or slave-pen, where girls were offered in sale to the highest bidder. In the past year, hundreds of Chinese girls had been imported and put to work as slaves to their procurers. Most had gone through the barracoon, exposed to the horrible maltreatment of the Old Mothers and the degradation of the slave block.

The procession moved slowly through the growing village of sand hills, tents, shacks and a few recently-built brick buildings. White men with dirty beards and big boots shouted obscenities at the passing group, while half-naked brown men and ragged black men watched from a distance. Horse-drawn wagons reeking of rancid fish rumbled by, followed by yelping dogs.

"Stay in line, dimwit!"

Kulien cried out from another blow of the stick against her cheek and stumbled to the ground. She staggered to her feet, wiping horse dung from the Chinese trousers Ben had procured. On they marched, up one dusty street and down another, under the scrutinizing gaze of barbarian eyes. When they reached the Chinese Quarter, the old woman herded them into a dark, foul-smelling alley. Rats, undaunted by human intrusion, continued to feast on piles of garbage. Filthy rags, broken bottles and slimy refuse obstructed the path, but if any one of the women stepped aside, they were rewarded with a barrage of curses and a blow to the head.

When they reached St. Louis Alley, they were crowded down a flight of stairs to the barracoon, a basement room large enough to hold many people.

The sallow hag in black pants and jacket jangled keys hanging at her waist. "I am Old Mother," she announced in a gravelly voice. "I hold the papers of you wretched slaves—twenty-five today. You be auctioned off tomorrow. Then I turn your papers over to new owners. But now," the old woman shoved two girls out of line and tugged at their clothes, "let me see what you have to sell!"

One of the girls, no older than ten, began to cry. "But I am not a slave. I have a marriage contract. My father arranged for me to marry a wealthy merchant."

The hag spread the girl's papers out on a splintery table. "You can all forget that lie. Just read what your papers say, turtle droppings."

The young girl's wide eyes searched the faces of her companions. "I cannot read! My father said that girls don't have souls, so we cannot be taught to read and write."

The girls looked at each other, nodding in agreement. Kulien lifted her chin and stepped out of line. "*I* read," she announced, taking the papers from Old Mother. "*I* have a soul." She fastened her eyes on the pitiful gathering. "And so do *you!*"

Before the old woman could snatch the papers away, Kulien scanned the Chinese ideograms. Spoken Cantonese was not yet completely familiar to her, but because every group and region of China used the same basic written form, Kulien was able to read the contract. "It says, 'Ah Ni,'" she looked up to acknowledge the wide-eyed child, "'agrees to give her body for the service of prostitution for the term of five years.'"

Kulien touched the little girl's shoulder. "I'm sorry. The old woman is right. The document records the sale of a prostitute."

Old Mother laughed and seized the papers. "What I tell you? Every one of you, no exceptions, for sum of your passage has promised use of your bodies for prostitution!"

"My papers do not say that," Kulien blurted.

"Ha! Your papers say you coolie. You promised to work out your 'credit ticket' in the mines. I could sell you to miners. You would be good diversion for them, but let them come here. More gold here than in mining camps!"

A tremulous voice spoke from the shadows, "I had no choice but to put my thumb print on the contract. But it is for only five years." Her eyes pleaded with the others. "Our shame will not be forever. Five years, then we will be free."

The old woman thrust out her toothless jaw. "Not so, my witless friend. Your papers also say monthly sick days be counted against your time."

"What does that mean?" Kulien demanded. She crossed her arms in front of her waist and glared at the wretched woman.

"It means that you make up your sick days—two weeks for one day, another month for each additional day!" Her words ended in a chuckle.

Kulien calculated the figures in her mind. For the five or six days the "crimson snows" lasted each month, the girls would never be free. She would never be free! They were all doomed to a lifetime of prostitution—or death by disease. There was no way out.

As each one came to the same conclusion she began to cry. At last the old woman shouted, "Enough! Listen to me you she-dogs! Depending on your looks, you have many choices. If rich man buys you, could mean elegant house, jewels and silks. If you have scars or deformities, you be placed in a bagnio."

"What's a bagnio?" a dull-eyed older woman asked in a scratchy voice.

"You'll find out soon enough, stupid," replied the hag. "But I tell you little bit now." She paced back and forth in front of the cowering women as she spoke, obviously enjoying the shocked expressions and distress of her charges.

"A bagnio. Ha! It *lovely* place, you see. It a small room with table and chair for eating; basin for water, and straw mat." The guttural voice erupted into a hideous laugh. "Straw mat. For *business*." She paused for effect before going on. "Little screened window opens to dark alley, and you paint yourselves and attract men by tapping on screen. You get many customers. The more men you service, you treated better. Your owner comes each morning to collect the earnings. If you do him well, you may be moved into upstairs rooms in better part of Little China." She stopped to stare at the whimpering group. Kulien's heart fell as she heard the words. It was much worse than she had even imagined.

"Enough talk. Now, you!" She pulled the jacket off the nearest girl. "Take off clothes and get up on platform so I see what I'm selling."

One by one, the girls and women slowly shed their clothing while Old Mother poked and probed them for scars and open sores. Some were motioned aside for a Chinese physician to examine, while several older women admitted to having relations with white sailors in the open ports of Canton and Hong Kong. Old Mother seemed to think they were the most immoral of the group, and consigned them to the corner of the room.

Kulien was the last to be stripped and examined. The shame was almost more than she could bear, but she willed herself to remember Dr. Ben's promise, "You will *not* be sold into slavery!"

As the foul-smelling woman circled, poking and prodding, Kulien forced her mind back to that morning. She imagined her tiny baby at her breast, his hungry mouth searching for nourishment. At the thought of him, a drop of warm liquid slid down her bare skin. The old woman's voice shattered her fantasy. "What's this?" She pulled Kulien's hands away. "You have a child! Where is it? I own you. And I own your offspring!"

Kulien covered herself with open hands. "Two weeks ago, I gave birth to a barbarian. It died yesterday." She lowered her head before continuing, and the tears came naturally. "The father was English, and I cannot say if I am infected with the pox or not. It is likely that the baby died because of the disease." Kulien wondered at the ease of her lies, but it was to protect Baby George, and she would gladly lie, even die for him.

The woman rattled her keys. "No matter. You look good. No scars—except on your back. Looks like fingernails did that." She snorted. "I think of way to make money off you."

Dark and damp. Stench of putrefying sores, unwashed bodies, and human waste soaked into the mud floor. The squeaking and gnawing of rats in the corners of the barracoon sent waves of fear through Kulien's body, and she began to shake uncontrollably. Her breasts throbbed with pain, and she burned with fever. The Old Mother had made the bindings so tight she could hardly breathe. "In day or two," said the old woman, "milk dry up. I not hold auction until I get a good price for you! Most of these girls are property of someone else and I get only a part of selling price, but you," she said, poking a finger at Kulien, "you mine!"

Sighs of relief rose from the group of women huddled together to keep warm. They would have two days reprieve before a lifetime of bondage. But the two days would only add to their growing fears.

Kulien nudged the woman beside her. "We may be able to escape. I know of Americans who have rescued some of the slave girls. They took them to a mission where they can be free."

There was a grunt of disbelief. "You're a fool. It is known by all that the foreign devils at the mission eat Chinese girls. They also pull out the fingernails of singsong girls, and then they scratch their eyes out."

"What?" Kulien turned toward the woman. "Where did you hear such a thing?"

"Everyone knows it's true. They did it in China, and they do it here. Not only that, before they eat their captives, they boil them in oil because they like them crispy. I'm surprised you didn't know this. The foreigners also drink their victim's blood after it's been mixed with brandy."

Kulien strained her eyes to see through the darkness. "That's not true. I lived with Westerners in Shanghai, and they were always kind to me, and to all the girls who lived in the mission. What you heard was a lie!"

"Believe what you want. None of us has any control over what happens to our lives anyway. We were born as unfortunate females and we'll die the same way."

Kulien shuddered and turned to her other side. Would the pain, the throbbing ever cease? Her stomach churned with hunger, but the thought of food in this vile place sickened her. She remembered how she had survived the long voyage across the sea by turning her thoughts to pleasant memories. Her first and continuous thought was of her precious baby. She felt a sense of comfort knowing he was safe with the O'Kelly's. Even if they found no way to rescue her, at least Baby George would have a home. She shivered again and wrapped her arms around her body. Suppose she had given birth in Ahtoy's house? Her child would have been born into slavery without ever knowing freedom.

Freedom. Wasn't that the thought behind all she did— even as a child? Although she had determined to put the distant past away, throughout the next two days and nights her mind slipped repeatedly to her life in the Kuang compound.

I was free compared to my girl cousins. With unbound feet, I could run and climb trees and hide behind screens when my father met with dignitaries. I learned the Chinese classics, and received instructions in English. I loved to carry on conversations with Elizabeth Whitfield in my own private courtyard. Why had I always been so discontented, sensing that there was more to life than what I knew behind high walls?

With eyes closed, she could almost feel Jiang pulling the bamboo comb through her long hair. She could hear her soothing voice, as well as her scolding words. *Dear, dear Jiang. If I'd been an obedient, respectful daughter, she would still be alive.* She recalled the misty mornings in the gardens and the fragrance of jasmine blooming on the compound wall. And oh, how delicious were her scented baths in the porcelain tub, and the feel of satin slipping over her freshly scrubbed body.

Then Marshall Whitfield's face filled her imagination. He had loved her, and taught her the elements of love that had produced their son. That one night in his arms had led her here, here to this filthy place across the wide ocean. Would she ever see him again? Her heart ached with the remembrance of being with him in Hong Kong, looking into his eyes again, feeling his warm breath against her face. She thought they were together forever when she was suddenly snatched away and consigned again to that dark galley. Where was he now? Did he have any knowledge that she had borne his child?

Her musings were interrupted by the sudden opening of the door at the head of the stairs. Daylight streamed in, sending rays of gray light into the dark basement. Rats and cockroaches scurried for cover; and the girls and women closed their eyes against the unfamiliar light and drew themselves up into tight balls against the coming events.

Men tramped down rickety stairs that creaked and moaned under the weight of many feet. Shrill voices called to each other as laughter echoed through the spacious room. A few of those descending the steps were Chinese who wanted to purchase wives. Most, both white and yellow, had contracted for five or more girls to work in brothels. Some had come only to ogle and pinch.

One by one, Old Mother brought each cringing girl to the auction block, stripping them of every bit of clothing before taking bids. And one by one, they stood lifeless and stiff as roast pigs hanging in the marketplace. Feet shuffled. Voices bargained. Laughs roared. Occasionally a girl would shriek with pain when a sensitive place on her body was pinched or jabbed.

The pretty young ones went quickly for the bids were high, but the older, unattractive women were practically given away.

Kulien could not bear to look at the shame parading before her. She closed her eyes and covered her ears with both hands. Then it was her turn. "Get up there, donkey dung. And open those big green eyes. Men be surprised to see demon-eyes. I want them know you not blind!" The old woman pushed her onto the raised platform. "And smile! You got all your teeth, so show them!"

Kulien's stomach convulsed and she swayed, almost falling as she stood alone before the sea of glowering lustful faces. She focused her eyes on a swarm of moths circling a lantern that hung from a rafter—anything to avoid the sensuous gestures and words of the seething crowd.

"Face is good. Show us the rest Old Mother!" shouted a voice near enough to reach out and touch her feet. She drew back and grasped at the edges of her blouse.

The hag jerked at her sleeve, ripping it from her shoulder. Before she could pull the blouse off, a voice called from the back of the room in strong Cantonese, "I'll buy that girl, sight unseen!"

Instantly the wrinkled old woman lifted her head to see who made the bid. "What do you give?" she croaked.

Another voice, nearer the auction block shouted, "I will pay two long strings of cash for that one. But I want to see more."

Kulien shut her eyes and waited for the old hag to yank off the rest of her blouse, but as she tugged at Kulien's clothing, she laughed, "Oh, this one's worth more than that. See how strong she is! And she even reads."

Over the din, someone else cried, "She looks sick, but young. I have three gold nuggets to give."

"Good, good. You have yourself a slave." She whispered in Kulien's ear. "That's twice what I pay for you. Hold out your hand, you turtle. The money goes into your palm before it ends up in mine."

But before the last bidder could make his way through the crowd, the first voice called out again, this time closer to the auction block. "I have two hundred American dollars. The girl is *mine*!"

THIRTY-FIVE

"Two hundred American dollars!"

Kulien recognized the voice of the carefully pronounced Cantonese words and opened her eyes to see Dr. Benjamin O'Kelly place gold coins in her open hands.

The hubbub of voices rose in intensity until the Old Mother shouted, "For two hundred American dollars you have a slave, barbarian!"

She snatched the money from Kulien's palms with one wrinkled hand while thrusting the contract at the redheaded man with the other. Dr. Ben stepped onto the platform and smiled down into Kulien's grateful face. He draped a large swatch of blue silk around her shoulders. "Let's get out of this place, Colleen," he said, only loud enough for her to hear. "There's a baby at home who needs his mother."

They shoved their way through the press of men who stood aside, awed by the excessive price paid for a slave. Voices rose in high-pitched chatter as the tall doctor led Kulien up the wooden steps to freedom. Once again she walked through the garbage-strewn alley littered with filth, but this time instead of fear Kulien's heart raced with gratitude. How could she ever thank this man for what he had done? She felt certain he had used the last of the money he and Lucy had saved from their trip west.

She lifted her eyes beyond the wall of shacks, rising on both sides of the pathway, to a blue sky dotted with white, fluffy clouds. She was free! She was going home to her baby! Home? When had she begun thinking of the O'Kelly's residence as *her* home? She paused to realize that it was when she knew there was someone there who needed her—someone she loved. Hot tears filled her eyes and poured over her cheeks, cleansing away the dread and horror of the barracoon.

They stepped out of the alley and Dr. Ben, with his arm still wrapped protectively around her shoulders, nodded toward the horse and cart tied up in the street. "You will be home soon, Colleen." A deep crease appeared between his eyebrows. "Are you ill? Were you harmed in any way?"

"No. I'm tired and hungry; that's all."

"And I can see that you are very weak. I'll lift you into the cart. There's clean straw and a quilt in the back. You can be resting on the trip home."

After tucking the quilt around her, Ben climbed onto the seat and shook the reins. "Giddy-up! Let's get this mother back to her son."

Kulien rested her head on the fragrant straw and closed her eyes. Free! She knew she should thank the gods, but perhaps it was Benjamin and Lucy's God who had set her free. Just to be safe, she thanked Kuanyin, Goddess of Mercy, and the Most High God.

Her concept of freedom seemed to change with each new event in her life. She had thought she was a prisoner when she learned of the marriage contract to Kong Li Tang. Yet in her home she had been free, taking it for granted. She had been free to run about the gardens, free to practice *taichichuan* every morning with her father. The barracoon, the bagnios, the illiteracy of the women—that was real bondage! The horror awaiting those girls was beyond understanding. Yes, now she could appreciate freedom as never before.

She opened her eyes to the sapphire sky, thinking back to her days in China. Although she had been free to run and play, her future had been decided. If she *had* submitted to her father's control, she would be nothing more than a body used to produce sons for Kong Litang. That was another kind of captivity. She must never forget the slavery of her Chinese sisters, whether here in America or across the Sea of Great Peace.

We do have souls, she said to herself. *We are capable of making choices that affect our lives.*

Kulien sat up in the cart and inhaled deeply of the cool breezes that blew off the bay. As the horse plodded over bumpy streets, the sights and smells of the barracoon disappeared in the distance. But the memory of those cries of anguish; the cold, pebble-hard eyes of lustful men; and the soul-draining humiliation of the slave block only added fuel to her determination. Somehow, some day, there must be hope for the women of her race. How, she didn't know, but she would find a way!

As the horse's hooves *clip-clopped* over the rocky roadway, Ben called over his shoulder, "See here, Colleen, we're approaching the docks. Have you any idea what those boxes contain?" He reached out an arm and pointed a long finger toward stacks of wooden crates.

Kulien rose to her knees and blinked her eyes at the bright rays of sun bouncing off the water. Rows of boxes measuring about three feet long and two feet wide waited at the dock's edge. She supposed they contained rice or bolts of wool to be transported across the ocean. "No, I don't know, Dr. Ben. Have you the answer?"

He laughed. "I thought you might like to see how some of your countrymen have booked passage back to China."

Kulien shielded her eyes with a hand and leaned against the side of the cart, balancing her weight on one elbow. "I do not understand." She strained to read the writing on the crates, but after days and nights of sleeplessness, the Chinese characters were nothing more than a jumble of illegible lines.

"Whoa!" Benjamin pulled on the reins and the cart jolted to a stop. "Come up here and sit beside me, lass. You can use the fresh air before returning home."

"I am too ashamed." She paused and wrinkled her nose. "I have the stink of night soil on my clothes, and my arms ache to hold my baby."

"I know," Ben answered. "But little George sleeps long this time of day. Now come on," he urged, leaning over to assist her. "You sit up here and look out across the bay. What I have to say will interest you."

"As you wish, Dr. Ben." Kulien's body still ached with fever, but the cool breeze was a balm. And how could she not obey her benefactor?

With Benjamin's help, she managed to climb over the front of the cart, and, easing onto the padded seat, she leaned against the backboard.

""Do you know what happens to Chinese men who die in the Land of the Golden Mountain?"

Kulien shook her head. Why did he speak of death on a day like this?

Benjamin continued to watch the unfolding scene as he talked. "See how many boxes are hoisted onto that ship? That many Chinese men have died this past year!"

Kulien lifted her eyes to follow Benjamin's gaze. One by one, the wooden crates, which numbered in the hundreds, were carefully lifted by coolies who carried them up the gangplank where they disappeared into the hold.

"There are men in those boxes?" Kulien frowned. How could a man fit into such a small crate? She looked at Dr. Ben with renewed interest. "What are you telling me?"

"That your people amaze me. I've been studying the Chinese culture for years, and when I learned that I might have the opportunity to practice medicine in Canton, I answered the call."

By now the activity on the wharf had accelerated. Men shouted to one another; vendors hawked their wares; bells rang; horns blew. Kulien's blood raced with the unfolding drama of cargo being loaded on ships as well as the men who scrambled ashore when they had finally reached their destination after long months at sea.

"You have not yet explained why we stopped here, or how a man could fit into such a small box."

"It has to do with the spirit chain of male ancestors, buried side by side."

Kulien nodded. "Yes, that is true. We have a great celebration to honor our ancestors. We believe that the spirit remains in the tomb to watch over the conduct of the rest of the family. So on *Ching Ming,* or Pure Brightness Festival, the family travels to the countryside to sweep the graves and repair the tombs. My father, as well as the other men in our compound, bowed three times to the ancestors and flew kites, but the girls were allowed only to watch."

"The belief continues here, Colleen. Every Chinese male who comes to America is guaranteed in his ticket that his bones will be returned to China for burial beside his ancestors."

Kulien's eyes followed the coolies who loaded the boxes on board. "I know now what you tell me. There are bones in the boxes."

"Yes, after decomposition, the bones are separated and dipped in a solution of brandy and water. Then professional bone-scrapers polish them with a stiff brush until they shine like glass." He clucked his tongue and scratched the stubble of coppery bristles on his chin. "I find the practice very interesting!"

"I think your heart is Chinese, Dr. Ben."

Benjamin's pale green eyes crinkled and his wide mouth opened in a grin. "Perhaps you're right Colleen." He shook the reins to get the horse moving along. "But let's get you home. There's a little boy who is waking up about now."

Another week passed before Kulien was strong enough to assume full care of her baby or to help Lucy, who seemed to grow weaker each day. Most of the day, Kulien gazed into the baby's small face and sang ancient melodies in her native tongue. "My dearest treasure," she whispered to the sleeping child. "Because you are the *brightness* of my life, I will call you *Ta Ming*. Although you are a son of both East and West, and I have given you a Western name, you must always remember your Chinese heritage and the family of Kuang. My prayer is that one day you will bring harmony between East and West and a bright light to darkened minds."

When Kulien announced the Chinese name she had given Baby George, Lucy and Ben repeated it several times. "Ta Ming. Ta Ming. It is a beautiful name for a most handsome boy, Kulien," Lucy said. "He will make you proud. Of that, I'm sure!"

As Ta Ming grew fatter each day, Little Katie's health declined. She fretted constantly, and slept little. Lucy, too, was listless and anxious that her milk was insufficient.

One night, Lucy, with Ben at her side, awakened Kulien. "Forgive me, my friend, for waking you, but Ben and I were wondering…since Ta Ming is so strong and, well, we wondered if you would be willing to be Katie's wet nurse? It would be for just a few weeks until she grows stronger."

Kulien rubbed her eyes and sat up on the narrow cot that had been placed at the side of the small living room. She glanced from Lucy's worried face to Ben's. Were they asking her to give of her own substance to the foreign baby? To be Katie's *amah?*

"I am confused," she stammered. "Have you no milk, Lucy? Would you put your baby to the breast of a heathen half-breed?"

"Kulien, how can you use such words about yourself? You're no more a heathen than I am; we all have more than one ancestry in our backgrounds!" She reached out to touch Kulien's shoulder. "I love you as I would a sister. I'm just so sick. There's a burning deep inside that takes away my energy. I worry that Katie isn't getting the nourishment she needs. She's so thin and frail." She turned to look into her husband's face. "Ben, you're a doctor. Won't you please tell me what's wrong with our baby? Please?"

Lucy fell to her knees beside Kulien's bed and covered her face before she began to sob. Ben dropped to his knees beside her and put his arms around her shoulders. Kulien's eyes widened at the remarkable display of emotion. She pulled the quilt up around her chin and began to tremble, waiting for Dr. O'Kelly to answer Lucy's plea.

"Oh, my darling, my love! Can you ever forgive me for bringing you to this godforsaken country?"

Lucy stopped crying long enough to wipe her eyes and look at Ben. "You didn't bring me here against my will. I wanted to come. I wanted to go to China. It's not your fault we're stranded!" They both seemed oblivious to Kulien's presence as they spoke to each other. "But how about Katie?"

Benjamin lifted Lucy to her feet and led her across the room to the sofa. "You're not well, my love, and I'm afraid the journey was too much for you."

"But I lived, didn't I? Many didn't make it, Ben."

"I know, but you were very ill long before we reached California, and when you became pregnant...." He covered his face with his hands. "I'm sorry, so very sorry!"

"Ben, please. Of course it was difficult being so sick on the trail, but we have our baby. We have our Kathleen! Just tell me what's wrong with her. Am I at fault? Is it because I'm not well?"

Ben pushed back the hair that fallen over his forehead, his face twisted in despair. "No, Katie's problem came from me. It's my fault."

"What do you mean?"

"There's something wrong with Katie's heart. The rhythm is off. I could tell as soon as she was born. My sister was born with the same physical defect. If we lived in New York, there would be help; there would be hope. But here?"

"Why didn't you tell me about this before? We must return to New York. Maybe we could sail through the Isthmus instead of traveling by wagon. Oh, Ben, there's still hope. Please tell me there's hope for our baby!"

Ben bowed his head. "Katie couldn't survive that long trip and neither could you, I fear. We'll just have to wait and see what happens."

Lucy jumped to her feet, waving her hands overhead. "Wait and see? Wait and see? Is that all you can say? Why did you spend all those years in medical school if you can only tell me to wait and see?"

At Lucy's outburst, Kulien burrowed deeper under her quilt and covered her head. She felt shame for listening to the heart-rending cries of her distraught friends. Her heart ached at the pleas of Dr. Ben. She wished to be far away from the disagreeable words between husband and wife.

Finally she could stand it no longer. She slipped off the cot and ran to the bedroom to comfort the crying baby girl. Holding her close, she stood quietly in the middle of the living room tapping a foot. Lucy and Ben stopped arguing and turned to Kulien, their eyes wide with surprise.

"You have forgotten Katie," Kulien said firmly. "At this moment I think it matters not *where* you live or *why* you are here! Enjoy this lovely little girl for as long as possible."

Kulien returned to her bed and discreetly opened her nightgown. Katie's crying stopped when she found nourishment and security in Kulien's tender and serene embrace. "She is a most beautiful child," she said, as she twisted a bright golden curl around her forefinger. "And she has fine, loving parents." She lifted her eyes to Ben and Lucy. "I am honored to be Katie's *amah.* She will always be fed first because she is weak and will not take much. Ta Ming is fat and healthy. What is left will be enough for him."

THIRTY-SIX

Katie immediately took to Kulien's new role as her *amah*, and began to sleep peacefully from one feeding to the next. Outwardly, life appeared normal in the little house on the edge of the Chinese Quarter, but inside an increasing tension hovered over the inhabitants like a dark cloud. Lucy spent hours in bed behind a closed door, and Benjamin often left for the Chinese Quarter before dawn and returned home long after dark.

Each day Kulien took on more of the responsibilities left by Lucy. She prepared the meals, baked bread and pies; and she scrubbed the family's clothes on a washboard until her knuckles were raw. The high points of her day were the moments spent with the growing babies; and she felt a deep sadness that those times passed so quickly.

The warm, balmy days of summer faded into autumn. Crisp, clean breezes painted the trees with shades of gold and russet, and brushed the babies' cheeks an apple-red. As season merged into season, not only did Ta Ming and Katie change, but Kulien emerged from the cocoon of girlhood into a woman of poise and serenity. On the rare occasions that Lucy felt well enough to help in the kitchen, she refined Kulien's art of cooking and sewing. Lucy shared her longing to return to New York as they rolled out a pie crust or sat at the table creating multicolored flowers on swatches of fabric with strands of silk thread.

"I know I shouldn't complain," Lucy would begin. "I have so much to be thankful for Kulien. If you weren't here to nurse Katie, I'm sure she would have died."

Kulien snipped off the end of a crimson thread and nodded. "I, too, would be dead if you had not allowed me to live here all these months. I can never repay you and Dr. Ben for your kindness."

"You've more than repaid us! You are a gift from God."

"You make me think of my friend, Elizabeth Whitfield. I have told you about her, haven't I?"

"Yes." Lucy's brow furrowed and she bit her lower lip. "You spoke of her the day you told Ben and me about Ta Ming's father and your voyage to America. You said that she taught you

English, and protected you in a mission in Shanghai. She is also your husband's sister; so in a way, she's your sister, too."

Kulien nodded. "Elizabeth tried to understand me, but I know it must have been difficult for her. She was very unhappy about Marshall, and believed he took advantage of an innocent girl." A smile brightened Kulien's deep green eyes. "But I was not innocent. I loved him; and although what we did was against the rules of her religion, we said vows before our gods." She tipped her head when she looked at Lucy. "Do you think your Invisible God is angry with me?"

Lucy sighed before answering, "I don't know, Kulien. I do know this, though; God does forgive the wrong things we do. That's why He sent His son, Jesus, to die on the cross."

Kulien squirmed at Lucy's reference to the gruesome death of their God, and held up the garment she had been embroidering. "Do you like the shirt I'm making for Ta Ming? I have almost finished the red and gold peonies. Then it will be ready for him to wear."

Another week passed before Kulien completed her needlework; and she dressed Ta Ming in the outfit to perform an ancient ritual. Although not totally convinced that the old ways were truly the best, to appease the spirits, she prepared her son. "I must take Ta Ming to look down the well. It will give him a bright, clear mind and produce courage and understanding." Even as she spoke the words, she doubted the superstitions taught by her father.

As months passed, Ta Ming's mixed heritage became more evident. The fine black hair grew rapidly, and Kulien plaited it together with strands of raw silk to create a short queue that reached his soft pudgy back. His eyes, though blue like his father's, were almond-shaped like hers. His chubby face dimpled and his arms and legs constantly moved, reaching for whatever was close, and climbing onto the sofa or any lap he could find.

Kulien's love for Ta Ming occupied most of her thoughts; when he was awake she held him close, stroking his hair, speaking to him of his goodness and beauty. She told him that his English name was for his paternal grandfather, Lord George

Whitfield, and that one day, he, too, would be a great statesman and a scholar. He would be acknowledged by the Whitfield clan as a gentleman, the son of Lord Marshall Whitfield. Then she let him touch the shiny signet ring, and promised to give it to him when he was older.

One day, almost a year after Kulien had come to live with the O'Kellys, Benjamin walked into the kitchen, his shoulders hunched, and deep creases lined his brow. Kulien looked up from the loaf of bread she had formed into a heavy iron pan. His expression sent a pain of anxiety racing through her heart. "Is Lucy all right?" Throughout the past month Lucy had become weaker, and Kulien often heard her crying in the night.

Ben cleared his throat before wiping his face with a red square of cloth. "No, Colleen. She grows weaker every day." He walked to the kitchen window, and stared with unseeing eyes at the blue morning glories climbing the back fence. "I've treated her with every known tonic, and she only gets worse!" Tears glistened in the corners of his eyes, but he seemed unaware of them until they spilled over onto his cheeks. With a quick swipe of his hand, he turned to Kulien.

"Lucy wanted to spare you, Colleen, but you must know that she's—she's dying."

Kulien wiped the flour from her hands. "I know. I've seen death before. And I heard her cry last night, harder than usual. Her pain must be unbearable. I see her take many doses of laudanum throughout the day." Kulien stifled a sob and turned back to the stove.

"Last night," Ben said, choking out the words, "she begged me for full strength opium. She *begged* me!" He turned away. "I'll have to find some in the Chinese Quarter."

"Kulien!" Lucy's weak voice penetrated their grief. "Please come to me. Please!"

Dr. Ben placed a hand on Kulien's shoulder. "Go to her now. She wants a last word with you." His voice ended in a sob.

"A last word?"

Although Kulien had been expecting this news for several weeks, her heart seemed to stop. She loved Lucy as a sister and a friend. Their spirits had become one. She had nursed Lucy's baby at her own breast; her life flowed together with Lucy's in Katie's spirit.

Kulien untied the large apron from around her waist and folded it over the back of a chair before lifting her chin. "I will go to her with courage, but my spirit is broken."

Ben slumped into a chair and combed fingers through his thick unruly hair. "I know, Colleen, I know." He wiped at his eyes. "At least, my Lucy will soon be free from pain!"

"Kulien, come quickly!" Her voice was barely audible now.

Kulien ran from the kitchen to her cot. She pulled out a box from the corner and lifted a small red bag she had recently made. Holding it in her hands, she tried to remember if she had placed everything in the bag that was necessary to provide comfort to Lucy as she went on her journey into the spirit world. Surely those who called themselves "Christians" needed provisions in the after-life also. The Chinese custom was to hang the bag on the buttonhole of the dying, then as the breath left the body, the bag was put into the deceased's mouth so she might have food to eat on her journey.

Kulien turned the bag over in her hand. There was a bit of gold dust for her to buy necessities, a pinch of tea and a piece of candy. She had also added a page from the black book Lucy read so often.

As she stepped into the room, Lucy lifted a hand, beckoning her to come in. "Please come here. I have to know…" She stopped to draw in a shallow breath. "I have to know what will happen to Katie!"

The words were so soft that Kulien had to put her ear close to Lucy's face. As she leaned toward her, she placed the bag on the frail woman's chest.

"What is this?" Lucy's fingers touched the shiny silk bag.

"It is for your journey beyond the Dog Mountain and the Yellow Springs."

"Oh, my dear, friend," her voice seemed stronger. "I don't need anything." She reached up to touch Kulien's cheek. "But thank you."

Kulien felt alarm and pressed the bag into Lucy's hand. "You must not take a chance that you'll be hungry or have any kind of need on your way."

A slight smile flickered over the pale face. "No hunger in Heaven." Lucy grimaced and clutched her abdomen. "Oh, the pain. It's unbearable!" Lucy's eyes widened. "My baby. My husband." She grasped Kulien's hand with unnatural strength, and spoke each word as if it were her last. "A favor." She paused, heavy sighs escaping her open mouth. "Will you care for Katie? And for Ben? Please?"

Tears welled in Kulien's eyes and she brushed at them with the back of her hand. Take care of Katie and Ben? What was she asking?

"I will do what I can," she said, holding Lucy's hand close to her heart. But I must tell you the truth," she glanced over her shoulder where Ben stood holding Katie, tears streaming down his face. "I hope to return to China as soon as I can arrange passage. Marshall Whitfield is surely searching for me."

Lucy's eyes fluttered as she slipped her hand under her pillow, drawing out a letter with bold English letters on its face. She spoke with effort. "Months ago—I—I wrote to your friend in Shanghai. . .."

Kulien turned to look at Ben who raised his eyebrows and mouthed, "I didn't know."

"I told her that, that you were safe. And I told her about Ta Ming."

Kulien's heart seemed to stop as she listened to the surprising words coming from Lucy's mouth. She watched as Lucy grasped the letter and held it to her chest. "This is her reply. I. . .," Lucy began to cry. "I'm sorry, Kulien. I couldn't tell you. Please forgive me."

Kulien stared at the piece of paper and then back at Lucy. This was a letter from Elizabeth Whitfield? Had she sent news of Marshall? Why hadn't Lucy given her the letter before now?

"Please," Lucy's voice was weaker. "Please say you forgive me!" Her mouth twisted in pain as she tried to lift her head. "And please care for Katie and Ben." She fell back on the pillow, barely breathing.

Lucy's words hung over the room like a winter cloud, but Kulien forced herself to answer as she took the folded parchment from Lucy's fingers.

"You are free to leave, Lucy. I will do as you ask. And of course, I forgive you. I'm glad that you wrote to Elizabeth!"

A smile flickered at the corners of the dying woman's lips, and she raised herself to one elbow and with her eyes focused on the ceiling, said, "A bright light! I see Jesus—and my mother!" A smile of recognition lit Lucy's face before she gasped and the breath left her body in a sputtering stream.

Barely conscious of Ben's looming figure in the doorway, Kulien stared at the still form. Lightly brushing her fingers over the staring eyes, she closed Lucy's eyelids. She quickly picked up the red bag, and hid it in the folds of her sleeve along with the letter. There would be no need for the silk bag. Lucy was gone to where she believed her God lived. Perhaps now she would find peace and rest.

THIRTY-SEVEN

Lucy dead! Kulien could not grasp the loss of her dear friend. Turning from the bed, she only had time to glance at Benjamin's stricken face as he rushed to the still form. Although knowing the danger of leaving the safety of the enclosed yard, Kulien could not stay in the house a moment longer.

The day was cool, yet the sun had broken through and spring blossoms dotted the hillside beyond the road that led from the O'Kelly home. Kulien set her focus on the large tree at the top of the hill where Dr. Ben had first shown her the San Francisco Bay glistening in the distance. The remembrance of the view and refreshing breeze drew her up the hill as her mind turned over the events of the morning.

Lucy had asked her to care for Ben and Katie! What could her friend have meant by those words? To continue nursing Katie until time for both babies to be weaned was a possibility; but what about Dr. Ben? Of course, she was also willing to prepare his meals and clean his house, but what else did Lucy expect of her? And the *letter* to Elizabeth Whitfield! Why had Lucy kept such a secret? She would have known how eager Kulien would be to have news from Elizabeth about Marshall.

Arriving at the tree, Kulien found a large boulder where the sun shone around it, and sat down, removing the letter from her sleeve. So many emotions filtered through her mind that she didn't know whether to cry for Lucy or to be angry that she hadn't given her the letter earlier. She was both eager to read how Elizabeth had responded to Lucy's letter, and fearful that the news from China would cause more grief.

Kulien held the letter on her lap, her eyes tracing both the English letters and the Chinese marks. It must have taken months to travel by ship from China to America. Whatever Elizabeth had written would be old news by now. Her eyes lingered on the familiar scroll of her English teacher. How often she had seen those carefully written letters as Elizabeth taught her the English alphabet and words.

Kulien realized that her hands were shaking as she slowly examined the broken wax seal and unfolded the page. The yellowed parchment was wrinkled and stained as if it had been handled many times. Lucy must have struggled greatly over the decision to tell Kulien about her correspondence with Elizabeth Whitfield.

With the sun's rays shining through the branches of the tree, she concentrated on each carefully written word: "My dear Mrs. O'Kelly," it started. "I cannot begin to express my gratitude in learning about my former student, Kuang Kulien. Reverend Mortensen and I have been most concerned about her situation these many months."

Kulien closed her eyes and meditated on the words. The morning she left the mission, disguised as a coolie, had been a sad, yet hopeful parting. Surely Marshall had contacted her about their meeting in Hong Kong and the way she had been snatched away from him!

She lifted the letter from her lap to continue. She wasn't sure she even wanted to read the rest of the letter as she thought about Lucy's anxious words, and pleas for forgiveness. If the letter held good news, there would be no need for forgiveness.

She had to read further; it would profit nothing if she didn't know the truth. A word from Elizabeth's Bible came to Kulien's mind, "Ye shall know the truth, and the truth shall set you free." That had always been her greatest desire—to be free—she must read on.

"Marshall sent me word that he and Kulien had actually met and were about to leave the dock when a gang of Chinese laborers surrounded her and dragged her back aboard the ship. He was most distressed, as was I. The most dreadful thoughts filled my mind. Had she died on that ship? Did she reach America? As you must have learned, Kulien was pregnant with my *brother's* child."

Kulien gasped at seeing the bold words. Elizabeth had been ashamed of Marshall, yet she had taken care of Kulien as if she were a young girl who had been abused by her brother. No amount of talking would convince her that Kulien had willingly chosen to give herself completely to the man she loved. Oh, if only they had been able to marry legally in Hong Kong, her life and the life of their son would have been so different.

Kulien laid the letter on her lap where the sun warmed it before pressing fingers against her temples. She wanted to forget those months at sea. There was so much death and despair. Kulien had been filthy and hungry, tired and in pain; and had feared the men would discover she was a woman, and then. ...

Jack Burton, though rough and uncivilized, had not only protected her but he had treated her kindly. But what about Marshall? What did he do after he saw the ship sail out of sight? Did he take the next ship to America with the hope of finding her? Perhaps Elizabeth had the answers to her questions, but she wasn't sure she was prepared to discover those answers.

She picked up the letter and continued to read. "Marshall was desperate for weeks, and then I received word that he had been ordered to sail for Great Britain immediately. The orders came from our father, and of course, he had to obey. Reluctantly he put his plans of searching for Kulien aside."

Tears began to fill Kulien's eyes and roll down her cheeks. He didn't come looking for her? He had returned to England without her! Why had his father insisted he come back home? Perhaps he had learned about Kulien and was disgraced as her own father had been.

"I want to thank you for telling me about the birth and well-being of Kulien's child," Elizabeth wrote.

"He's *Marshall's* child too," Kulien said aloud to the open fields. Why doesn't she rejoice that Marshall now has an heir?

"I'm happy that Kulien is with fine Christian people, and that she has a future there in San Francisco. I'm not sure when you will tell Kulien what I'm about to reveal; I'll leave that to your discretion.

"Marshall had to return to Great Britain to fulfill the promise our family made to another family of nobility. Rebekah Halliwell, their only daughter has long been betrothed to Marshall. If he had not been assigned to China when our father was ill, the marriage would have taken place last year."

Kulien crumpled up the letter, holding it against her heart. Who was this Rebekah Halliwell that had been betrothed to Marshall? Did the British practice the same rules of marriage as the Chinese? Did Marshall love this woman? Kulien knew that he could not have. He did not mention her once; and he had pledged his love to her. She had his signet ring to prove it. He married her! He gave her their son!

Kulien wanted to tear the letter to pieces and let the sea breezes blow them into oblivion, but she couldn't. She had to know the truth, regardless of the pain and hopelessness it would bring.

By now, the sun had set lower on the horizon, but the light was enough for her to see the words blurring before her tear-filled eyes. "Marshall and Rebekah (a longtime friend of the family) were married two months after Marshall's return to Great Britain. They had a large, elaborate wedding, and have settled in an area known as the Cotswold's, in a beautiful countryside mansion.

"I did not tell Marshall about Kulien's baby, nor did I tell him that I received a letter from her benefactors. His responsibility now, as it was back in those months he served in China, is to Rebekah, his legal wife. She has been frail and somewhat sickly since her youth. I would be grateful for your prayers on her behalf. She wants to produce a son for the Whitfield legacy, and that is Marshall's desire as well."

Kulien shouted to the sky, "You have a son! You have a beautiful son—right here with his mother!"

Kulien felt a hand on her shoulder and turned, thinking she had somehow brought Marshall back to her, but when she looked up, she saw Benjamin, his eyes wide with surprise, yet red from weeping. "Colleen, I don't know what you've read in that letter," he motioned to the paper clutched in her hand, "but I need you now. Katie needs you, and so does Ta Ming. Please come back. It's getting dark, and we have to decide what to do about Lucy."

Lucy! Oh, yes, dear Lucy must be laid to rest. There was much to be done, and she had promised that she would care for Ben and Katie. She smoothed out the letter and carefully folded it before replacing it in her full sleeve. Inhaling deeply of the cool air, Kulien turned to follow Dr. Ben down the hill to the little house where the babies awaited nourishment that only she could provide. After feeding them and getting them settled for the night, she would try to help Dr. Ben decide how to care for the burial of his wife.

The day following Lucy's death was filled with confusion as Kulien beheld the strange customs of the Americans. Families who had traveled west on the Overland Trail with Lucy and Benjamin came to see the body before it was buried. They came with sorrowful faces and low voices. Those customs were familiar to Kulien, but she found it strange that they wore black for mourning instead of white. In China, the symbols were reversed: black the color of virtue; white the color of deceit and mourning.

The people brought food as they did in China, but the food was for the living, not the dead. The children brought no food for a Heredity Jar that would assure Lucy many descendants and there were no hired mourners or musicians.

Reverend Clark from the Presbyterian mission wore a deeper frown than any of the others, and although he spoke of "eternal life" and "hope," Kulien felt that his demeanor of gloom spoke louder than his words of hope.

Dr. Ben and his friends believed that Lucy's spirit had gone to Heaven and that she no longer had need of anything; but Kulien believed differently. She dressed in white cotton mourning garments and knotted a white scarf around her neck to show her bereavement. Then, under the cover of darkness, she secretly burned paper money for Lucy's journey into the unknown. Perhaps her dear friend could use the spirit money to purchase a violin so she could once more enjoy the music she loved.

For days after Lucy had been laid to rest outside the village of San Francisco, Dr. Ben would sit for hours at a time with his head in his hands. Kulien wished to comfort him but because he would neither speak nor look at her, she filled her days and nights with only the companionship of Katie and Ta Ming.

As weeks passed and the weather grew warmer, Kulien spent more time outside where she could entertain the children with games and stories. The splintery fence enclosed the small dusty yard and Kulien felt safe there even though Dr. Ben had warned her to stay inside the house when he was away. Her occupation with the children kept her mind and heart from dwelling on the marriage of Marshall Whitfield, and of her great loss.

How she enjoyed the children. They were funny little creatures who sometimes crawled, and sometimes walked on wobbly legs. They babbled strange baby words to each other that only they understood. As she cared for them, her own youthfulness began to blossom and her sadness began to wither. She laughed often, forgetting she was a mother who had suffered more than most women much older than she.

"Come, babies," she called in Mandarin. "Sit here beside me, and I will tell you a favorite story, one I heard at my father's feet."

When she finished, Kulien closed her eyes, remembering the visions of romance the story had conjured in her as a child, the children nestling close to her. With their dimply hands clinging to her blouse, she sighed in contentment.

"Colleen." The low voice startled her. "Please come inside."

Dr. Ben had returned from the growing Chinese settlement. His eyes drooped with weariness and his mouth was set in a straight line. Kulien studied his face a moment as he reached down to lift Katie into his arms; then with Ta Ming in her own, she followed him into the house. They laid the sleepy babies in their beds and walked into the kitchen to sit on high-backed pine chairs where they enjoyed the lunch Kulien had prepared earlier.

Ben raked fingers through his thick hair. "Since Lucy's death I've been thinking about the future." He fastened his eyes on a small window behind Kulien, and then lifted himself out of the chair to pace in front of the woodstove. "I'm concerned about Katie. The children are weaned now, and I know that you can't stay here much longer. But where will you go? What will happen to my Katie?"

Kulien sat without moving, her smooth black tresses spread over her shoulders like a silk cape. She kept her eyelids lowered, her vision focused on slender fingers entwined in her lap.

"The people at the mission say it's not proper for you to stay here with me, a young woman alone with a widowed man." He stopped beside Kulien a moment before continuing his pacing. "I've heard there is talk in the Chinese Quarter."

"Talk? What is this talk?"

"It is talk that could be trouble. There's a plot to kidnap you and force you into prostitution."

"But Dr. Ben, you bought my papers. You sacrificed all you had to purchase me. You said that I am free!"

"And you are! But that means nothing to those who left their wives in China. They're lonely and restless here. And there are thousands of Celestials, Chinese, in the foothills. Those men are not only lonely, but they are mistreated, and sometimes murdered, simply for the sport of it. What they wouldn't give for even one woman in their midst!"

Dr. Ben's words sent a chill through Kulien's body. "Perhaps there is a way for me to return to China. If I'm not able to stay in your home, it is time for me to go back to my own land."

"If only it were that simple," he replied. "You could not travel in safety alone; and there's no money for passage." He stopped pacing and sat at the table.

She leaned forward, waiting to hear his solution to the problem. Her small heart-shaped face had grown more beautiful in the passing months. No longer strained by fear and sadness, she was alive with health and youth; her porcelain skin glowed from hours in the sunshine, and her deep green eyes sparkled with enthusiasm. "Do you have an answer to this riddle, Dr. Ben?"

"I believe I have," he said, his voice becoming serious and his eyes fixed on hers. "If you were a member of my family, no one would dare kidnap you."

"You want to adopt me as your daughter?"

A crimson flush began at Ben's open collar and spread upward to the roots of his red hair. "Uh, not exactly."

"A niece then?"

The usually self-confident doctor cleared his throat before rising to dip a cup of water from the basin. He sipped slowly while Kulien waited for his answer. When he returned to the table, he moved his chair closer to Kulien's and covered her hands, now folded on the table, with his. "Colleen, you were close to Lucy, and," he motioned toward the sleeping babies, "you fed Katie with your own milk. That took so much of your strength that you had to wean them both much earlier than is usually done." He paused and glanced down at their hands folded as one. "As far as Katie is concerned, *you* are her mother and Ta Ming is her brother." The russet glow washed over his face again. He let go of Kulien's hands and rose to stride across the room and stared out the window.

Kulien weighed the words, the actions, and the expressions. Could Dr. Ben be suggesting that they marry? He was a kind man, a good man, but he was Lucy's husband, and much older than she. What should she do? He had done so much for her, and would lose face by her refusal. But she didn't love him. Not like that. Even though Marshall Whitfield was married to another, she continued to think of him as her husband, the only man she would ever love as a woman loves a man. Yet Dr. Ben had saved her life; he owned her papers, therefore, he owned her. She made her decision, and must choose her words carefully.

Rising from the chair, Kulien crossed the narrow space between them before gently touching Ben's arm. He turned to her, his face alight with expectancy. "Do you know what I'm suggesting, Colleen?" He took a white cloth from his pocket and wiped at the moisture on his brow. "Can you give me an answer?"

THIRTY-EIGHT

"Yes, I do know what you are saying, Dr. Ben. Your very fine wife, and my dearest friend, is in the grave, and now that Katie is weaned it is time for me to leave this house."

Benjamin began to speak, but Kulien held up a hand. "Forgive me, but I think what you suggest is not possible; so I would like to move into the Presbyterian mission house on Sacramento Street. Lucy spoke of that place often, and she said they would like for me to come help them." She turned her head away from Ben's frown and downcast eyes. "I can cook and clean, and teach English to the slave girls who have been rescued by Reverend Clark and his helpers. I believe there are living quarters in that large house for Ta Ming and me." She ventured to meet his eyes. "It is time for me to care for myself and my son."

Ben's teeth clenched as he lowered his head, his ruddy complexion was now pale, and his eyes vacant. A gasp of air escaped his partially opened lips. "You *want* to leave? That is *not* what I had in mind for you, Colleen!"

Kulien nodded and folded her hands in front of her. "It is the only solution. I will be protected at the mission; and there will be no more bad talk. Perhaps they can find someone else to care for you and Katie, even though I promised Lucy I would be here for both of you." Her face warmed as she imagined the talk that went beyond a kidnap plot.

"But Colleen, I hoped. . .."

"Dr. Ben, sir, you are my good friend. You saved my life, and the life of my child, and I will be forever grateful. The gods brought me to your home, and I was able to take Katie to my breast until she became stronger. She will be fine without me. I learned many things about living in America here in your home; but now it is time for me to leave."

Before he could make another objection, Kulien turned and moved quickly across the room to the cot at the far end of the small living room. She dropped to her knees and drew a small chest from under her cot. "In the morning, Ta Ming and I will move to the mission house. Will you please advise them that I am coming?"

Kulien's last night in the house of Dr. Benjamin O'Kelly was long and dark. The moon hid its face; the stars refused to glow; the house sighed in the stillness; and Kulien tossed and turned. Lumps in the cot jabbed into her back, and Katie, who slept in a small crate next to Ta Ming, woke up crying. When Kulien heard Benjamin pacing behind the closed bedroom door, emptiness swelled within her heart, threatening to change her decision. After she quieted Katie by patting her back and humming a song, she slept fitfully. There were dreams, dreams of barbarians kidnapping Ta Ming and of Katie suffocating in her sleep. When night visions brought Lucy from her grave, accusing, "You promised to take care of Katie and Ben," Kulien sat up, her nightgown damp with perspiration.

Had her decision to move to the mission been a mistake? What kind of life could she expect to have there with strangers?

By the time a faint light filtered through the curtains, though, Kulien was convinced she had made the right choice. She would miss Dr. Ben, of course, but her greatest loss would be Katie. She loved that baby! What would become of the tiny little girl with emerald eyes so like her own?

"Are you sure this is what you want?" Ben asked the next morning. His eyes were circled with red and he thrust his hands into his pockets.

"It is best," she answered, buttoning the frogs on her quilted jacket. "I think the bad talk is about a Chinese woman and an unmarried white man in a house alone. You will lose the trust of those you came to help if such talk continues."

"But if you would only listen to my plan. . .."

Kulien turned away before he could finish his words, and leaned over Katie's bed to touch the soft forehead with the back of her hand. The fever was gone. The little girl opened her eyes and reached for Kulien. "Mama!"

Kulien's heart sank as she lifted the baby and held her close. "My little cricket! You must promise to come see me at the mission." She closed her eyes and pressed her face against the soft curls.

"She calls you, 'Mama'. I don't want you to leave, Colleen. I couldn't speak my intentions last night. You must know that I don't want to adopt you. I want to *marry* you!" His voice faltered, and even in the early morning light, the rosy glow was visible as it spread over his face.

Kulien ignored his proposal and busied herself by changing Katie's clothes. She tried to form the right words in her mind, words that would convince, but not hurt Dr. Ben. To marry him would solve many problems. She and Ta Ming would have a permanent home and protection. Her beloved Katie would be a true daughter, and Ta Ming would have a sister. Yes, so many problems would be removed.

She set Katie back in her little bed with a rag doll and faced Benjamin. "I am honored beyond words that you would want me to be your wife." She bowed her head and clasped her hands at her waist. "But this is not my destiny. Although Marshall Whitfield has taken another wife, he will always be my only husband."

Ben nodded and rubbed a hand over his stubbly chin. "I understand, Colleen, and I hope that someday you will find the happiness you deserve, happiness I hoped to give you."

"Thank you, Dr. Ben. I believe you would be a most wonderful husband to me, and father to Ta Ming. But as you know, I have experienced married love only one time, and that is enough for me." She felt the blood rise to her face as she remembered that night in the summerhouse.

The ride to the mission house on Sacramento Street was less than a mile west of Dr. Ben's house, but to Kulien it seemed that the trip was to the other side of the world. For the passing of several seasons, she had lived within the safety and familiarity of the O'Kelly's home and fenced-in yard; now she was leaving the past behind once more.

Dr. Ben directed the horse to take them through the Chinese Quarter so Kulien could get a clear vision of the area where her people had settled. She sat on the bench beside Dr. Ben holding Ta Ming on one knee, and Katie on the other. There were mostly men on the streets, men with black pants, jackets and flat black shoes, their queues hanging down their backs like long tails. They passed open stores where the aroma of freshly roasted ducks wafted past them. Hawking their wares, storekeepers called from the doorways. The street was bumpy with cobblestones, and Kulien feared that the children would be shaken from her arms.

Dr. Ben didn't speak as they jostled up one street and down the next. Buildings of brick and some of clapboard had sprung up in every direction since Kulien had arrived in San Francisco. Merchants of every kind had opened shops or operated from a corner near the road. Men stopped to stare and point at Kulien and Dr. Ben as the cart rumbled past. She blushed when she heard some of them call her names, linking her in a familiar way with Dr. Ben. He glanced at her and said in a low tone, "Ignore them. They're ignorant and are only repeating what they've heard."

Katie sat quietly without a sound, while Ta Ming waved his chubby arms at the sight of jugglers and acrobats performing on a street corner to a gathering crowd. "Quiet, son," Kulien whispered, holding him closer. "We will soon be at our new home. Then you may laugh and run as much as you wish."

Outside the section known as "Little China," there were many more unadorned two-story brick buildings and wooden shacks. They climbed from the water's edge on the east to the top of the hill rising in the west. On the flat ground at the foot of the hill were rows of markets, and nearby, on the rise of the hill, many of the merchants had built homes. Although there were houses going up in the north and south, most of San Francisco's population had settled on the eastern slope of the hill where the weather was the mildest.

Surprised to see the multitudes of her race mingling with foreigners, Kulien watched bearded miners shove the reticent citizens of the Middle Kingdom as they passed. The Chinese only nodded their heads in apology and shuffled on, their queues swinging across their backs. There was cursing and shouting, and Kulien covered Ta Ming's and Katie's eyes with both her hands when she saw a barbarian waving a large pistol in the face of another man.

Only a few white women were on the crowded streets, and they held fast to their husbands' arms, their eyes straight ahead. They wore the same clothing she remembered seeing on Elizabeth Whitfield: heavy skirts of dark cloth, jackets buttoned to the chin, and hair hidden under flower-decorated hats. But there were no Chinese women in sight.

She had begun to wonder if they would ever arrive at the mission house when Ben jumped from the cart to tie the horse to a wooden post. "Here we are," he said without a hint of enthusiasm in his voice.

Kulien stared at the building that was to be her new home. The brown two-story, frame house with tall windows and a very high roof, was much larger than the O'Kelly's, but she knew they housed many Chinese girls rescued from the bagnios.

"Let me help you." Ben put out his hands to take Ta Ming first, then a tearful Katie from her arms. He set the children on grass that bordered the road before helping Kulien down from the cart, letting his hands rest on her waist longer than necessary. Speaking comforting words to Katie, Ben motioned to Kulien, who now held Ta Ming, to follow him up the steps and onto a wide porch.

Anna Clark opened the door before Benjamin knocked. "Dr. Ben, you have brought Kulien and her lovely son to us! We are so delighted that you've decided to come help us," she said to Kulien. She held out her arms, speaking softly to Ta Ming. "Come in, dears," she said in faltering Cantonese. "This house is known throughout San Francisco as the 'Home for Slave Girls.' You are most welcome and safe here!"

Benjamin nodded at Mrs. Clark, and then glanced at Kulien. "As I told you last night, Colleen speaks excellent English, even though her first language is Mandarin Chinese. She does understand and speak a little Cantonese."

Kulien spoke for herself, "I hope also to improve my Cantonese because I understand that most of the Chinese here are from Southern China."

"Well, my dear, I can only say that we are most delighted to have you live in this home! We will do all we can to help you and your son adjust to living in a mission house."

"Thank you," Kulien said. She set Ta Ming down on the faded, but colorful carpet, and folded her hands at her waist before bowing to Mrs. Clark.

"Oh, child," she said, touching Kulien's elbow. "You needn't bow to me. We are all God's servants here. There is no bowing, but we are respectful of each other regardless of whether one comes from the bagnios or from a European university!"

Dr. Ben stepped aside and with a flat and unemotional voice, said, "Mrs. Clark, your husband thought it would be better for Colleen, that is, *Kulien*, to live here since Lucy is gone." His eyes rested on Kulien, who looked up at him with gratitude.

"I am glad you took my husband's advice." Mrs. Clark watched Kulien take Katie from Ben's arms and hold her close. Tears, like brilliant emeralds, glistened in her eyes, but she didn't bother to wipe them away. She kissed Katie's thin face and tipped her chin to look in the child's eyes. "Oh, my little cricket. Don't forget me!" Without looking at the doctor, she spoke in a commanding tone, "You must bring her often. It is too much for this baby to lose both her mother and her *amah* in so short a time."

"If it is agreeable with you?" Ben asked, his attention on Mrs. Clark. "Kulien has been like a mother to Katie for months—even before Lucy passed on." He shifted from one booted foot to the other. "I don't know how we, that is, *she* will get along without her."

Kulien felt a stab of guilt and remorse as Dr. Ben reached out to take Katie.

"Of course, you may bring her anytime!" Anna Clark lifted her chin and smiled at Kulien. "Now I must ask you to say, 'good-bye.' It is nearly time for our dinner."

Kulien kissed Katie's head, inhaling deeply of the soft golden curls; and with a sense of desolation, she handed her back to Benjamin. He held the crying child in his arms, cooing tender words of love and comfort. His eyes were on Kulien, but he neither smiled nor spoke.

She opened her mouth to speak, if only to wish him well, but she had no words either. It was time again to leave those she loved. Time to begin a new life.

THIRTY-NINE

The next month passed quickly as Kulien and Ta Ming settled into the mission house as the newest members of a large family. The young girls and women, who had been rescued from the bagnios and bordellos of San Francisco, had immediately received Kulien as their teacher and confidante. Ta Ming, with his antics and baby-talk, that mingled both English and Mandarin, delighted the girls. For the first time in many months, they smiled and laughed as they chased Ta Ming through the house and watched him smear porridge on his face. The secure and loving atmosphere in the mission gave Kulien, as well as the other girls, a sense of home.

One evening, with her attention fastened on the moon overhead, Kulien sat with six girls on the front porch of the "Home for Slave Girls." *It's time for "Moon Festival" throughout China*, she thought. Even in America, the Chinese celebrated the mid-autumn holiday. Mrs. Clark had purchased moon cakes to comfort the girls and remind them of happier days in China. Receiving them with open hands, the girls smiled shyly, their eyes brightening with joy. They whispered among themselves as they examined the round cakes decorated with images of rabbits, flowers or fish. Reverend Clark said nothing when the cakes were presented, but only scowled and turned away.

"Oh, Horace," Anna Clark said, as he walked off the porch, "it's not a sacrilege to bolster these dear spirits with a remembrance of more pleasant days."

"It's a heathen custom, Anna, and I simply do not approve!"

Anna Clark continued to distribute the delicious cakes filled with sugar, almonds and orange peel. "It all depends on how you look at it," she argued. "We put up a Christmas tree in December. Some folks consider that a heathen custom."

As Horace Clark continued to scowl, Anna set him straight. "The Moon Festival is only that—a festival. Beautiful poetry has been written about this night." She sighed with exasperation. "Well," Anna said, with renewed energy, "perhaps we can use their symbols to teach them about Christianity." She turned toward Kulien, who listened intently to their discussion. "Kulien, will you please tell the girls that the round shape of the cake is symbolic of eternal life?"

Kulien, although unsure of Mrs. Clark's meaning, repeated the words.

"Say that the God we worship loves them and gives eternal life to all who believe in his Son. Tell the girls we love them too."

Kulien spoke the words in her rapidly-improving Cantonese dialect, and watched the pitiful girls nod as they held the cakes in their hands, inhaling deeply of the delicious aromas. Even as she repeated the words, she felt confused about the Invisible God of whom the missionaries were so convinced.

Later that night after Kulien had put Ta Ming to bed and the other girls had retired, she went back to the porch to watch the moon glide across the sky. Unfolding the napkin in her lap, Kulien pinched off a bite of the moist cake hidden in its folds, savoring the sweetness and remembering the happy days of childhood—Father—Jiang—home.

Anna stepped through the front door, her petticoats swishing as she walked. She sat on the step beside Kulien. "What is it dear? Are you feeling lonely?"

Kulien nodded. "I have been in America for more than a year, and not a day passes that I don't think of my country and my family." With her gaze still fastened on the heavens, she added, "I find comfort knowing the same moon smiles on my father's garden. I often wonder if I'll ever see him again or if Ta Ming will one day stand on the land of his forefathers."

"Well, my child," Anna said, "if that is what you want, and it is God's plan, you and Ta Ming will return to China one day."

Kulien glanced down at the partially eaten cake in her hands. "I don't understand your God; and I'm not even sure what it is that I do want."

As autumn faded into winter and dark clouds released their burden to quench the earth, Kulien buttoned her quilted jacket high under her chin and hid her unhappiness under a coat of activity. When she finished conducting English classes of reading and writing, she kept busy in the kitchen helping to prepare meals for the growing number of rescued slave girls.

Evelyn Timmons, a young unmarried woman, had recently arrived from the east coast to assist in the rescues, and Kulien felt gratitude at having an American friend close to her own age.

"Kulien," Evelyn said one morning as they were cleaning up the kitchen, "I think you are very beautiful."

Warmth spread over Kulien's face and she lowered her eyes, speaking softly, "I—I am the same as any other Chinese girl."

Stepping closer, Evelyn's voice was persuasive, "Oh, no, you are nothing like the poor wretches we bring to the mission. I know you haven't been subjected to the tortures they have known, but your features are so fine—elegant actually. And your green eyes! Well, I've never seen another Chinese with eyes that color!" She paused and smiled as Kulien lifted her head. "You know what I think when I see you? You remind me of an ivory carving I once saw in a museum—a carving of a Chinese empress."

"You're very kind," Kulien said, her long lashes veiling her eyes as her full lips parted in a smile. "I thank you for your words. Perhaps I resemble the mother I never knew."

"Your mother? Would I be too forward if I asked you about her?"

The silence stretched between them before Kulien answered. "I don't know much about her. My father met and married a British woman when he went to England to study as a young man. My unusual coloring is a result of their union. My mother died soon after my birth. As for my father's family, I've been told that his ancestors were of royal blood, dating back to the Ming Dynasty."

"That's fascinating!" Evelyn responded, her eyes wide with wonder. "Now I understand why you carry yourself with such dignity, and why the girls show you so much respect. They listen to everything you say and I overhear them talking about your kindness to them."

"I do care about them." Kulien lowered her eyelids again, bringing the horrors of the slave block to mind. "No woman deserves to be treated as they were—like animals!"

Kulien's first months at the mission were so occupied with teaching English classes and instructing the girls in the arts of cooking and sewing that she had little time to think of Katie or Dr. Ben. When her questions about them were ignored by Anna Clark, she stopped asking. She had even relegated Marshall's memory to the most hidden part of her soul.

Kulien found happiness in the hours given to Ta Ming and his newly discovered skills of running and hiding. His constantly busy arms and legs and perpetually happy disposition kept everyone in good spirits. A small child in a household of women gave the home a feeling of normalcy and hope; and Kulien, with the others, laughed when Ta Ming toddled into the parlor with a flour-dusted face, or when he fell asleep under a large pile of laundry.

One night, after Evelyn and the Clarks had left for a raid on the bagnios, and Ta Ming was tucked safely in his bed, Kulien decided to pay Dr. Ben and Katie a visit. Anna Clark's silence about them concerned her. Was there sickness? Did Dr. Ben continue to suffer from Lucy's death—and her rejection of his marriage proposal? Since no one brought news of her former family, she would just have to discover the answers for herself.

"Watch Ta Ming," she instructed one of her more dependable students. "He sleeps now, but if he wakes, you may give him a drink of water. I'll be gone for an hour or two," she added.

"Without a protector?" The woman covered her mouth and her eyes stared in disbelief.

"I will be careful. See, I dress like a man." She pointed to the full trousers and padded jacket. "And I wear a man's hat." Kulien had braided her long hair into a queue, and pulled a dark skull cap over her forehead. "I shall return before dawn. Stay in my room and sleep in my bed. I won't be missed."

The streets at night reminded Kulien of a darkened room invaded by cockroaches. Now and then, in the glow of recently installed gas lights, a figure darted furtively from the shadows only to disappear into an alley or behind a closed door. She felt, more than saw, Chinese men, as they shuffled among the whites, speaking to one another in soft tones. She scurried past alleys where men searched out women for hire, staying in the darkness so that she would not be recognized. She heard the singsong calls of prostitutes as they tapped on screens of their cages vying for customers. The pounding of her heart rose and fell with the rhythm of the city—one moment it raced with fear; the next, sinking with sorrow.

The thoughts urging her up one dark street and down another were that she must see Katie to be assured that the little girl was well. Why hadn't Dr. Ben brought the child to see her as he had promised? As she considered these things, she felt a dark foreboding that there was trouble at the O'Kelly house.

By the time she reached the little home, surrounded by a picket fence, the night air swirled around her in billows of fog. When she opened the creaking gate, Ben appeared in the doorway holding a kerosene lamp overhead.

"Oh, thank God! It's you, Colleen!" His words carried a message of grief to her troubled soul. "What are you doing out at night? Don't you realize how dangerous it is?" He rushed to meet her, holding out a hand. "Please, come in! You're an answer to my prayers."

Like the claws of a predatory bird, alarm clutched Kulien's chest. Her hand went to her heart. "What is wrong? Oh, please tell me that Katie is well!"

Still holding the lantern overhead, Ben warned, "Before you come in, I must tell you something." He set the lantern on a table inside the doorway and Kulien watched the orange glow flicker over the room in melancholy waves.

"I was worried about Katie," she said, pulling off the skull cap. Long strands of hair, like black silk threads fell over her face, and she brushed them aside.

"I thought you would sense that there was trouble. You were always so attuned to Katie—to her every need and mood." Benjamin put an arm around her shoulders, and brushed his lips over her head. "I don't know how to tell you, but. . ."

"It *is* Katie, isn't it?" Kulien felt as if her heart had stopped and the floor began to move under her feet. Swaying, she leaned against Dr. Ben as he led her farther into the room.

Inside the familiar living room, quietness hung like a shroud. Katie's wooden crib stood in the center of the floor, candles flickering at both the head and the foot. A small figure was lying on the bed, covered with a soft pink blanket. Kulien shivered, and fighting panic, she stepped away from Benjamin and edged closer to the still form.

"Katie!"

Golden curls framed the tiny face, pale in death. Emerald eyes had closed for the last time. Rosy lips would never smile again. With a shaking hand, Kulien reached out to touch Katie's cheek. Her skin was cold and hard to the touch. "Oh, no, my little Cricket!" Kulien fell to her knees, her eyes still on the dead child. "Where have the gods taken you? Why, you? Why?"

Kulien prostrated herself on the floor, the questions rising with each sob. How long she lay there, she didn't know, or care; but in the deep recesses of her broken heart, she was aware of Ben's voice. His hand rested on her shoulder. "Come, Colleen. I know this is a terrible shock to you. I should have let you know that she had been failing."

Kulien rose to her knees, and Ben helped her stand. He drew her close, pressing her head against his shoulder. Minutes passed before she spoke, "When?"

"Early this morning. You know that she's always been sickly, but she had been very ill for only a few days."

"Why wasn't I told? For weeks, I asked Anna about you and Katie, but she would tell me nothing." Kulien made no effort to move, but kept her face buried against Dr. Ben's rough flannel shirt.

He stroked her hair before answering. "I asked them not to tell you. I didn't want you to worry or to blame yourself."

"Blame myself? Was it my fault that she died?"

"No! Of course not!" Ben sighed and rested his chin on her head. "She did miss you—and so did I. But you know that she has always been frail. Then when she got the fever, she stopped eating. She cried for you, Colleen."

"Now I cry for her." Years of pent-up grief finally broke through Kulien's façade of serenity. It no longer mattered if she lost face. Everyone she loved had departed, one by one.

Unaware of how long she sobbed, she finally pulled away and stared first at Katie, then let her tear-filled eyes rest on Dr. Ben. "To give one's heart to another brings much pain," she said, enunciating each word. "My father once told me that to know pain is to know life; and to experience sorrow is to appreciate joy." She stopped to wipe away the tears. "Do you think Lucy's invisible God will somehow bring joy through this great sorrow?"

"I don't know, Colleen," Ben replied. "But you must know that you bring me joy. I can't tell you how much it means for you to be here tonight." Ben's fingers traced her chin as he gazed deeply into her eyes. His face flushed and he drew back. "But I think it is for the best if you leave now. I'm not sure I trust myself."

"I don't understand." Kulien frowned, suddenly feeling deserted.

"It's just as well." He cleared his throat. "I'll take you home in the cart. As the hour grows later, your presence on the streets becomes even more dangerous."

FORTY

Kulien was back in the hold of a ship, riding out a violent storm—up one giant wave and down the next. A loud explosion, then a sharp jolt awakened her from her dream. Terrified, she stared through the darkness as the rapid vibrations continued. Ta Ming cried out, and as Kulien rose to comfort him, the floor shifted and she fell to her knees.

Lifting Ta Ming from his bed, Kulien suddenly felt sick to her stomach. What had happened? Just as suddenly as the shaking started, it stopped. Voices called out, feet shuffled, pans clattered. "Is everyone all right?" Horace Clark's voice boomed through the mission house. "I believe we've had an earthquake. Come to the kitchen at once—all of you! We must pray for the people of our city!"

With a woolen cloak wrapped around Ta Ming and herself, Kulien obeyed the orders along with the rest of the occupants. An earthquake? Could it be possible? Here in San Francisco?

By the time all the slave girls had made their way to the kitchen, Reverend and Mrs. Clark had lit the lamps, and Evelyn stood at the wood stove boiling water for tea. Even before Reverend Clark asked them to bow their heads, he began to pray. "We thank Thee, Almighty God, for sparing our lives. May we continue to serve Thy people as long as Thou givest us breath."

As soon as he stopped praying, the chatter rose in pitch as the girls became aware of what had happened. "But I thought," Kulien said, when Evelyn joined her with a cup of tea, "that the newspaper said it was unlikely that San Francisco would ever have an earthquake."

"You're right," Evelyn nodded. "After that heavy quake in Los Angeles last July, those, who seem to know about such things, reported that we here in the north should have no fear of earthquakes." She shrugged her shoulders. "But I suppose February 15[th]1856 will be in the history books now."

Most of the day, the inhabitants of the mission discussed the unusual phenomenon; however by evening, the excitement had subsided. While preparing dinner for the girls, Evelyn drew Kulien aside. "Mrs. Clark told me that we are expecting a guest tonight." Her deep gray eyes shone with interest. "He's a friend of yours."

Laying aside a large ladle, Kulien tilted her head. "A friend of mine?"

Evelyn smiled. "Dr. O'Kelly is coming to talk to Reverend and Mrs. Clark—about spiritual matters, they said."

Kulien felt the warmth spread over her cheeks. "He is a fine man. I haven't seen him since Katie's funeral. That was months ago."

"Anna said he requested that you be present when he calls."

After the girls retired for the night, and Kulien had put Ta Ming to bed, she joined the Clarks and Evelyn in the parlor. The women sat on chairs against the wall while Benjamin O'Kelly and Reverend Clark sat near the fireplace, discussing the earthquake's destruction and other events of the day. They talked about a man by the name of Jose Limantour, who claimed title to one-third of the city.

"What is one to think?" asked Horace Clark, pulling at his beard. "It seems strange to me that the man claims Mexico granted the land to him in '43, yet he waits until now to come forward."

As the men's voices droned on, Kulien's mind wandered, hearing only bits and pieces of a conversation about a court trial concerning a man who murdered General Richardson. In China, she mused, the judgment would have been quick—and final.

Evelyn nudged Kulien. "Prior to your coming into the room, Reverend Clark introduced me to your friend." She lowered her head, "He does seem very nice—as you said."

Before Kulien could respond, Benjamin spoke, "I'm sure you're wondering why I wanted to speak to you tonight," he said to Horace Clark. "And you, too, Mrs. Clark." Pausing, he motioned toward Kulien. "I wanted Colleen to hear what I have to say."

Benjamin combed fingers through his unruly red hair before he went on. He leaned forward, his face intense, his hands gripping the arms of the chair. "At one time, I was a believer. Lucy and I planned to serve God in China where I believed I could help heal souls as well as bodies." He inhaled deeply before continuing. "There was so much death on the trail—women—babies. Something changed in me." His eyes swept a slow glance across the room as if he were again seeing the suffering. "I asked myself—and I asked God, 'Why do these innocent people have to endure so much pain? Why?'"

"But Ben," Horace Clark said, in a soft voice, "you *are* a doctor. Surely you had accepted the reality of death and disease."

"I thought I had, too. But then I lost Lucy—and now Katie. At times, I feel it's more than I can bear."

Horace placed a large hand over Ben's. "What is it that you want me to do for you?"

"I want to change." He pulled a handkerchief from his pocket and blew his nose. "I saw Lucy's faith, and even felt an unseen strength when Katie died." His eyes met Kulien's. "Even this dear girl from the other side of the world was used by God to comfort me."

Kulien squirmed at his words and passionate expression.

"What I'm trying to ask is, will you pray for me? I want to come back to God, and spend the rest of my life serving Him."

Kulien watched in amazement as Evelyn joined the others who knelt on the floor to pray. When Horace Clark finished and they all rose to their feet, there seemed to be a festive spirit in the room. Kulien could not comprehend the ways of these foreigners, but only watched and listened. Perhaps one day, she would understand their belief in only one God.

Pink hues of the spring sky began to overcome the somber shades of winter, and Kulien grew restless. Her longing for home, for China, increased daily. After mentioning how she yearned for her birthplace to Anna Clark, that very day Anna and Horace took her into the heart of Little China.

Sitting on the wagon seat between them, Kulien stared in wonder at the changes that had taken place since arriving two years earlier. Stores now spread down Dupont Street, spilling onto both sides of Jackson between Stockton and Kearney streets.

Reverend Clark waved an arm as if pronouncing a benediction. "Your people have made themselves at home here,

Kulien. They have general stores, doctors, restaurants, boarding houses, silversmiths, and even a candle factory. I am proud to know such an industrious and self-supporting people!"

The cool morning air caused Anna Clark to snuggle deeper under her high coat collar. "But Kulien", she said, "as you know many of the San Franciscans are strongly opposed to the Chinese. That's one more reason for you to be careful about going out alone."

Long queues swinging at their backs, hordes of men walked quietly by, tending to their business. Moments passed before Kulien spoke, "Why do the people oppose them? They cause no harm."

"It's the politicians. The Chinese arrive daily by the shipload. At first, they were looked upon as interesting and colorful, but as time goes by Europeans and other whites complain that 'John Chinaman' takes gold out, but gives nothing back. They accuse the Chinese of being ignorant and uncivilized..."

Anna Clark interrupted, "But our so-called *enlightened* countrymen choose to ignore China's six thousand years of established order." She shook her head. "While our ancestors were living in caves and wearing animal hides, your ancestors were building pavilions of lacquer and gold, and clothing themselves in satin and silk."

Kulien felt a warm surge of affection toward these usually serious people. They truly loved the Chinese, and showed no partiality to those who shared their skin color. "Perhaps the Americans are only afraid because they don't understand our customs." As she finished speaking, they heard strains of music coming from a gambling club. Kulien smiled at the sound of the *erhu,* a two-stringed fiddle. "I can understand that our music is not tuned to Western ears."

They passed a garbage-strewn alley, and Kulien covered her nose with the hem of her jacket. "But I feel certain that the Americans are as distressed over the bagnios and slave traffic as we are!" Thinking of the slave girls held in caged rooms down that alley, she shuddered.

"Oh, the Chinese aren't the only people dealing in prostitution in this city." Horace Clark shook the reins and the horse turned down the road leading back to the mission house. "There is sin and vice on every side, among all people." He spoke so low, that he seemed to be talking to himself. "I pray that we can make a difference in some of the lives."

"We do, Horace," Anna assured him. "We do!"

Kulien agreed. For as the days and weeks turned into months, slave girls were rescued and brought to the mission, girls that had been imported by the thousands through the Hip Yee Tong, the secret society that dealt with prostitution trafficking. The girls and women ranged in age between sixteen and twenty-five, and were consigned to the bagnios and brothels of Spofford and Sullivan Alleys. Some of the rescued girls left the mission as wives of Chinese merchants, only to be sold again to the dealers in flesh. At times, it seemed like a hopeless task, but as Evelyn Timmons joined the Clarks in the rescue operations, one more person caught the zeal to aid the "Daughters of Joy."

Kulien noticed that, in the last few weeks, another interest had brought a sparkle to Evelyn's eyes. Dr. Benjamin O'Kelly had begun visiting regularly, and often accompanied Evelyn and the Clarks on their excursions to the alleys of Little China.

When arriving at the mission, Dr. Ben always greeted Kulien with affection and brought a little trinket to Ta Ming; but his eyes sought out Evelyn. When she entered the room, his cheeks flushed; and he often spilled tea on his clean shirt, or bumped against a chair as he rose to bow to her. Evelyn, also, became flustered in his presence; and her usually low voice rose in pitch before she ended her sentences with soft laughter. It was obvious to Kulien that her friends were falling in love, and she felt only joy for both of them.

As crime rose in the city, the missionaries' conversations were often given to the problems of sin and death, and their beliefs about Heaven and Hell. They also discussed how the Vigilance Committee had taken it upon themselves to bring about justice by hanging James Casey, the man who had murdered the editor of the *Evening Bulletin,* and then executing Charles Cora for the murder of General Richardson. Their discussions often ended in prayer for both the criminals and their victims. Kulien tried to align their words with what she had learned from Elizabeth Whitfield, but she continued to pray to the gods she had known from childhood.

One day in early summer, Evelyn, holding a newspaper, approached Kulien with a scowl on her pretty face. "Kulien please help me understand what I read in the paper today."

Kulien shrugged her shoulders, a question on her face. "I don't know how I can help; but what did you read?"

"I hope you won't take this as a criticism, but you are the only Chinese person I know who is well-educated."

"Yes, what is it, Evelyn? Don't be concerned about offending me."

"This is what I read in the paper today," she said, pointing to an article on the front page. "One of the many reasons people are so up in arms about the Chinese is how they put strangers out of their houses when death is near. It is said that because the Chinese are superstitious, they think it is bad luck for a stranger to die in their house."

Kulien closed her eyes, trying to remember what her father had taught her about that custom. "Evelyn, I am not saying that this practice is a good thing, but the reason is practical, not superstition. If a person dies in another's house, the living one is liable for funeral expenses. My people have seen much poverty and starvation; they conserve what they have for the living."

Evelyn seemed to be satisfied with Kulien's answer, and set aside the newspaper to reach for Kulien's hands. She inhaled deeply and bit her bottom lip as a pink glow spread over her cheeks. "I have something to tell you. I want you to be the first to know." Her voice sang with excitement. "Benjamin wanted me to tell you before we give our goods news to the Clarks."

Kulien's spirit rose with joy as she waited for the news she had been certain was forthcoming.

"Benjamin and I are to be married!" Evelyn's dove-gray eyes sparkled with happy tears. "I can't believe it! He loves me, Kulien! And I love him. I am so blessed!" She raised her eyes heavenward, before asking, "Oh, have you ever been in love?"

Kulien lifted Ta Ming, who had been playing at her feet, and held him close. "Yes."

Evelyn covered her mouth and her eyes widened. "Please forgive me. Of course you have! That was a foolish and rude question."

Kulien only held Ta Ming closer, wondering why she felt a mixture of joy as well as sadness at Evelyn's announcement. "When will you be married?"

Evelyn lifted her shoulders and the white lace collar caressed her softly rounded chin. "Soon. Benjamin wants to marry this summer. It's his desire to take me to New York to meet his family. We'll sail around the Cape before the winter's storms."

Reaching out to touch Evelyn's shoulder, she said what was in her heart. "I have only happiness for you. Dr. Ben is a good man, and you'll be a fine wife for him."

Surprised that she had shown the kind of emotion usually expressed by Westerners, she watched Evelyn leave the room to tell the Clarks her good news. She recalled the warmth and passion she had seen in Benjamin those many months ago. He needed a wife, and Evelyn would make him happy. She would give him fat, healthy babies, and put a smile back on his face.

FORTY-ONE

That summer afternoon, a hazy blanket lingered over the bay; but the weather mattered little to Evelyn Timmons. The entire direction of her life was about to change; it was her wedding day. "Oh, Kulien, I'm so nervous!" Evelyn pressed fingers against her rosy cheeks. "I love Benjamin so much, it frightens me."

Kulien brushed Evelyn's long wavy hair, remembering Jiang's loving touch as she prepared her charge for a Chinese wedding. What a contrast! Instead of a heavy red gown, a blue satin one; there was no cumbersome headdress, but instead, a matching blue hat decorated with white roses. The greatest contrast was that Evelyn knew and loved her groom.

Kulien twisted golden strands into a chignon and fastened it with ivory pins. "It's good to love the man you marry," Kulien said, remembering the vows she and Marshall Whitfield exchanged. "You will be happy and have beautiful babies."

Evelyn's cheeks flushed again. "I know nothing about marriage, Kulien. I've seen only the result of men's passions in the bagnios, and I'm afraid of the intimate part."

Kulien's dark green eyes twinkled as she caught Evelyn's reflection in the mirror. "You don't need to be afraid of Dr. Ben. He will be a kind and considerate husband."

"How can you be sure?"

"Ta Ming's father and I loved one another. He was most gentle and patient in taking my maidenhood. There will be some discomfort; but you won't mind because you love him."

As Kulien placed the wide-brimmed hat on Evelyn's head, the sun broke through the fog, splashing glorious rays across the room, and lighting Evelyn's face with a heavenly glow.

"Thank you for your words!" Before brushing Kulien's cheek with a kiss, she hugged her tightly. "I will miss you so very much. And so will Benjamin."

Drawing a deep breath, Kulien asked, "Will you return to San Francisco after your trip to New York?" She would miss both of them as well, and hoped that she would see them again.

"Oh, yes! Ben anticipates raising enough support for us to go to China. That's where we both want to be."

"That's where I want to be also," Kulien said, her mind far across the Peaceful Sea. "Perhaps one day we will find ourselves visiting one another on the banks of the Yangtze."

The rest of the day was a whirl of activity: the wedding at the Presbyterian Church, a dinner reception in the dining hall, and finally, a tearful departure at the docks.

As Evelyn and Benjamin O'Kelly waited to board the steamer, *John L. Stephens*, Ben explained that he had made arrangements to go through the Isthmus of Panama, a much safer journey than around Cape Horn. "We'll have a new experience of riding in a train for the seven miles across the Isthmus before boarding another ship bound for New York Harbor."

Before taking Evelyn's hand and starting up the gangplank, Benjamin whispered in Kulien's ear, "Keep your dreams, Colleen. You're in America for a reason. One day you'll know your purpose and the freedom you've been searching for."

There were more "goodbyes" and a few tears as Kulien and the Clarks watched Benjamin and his bride wave from the deck rail. They continued to wave until the steamer disappeared from sight.

As the days grew shorter, so did Kulien's patience. "I thank you for your care and kindness," she said to Anna Clark one morning, "and I do enjoy teaching the girls, but I wish to do more." She paused before going on. "Would it be possible for me to assume Evelyn's work? I want to help in the rescue operations."

Anna Clark glanced across the breakfast table at her husband. "What do you think, Horace? We certainly could use more help since both Evelyn and Benjamin left." She waited until she had his full attention. "I think Kulien would win the confidence of the girls, especially since she's Chinese."

Horace Clark's heavy eyebrows drew together, and his jaw clenched under his beard. "No."

Never one to accept a blunt response, Anna walked to his side of the table with hands on her hips. "No? Is that all you have to say? You must have a good reason to answer so quickly, and without any consideration of my words."

"I have considered the possibility. It's too dangerous for her to be seen in the Chinese Quarter."

A heavy sigh escaped Anna's lips. "They *know* she's here, Horace. We've taken her with us when we went shopping. Besides, there are no secrets in Little China. Her people know about the 'big-foot, half-breed Chinee girl who live with 'Mericans,'" Anna said, affecting Pidgin. "I think they would be afraid to kidnap her!"

Tugging at his beard, Horace peered over his round spectacles at Kulien. "Well, wife, you do have a good argument. You might even be right." He shrugged his wide shoulders, looking up at Anna. "We could use the help."

Kulien leaned forward in her chair to hear every word, and smiled within herself as, so often in the past, the minister gave in to his wife's arguments.

The following night, after Kulien had been disguised in the clothes of a coolie, Reverend and Mrs. Clark, accompanied by a red-faced policeman, warned her about her first of many trips into the dark alleys of Little China. "Kulien, you must be very quiet and make no movements on your own." Horace nodded toward the uniformed officer. "Sergeant O'Day will do the talking. He has made arrangements with a merchant who is sympathetic to our cause. Dr. Li Kow is a Chinese herbalist who is respected by the community. Thus far he has been able to aid us without harm to himself or his business."

Blinking her eyes to show her understanding, Kulien felt that her heart would burst with excitement. Finally, after years of waiting she was going to help another Chinese woman break free from the bonds of slavery.

After assigning an older woman, who had been at the mission for almost a year, to watch over the household, the four rescuers furtively emerged from the two-story house to climb into the cart waiting to take them to Cooper's Alley. In the back, blankets had been stacked to cover as many girls as they could rescue. Kulien sat next to Anna Clark as the horse trotted down the bumpy road leading to the heart of the Chinese Quarter. "Dr. Li Kow not only dispenses herbal medicines," Anna said, "but he also operates a joss house where many of the men go to worship. We're thankful for his help. Most of the Chinese don't trust Americans, especially missionaries."

"This doctor *trusts* you?"

"Perhaps it would be best to say, 'he fears us.' But his fear is not so much of *us* as it is of John O'Day. This big Irishman must look like a giant to him."

When the horse stopped in front of the medicine shop, four figures slipped silently into a narrow doorway. Sergeant O'Day tapped on the door once. They waited a moment before a roly-poly man shuffled out to join them. Li Kow's eyes darted to each person, resting longer on Kulien than on the others. After glancing over his shoulder, he edged through the doorway beckoning them to follow him down a dark alley.

They followed the man in and out of narrow passages and through low doorways. The stench of the squalid alley was intolerable, and Kulien fought against the hot bile rising into her throat. Several times, she slipped on a slimy substance, thankful that she couldn't see the vileness under her feet. Anna Clark gave no evidence of her dismay, but simply lifted her skirts high enough to avoid contact with the litter.

The policeman carried the only lantern, which cast a flickering glow on the dismal and depressing passage. At last they arrived at a door no more than five feet high. The Chinese herbalist tapped three times.

A peephole opened.

The doctor spoke only one word, "Me."

Down a dim hallway lit by a flickering gas light, they followed yet another man into a large smoky room where men sat around tables playing *fan-tan* and *pai-gow*. The gamblers paid no attention to the intruders as they crossed the room leading to another door and an even smaller room. The men, smoking cigars, turned in unison as an extremely fat man clothed in a red silk gown signaled the gamblers to leave.

Waddling across the room to a large painting of a bulbous-eyed god, the man lifted the picture from the wall revealing a small trapdoor. One by one, following Officer

O'Day, they squeezed through the door into a clammy cubicle reeking with human excrement and death.

The policeman lifted his lantern higher so the Clarks could see through the shadows. There was a small table against one wall with an oil lamp that held no oil, an empty rice bowl and a dry water cup.

"Here's one," O'Day said, bending over a still form. "We're too late. She's dead."

Kulien felt faint as she looked on the emaciated and scantily-clothed body of a young girl, probably no older than twelve years old. Too late? Why?

With a groan, Horace Clark gently wrapped her in a blanket before lifting the light corpse in his arms. "We'll take her with us. She deserves the dignity of a decent burial."

The return trip through smoke-filled rooms, down putrid alleys, and back to the mission house was no more than a blur of hazy images to Kulien. Memories of her confinement in a barracoon flooded her mind, rekindling her desire to help the unwanted females of China. She stared at the lifeless bundle in the back of the cart. "Why was that child left to die?" she asked Anna. "There was no rice or water. No light."

The older woman put an arm around Kulien's shoulders and drew her closer. "There is much evil in this world as you know. I'm sorry your first trip to the bagnios had an unhappy ending." Anna's voice revealed her own weariness and heartache.

"These girls can survive what we call a social disease for only so long. When a prostitute is infected with the 'pox,' and can no longer make money for her owner, she must submit to a death sentence. She is taken to a barren room, like you saw tonight, with only enough rice and water for a day or two." Anna waited for Kulien to nod her understanding before going on. "The man in the red gown, Gao Ping, knows how long the oil and food will last and how long the victim will live." Anna's voice caught in her throat. "Some of these unfortunates take their own lives; others die of starvation. We've heard that when the so-called 'doctors' return, despite the condition of the girl, they leave with a corpse."

Kulien gasped. "You mean if she's not dead, they would kill her?"

Anna nodded, and squeezed Kulien's shoulder. "We do save some, thank God. And you give them hope by teaching them to read and write. Although we didn't save any girls tonight, there's always another night"

When they reached the mission and Kulien had bathed and slipped into her bed, she reached over to touch Ta Ming, who slept soundly on his own little cot beside her. She knew the love Reverend and Mrs. Clark had for her as well as the girls in the mission. If even one suffering girl could be saved and know the same love, the danger and misery would be worthwhile.

As she lay in the dark room, alone with her child she began to think of the changes that had so recently taken place. Evelyn had married Dr. Ben and would spend the rest of her life with him; and Kulien now had the opportunity to be involved in rescuing young women from the bagnios. Where that would lead, she had no idea, but she soon fell asleep, content that she had chosen the right path.

FORTY-TWO

Throughout the next month, Kulien continued to be part of the rescue team; twice they were too late, but three girls, still alive, yet in dire condition, were brought to the mission house. Each day with proper medication and food the Clarks saw a marked improvement in the growing members of their household. Although most of the slave girls would not live long because of disease, their final days would be the happiest they had ever known. Kulien watched and listened with interest, as Horace and Anna Clark spoke to them of God's love. They demonstrated their faith by applying medicine to oozing sores, and cleansing bound feet that had been invaded by maggots. Some of the girls responded with tears of joy when they heard that the Most High God loved them, while others only sneered and smirked, even laughing aloud at such a preposterous idea.

The death and disease of Chinese women and girls took its toll on Kulien's life as well. She often woke in the night, drenched with perspiration, and crying out in fear. Always her nightmares took her into the dark alleys, where tortured women screamed pitifully and grasped at her clothes with claw-like fingers.

One morning, after a sleepless night, Kulien squeezed Ta Ming so hard, he groaned. "Oooh, Mama, you hug too tight!"

"But I love you so much, my son. It's not good for you to stay inside this house when the sun shines brightly and the leaves change from green to many other colors!" Kulien had been careful not to venture outside alone because of the danger; but she avoided mentioning her concern to Ta Ming. She would ask the Clarks to accompany them on an outing.

Holding Ta Ming's hand to keep him from running off to climb up and down the staircase, Kulien approached Anna, who had just finished drying the last of the breakfast dishes. "Anna, I do thank you for the care you've shown me and my son," she began. "I am ashamed to admit that I'm dissatisfied, but. . .."

Anna glanced over her shoulder and folded the towel, hanging it carefully on a hook before she acknowledged Kulien's comments. She nodded her head and clucked her tongue. "I've noticed that you've been restless lately. Is it your longing to return to China?"

Kulien glanced down at Ta Ming, and back at Anna's concerned expression. "It isn't only that. It's true that I want to return to the land of my people one day, but I know that time hasn't come yet."

"What is it then, dear? What's troubling you?"

"Please forgive me if I seem ungrateful. It's only that, for our protection, Ta Ming and I must stay inside when the sun is so warm and bright. I only go out when it's dark, and my spirit yearns to walk through the grass, or spend time in a garden with my son."

Anna nodded with vigor. "Oh, I do understand. We've been overly protective of you. On such a beautiful day, you and Ta Ming must go to the hillsides nearby." She clapped her hands. "I'll speak to Horace at once. I believe a short trip out of the city would do us all good. I become restless, too, especially since it will soon be winter. You know, we have only four girls living here now, including that beautiful woman we rescued from the docks last night. Poor thing, she says an American bought her, and she expected to live in a wealthy home. Anyway," she said, removing her apron, "we'll lock up tight. Our young women are busy with their sewing, and will be safe for a few hours."

An hour later Reverend and Mrs. Clark smiled at Kulien and Ta Ming as they bounced along the rutted road in the back of the buggy. With her attention on Ta Ming, Kulien pointed out objects of interest, speaking both English and Chinese. Her heart pounded with enthusiasm as they left the outskirts of the growing city to ascend the sandy hills on the eastern borders.

"This is beautiful," she said, sweeping her hand to encompass clumps of trees and long grasses, now turning shades of burnished brass. Spreading their wings, birds rose above the clouds, lifting Kulien's spirits as she watched them defy gravity for the freedom of the open sky. In another month, the days would be even shorter, and cold winds would blow off the bay. "May we stop here for a while? The autumn sun is warm, and I want to tell Ta Ming more about the land of his birth."

"Yes, of course. I've brought some cakes and oranges for lunch, and I imagine we're all hungry by now. Horace," Anna said, pointing to a shaded hillside, "you can tie the horse over there."

After they had alighted from the buggy, Kulien shivered with excitement. "Would it be agreeable for me to walk with Ta Ming alone? There is much I want to show him—things he has never seen." She smiled at her son's squeals of joy as he tugged on her hand.

Horace removed his wide-brimmed hat and stroked his beard before sitting on the blanket Anna had spread under the trees. For several quiet moments, he studied the scene around them, and then gave his permission. "You're safe here; there's not a soul for miles around. Just keep this mound of trees in sight so you don't get lost." The man stopped talking and waved at Ta Ming, who gamboled up a slight rise before falling face down in the dirt.

Laughing, Kulien dashed to his side, and in one quick movement had wiped his face, and had taken his hand in hers; then together they started out to explore the rugged terrain.

"Mama, see!" Ta Ming held up a pudgy fist. "Cake!"

"No, son." Kulien shook the cow pie from his hand and led him to a pile of rocks. She squatted in the grasses and carefully plucked a scrap of fur from a bramble. "See, Ta Ming. An animal left some of his fur on this bush so a bird might line her nest with it." She tickled the boy's chin with the brown fuzz and laughed as he crinkled his nose.

At the sound of chirping from a nearby tree, Ta Ming started hopping up and down, "Birdie, Mama, give it to the birdie!"

Kulien held the piece of soft down in her fingertips an instant, and then they watched it float away on a cool breeze.

"Come, little George," she said, using his English name. "We'll go to the top of that knoll. Perhaps from there we can see the ocean; and I will tell you about your father who lives very far away." At the thought of Marshall living with his new wife in Great Britain, Kulien's heart ached with longing. Would she see him again? Would Ta Ming ever meet his father?

"Fadda," Ta Ming repeated. "Where my Fadda?"

Kulien diverted his attention by walking on, stopping now and then to watch a squirrel scamper up a tree or a bird swoop close to the ground. With the warm afternoon sun on their faces, Kulien lost track of time and space. She glanced around to where she had left Horace and Anna Clark, but their camp was hidden behind the rise. No matter. To her it was more important that Ta Ming had a free and unhurried outing. When they reached the knoll, Kulien noticed that a dense grove of tall trees rose up behind it. She smiled with pleasure. So much beauty—such, clean fresh air. She turned toward the west where she caught a faint glimmer of ocean shining through a cluster of oak trees. "Ta Ming, breathe deeply. The air here is like perfume." She knelt beside him and sniffed, laughing at his imitation—his little nose in the air and his almond-shaped blue eyes closed tightly.

Suddenly he turned and ran back toward a shadowy object barely visible among the trees. He held out both hands. "Doggie, Mama!"

"Ta Ming! Stop!" The words caught in her throat. From out of their hiding place, two dark figures lunged at her; one man grabbed Kulien, and held her arms tightly at her side, while the other snatched up Ta Ming. She screamed and kicked until the other attacker struck her on the head with a large rock.

"Dirty yellow devil," one man shouted.

"Kulien!" Horace Clark's loud voice rang out over the space separating them.

"Leave the woman!" shouted the man holding Ta Ming. "I've got the kid!"

"Mama! Mama! Bad men!"

"Ta Ming! Nooooo!" With pain ripping through her head and blood streaming into her eyes, Kulien struggled to get to her feet. "No! Take me! Leave my child!" Her arms stretched out like leafless branches waving in the air. Her voice rose like the wail of the northern winds. "Noooo!"

But as quickly as they had appeared, the men were gone. Ta Ming was gone. The warm afternoon sunshine and laughter were gone. All that was left was a cold, empty chill.

Kulien forced herself forward: one step, two steps; down on her knees; up again. She must follow. She had to save her baby. She was drowning. She saw herself sinking, slipping under the filthy brown water of the Grand Canal—reaching—reaching for Ta Ming. But the little dimpled hand was just out of her grasp. She heard a shrill keening rise from the depths of her soul before she sank deeper and deeper into the mire.

Three days passed—three days of concern and sorrow—three days of constant vigil. Kulien remained unconscious. The mission doctor came to examine her, but only shook his head. "I'm not sure if her loss of consciousness is from the blow to her head, or because of the great emotional shock in seeing her son taken away."

Horace and Anna took turns watching over her, praying, coaxing her back from the dark place where she had escaped. On the fourth day, Kulien opened her eyes. Wincing in pain, she touched the hard lump on her forehead, "Have I gone beyond the Yellow Springs?" When she saw Anna Clark's wide eyes and Horace's creased brow, she knew something terrible had happened, but she couldn't remember what it was.

"You're here with us dear—at home." Anna's cool hand brushed Kulien's hair away from the ugly wound. "You were injured—quite seriously."

"And you've been asleep for three days," Horace added.

Trying to sit up, Kulien glanced at Ta Ming's empty bed. "I remember now! Oh, no, I remember! Ta Ming! Where is my baby?"

Images of shadowy foreigners loomed just below the surface of her mind. She saw cruel eyes and heard their curses. Dropping her head back onto the down pillow, she cried, "Ta Ming? Where is he?"

"We received a letter from the men who kidnapped him. He's safe. We will get him back soon." Horace's words barely touched Kulien's understanding.

"Ta Ming was kidnapped? But why?" She pressed a fist against her mouth to restrain a sob.

"The men who took him want an exchange—tonight!" Horace rested a large warm hand on Kulien's shoulder. "So don't be distressed. I'm certain these men will keep their word. We have what they want."

Anna interrupted, "Remember the beautiful young woman we took from the docks as she arrived from China?"

Kulien managed to nod.

"It seems that she is the property of a very influential citizen of this city—and he wants her returned. The exchange is Orchid for Ta Ming."

Words and images raced through Kulien's troubled mind, but she did remember the woman as being well-dressed and quite lovely. Orchid. Even her name was descriptive and suitable for such a delicate and elegant woman.

Horace continued, "Orchid is an extremely high-priced joy girl who will be working in a clean bordello that caters to 'respectable men.'"

Rising to her elbow against the mumbled concerns of Reverend and Mrs. Clark, Kulien grimaced in pain. "Tonight? We'll get Ta Ming back tonight?"

Aware of the slight shrug, Kulien noticed how Anna and Horace looked at each other before answering, "If all goes well, dear—and God shows us a way."

Anna patted Kulien's hand to reassure her, and repeated, "Yes, if all goes well, you'll have your son back soon—and in good condition."

As the Clarks left Kulien alone, the words played over and over in her mind, "If all goes well." Suppose it didn't go well? Somehow her thoughts drifted back to that horrifying experience she'd had at The Blue Chambers. At that time, she had prayed to any god that would hear for help to escape—and she had found a way! How would she know if the help came from one of her gods, or from the invisible God that the Clarks prayed to? What or who interrupted William Walker's advances that night?

She lifted her eyes to the ceiling of her room as she had seen the foreigners do when they prayed. Her words, in the familiar Mandarin dialect, were faltering, but her hope was strong. "*If* there is a living God as my friends have proclaimed, I humbly beg You to bring my son back to me."

She had no evidence that her whispered prayer had been heard. Did this God only hear words spoken in English? Just to be certain, she repeated the same request in the language of her new country.

Still tired and weak, she closed her eyes, contemplating a dismal future. *How can I go on living without Ta Ming? He is my only purpose in waking each day. He is my life.*

FORTY-THREE

As planned, Reverend and Mrs. Clark were waiting with Orchid nearby when men in black suits and hats arrived at their front door. No one spoke as one man stood on the steps holding a squirming bundle wrapped in a dirty blanket while another held out his hand to Orchid. As she left she glared at the Clarks, speaking in Cantonese, "How dare you take me away from the high life planned for me! May the gods bring you pain and misery for interfering with my American friends."

Horace Clark stepped out behind her to receive Ta Ming into his arms. Before the men left with Orchid, Horace took the boy out of the filthy blanket, and removed the scarf tied around his mouth. Ta Ming let out a loud, "Mama!"

Kulien, still reeling from pain and weakness, stumbled down the stairway, holding tightly to the smooth banister. "Ta Ming! Oh, my son, you're safe! Come to me!" She sat on a step and wrapped her arms around the little boy, and they both cried with relief.

"Well, this is a happy ending for *them*," Horace said. "But I don't believe, for a minute, that Orchid will be happy with the outcome of her rescue. No doubt, she'll be sold to the highest bidder."

"Oh, Horace, if only we could have kept her here. She's more refined than most of the girls we take from the bagnios; but like you, I fear she'll regret that she ever believed the lies that brought her to America."

As Kulien's health and emotions healed, her constant anxiety for Ta Ming's well-being consumed her. She never left a room without him in her sight; and at every possible moment throughout the day she would put her arms around him as if to protect him from any outsider.

One evening as Kulien sat rocking Ta Ming, Anna stood over her, the concern showing in her eyes. "Kulien, you can't hold onto him forever. Ta Ming wants to run and play. For his health, and also for yours, you must learn to let go."

"My strength is in my son," she replied, looking down on the sleeping boy's face. As she glanced back at Anna, she knew in her heart that the woman was right. She had felt her own vitality leave her body; she had no appetite and slept restlessly.

"But, my dear," Anna said, kneeling in front of Kulien on the carpeted floor, "have you considered what would happen to Ta Ming if you should die? You must take care of yourself!"

Anna's bold words jolted Kulien's sagging spirit to attention. "What are you saying?"

"If you don't eat or sleep, you will die. Ta Ming has no one else to care for him. He can't stay here indefinitely. He would have to be sent to an orphanage."

Kulien stared at the older woman. Anna's face showed no sign of compassion as a crease slashed across her high forehead. The words had been deliberate, meant to shock.

Kulien turned her attention back to the sleeping child. "Ta Ming needs me. I am all he has; and what you say is true." She relaxed her hold and leaned her head back against the high wooden rocking chair. When she opened her eyes, her voice was steady. "Yes, you tell the truth. It's time to take care of myself as well as my son. I have neglected my own health and must keep strong for him."

Anna rose from her kneeling position on the floor and smoothed her starched apron over the dark cotton dress. As she turned to leave the room, she fingered a strand of loose hair back into the roll on top of her head, and then paused at the door. "I'll bring you a tray of food then. But Kulien, regardless of how much you love your son, there is more to life. You're still young and have years ahead of you. You need to live your life and dream your own dreams. One day Ta Ming will be grown, and you must have a purpose higher than mothering your only child."

When Kulien's eyes met Anna's, they glistened with tears. "Ta Ming is my bridge between the past and the future. Without him, I *have* no life, no dream. Every person I have loved is gone, and I will *never* let Ta Ming be taken away. I *will* keep him within my sight!"

Anna turned from the doorway and strode back across the room, dropping to her knees again. She brushed a hand over Kulien's smooth cheek. "Oh, my dear girl, do you want a son who can't make decisions for himself? The natural world you love so much teaches the wisdom of letting go. A mother bird pushes her young from the nest so he can learn to fly. Would you do less for Ta Ming?" Her voice was gentle and soothing as she motioned toward the window. "There's life out there for Ta Ming—a life of fulfillment and accomplishment that he must discover for himself. Would you deny him that?"

Kulien shifted her position. Her shoulders ached from holding the growing boy, but she reveled in the pressure of his head against her chest. "I want only the best for him," she said at last. "But I fear that he'll be hated wherever he goes. Even in this house, I hear some of the slave girls call him names. 'Half-breed,' they say. And '*fankuei*, foreign devil.' He'll hear the same, perhaps even worse when he goes out among foreigners. He won't be accepted by either the Chinese or the Europeans."

"You don't know that! And you can't keep him in your arms forever. He will want to be free. Think of yourself; hasn't that always been your greatest desire?"

Kulien remembered a rebellious young girl whose yearning for freedom had taken her from the safety of a walled compound to the far shores of a distant kingdom. With a nod of her head, she shook the pictures from her mind. "Yes, my longing for freedom continues—and of course, I want my son to be free to choose. But he's still young; I must keep him close as long as possible."

Anna rose to her feet with a sigh. "How about the rescue work? And your classes in English? Are you going to give up these good works that help so many? Your neglect of duties harms these girls who need you!"

Wiping away the tears that had begun to flow down her cheeks, Kulien knew Anna was right, but her fears overcame the reality of what she said. "Please, try to understand. I can't leave my son yet." Her voice quavered with emotion.

"Very well, then," Anna said, turning once more to leave. "You may bring Ta Ming with you into the classroom; but please, please come out of this dark room and join the rest of us. We love you, Kulien. We want what is best for both you and Ta Ming."

The seasons changed as they had from the beginning of time. Every morning the sun rose in San Francisco from behind the eastern range of hills, and every night it sank into the deep blue of the Pacific Ocean. The passing months brought warm breezes from the south and cold winds from the north; and as one year evolved into the next, the city on the bay became a seething cauldron of nationalities and cultures. Ships from around the world brought men and women hoping to find their fortunes in the new land. By 1858, the estimated population of San Francisco was over sixty thousand.

Discrimination against the Chinese grew with the surge in population. Shouts of, "The Chinaman must go!" "Burn down their filthy shacks!" were not unusual. Fires broke out in Little China; and men disappeared from the streets never to be seen again. In the cities and mountains of California, the Chinese were beaten, hanged and slit open. A new breed of social ill rose out of the turmoil, and as Kulien heard the news of the "San Francisco hoodlums," her determination to protect her son grew even more unwavering.

When Reverend Clark read aloud the news regarding the growing problem of bigotry, Kulien listened carefully, trying to understand why the citizens of the Middle Kingdom had been singled out as objects of torment. Even the Digger Indians and black men from Africa received better treatment than the Chinese.

Although she didn't fully grasp the situation, she tried to be brave concerning Ta Ming's safety; and faithfully performed her duties as an English teacher to the rescued girls and women while Ta Ming played nearby. However, she now refused to leave him alone in order to accompany the Clarks on raids of the bagnios. Her great joy in living was spent alone with her son, teaching him to hold the writing brush, and guiding his small hand to form smooth strokes of Chinese characters. She read stories, taught her son songs, and instructed him in the simplest movements of *taichichuan.*

On the afternoon of Ta Ming's fourth birthday, Anna interrupted Kulien's teaching of the alphabet to her students. The woman stood in the doorway a few moments before blurting, "Kulien. Dismiss the girls. I have a most important matter to discuss with you."

Kulien's eyes darted to the corner where Ta Ming bent over a book carefully copying the words onto a large piece of paper. Yes, she assured herself, he was safe. She waved a hand at the students, watched them leave single-file, then with hands folded at her waist, she bowed slightly. "Yes, Anna, what is it?"

Anna Clark cleared her throat before guiding Kulien to a table where she motioned for her to sit. With a faint smile, she took an envelope from her pocket. "A letter was delivered this morning." She held it out for Kulien to see the postage bearing a picture of Queen Victoria. "This correspondence is a response to a letter I wrote nearly two years ago." She waited for Kulien's eyes to return to hers. "I wrote to your former teacher, Elizabeth Whitfield."

The blood drained from Kulien's face, and her heart began to flutter. Elizabeth Whitfield? But why? A cold chill inched up her back, and she folded her arms tightly across her waist to keep from shivering. "I don't understand. Why would you write to Miss Whitfield? And why did it take two years for her to respond?"

Placing the letter on the table, Anna replied, "You can see for yourself. Horace and I read it; but it concerns you."

Kulien's breath caught in her throat as she stared at Elizabeth Whitfield's familiar ornate scroll on the ivory parchment. Long-forgotten memories crept from the dark shadows of her mind into the glaring light of day. She found difficulty swallowing, and her breath came in gasps.

"Take Ta Ming with you, dear, and go to your room to read the letter. Horace will finish your classes for you." Anna patted Kulien's shoulder before leaving. "Give yourself time to think on Miss Whitfield's letter before you reach a decision. Remember it's never wise to make a judgment based on changing emotions. I think it would be prudent for you to wait several days, weeks even, before you speak about your thoughts regarding the letter."

Kulien did as Anna suggested, and retired to her room. Before opening the letter from the other side of the world, she read a story to Ta Ming and waited until he fell asleep. After preparing a cup of tea, she took up the letter and stared at it. Five years had passed since she had seen Elizabeth Whitfield; and the last time she had seen a letter from her teacher, she learned of Marshall's marriage. Would this letter also bring bad news? Moments passed before she began to read:

"To the Reverend and Mrs. Clark; Greetings from Great Britain. Please accept my apologies for the delay in responding to your letter dated February 20, 1856, addressed to the Orphanage of Shang Ti, Shanghai. Your correspondence reached China a month after my departure for England, but was not forwarded to me until more than a year had passed.

"In January, 1856, a group of dissidents, who call themselves, Triads, destroyed our complex, and murdered Reverend Mortensen in his attempt to shield the children. Several orphans were also killed, and five were kidnapped. Mrs. Mortensen and Dr. Gordon and his wife escaped. I was left for dead, having received a serious injury. For some reason, known only to God, I was spared. Three days after the attack, I was discovered under the rubble."

Kulien's heart froze as she imagined the frightful scene. Thinking about the death of the kindly white-haired minister overwhelmed her with sorrow. He had been so gentle and caring of her. She imagined the horror of Elizabeth Whitfield lying under the ashes and burnt timbers, unable to call for help.

Curious, she picked up the letter and began to read further. "Doctors at the British Consulate ministered to my needs; and although a lung was punctured, the knife wound healed, and I am, at last, well and back in England with my mother and brother."

Kulien's could scarcely breathe as she went on.

"My father, Lord George Whitfield, died the previous year, and Mother had been lonely, living in the manor with only the servants. Before I arrived, my brother spent as much time with her as he could spare away from his wife, Elise. Poor Elise is bedridden now, and under the constant care of a nurse."

So, it was true; Marshall had married the woman chosen for him by his family, a woman too ill to participate in his interests. Sadness tugged at the corners of Kulien's lips. Perhaps he was as unhappy as she had been. She rested her eyes on Ta Ming. At least she had their son. Did he have another son now?

She read on. "But I speak too long of personal problems. I must give attention to your inquiries and address the news you have written about Kulien. Yet who knows what changes have taken place since you wrote two years ago? Is Kulien still well? Is the boy safe? Your letter spoke of your concern for both of them. I, too, care about my former student; and of course, Ta Ming, George, is of my own blood. You suggested that money might be raised to send Kulien and Ta Ming back to China where she could live and work among old friends at the orphanage. Because of the horrible events there, that is out of the question since the orphanage is no longer in existence."

Kulien's interest rose and fell, leaving her weak and trembling. · She sipped the sweet green tea and watched the leaves swirl in the thin porcelain cup. If only she could return to China with Ta Ming. But where would she live? Her father would not accept her! She rose to tuck a quilt around the sleeping boy and allowed her fingers to brush against his smooth, round cheek. What would Marshall think of his son? When she returned to her stool and picked up the letter, she read the answer to her unspoken question.

"Now I come to the most important part of my correspondence. It was not until your letter finally reached me a fortnight ago that I told my brother about their son. Although he often had implored me to tell what I knew of her, I refused to give him any information. He knew that the clipper ship, *Houqua*, was bound for California, but he never knew if she had arrived there, or had possibly died en route.

"You can imagine his astonishment when I told him that Kulien had not only arrived in San Francisco, but that she had given birth to a healthy baby boy. This child is Marshall's only heir, as Elise is unable to bear children. As the heir, Ta Ming is beneficiary to the vast fortune of the House of Whitfield."

Kulien's heart began to pound. She folded the letter and put it aside for a few moments until she felt calm enough to proceed.

"I now come to my proposition and purpose in writing to you. You said that even two years ago, you feared for the boy because of his mixed heritage. I assume the situation may be worse now from the reports in the newspapers. I am ashamed to tell you that he could be in danger here as well. A child, with even some Asian features, would be denied the privileges of the upper class.

"However, with Marshall's influence and wealth, I strongly believe he should, and would assume full responsibility of the boy's safety—and future. Would you discuss with Kulien the possibility, and advantage, of allowing Marshall to raise Ta Ming here in England? He would have privileges otherwise impossible, including the finest governesses and the most advanced education in Great Britain."

Kulien could not believe the words on the paper! Would Elizabeth Whitfield, or Marshall, for that matter, believe that she would ever give up her son? Where he would go, she would go also. If Marshall wanted to raise Ta Ming, he would also have to take her as his only wife!

The letter concluded with the words, "After reading your letter to Marshall, he talked to Elise, confessing his 'youthful indiscretion' regarding Kulien, and that he now has a son who lives in America. She agreed that Ta Ming, young George, should be with his father, and. . . ."

A cry escaped Kulien's lips, and she fell across her bed. "'Youthful indiscretion'!" she cried aloud. "Is that all I am to him?" Her tears of anguish woke Ta Ming, so he crawled out of his own bed over to Kulien, where he wrapped his arms around her neck. As she continued to sob, Ta Ming's arms tightened, and his sweet voice barely reached her brokenness, "Mama, don't cry. God will take care of us!"

FORTY-FOUR

The day after reading Miss Whitfield's letter, Kulien replaced her dark blue jacket and trousers with a peacock blue gown. Her hair, the fragrance of roses, fell over her shoulders in sheets of fluid ebony. Neither Anna nor Horace Clark mentioned the transformation to Kulien, but privately discussed her show of false happiness.

The slave girls were not so shy about their comments. "Why do you dress in rich clothes?" one asked. "Are you going to a wedding?"

"Or are you the bride?" teased another.

"Why do you smile? Have you swallowed a feather?"

Kulien ignored the questions, determined to lift her thoughts from the anxiety that had engulfed her spirit. She must show a good face; it would not do for Ta Ming to see her cry again. He had become so frightened by her sobs that she could not calm him for hours. He must never know about the letter; and she put the suggestion to send him to England far from her mind. How could Elizabeth Whitfield ever imagine that Kulien would give up her son—her life? She would make the days so beautiful and charming for her boy that he would be content to stay with her forever.

Weeks passed while Kulien kept up the pretense that all was well. At last, she decided it was time to respond to Miss Whitfield's letter. In her most precise English scroll, she gave her reply, and then handed the letter to Anna for her approval.

Sitting on the settee in the parlor, Anna motioned for Kulien to sit opposite her on the wing-backed chair. After clearing her throat, she began to read aloud.

"To my honorable teacher and friend, Miss Whitfield;

"Your letter, written to the Reverend and Mrs. Clark, was delivered into my hand. Too moons have come and gone; now I am ready to reply. I am well, and protected by my American friends. My son, Ta Ming, is healthy and happy to be with his mother. He is now four years old, according to the Western Way of counting, and he is bright beyond his years. He knows and writes the letters of the English alphabet, and has already memorized and can write many Chinese characters. I am told that he is ready for school, and I will allow him to attend public school with the American children here in this great city. I see few, if any, Chinese children because the men have come to this land without their wives and families. Ta Ming will be accepted by the white children because his eyes, though slightly slanted, are blue. He will be known to the school children as George Kuang, George being the European name he bears in honor of his paternal grandfather.

"I humbly refuse the gracious offer made by your brother and his wife to educate *my* son. He would die without me—and I without him. Sincerely, Your former student, Kuang Kulien."

Anna looked up from her reading. "This is your answer?"

"There could be no other."

"As you wish; but plans to send Ta Ming to the American school may be thwarted."

"He is far beyond his years in knowledge."

Anna sighed. "That's true dear, but there are those who oppose any Chinese presence in this city so strongly that they have drawn up laws to forbid them to attend school."

Kulien bit the edge of her lower lip. "How can that be? There are people of every nationality and color in this city."

Nodding, Anna strode to the roll-top desk in the corner of the room and reached into a cubbyhole. "You're right; and at times I'm ashamed of my heritage. Those who happened to be born into the white race have taken it upon themselves to consider all others inferior! The California Superintendent of Education had a notice in a recent newspaper."

She unfolded the paper and began to read, "Had it been intended by the framers of the education law that the children of the inferior races should be educated side by side with the whites, it is manifest the census would have included children of all colors. If this attempt to force Africans, Chinese, and Diggers into one school is persisted in it must result in the ruin of the schools."

Shaking her head sadly, Anna continued, "The 'gentleman' goes on to say that the masses will not accept the inferior races as equal, nor will they allow their children to do so."

Anna rolled her eyes heavenward. "May God change the hearts of these proud, selfish men!"

"Is there a law forbidding my child to attend the white school?"

"Not yet."

"Then Ta Ming will take the name George; I will cut off his queue and dress him in Western clothes. He is not to be denied an education."

Kulien's letter to Great Britain was posted, and she relegated to the back of her mind the knowledge that somewhere Marshall Whitfield and his wife hoped for a son—her son.

She continued to carry her head high, always aware of her own proud heritage. Her father, a Mandarin of the highest order had married a British woman of wealth and elegance. Ta Ming bore a strong resemblance to both his Chinese and British heritage. Whatever the future held, he would be a strong leader of men.

As summer edged into autumn, Kulien reached her decision. Although Ta Ming was not yet six years old, she would not wait another year to enroll him in the public school. Before a law was enacted to forbid his attendance, he would already have proven his worth.

"My son," Kulien sighed, lifting a razor to his thick, shiny braid, "to cut off your queue would be considered a shame by your countrymen, but if you are to pass as a white boy, you must dress as they do and adopt their culture as your own."

Lifting his narrow shoulders, Ta Ming clenched his teeth, and answered, "I am a big boy, Mama. I will make you proud of me. I'm not afraid for you to cut my hair the way the white boys wear theirs."

"Each day, my son, you will be two boys—American at school, and Chinese at home. It will be difficult, but the gods will be with you."

Ta Ming stared at his mother and cocked his head. "Reverend Clark says there is only one God—I believe him."

Perplexed that Horace Clark would attempt to deny Ta Ming of his heritage, Kulien frowned and shook her head in displeasure. As she stepped back to survey Ta Ming's haircut, she saw a new boy. Her son had become a stranger--a different boy—one who thought his own thoughts. As he took off his loose-fitting clothes and began to dress in the narrow-legged trousers and stiff shirt collar of the American school boy, she realized his likeness to Marshall had become more pronounced with each passing year. Although his hair was black as charcoal, the sun filtering through the curtains seemed to sprinkle gold dust over his head. And his blue eyes were Marshall's, one moment staring back at her with intensity; the next, sparkling with humor.

Ta Ming's skin, the shade of weak tea, could pass as Caucasian, but his high cheekbones, sculpted with Chinese artistry, could not be denied. At almost five years old, his arms and legs were long and his body already more European than Asian. Kulien's heart swelled with pride; her son was a living portrait of two worlds.

In the fall of the year, Anna and Horace Clark accompanied Kulien to enroll the Ta Ming. The high recommendations impressed the schoolmaster who smiled benevolently at him.

"George Kuang?" he asked, after reviewing the application. His eyes rested on Horace Clark. "Is the father also Chinese? The lad appears to be somewhat European."

Reverend Clark nodded. "The boy's father is British, a member of a noble family. At present he resides in Great Britain. His mother," he said, with a hand on Kulien's shoulder, "as you can see from her features, also comes from British as well as Chinese ancestry."

"Hmm, I do see." The man adjusted his spectacles before peering once more at Kulien, then at her son. He pointed his long nose in the air and sniffed as if an unpleasant odor had surrounded him. "I cannot guarantee how long the boy may attend school. As you know, Superintendent Moulder opposes Chinese receiving education alongside our children."

Moving his hand to rest on Ta Ming's head, Horace nodded. "We understand; but George shows extreme intelligence—and he was born in San Francisco. That must mean something." Horace mopped his brow. "This child speaks

English as well as any child in your school. In fact, though he's not yet five, he reads and writes in two languages." Anna nodded her agreement. "Just give the boy an opportunity; that's all we ask."

Mr. Evans, the schoolmaster, tapped his foot and frowned down at Ta Ming. "All right, we'll take him, but when and if we decide to dismiss him, there will be no questions asked. Agreed?"

Kulien hardly knew her own feelings as she walked away from the school, leaving Ta Ming to the exacting headmaster who obviously resented his presence. She wanted him to learn the ways of his birth county, but at the same time she worried that harm would come to him.

"You've done the right thing," Horace assured her as they rode back to their house on the outskirts of Little China. "Ta Ming, George, will impress his teachers. You'll see."

To Kulien, the day seemed endless, and she had to force herself not run and greet him as her son walked down the steps of the schoolhouse to the waiting cart.

"Mama, we sang the same hymns Reverend Clark sings; and we had lessons in geography, writing and reading. The other children played together at recess, and I laughed at their games."

Kulien sighed with relief, but had a question, "Didn't you join in the games?"

"No. I'm not ready to talk with them yet."

As one day passed into the next, Ta Ming's answers were always the same. His lips smiled as he spoke, but Kulien sensed her son's anxiety as a small crease appeared on his smooth forehead.

It was two weeks later that Kulien saw Ta Ming's back when he changed from his school clothes. Deep red welts rose up near his underarms and shoulders.

"My son!" she cried, before he could conceal the injuries with the cotton shirt he wore at home. "What is this?" She touched the swollen marks with a forefinger.

"It's nothing, Mama—nothing." Ta Ming turned away, trying to put his shirt on quickly so she couldn't examine him further.

With hands on his shoulders, Kulien turned him around and gently traced the lumps. Ta Ming winced with pain.

"It's nothing," he repeated, his eyes on Kulien's worried expression. "The boys only tease me, Mama. They pinch and scratch me when the teacher isn't looking. They mean no harm." His voice had a pleading tone.

A lump formed in Kulien's throat, and she blinked back tears as she gathered Ta Ming into her arms. Angry beyond words, she held him as gently as possible.

That night after Ta Ming went to bed, Kulien approached Horace Clark who sat at his desk writing letters. "May I speak with you?"

"Of course, child, what is it?" Reverend Clark leaned back in his chair and fastened his eyes on Kulien.

"Ta Ming will no longer attend the school for white children," she said with a sigh.

The man's dark eyebrows rose over the edge of his glasses. 'I don't understand. He's doing so well, and the authorities have not forbidden his attendance."

To save face, Kulien didn't mention the cruelty of the children, and lowering her gaze to the floor, she said firmly, "I will educate him here at home."

"But you have no education in anything other than English."

"Perhaps you could purchase a book or two from the school and together, Ta Ming and I will study the ways of the West."

Reverend Clark's eyes narrowed in understanding.

Kulien's mind was again at peace as Ta Ming came under her constant supervision. He learned quickly from the books supplied by Reverend Clark; and as another year passed, he grew as rapidly in stature as he did in knowledge. Kulien knew he was lonely for companionship of children his age, but she dismissed the worry for the present. For now, she would spend her energy studying and teaching her son along with the rescued girls.

Over the years, she had found great satisfaction in teaching the slave girls. As their hope for a better life was kindled, they changed, and that expectation showed in their faces: dark eyes, shiny as wet pebbles, greeted Kulien every morning; turned-up lips, eager to recite the words written on the pages of books; clean hands, open to grasp the writing brush or pen. The students' attitude toward Ta Ming had changed as well. Instead of deriding him, they now called him, "Little Brother."

Several of the girls had resided at the mission for over a year, and these often came to Kulien after classes to learn more. To see once-ignorant girls, who had known only a life of prostitution begin to blossom into young ladies of refinement, inspired Kulien's dedication to reach as many as possible. Could it be that Anna Clark had been right when she said there was more to life than protecting Ta Ming?

As another year unfolded, Kulien became so preoccupied with her studies that she forgot Elizabeth Whitfield's letter; she forgot her fears for Ta Ming; she even forgot her longing for China. She had thrown herself into her work, hungering for yet more knowledge, and reaching out in love to her students.

Life was good. She had found contentment at last, if not the freedom she still sought. No troubling winds blew across the waters of her spirit. She was at peace.

FORTY-FIVE

Horace and Anna Clark seemed unduly concerned about climatic conditions. Not only did they endlessly discuss the unusual weather for this time of year, they had been jumpy for days. At the slightest provocation, they were at Kulien's side.

"Do you feel all right, Kulien?"

"Have you enough warm clothing for Ta Ming?"

"Did you sleep well last night?"

Their scrutinizing attention to her welfare worried her. Why the great concern? Was there bad news they were reluctant to discuss?

After a long day in the classroom and a simple meal of rice and vegetables, Kulien asked, "May I be excused from the evening meditations? I'm very tired tonight, and would like to retire early."

Anna shot a furtive glance at her husband. "Perhaps that would be wise, dear. Take Ta Ming to your room, and we'll see you in the morning."

Horace Clark's face relaxed. "Yes, you rest. One never knows what the next day will bring."

During the night, Kulien awoke when she heard the front door close. Reverend Clark must have gone out to rescue a slave girl. How kind he was to leave his warm home to go out into the stormy weather to save a woman most people considered useless.

The sun had not yet risen when Anna Clark tapped on Kulien's door. At first, Kulien thought it was rain pelting against the window, but as she rose to one elbow, she saw a beam of light shining through the crack under the door. Quickly, she threw a robe over her shoulders. "What is it?"

Anna's hoarse whisper came from the hall. "You must dress at once, Kulien. Don't wake Ta Ming. Come to the parlor—alone. There is—there is someone here to see you."

Without asking further questions, Kulien lit a candle, rinsed her mouth, and washed her face; she smoothed her hair back and fastened it with a long silver pin, wondering who would come so early in the day? And who would ask to see her?

As she slipped into a green woolen tunic and trousers, she continued to ask herself, *Has someone died? Have my papers been sold to a slaver?* The high collar concealed her long, slender neck, displaying only her flawless complexion and finely sculptured face. With one last glance in the mirror, she snuffed out the candle and tiptoed from the room.

Her heart beat wildly as she walked silently down the hallway. The sliding doors of the parlor were closed and she paused to catch her breath before knocking. Both Reverend and Mrs. Clark responded by stepping out into the hallway. Anna held a lamp in her hand, and the orange glow showed concern on the woman's face.

"Kulien, this is very difficult. We should have warned you this day was coming, but. . . ."

"But we were asked to keep silent," Horace said, finishing Anna's explanation. "Our early morning caller feared you would refuse a meeting." Although a cold draft flowed through the hallway, Horace Clark mopped his brow with a handkerchief. His eyes held Kulien's as she looked up into his face. "Your visitor requested a private audience," he said, turning away. "But if you need us, call!"

Now Kulien was more apprehensive than ever, yet curiosity drew her through the doors toward the fireplace. There, silhouetted in the bright glow of the flames, stood a tall man wearing a long coat and high boots. Her breath caught in her throat, and she stopped halfway across the room.

Struggling to find her voice, she said, "You asked to see me?"

The man turned toward her, his face still obscured in the shadows. "Kulien, I've found you at last."

At the sound of the familiar voice, the room began to reel. The past rolled into the present, filling the space with the forgotten fragrance of jasmine, the sound of wind chimes, the summerhouse, and an innocent girl with an Englishman.

Kulien braced herself, and walked deliberately to the sideboard where she lit a lantern. Marshall Whitfield didn't move, but waited for her to turn toward him. Neither spoke as the amber flame of the lamp flickered over their faces. They surveyed one another quietly, calmly.

The air crackled with tension as Marshall bowed from the waist. "It's been a long time."

"Yes," she said fastening her gaze on the worn carpet. "Nearly seven years." Her voice quavered only slightly. She licked her lips and beckoned toward the chairs in front of the fireplace. "Would you like to sit down, Lord Whitfield?"

The man's fluid movements, the shine of his hair, and the tilt of his head, struck a long-remembered chord in Kulien's heart. She thought she had erased her desire for him; she'd tried to forget him, and had even been able to go several days at a time without thinking of the love she'd once had. Their hours together had been short, and very long ago; and she believed she had stopped loving him. She often wondered if he had tried to follow when she was so cruelly taken away from him in Hong Kong. Or had he eagerly returned to Great Britain to marry an English woman?

Kulien held her breath, waiting for him to speak. Unable to relax, she sat on the edge of the chair and folded her fingers together in her lap. Marshall Whitfield leaned back in his chair, stretching long legs toward the warmth of the smoldering fire. After several minutes, he sat forward, hands on his knees, eyes reaching out to hold her. He cleared his throat, and then spoke slowly, his voice barely audible.

"I thought I would never see you again." He paused, and then the words came as a flood. "When Elizabeth told me you were here in America, I couldn't believe it. I thought I'd lost you forever! No one would tell me what happened to you." He rose from the chair to pace in front of her. "After you were grabbed by those men in Hong Kong, I tried to follow you onto the ship, but was attacked and beaten. They left me on the dock, unable to move. I must have been unconscious. Later, some men, I'm not sure who they were, dragged me away, and I was thrown into prison for three months. The charge: attempting to kidnap a slave who belonged to a man—Jack Burton, I think his name was." His voice dropped to a hoarse whisper, "Forgive me if I'm too familiar. I know that many oceans, and many years have separated us from what we once knew." His words burned with passion.

Kulien slowly lifted her head, filling her eyes with his presence. He was here—with her. His face, clean shaven now, had matured; the golden hair seemed darker, and his blue eyes less brilliant. There was a slight drooping to the broad shoulders as if they carried the burden of the world. Her heart swelled with emotion, but she didn't speak. She would leave that to him; she had no words to express her feelings. Why had he come? Surely Elizabeth had relayed her message denying him any right to Ta Ming. And hadn't he only considered her a "youthful indiscretion"?

"You've changed, Kulien, yet you seem to be the same-- determined and strong. His eyes swept over her face. "You're no longer a girl, but a woman, an even more beautiful woman."

Marshall sat down, and again leaned toward her. "I know you didn't expect to see me after you wrote to Elizabeth, and I hope you'll forgive me for coming secretly like this."

Kulien had no answer. Her mind wrestled between the past and the future. Seven years ago, this man had taken her maidenhood, and had given her a son. Had he come to claim him now? She shook her head to erase the worrisome thought.

Marshall watched her closely, and at the toss of her head, his brow furrowed. "You won't forgive me? I couldn't blame you. I know I've brought nothing but pain and trouble into your life."

Composed now, Kulien spoke slowly, clearly. "It is not for me to forgive or condemn you, Lord Whitfield. If I've suffered any pain, it came about through my own choices." She wouldn't let him see the turmoil raging in her heart. Oh, how can it be? She still loved him!

Willing the emotions back into the depths of her mind, she asked, "Do you have business in America?"

Seeing that Kulien didn't want to speak of personal matters, he answered, "Yes, I do, not only as a representative of my country, but my business is also personal."

Their eyes met and held each other. He went on, "The discovery of gold in California has attracted about 30,000 men and women from the British Isles. It's the Queen's hope that these people can be persuaded to return to England."

"Then, I suppose, you are still active in British politics?"

"In a manner of speaking."

Kulien knew he had come to California for a greater purpose than to serve his queen. He had come to take Ta Ming away from her. The thought left her feeling weak. "Did you sail across the Ocean of Great Peace," she asked, hoping to regain a semblance of serenity.

Marshall leaned back in his chair again. The sound of leather boots squeaked as he crossed one ankle over the other. "No, I sailed the Atlantic from Great Britain to Boston, Massachusetts. The British are importing goods to the New World, among them, shoes and furniture. From Boston, I booked passage to San Francisco around Cape Horn.

"I've wanted to see this country," he said, never taking his eyes from her face. "Some of my ancestors died on American soil, near Boston actually."

"In the War of Independence."

"Yes." He smiled. "I see you've been learning the history of your new country."

"I study history to be a better teacher for my son. This is *not* my country. My country, my home, is China. One day, *Ta Ming* and I will return."

"I understand," Marshall said softly. "Elizabeth received a letter from Reverend Clark requesting sponsorship for your passage to China."

Now Kulien leaned forward. "Elizabeth. How is she? I was most grieved when I learned of her tragedy in Shanghai!"

"She's in good spirits, actually. She sends her best wishes and love."

And you? Kulien asked herself. *Do you have any love left for me? Were our vows of marriage nothing but a 'youthful indiscretion' to you?* "I think of her often," she said, lowering her eyelids to stop the tears that burned behind them. "She opened the windows of the world to me."

"And the entrance to your family compound to me."

No sooner had he spoken than Anna tapped at the closed door. Without waiting for a response, she entered. "We're ready to partake of our morning meal, Lord Whitfield. Would you honor us with your presence?"

Marshall glanced from Anna Clark to Kulien. "Is it agreeable with you?"

"Mrs. Clark has offered an invitation. Respond as you wish. This is not my home; I'm but a guest here."

Marshall rose to bow to the older woman. "Thank you, I would like that."

Before turning away, Anna beckoned to Kulien, "I'll show Lord Whitfield to the dining area. There's someone in your room who needs attention."

Ta Ming had dressed and waited patiently for his mother. Anna Clark had given him strict instructions not to leave the room until his mother came for him.

"What secret visitor has come?" Ta Ming asked as soon as Kulien opened the door.

"Whatever are you talking about, son?" Kulien bustled around the room for several minutes before answering his question.

"Mrs. Clark said you had a secret visitor in the parlor. Is it someone from the school? I hope you changed your mind about the American school. You're a good teacher, Mama, but I want to go to a real school." Ta Ming's wide eyes shone with excitement.

"No, son, there's no one here from the school; it's a visitor from across the seas. Someone I knew in China."

"Oh, may I meet the visitor? Who is it?"

Kulien leaned against a table as strength drained from her body. What could she say? She had, on occasion, spoken to him about his father, yet she had not foreseen this day.

"Yes," she said, after inspecting Ta Ming's attire. "I'm certain the visitor would like to meet you as well."

When Kulien and Ta Ming walked, hand in hand, into the dining room, Marshall rose from his place at the table. With his eyes fastened on Ta Ming, he bowed after Kulien's introduction, and then held out a hand. Ta Ming also bowed before extending his small hand to the foreigner. Marshall's face flushed as he gently took the boy's hand in his.

"My mother said you are a friend from China. I expected a Chinese—an old woman," Ta Ming said in clear, concise

English, his red lips curled up in a bright smile. "You're not Chinese—and you're not an old woman!"

A low laugh escaped Marshall's mouth as he studied Ta Ming's face. Then, with a smile that reflected the boy's, he said, "And I expected to see a Chinese boy. Instead I see a young man—a European, at that!"

Reverend Clark coughed uncomfortably and motioned for everyone to be seated.

"Our girls are having breakfast in the kitchen today," Anna said, after grace had been offered. "We don't often have visitors from abroad."

Marshall took his eyes off Ta Ming long enough to reply. "Last night when Reverend Clark met me at the customs house, and helped me find a hotel, he spoke about your work." He wiped the edge of his mouth with a napkin. "I had no idea the Chinese were treated with such cruelty. One would think that in a new country, people would be more accepting." His eyes, filled with sadness, brushed over Kulien to rest on Ta Ming.

"I can't attend school," Ta Ming blurted. "I am hated because I look Chinese. People call me, 'yellow dog.'"

A vein at Marshall's temple began to throb, and his eyes bored into Kulien's. "He doesn't look Chinese to me. He could pass for a White."

Kulien, ignoring Marshall's insensitive statement, slipped a protective arm over Ta Ming's shoulder. "I teach my son to read and write both English and Mandarin. I also teach him to be proud of his Asian heritage!"

"Kulien *is* an excellent teacher," Horace Clark said, after another fit of coughing. "However, I must be excused Lord Whitfield. It's time for morning devotions, and the girls are waiting." His glance touched Kulien before returning to Marshall. "Kulien is free today if you want to spend some time with her away from the mission, Ta Ming will stay with us."

Marshall, without looking at Kulien's surprised expression, fingered a brass button on his coat. "I would appreciate that, if Kulien will agree. As I said before, I do have personal business to discuss with her." His eyes fastened on Ta Ming before meeting Kulien's frown.

Kulien realized at that moment that she felt both hatred and love for this man. Surely he couldn't ask her to surrender the one thread that held her life together.

Before she could object, Reverend and Mrs. Clark walked out of the room, leaving Marshall alone with Kulien and Ta Ming. He rose to stand beside Ta Ming, and placed a hand on his head. When he looked at Kulien, his eyes softened and his mouth relaxed. "You have a fine son. I hope that I can get to know him better."

"Another time, perhaps. It seems our day has already been ordered." Kulien rose to stand beside Marshall Whitfield.

"Oh, Mama, may I please be excused from my studies today? Are you going to the country? I want to go with you."

Kulien was gentle, but firm in her answer. "Lord Whitfield will be here for several days, my son. There will be time for you to become better acquainted."

Ta Ming cocked his head, first at his mother, and then at the English gentleman. "I think, I think," he repeated, with his eyes traveling from Kulien to Marshall, "that Lord Whitfield is the father I've never known!"

The color drained from Kulien's face, leaving her weak with fear. "And I think you speak out of turn, young man." With her hands on his shoulders, she stood him in front of her. "You are dismissed from the table, and I will talk to you about this later."

His eyes shining with excitement, Ta Ming made a small bow before Marshall Whitfield. "I am most happy to know you, sir," he said, holding out his hand. Marshall's warm clasp and nod confirmed Ta Ming's suspicion.

"And I, too, am happy, my boy."

FORTY-SIX

Bright rays of sunlight pierced through the dark clouds forming on the horizon. Here and there, on the low hills, patches of golden wildflowers bobbed their heads to the westerly breezes. Looking toward the right side of the graveled road, Kulien could see white foam riding the crested blue-gray waves of the bay. She sat beside Marshall Whitfield in a covered buggy drawn by an amiable horse that seemed to enjoy the outing as much as its passengers. Neither spoke as they headed away from the city. For the past hour, to avoid any personal conversation with Marshall, Kulien recited information she had learned about the growing city of San Francisco.

Earlier that morning, while Kulien prepared a lunch basket, Marshall had gone with Horace Clark to rent a horse and buggy from the livery stable. Contemplating a day alone with Ta Ming's father, Kulien's emotions raged from fear to longing. What would they talk about? Seven long years of change had passed since their nightly meetings in the summerhouse. She had been afraid when Sunfu asked her to care for Marshall Whitfield's wound, but her daily ministrations to him had opened her mind and heart to words of commitment as they recited marriage vows to each other. Her life had begun to change from that night of love until this very day.

As she continued to add pieces of fruit to the basket, she wondered if Marshall could even imagine her life after they had reunited for such a brief moment in Hong Kong. She had escaped a life of prostitution, and survived the long voyage across the Peaceful Sea, only to escape the life of a joy girl once again. Then an Irish doctor had safely delivered her baby, and had rescued her from the slave block. Today, the only thing she and Marshall Whitfield had in common was the most important person in her life—Ta Ming! And she didn't want to talk to Marshall about him, because she knew his purpose in coming to America was to take him away from her to live in Great Britain.

Now as they proceeded on their trip to the outskirts of the city, she had become a reservoir of information, beginning at Little China and continuing up and down the busy streets of San Francisco.

"On the top floor of that building," Kulien pointed at a house with a small red door decorated with gilded plaques, "is a joss house, a Chinese temple, where men light incense and burn paper messages to the gods. Americans call my people pagan, but they *are* religious, and find comfort in the familiar."

Marshall scanned the narrow streets. "I'm reminded of Shanghai." He covered his nose with a handkerchief as they passed an alley. "It even smells the way I remember it," he said, smiling.

As the horse *clip-clopped* down the bumpy road, Marshall nodded toward the groups of men who squatted in front of stores gambling. "At least they aren't lonely."

Kulien, continuing to avoid the subject of Ta Ming's future, launched into another discourse. "The men have formed *tongs*, family associations of people with the same surname. Through the organizations they find mutual aid in a country opposed to their coming." She spoke as if she were reading from a book.

Nodding absentmindedly, Marshall added, "It's strange that there are no Chinese women to be seen. Where are their wives and children?"

Kulien repeated what she had learned from Dr. Ben, "The men who come primarily from southern China plan only to stay long enough to make money to help their families. Their wives and children wait for them to return to lands that have been ravaged by floods and famine."

As they traveled through the town, Marshall watched people from many nations go in and out of banks, theaters and gambling halls. "What a mixture of races! And I thought London was exciting."

At the lilt in his voice, Kulien turned away from the busy street. She remembered his enthusiasm when he told her about England and life outside the walls of her family compound. Her heart fluttered at the memories, but she reminded herself of his reason in coming to America, and glanced away.

As the faint morning sun moved higher overhead, almost disappearing behind slate-colored clouds, the horse headed southeast toward the gently rolling hills. Sitting side by side, neither Kulien nor Marshall spoke, each wrapped in private thoughts.

It was almost noon when Marshall rubbed the back of his neck. "You must be hungry; I know I am, and I'd like to walk around a bit. It's been awhile since I've held the reins, and I'm starting to feel the results!" He leaned out of the buggy, and then turned to smile at her. "There's a grove of trees ahead. Let's stop there and have our lunch." He glanced up at the threatening sky. "It looks like it might rain again."

After tying the horse to a tree, Marshall took Kulien's hand to help her step down from the buggy. Holding the basket on one arm, she quickly withdrew her hand, extremely aware of his touch. Shaken from her response, she glanced away while he spread a blanket over a carpet of long grasses under a large tree. Removing his hat, he shook off the raindrops that had begun to fall. "I hope this gives enough protection if it starts to rain harder!"

The low branches, covered with young tender leaves, formed a canopy of pale green overhead. Although the rain splattered all around them, Kulien and Marshall were sheltered from the afternoon storm. As they stood looking out at the rain, Marshall's presence overwhelmed her. The scent of his wool coat and highly polished boots filled her mind with past memories. Tall and noble in his bearing, she recalled the night he had dressed in her father's robe, and stood waiting for her in the moonlight. He was a different man then, and she was only a young girl. Repressed longings for physical love stirred deeply within. After so many years he was here beside her. Her head began to whirl; the grassy meadow rose up to meet the dark clouds, and she had difficulty breathing. She reached for Marshall's arm to steady herself. Before weighing her words, she blurted, "Oh, Marshall, I can't believe that you're here—at last!"

Marshall covered her hand with his, concern showing on his handsome face. "Kulien, you're pale. Come, let's sit down. I think we'll stay dry here; and the rain seems to be letting up."

Still holding her hand, he led her to the blanket and sat beside her, his shoulder touching hers. "I know it's been a shock seeing me after so many years, but I had hoped that. . .."

Not allowing him to finish his thoughts, Kulien removed her hand and edged away from him. "Yes, I know. I, too, had hopes, dreams actually. I hoped that we would have a lifetime together, but it was a false hope—a dream that died years ago."

Marshall said nothing, and except for the spatter of raindrops rattling the leaves outside their shelter, silence rose like a wall between them. Kulien's breathing was shallow; and her heart pounded erratically as she tried to gain control of her unwelcome emotions. Shivering, she folded her arms close to her body, and inhaled deeply of the fragrant rain-cleansed earth.

Watching Kulien carefully, Marshall removed his coat, and said, "You're cold, and if you'd permit me, I'd like to give you this."

Kulien glanced at his concerned expression and nodded. "Thank you."

He rose to his knees and gently draped the dark wool garment over her shoulders. He was so near, she could smell the spicy scent that she remembered. She caught her breath.

"Kulien," he said, tilting her chin with a finger. "You don't need to be afraid of me." His hands moved to her hair, and he removed the silver pin that held it in a roll. His eyes still on her face, he spread her long hair over her shoulders. "There! That's how I remember you. Kulien," he whispered, lifting her to her knees, "we *are together* today, and we can reclaim those lost years."

Suddenly, a gust of wind blew through their enclosure lifting her hair, swirling it across her face. Marshall's hands were on her waist, raising her to her feet. His eyes glowed with passion as he searched her face for an answer.

Kulien felt as if she were caught up in a storm with no way of escape. She didn't move away, but after drawing the strand of hair from her face, she rested her hand on his arm. The wind continued to blow as his coat slipped off her shoulders. Marshall lifted her other arm to encircle his neck, and drew her closer. "I've never forgotten you, my Abishag." He buried his face in her jasmine scented hair. "I tried; I knew I must in order to be the man my family expected."

Marshall's hands on the small of Kulien's back spread warmth throughout her body. She felt utterly weak, unable to speak or move. His lips brushed her forehead, the tip of her nose, and before she could refuse, his lips were on hers. She felt her mind had left her body; all she wanted was to be one with him as they had been that night so very long ago. As if starved, she responded to his kisses with a hunger she'd never known.

Breathlessly, Marshall drew back long enough to gaze into her eyes with longing. As she returned his gaze, he began to remove his tie, and unbutton his shirt. "We're alone here, Kulien. The storm has stopped; it's dry, and," he glanced at the blanket spread out on the layer of dry leaves, "we can reclaim the love that we both want. I still think of you as my wife."

Kulien struggled between the desire for his touch, and what she knew in her heart was right—and wrong. He was married, and his legal wife waited for him in England, trusting him, perhaps loving him as much as she did.

The moment Marshall began to unloose the fastenings of Kulien's jacket, brilliant rays of sun washed the shadowy enclosure with light—pure, cleansing light. Kulien stopped Marshall with a hand on his. Confused at her change in attitude, he stared at her firm expression. She could see a rosy flush begin at his throat and spread upward over his face.

"I don't understand! I thought you wanted me as much as I want you!"

Kulien lifted his hand to her lips and kissed his fingers. "Forgive me for being so weak, Lord Whitfield. You are an honorable man, and I know that if we should give in to our desires, we would both regret it." She let go of his hand, and refastened the top button of her jacket. "Your wife, Elise, trusts you. She is not here to remind you of your vows to her."

Marshall, still flustered, began to button his shirt. He turned away from her, his back straight, his neck stiff with indignation. "*We* made vows, too, Kulien. And we made a child! Surely, I have *some* rights!"

"*You* have some rights?" Kulien's words came in a rush of anger. "You gave up your rights to me when you married your childhood sweetheart!"

"But our son. . ."

"*My* son," she said. "I carried him nine months in my body; I almost died when he was born. I nursed him; I loved him; I taught him all he knows. I am his mother—and the only parent he has ever had. You produced the seed, but that is *all*." She paused, her indignation continuing to rise. "I confess that I *was* tempted to lie with you just now; but I've changed. I'm no longer that innocent girl who knew nothing about the world and its evils."

"Do you hate me so?" Marshall's eyes glistened with tears. "Only moments ago, I thought you still loved me."

Kulien had bent down to fold up the blanket, and she handed it to Marshall. With the uneaten lunch still in the basket, she picked it up and walked out into the open meadow, now sparkling like diamonds from the remaining raindrops. Marshall followed her to the buggy, and before he could assist her, she had climbed up and sat down, her eyes straight ahead.

"So is this how it's going to be?" he asked, after shaking the reins. Turning the horse toward the city, his voice had a pleading tone, "Kulien, forgive me if you think I took advantage of our situation today. I thought you felt the same about me as I do about you. Please don't shut me out of your life—or away from Ta Ming. Regardless of your opinion, he *is* my son, too."

Without looking at him, she answered, "Lord Whitfield, you need no forgiveness from me; and I certainly don't hate you! I was at fault in giving in to my weakness. As far as Ta Ming is concerned, we won't talk about him today. Enough has been said."

Kulien had spoken the truth. On the long ride back to the mission house, neither said a word. However, in their minds, both Marshall and Kulien continued to rehearse the events of the day, each wondering what would have happened had they given in to their desire.

FORTY-SEVEN

When Kulien and Marshall arrived at the mission house, Anna and Horace greeted them at the door. Anna, wearing a starched apron over a gray dress wiped her hands on an embroidered tea towel and blurted, "Lord Whitfield, won't you please honor us by staying for dinner? I've prepared a turkey with potatoes and garden vegetables." Smiling with anticipation, her eyes crinkled as she waited for his answer.

Unsure of how to answer, Marshall glanced at Kulien. She had lowered her eyes and set her mouth in a compressed line. In a solemn tone, he replied, "I'm afraid Kulien is quite exhausted after our long ride." He brushed hands over his damp coat and added, "As you can see, we didn't escape that sudden downpour!"

Shaking her head with disapproval, Anna stepped onto the porch, and took the basket from Kulien's arm. "Why you didn't eat your lunch! You must be starved. A fine dinner will refresh both of you." Still holding the basket, she spoke in a compelling tone, "Come along now, we won't accept any excuses." Her eyes sparkled with humor. "My famous roast turkey will fill your stomachs, and bring a smile to both of your faces!"

"It will bring a smile to *this* old face," Horace said, before clapping Marshall on the back. "Now, as you heard her say, the wife has prepared a delicious meal; and we won't take 'no' for an answer, Lord Whitfield." Horace nodded toward the doorway, "And Ta Ming has been waiting all day to see you. It isn't often we have foreigners visit our home."

Marshall lifted his broad shoulders in a question, awaiting a reply from Kulien. She felt trapped as they all turned their eyes on her. It had been one of the most unpredictable days of her life—spending time alone with the only man she had ever loved. He had wanted her to forget the years since their wedding night; and surrender herself to him as she had then. It had taken all her power to deny him, because she had also wanted to erase the years of pain for a moment of love and connection. And now, here she was, asked to be with him for another hour—so close, yet so far. And there was her son, who already believed that

Marshall Whitfield was his father. She would have to tell him—soon. She forced a smile. "Yes, of course you must stay, Lord Whitfield. It will be a treat for all of us to have you join us for a meal. Perhaps you could even meet the girls who live here. After several months of good food and learning to read, they're becoming young ladies now." Her eyes met Anna's, "We're quite proud of them."

While Marshall went to clean up for dinner, Kulien followed Anna into the kitchen. "The food smells delicious, as usual. And you're right about not eating lunch. We had traveled quite a distance before the rain began to fall. There wasn't time to stop and eat." She didn't mention taking refuge under the trees, but quickly went on, "I'll help you get the platters on the table." Warm steam from the stove added to the heat she felt rising to her face.

Anna turned away from the stove to take Kulien's hands in hers. "We knew this wouldn't be easy for you, my dear—being with Ta Ming's father after all these years. You haven't told us the details that led to his birth, and that's fine. You have a right to your privacy. God knows all about your past, and He has mercy beyond what you have *yet* to believe. Horace and I prayed that God would give you strength to do and say what you knew to be right." Listening to Anna's kind words, Kulien blinked away gathering tears, and forced a weak smile. The woman, still holding Kulien's hands, nodded her understanding. "We were concerned that you might be tempted to do something you'd later regret."

Kulien's innermost thoughts whirled about in her head as each day she learned more about the Clarks' faith. How was it that they seemed to sense every mood and change in her life? Anna was right about the temptation. If they only knew how close she had come to setting aside her new morals, and yielding to her desire. Withdrawing her hands, she nodded, "Thank you. Although I don't understand who this God is that you talk to, it seems that He hears."

As if perceiving what Kulien had faced that afternoon, Anna smoothed her apron, and with a smile and gentle voice, said, "Let's take this food into the dining room; I know a little boy who's not only hungry, but also quite curious. He's been waiting hours for your return. He's run to the window so many times, I fear he's worn a path in the carpet." Handing a large bowl of steamed vegetables to Kulien, she lifted a platter of sliced turkey, surrounded by browned potatoes, and started out of the kitchen. "The girls went to their rooms to study; Lord Whitfield can meet them later."

After they were seated, and Horace Clark had offered a prayer of thanksgiving, each person took generous servings of the sumptuous fare. Several quiet moments passed before Marshall Whitfield began to talk about his long voyage around Cape Horn. Ta Ming was full of questions, and Marshall was only too eager to answer, his face alight with joy in seeing the intelligence of his son. The little boy sat next to Kulien, across the table from his father. Kulien had thought about when and where she would tell Ta Ming about Marshall, and had reached a decision. For now, she preferred that he only know the man as a foreigner who had come to visit.

Still protective of Ta Ming, and hoping to avoid any questions he might ask Marshall Whitfield, Kulien excused herself soon after they finished the meal to put the child to bed. When she returned, Marshall was waiting in the parlor. "Reverend and Mrs. Clark have gone to see about the girls, and suggested that you and I might have more to say to each other—alone."

"I do have questions I'd like answered before Ta Ming is formally introduced to you as his father." She stood in the archway and nodded her head toward the front door. "The evening is pleasant, and we can sit outside on the porch so our words won't be heard." She took her jacket from a hook in the entryway, and Marshall, putting on his coat, followed her down the hallway and out the door.

Sitting beside one another on a bench, Kulien's voice was cool and controlled. "I know that you're still unhappy about my behavior this afternoon, but I cannot forget that although you *married me*, you have taken another woman to be your wife." There, she had said it. She wondered if he sensed the hurt in her voice. His eyes never left her face, though he said nothing. As moments passed, she could feel the tension growing between them. Turning away, she watched the sky as the sun sank deeper into the horizon, casting shades of purple and pink over the city.

When Marshall finally spoke, his voice was tender, his words slow and deliberate. "I want you to *know* that I had no choice in the matter. Please believe me when I say—I took our vows as seriously as you did."

Lifting her chin, she turned her eyes to him, attempting to respond with a calmness she didn't feel. "You told Elizabeth that our marriage was only a 'youthful indiscretion.' Why would you say that when you led me to believe that you truly loved me?"

Without warning, Marshall's arms went around Kulien, pulling her close—so close she could feel his heart beating in rhythm with her own. His mouth moved in her hair, his words so soft, she could scarcely hear. "Can you—will you forgive me?" When she didn't answer, he added, "I admit I was wrong to say that, but my true feelings for you haven't changed. I want you to understand that even though my sister tried to help you reach me in Hong Kong; neither she nor my mother will accept what happened between us." With a forlorn expression on his face, he continued, "My darling, although Elise is my legal wife according to British law, she is not a *complete* wife to me." He released his hold, and tipped her chin with a forefinger so he could look into her eyes.

His closeness revived her sense of weakness. Would she ever be able to let go of her love for him? Could she trust him? Her voice quavered as their eyes locked, "I don't understand. What do you mean, she isn't a complete wife? Elizabeth wrote that you had a lavish wedding, and that you live together. You *are* married to Elise!"

As Kulien inched away from him, Marshall bowed his head, and bracing his arms on his knees, he tried to explain. "Elise and I grew up together as family friends. As a child, she contracted a disease that left her paralyzed from the waist down." He glanced over at Kulien to see if she was listening before he went on, "As her closest friend, I took her to social events and became known as her escort, and eventually, her fiancé."

Kulien sifted his words, searching for the true meaning. "Do you love her?" Her voice quavered with a child-like tone.

Sitting upright again, he reached for Kulien's cold fingers, and pressed his lips against them. "Yes, I do love her, but only as a very dear friend. She loves me as she always has—a friend who helped her feel accepted in social situations. But friendship is the *only* relationship we have, Kulien. I promise you!"

The warmth of his lips on her fingers remained, and his words of comfort tugged at her heart. "To be a friend with the woman you marry is a good omen. I don't understand what you're trying to say." Her own words sounded false to her ears. She did know what he meant, but wanted him to tell her plainly, and without deception.

"We have never made love—as you and I did that night in China. When I say that Elise is unable to be a complete wife; I'm telling you that we cannot have children together; we don't sleep in the same bed—or in the same room."

Continuing to hold her hand, Marshall turned to place his other hand on her face, looking deeply into her eyes. "I still think of you as my wife."

Kulien lowered her eyelids, smiling within herself. She felt sadness for the paralyzed woman, but happy that she was denied Marshall's manhood. Feeling his eyes still on her, she was thankful that as the hour grew later, darkness veiled their faces. "But I am *not* your legal wife; Elise is." Despite the woman's lack of a physical relationship with Marshall, Elise still bore his name and prestige. She, not Kulien, had been accepted by Marshall's family as Lady Whitfield.

Marshall continued talking, his words soft and caressing. "Kulien, you are the mother of *my son*, the only heir to the Whitfield name and fortune. Surely that means something to you."

Rising from the bench, Kulien folded her arms across her waist, looking down on him. In the twilight-darkness, Marshall's somber face was in the shadows, and although her love for him was as strong as when she was a young girl, his plan to take Ta Ming away, built a wall between them. Gathering strength, she said in a breathless, but decisive voice, "We are no longer married. As I told you earlier, I'm *not* the same innocent girl you met in China many years ago." Struggling against the memories crowding her mind, she spoke the words she had been delaying, "However, I do want Ta Ming to become acquainted with you *as his father* before you leave America." She glanced away for a moment, then announced in a strong voice, "Tomorrow we will take him to see the ocean; there you can say 'goodbye' to both of us."

The next morning, Ta Ming could scarcely contain his excitement when Kulien informed him that they were going to spend the afternoon with Lord Whitfield. He had already expressed his suspicion that Marshall was his father; and she had chosen the time and place to tell him the truth.

After the midday meal, Kulien buttoned Ta Ming's warm coat under his chin, put on her own quilted silk jacket and combed through her long hair, leaving it loose to spread over her shoulders. As her son waited in the hallway, Kulien entered the dining room, speaking in a low tone, "Anna, Lord Whitfield will arrive soon to take Ta Ming and me for a ride." She fingered the buttons on her jacket. "It's time for my son to know his father."

Nodding in agreement, Anna's eyes brightened with interest. "Have you discussed the boy's future with Lord Whitfield? Did you come to a decision about where he will grow up? I must confess I had hoped you would have come to a mutual understanding last night."

There had been no discussion, and certainly no agreement regarding Ta Ming's future. Kulien had determined that he would never leave her; but Marshall could be persuasive; and she knew her own weakness. The hours she and Marshall had spent under the sheltering trees the day before, passed quickly through her mind, and she trembled at the memory of his warm lips on hers. She shook her head to dispel the passionate scene and closed her eyes.

Anna watched Kulien's expression change. "Forgive me, dear, for upsetting you with my words. Horace and I know that this is a heart-searching decision for you, but we're praying that you'll do what is best for Ta Ming. He's a bright child, and he does deserve the *formal* education he would receive in Great Britain."

Kulien felt like shouting at Anna and covering her ears; but instead she hurried out of the room, and taking Ta Ming's hand, went outside to wait for Marshall to arrive with the buggy.

Although Anna's declaration, *"He deserves the formal education he would receive in Great Britain,"* brought pain, Kulien continued to consider them as she and Ta Ming sat beside Marshall in the covered buggy. However, she wasn't able to dwell on the worrisome words for long because Ta Ming could not contain his joy. Sitting between them, the boy wiggled and squirmed, and hopped and bounced. "My son," Kulien looked at him, her eyes twinkling with amusement. "I believe the egg you ate this morning has hatched into a chick! You are unable to sit still!"

Marshall patted Ta Ming's leg. "This is an exciting day for you, isn't it? Your mother tells me that you love the ocean. Would you like to ride out to the Golden Gate where the water stretches as far as your eyes can see?"

"Oh, yes, sir. That would make me most happy."

Again, the seat began to jiggle with Ta Ming's enthusiasm. Marshall smiled at Kulien over the boy's head, and she felt her heart swell with gladness. If only they could always be together as a family. Today was a fulfillment of her girlhood dreams; and although she knew the joy would not last, she would have these moments to remember. Glancing beyond Ta Ming's head, she studied Marshall's fine features. He was even more handsome than when she first saw him on her sixteenth birthday. A few silver hairs, mingling with the gold at his temples, added to his distinguished appearance. No longer wearing a moustache, his face was now smooth and clean-shaven—and she liked it. He seemed oblivious to her perusal while he talked with Ta Ming, so she continued to gaze upon him: the high forehead, the long, straight nose, full expressive lips, and finely chiseled chin. She watched what the foreigners' called, "an Adam's apple," move up and down as he talked and delighted in his broad shoulders and muscled chest—remembering their one night together. Stopping her imagination before going further, she felt the heat of desire spread throughout her body. It was all she could do to stay composed as pent-up emotions rose to the surface of her mind. How she longed to be one with him, if only one more time since she knew that he still desired her.

Yet there was something within her mind and spirit that needed much more than Marshall was willing—or even able to give. It would not—could not happen again.

After bumping along the road for several miles, a sudden jolt of the buggy brought Kulien to her senses. "There, Ta Ming, see where the ocean meets the sky!" Marshall, pulling on the reins brought the buggy to a halt. "On the other side of that water is China. That's where your mother and I first met." Marshall lifted the boy from the buggy and held him in his arms as he walked out to the point; but his eyes were on the expressive face of his son, not on the surging tide.

As Kulien joined them on the rocky ledge, Marshall shifted Ta Ming to one arm and wrapped his other arm around her shoulders. Holding Kulien and Ta Ming close to his body, he spoke above the roar of the waves crashing below, "Here we are—together as a family, at least for a few hours."

Kulien smiled within herself. Yes, they did have these moments—glorious moments she would never forget. No one spoke as they listened to the pounding surf, and felt its salty spray on their faces. Kulien broke the tranquility of the moment with a commanding voice, "It is time to speak to Ta Ming of his past—and his future."

The wind whipped the words from her mouth and blew a strand of raven hair across her cheek. She pushed it behind her shoulder, aware that she could no longer postpone the inevitable. Ta Ming had a right to know his father, if only for a short time.

"Ta Ming," she said, after they had sat down on large boulders near the cliff, "you were correct yesterday when you said you believed Lord Whitfield was your father."

Standing beside Marshall, Ta Ming's blue eyes sparkled and he leaned against Marshall's arm, his hand on the sleeve of the woolen frock coat.

"Yes, son," Marshall added, looking into Ta Ming's expectant face. "As I mentioned before, your mother and I met many years ago in China. We had to be separated because of my position in the British government. I learned that I had a son only a few months ago. You're quite a big boy now—six years old, and I regret that I wasn't here when you were a baby. I would have been able to hold you; and as you grew older, I would have taught you the affairs of men." His eyes connected with Kulien's.

Lifting Ta Ming onto his lap, Marshall smiled with surprise as the boy put his arms around his neck and nuzzled his face against his father's.

The three sat quietly on the rocks, each absorbed in private thoughts. The only sounds were the squawking of sea gulls and the rhythmical crash of waves on the rocks below. Kulien's eyes swept over her son and his father as they seemed lost in each other's presence. Marshall stroked Ta Ming's shiny black hair, and he studied the boy's upturned face as if seeing his own image. The sky reflected the same deep blue in Ta Ming's eyes as in Marshall's, and his smile flashed from the same impressive mouth. Turning to Kulien, Marshall broke the spell, "He does look like me, doesn't he?"

"Yes, I see it more today than ever before. Except for Ta Ming's high cheekbones and thick, black hair, I would say he is more your child than mine."

"He is both yours and mine—yet—I feel somehow that he belongs to neither of us."

Ta Ming slid off Marshall's lap and ran to stand near the brow of the cliff where he watched gulls soar on the drafts of wind. Glancing over his shoulder at his mother, he saw her motion with her hand, and stepped back a safe distance from the ledge.

"Who knows what his future will be," Kulien said, with an audible sigh. "I do want him to stay here with me; he is my very life, yet. . .." Her face clouded with uneasiness. "I know you want to take him with you." She could hardly speak from the dryness filling her mouth. Breathing in short gasps, for a moment she thought she would faint when Marshall reached out to cover her hand with his. At his touch, her words returned. "I understand that he would have greater opportunities there. But he is still young. He needs a mother. He needs *me*."

"Of course, he does, and no one could take your place; but you may be assured that my entire family would love him."

"Even your *wife*?" The words tasted bitter in her mouth.

"Elise is known for her gentleness and generosity. She desperately wants a child; and hopes that Ta Ming will return with me."

Pulling her lips into a narrow line, Kulien closed her eyes, thinking—deciding. When she looked up, she asked, "How about Elizabeth? And your mother? Would they be willing to accept a child of mixed blood into their family?" More worries filled her mind, and before he could answer, she went on, "And then there are other boys. Ta Ming was treated cruelly here; and from what I've learned of your people, they're not even as accepting of other races as the Americans are supposed to be."

Dropping to his knees on the rocky ground, Marshall took both of Kulien's hands in his and looked up at her, his eyes pleading. "He would attend a private school where all the boys are treated equally. There would be riding lessons, music— anything that interests him."

As he turned to watch Ta Ming toss pebbles over the edge of the wind-swept cliff, he added, "I feel that I've known him since his birth, yet I've missed all of his growing up. Kulien, you've had him for six years! Isn't it time for him to know his father, and the British side of his heritage?"

Resting his forehead on Kulien's knees, he breathed deeply. Kulien, keenly aware of his longing, combed her fingers through his golden hair, wanting to ease his pain—and hers. But she was unable to speak the words he wanted to hear. Wasn't it enough that Marshall would sail away from her? What right did the paralyzed woman have to both her lover and her son? All the people she had cared about had gone away from her. How could she let Ta Ming leave? At this moment she felt her life hanging by a silken thread.

When Marshall lifted his head, his eyes burned with a faraway look. "I do want him to go with me, but I've already brought you so much pain. I don't think I could take the boy away from you; he's the center of your life."

Marshall stood and lifted Kulien to her feet. He held her close enough for her to hear his low voice, "Will you please believe that I don't want to hurt or deprive you of happiness?"

Kulien's answer was to pull his face to hers and stop his words with a fleeting kiss. They held each other for several minutes, not speaking, but turning their heads to watch their son.

Nestled in the warmth of his arms, Kulien asked, "When do you need an answer? I'm so afraid." She looked up into his face, her green eyes questioning. "I was certain I would never let Ta Ming go; but I must think more of him and his future than of myself."

Tenderly, Marshall took Kulien's face in his hands, desire shining in his eyes; then his mouth was on hers—kissing her with such intensity, that when he lifted his head, she could scarcely breathe.

He moaned, his eyes resting on her full lips. "My ship leaves in a week."

Stepping out of his arms, Kulien called to Ta Ming, and smiled wistfully as he ran to her, his cheeks rosy from the ocean breezes. "Our son is young," she said, "but he should help decide his future."

With a hand on his narrow shoulder, Kulien stooped to look into the boy's eyes. "My son," she began, "your father has come from across the sea because he would like to take you to live with him in England."

"England? But isn't that far away, Mama?" He looked at Marshall, then back at Kulien, a frown appearing on his smooth forehead. "Will you come with us?"

"No, son, I'm needed here to work with the slave girls." She bit her bottom lip as she forced herself to speak the dreaded words. "You would have a good life with your father; and grow to be a fine English gentleman. Wouldn't you like that?"

"But what about you, Mama? I don't want to leave you. Please come with us!"

Without looking at Marshall, Kulien answered in unhurried, purposeful words, "Your father has an English wife. She's a very fine lady, but is unable to bear a child." Her voice trembled in spite of her resolve. "You would be her son while you're away from me."

"No," Ta Ming, said, frowning. "You are my *only* mother." He glanced up at Marshall's hopeful expression, and added, "But I could try to be her friend."

Marshall placed a hand on Ta Ming's head as if declaring a blessing. "Think about this carefully, son. Even though you would receive many benefits in England that you are denied here, you would miss your mother, and she would miss you."

Looking first to Kulien, then to Marshall, Ta Ming tried to make a much-too-large decision for such a small boy. "Mama, I *would* like to go to school. And," he said, slipping his small hand into Marshall's, "it *is* a fine thing to have a father. I want to go, but I don't want to leave you." Tears filled his eyes and streamed down his cheeks.

With one hand on Ta Ming's shoulder and the other on Marshall's arm, Kulien heard only the hammering of her heart. "Your father would bring you back for visits—wouldn't you?" Her question was more a statement than a request.

Although tears continued to spill from Ta Ming's large eyes, his lips turned up in a smile as he looked into his father's face. "If I may visit my mother, I will go with you."

Marshall knelt on the ground to meet Ta Ming's eyes. "I promise to bring you to see your mother as often as possible."

As he spoke, Kulien knelt beside them, her voice seeming to come from far away. Feeling numb, she barely heard her own words. "It will be a fine adventure for you, my son. I'll write letters to you, and you can write to me, and tell me of all the new things you're learning."

She had said the hated words. She had encouraged her most beloved son to leave her—to go to the other side of the world.

Ta Ming's head turned from one side to the other, first studying his father's face, then his mother's. "I will go with you, my father," he said at last.

Panic, like a fist, closed around Kulien's throat, but she swallowed deeply and lifted her eyes to Marshall's. "Then it will be as you wish. We must accept this as our destiny." Reaching for her child, she held him so tightly, he groaned. "Ta Ming, my son, we have only a few days before you leave." Trying to sound cheerful, a hollow laugh accompanied her words. "In the short time we have left, we'll have to make many new memories— memories to last us a very long time."

Looking away at the horizon, she said softly, "Anna told me that 'faith is living with pain.'" With an expression of defeat, she thought, *If she's right, then perhaps one day I will become a woman of great faith!*

FORTY-EIGHT

Because he wanted to arrive in England before winter, Marshall had booked passage for himself and Ta Ming on the next ship leaving for Boston, giving Kulien only a short time to prepare Ta Ming for the long separation from her. As each day passed, she grew more apprehensive, more depressed. Had she made the right decision? Was Ta Ming too young to decide for himself? Could Marshall give his son as much love as she had—the love he needed?

Anna and Horace Clark expressed their approval of Kulien's conclusion. "It will be best for the boy. You'll see," Anna said, every time she and Kulien were together in the same room.

"Yes, Ta Ming will be safe in England," Horace encouraged her. "Times are growing worse, not better here. I'm afraid there's going to be even more open opposition to the Chinese. The child would be in danger." He stroked his beard and squinted over the top of his glasses. "You aren't safe, either. You must be extremely careful."

Marshall came to the house only twice that week. Kulien supposed he was allowing her more hours alone with her son, and she was glad for every moment; but she missed him, too. Soon they would both be gone, and Marshall had told her it could be as many as five years before they would be able to return—five years!

Two days before the ship's departure, Marshall arrived at the front door with a wide smile and an enthusiasm that echoed Ta Ming's. "I have a surprise for you," he said, when he and Kulien were alone in the parlor. "But first..." He walked to the sliding door and latched it. "First I must hold you, and perhaps persuade you to change your mind—about us—when we're alone?" His eyes twinkled with mischief.

She went to him and lifted her face. "Thank you for your patience with me. I can't explain my feelings. I know I love you, and my desires are the same as yours; but there is something within me that remembers your wife. She trusts you!   And to give up my son, I must trust you also."

To keep tears from overflowing, she blinked and smiled. "You said you have a surprise. What is it?"

"I also want the Reverend and his missus to hear what I have to say." With Kulien's hand in his, he walked to the kitchen to ask Anna and Horace to join them in the parlor.

When they were all seated, Marshall opened up his frock coat, and drew a shaft of papers from the inside pocket. "I've taken this upon myself, but if you," he directed his attention to Kulien, "or either of you," he said to the Clarks, "are uneasy about my proposition, please speak up. I want only what is best for Kulien." He took Kulien's hand and, with his eyes on her face, pressed his lips into her palm.

Kulien felt the blood rush to her cheeks and lowered her eyes. Marshall was behaving in a most unusual way in the presence of Horace and Anna Clark. Were they shocked at his open display of affection? Glancing over at them, she saw they had turned their eyes away in embarrassment. But Marshall gave them no heed, and continued to hold her hand. Then kissing her fingertips before releasing her hand, he began to open the documents.

"I have in my possession the deed to a house not far from here. It's a large and very comfortable house built by a man from the state of Virginia. As a prospector, the man made a fortune in gold then decided not to stay in California, but to return to the east."

Kulien and the Clarks looked at each other, questions filling their minds.

"It's my obligation, and within my power, to provide for Kulien as is fitting a member of the House of Whitfield. Although she is not my *legal* wife in the eyes of the commonwealth, I am committed to care for her needs."

Anna and Horace Clark sat dumbfounded. Kulien, too, was puzzled by Marshall's words; but no one spoke.

"This deed is in Kulien's name. Whatever you decide," he said, directing his words to her, "the house is yours to do with as you please." He unfolded another paper.

"I've also opened a bank account for Kulien," he looked up at the Clarks, "and with your help, she can learn how to use it.

I'll regularly deposit a sum of money that should be sufficient for any needs she might have."

To Kulien, "If you decide to continue your work with the slave girls, you have your own home." He lifted dark eyebrows. "Or if you decide to return to China, you may. I want you to know that you're free to pursue your life as you wish." His blue eyes never left her surprised face. Nodding at the silk rope around Kulien's neck, he went on, "With that signet ring, you possess my family crest; and to withdraw monies from the bank, you must use the ring, and the family name—Kulien Whitfield."

Marshall's words hung over the room like a bomb ready to explode. Kulien's mind went back to her youth when firecrackers and rockets crackled through the air on New Years' Day. They all held their breath, waiting for someone to speak— to break the spell.

Finally, Horace practically leaped from his chair, and reaching for Marshall's hand, he pumped it vigorously. "You've done a good and decent thing here, Lord Whitfield. Kulien will be living up on the hill with the rich folks, but close enough to reach us if she has any needs." Smiling, he turned to Kulien. "This is a fine gift, my child. As you know, I cannot bless what happened in the past; but I believe the Englishman makes restitution for his sins."

Later that afternoon, the Clarks accompanied Marshall, Kulien and Ta Ming as they made a stop at the bank. Before heading up the hill to Kulien's new home, Horace said, "We'll return to the mission while you go to your property. You can tell us about it when you return."

Kulien's head whirled with the transformation her life was about to take: a generous bank account, a new name, and a home to call her own. After guiding the horse over a narrow lane, up a hill, and through a wooded forest, the buggy stopped in front of a magnificent white house surrounded by an elaborate iron fence.

Waving his arm in the direction of the imposing structure, Marshall's voice rose with excitement, "Here we are!" Kulien couldn't speak as she watched Marshall take Ta Ming from the buggy; then with his large hands encircling her waist, he lifted her to the ground. Staring at the house, surrounded by well-kept lawns and gardens, her eyes reflected the surrounding trees. Marshall's expressive blue eyes met hers. "You are the most beautiful creature I've ever seen!" His breath, warm and spicy, brushed over her senses.

"This is the house you purchased for *me*?" Her lips felt numb, and the words were halting.

"Yes, this is just for you. Do you like it?"

"But it is much too large for one person."

"Too much for you to care for, I agree. But you needn't be concerned. I've hired groundskeepers for the outside and servants for the inside. A dressmaker has been engaged to outfit you in clothes worn by a woman of wealth—in whatever style you prefer, of course."

"But I don't deserve. . .."

"That you have allowed Ta Ming to come with me is the greatest sacrifice a mother could make. I only wish I could have given you more." His lips rested gently on her forehead before he added, "You'll never want for anything again. The Americans will no longer snub you because you are part Chinese. The white man judges not by the color of skin, but by the color of money—and you'll have more than enough for as long as you live."

Kulien struggled to understand the extent of all Marshall had said. Was she actually to live in this mansion? And to do as she wished?

As if reading her mind, Marshall said, "Bring your slave girls here if you like. You are *free* to do as you please! Isn't that what you've always wanted?" He stopped talking long enough to briefly kiss her nose and lips. "The Americans will give you respect now." He pressed a warm hand on the small of her back. "Let's go inside."

As Marshall led Kulien through the expansive house, she tried to absorb the immensity of her new possessions. Not only was the twelve room house staffed with a cook, housekeeper, gardener, and guards, it was also appointed with the finest furnishings. It was obvious to Kulien that Marshall had made the purchases before he arrived in America. How could he have been so certain of her decision to relinquish her child to him?

She didn't question him, but gazed in amazement as they surveyed each room. There were treasures from around the world: paintings from France, sculptures from Italy, finely crafted furniture from Great Britain, and Oriental carpets of the highest quality. When she walked into her bedroom, a smile lit up her face. Exquisite Chinese screens, fashioned of ebony and ivory, divided the large suite into separate sections for both study and sleep. High-backed chairs with carved arms and legs had been placed in front of a marble fireplace. She suddenly yearned for her childhood home as she admired the familiar objects. At the other side of the room was a vanity, a table and lamp, and most imposing of all, a luxurious bed, enclosed by a sea-blue silk curtain.

Inhaling deeply, Kulien could hardly speak. "My gratitude is beyond words." Her voice was husky, her attitude shy. "I'm not worthy to live in such splendor when others of my race suffer in the alleys of Little China."

"You are more than worthy, my lovely Lotus Blossom. I know you'll use these possessions to the best of their advantage. Here in this place, you can do far more for your people than you could ever do on Sacramento Street."

The next day, Kulien, with the Clarks' help, moved into her new home. Ta Ming dashed from room to room, running up and down the stairs, asking questions with every breath. "Mama, don't you want me to stay here? Does Lord Whit..., I mean, does Father have as fine a house as this? Will you miss me? Where does that door lead?"

Kulien kept busy enough to mask her grief over Ta Ming's imminent departure. How would she survive without his countless questions, his boundless energy, and his arms around her neck? With only one more night together, she must not allow him to see her sadness. At every opportunity, she joined in his adventure of discovery. She raced up the stairs after him, catching him, pinning his arms, and tickling him until they both lay on the floor, exhausted from laughter. They played hide and seek, constantly finding new places to escape from each other. By the end of the day, they were both tired and happy.

After taking baths, and dressing in their finest clothes, they waited for Lord Whitfield to join them for dinner. Ta Ming held Marshall's hand while the three of them went from room to room, showing him what they had accomplished.

Later, as they sat in the formal dining room, servants stood in the shadows ready to respond to their slightest needs. After Marshall dismissed them, Kulien relaxed and began to talk. "Must Ta Ming be away from me for so many years? When I think how much he will have grown in five years, my spirit melts."

"I know it's a long time." Ta Ming sat between Kulien and Marshall at the dining table. "But it's also a perilous voyage from Great Britain to San Francisco." His eyes rested on the child who was intent on only one thing—the meal in front of him. "George would miss at least a year of schooling whenever we travel so far; and I know his education is one reason you've permitted him to go with me."

Kulien's heart beat wildly. "You called him, 'George.' Why don't you use his name—the name he knows?"

"When he's in England, he will be George Whitfield. He may as well get used to the change now." He smiled at Ta Ming. "Don't you like the name, 'George'?"

Ta Ming's round face dimpled. "I like whatever name you wish to call me, Father."

Kulien, though surprised by Marshall's words, continued to worry about the time her son would be gone. "But five years!" She put an arm around Ta Ming's shoulders. They felt so narrow and thin. "By the time he's eleven years old, he'll be almost grown!" She let her hand brush his cheek. Would he have hair on his face by then? Would he forget his mother and his Chinese heritage? She glanced up at Marshall as if he had heard her unspoken questions.

"If possible, I'll come sooner." He wiped his mouth with the edge of a napkin. "He'll miss you—we both will. But he'll grow strong through the experience."

"And what about me? Do I need more experience—more growth? Must I lose all that matters in life to grow strong? You know that I've lost enough in my twenty-two years—my birth family, my husband, and now my only child." She bit the inside of her cheeks to keep the tears from forming in her eyes.

"May I be excused from the table?" Ta Ming looked from his mother to his father, a slight frown on his forehead. "I would like to play in the upstairs rooms before I go to sleep."

After Ta Ming disappeared into the upper recesses of the house, Marshall followed Kulien into the lavishly appointed parlor. A low fire crackled in the fireplace, casting shadows on the high ceiling. A satin brocade settee glistened in the warm glow, and the polished furniture shone against richly-colored carpets from the Orient. Vases, statues, and pictures from around the world gave the room an international flavor. Kulien looked around, grateful, yet sad. There was so much. Too much. A sigh escaped her lips.

Marshall stood behind her and wrapped his arms around her, drawing her close against his body. "Are you happy?" he whispered into her hair. "Please tell me you are."

Silently, Kulien watched coral flames dance across the logs. When she finally answered, her cool tone belied her overwhelming emotions. "I'm as happy as I can be without you and Ta Ming."

With his hands on her shoulders, he turned her to face him. "You are, without doubt, the strongest woman I know. I understand that you're sad tonight, but your beautiful face will again shine with happiness." He touched the dimple in her cheek. "You'll miss George, Ta Ming, as deeply as he will miss you; but I have no doubt that both of you will make the best of it. Kulien, you persevered through that harrowing journey across the seas; you overcame the horror of the slave pen, and . . .."

"I had reason to live then—for my child—for you."

Drawing her closer, Marshall breathed deeply and moaned. "Oh, my lovely one, it isn't too late. If you've changed your mind about Ta Ming coming with me, I'll leave tomorrow without him." Stepping back, he searched her face. His jaw clenched in the firelight and his hands tightened on her shoulders.

"I don't want to make a mistake." She lifted her eyes to his, holding her breath.

Marshall's forlorn expression melted her heart. She couldn't change her mind, not now. "I know it will be good for our son to go with you; yet I also know that I'm good for him." Pulling away to quiet her tremulous emotions, she started for the stairway. "He's very quiet—too quiet. I should see what he's doing."

Waiting at the foot of the staircase, Marshall watched her slim form run up the stairs, full silk trousers swirling around her ankles.

Several minutes later, she came back down, smiling. "He crawled into bed in the guest room, and is sound asleep."

Reaching for her hand, Marshall smiled down at her. "Then we're alone. We have this one last night." He led her into the parlor where he sat on the rug in front of the fireplace. Looking up at her with longing, he opened his arms, and she went to him as a moth to a flame. "If you could put aside this new morality of yours," he whispered, "we could make memories to keep us warm while we're apart."

What he said was true. Why did she hold back the intense desire burning throughout her body? He was the father of her son, the only man who had ever possessed her body and soul.

Wrapped in his arms, Kulien melted in his embrace and surrendered to his kisses. She closed her eyes, enraptured by his every touch. One hand moved from her shoulders to her neckline where he began to undo the fastenings of her blouse, while the other hand went to her waist, drawing her closer. Kulien was only slightly aware of his movements, deeply satisfied with the fervor of his kisses. When, as one, they lay back on the rug, Kulien felt her inhibitions soar out of reach, her passion unleashed.

Groaning as if in pain Marshall rose to his knees. "We do have a bedroom tonight, a place where we will be undisturbed." With ease, he lifted her in his arms and started for the stairs.

Suddenly Kulien tensed and pushed out of his arms. She stood facing him. "No, Marshall. I can't do this. You know I want to—but I can't."

Marshall's face froze in disbelief. "Why not? You love me. I know that. What more do you want?"

"I want to be your legal wife. I want to be Elise!"

Trembling, Marshall shook his head and dropped onto one of the stairs. "I can't believe you're denying us this one last hour of love!" For several moments, his eyes bored into hers. Then he stood and lifted his proud chin. "But perhaps you're right. Forgive me for bringing more complications into your life."

Kulien took Marshall's coat off the hook by the door, and watched him put it on, slowly fastening each brass button. With a hand on the side of her face, he slowly traced her lips with his thumb. "You've been much stronger than I have, Kulien. I admire you for that."

After a quiet moment, she rested cool fingers on his hand. "And I thank you for providing so well for me. Now I begin a new life—a life without a son or a husband."

Bowing from the waist, and with his eyes on her face, Marshall took her hand in his and kissed it. "It is time for me to leave then."

Kulien followed him to the door, holding her head high and her emotions in check. She watched him take his tall hat from the table near the door, and brush at an invisible spot. When he turned, his expression was grim. "I'll miss you, Kulien. I will always remember you and the depth of love you have brought to my life. "

"You take care of Ta Ming. Be proud of him." The words caught in her throat. "Go in peace, and enjoy every day, every moment with our son."

Marshall hesitated before stepping onto the veranda. "I'll see you tomorrow; and we'll have our final farewells then."

Holding up a hand, Kulien shook her head. "No, Ta Ming will be ready when you arrive. I will not say goodbye or watch you leave with my son."

Marshall closed the space between them to take Kulien in his arms one last time. They held each other as if, letting go, they would drown. When their lips met in a final kiss, it was as tender and light as a summer breeze. Then, without another word, he turned and walked away.

Watching his every movement, Kulien filled her vision with his image—golden hair glistening in the moonlight; long legs striding in masterful purpose.

She wrapped her arms about her waist and closed her eyes, etching his portrait on her heart. She would never forget him—never.

The Harvesting Season

*"Let both grow together until the harvest, and at harvest time I
will tell the reapers, Gather the weeds first and bind them in
bundles to be burned, but gather the wheat into my barn."*
~~~Matthew 13:30 ~~~

FORTY-NINE

Kulien's first weeks in the big house on the hill had been
the loneliest period of her life; not only did she long for Ta Ming;
she had no companionship other than the servants. At times she
felt she had been set down in another world, separated from all
that was familiar. The large house creaked and moaned in the
darkest hours of night; and although the food, prepared by a
Chinese cook, reminded her of childhood meals in the Kuang
compound, she felt even more isolated at mealtime with no one
to share her table. Her soul yearned for Ta Ming's contagious
laughter, for Marshall's expressions of love, and for the Clarks'
words of hope. She knew, from past experience, that her life
would change for the better as time went by; so she exercised the
patience learned in her father's home.

One afternoon, two months after moving to the hill, her
friends from the "Home for Slave Girls" arrived at the front
entrance. Before that day, they had occasionally visited,
bringing a rescued girl to meet Kulien; but this time they were
accompanied by a young Caucasian woman with brown hair and
eyes.

"Kulien, forgive us for arriving unannounced," Reverend
Clark explained. "But we have someone we want you to meet
before making a proposition to you."

Dressed in a new gown, which accentuated her slender
beauty, Kulien stepped aside to wave them into the parlor. The
sky-blue dress, made according to Chinese fashion, was simple,
but elegant. The high collar and smooth straight lines covered
her from chin to ankles—the only decoration, a chain of

intricately embroidered white lilies at the throat. With her glossy-black hair smoothed away from her face and fastened at the back with a silver pin, Kulien seemed to have added years of serene maturity in only eight weeks.

Anna's eyes swept over the changed appearance several times before she relaxed on the settee beside the young woman they had brought with them.

Folding hands at her waist, Kulien bowed slightly, and sat opposite them on a wing-backed chair.

"How are you faring, child?" Reverend Clark peered over his glasses at Kulien after taking in the ornately decorated room. "We know you have your every physical need supplied," he said, leaning toward her, "but we're concerned that you must be lonely up here by yourself."

Nodding in agreement, Anna looked first at Kulien, and then rested her eyes on the young woman seated beside her. "We've brought a friend of ours to meet you—Martha Johnson. She recently arrived from Pennsylvania, a state on the east coast. She's a fine teacher, and is extremely interested in our work!"

Kulien smiled at the woman, wondering what Anna and Horace had in mind.

"We'd like to transfer some of our more advanced students up here—to stay with you." Anna glanced at Horace and back to Kulien. "We thought Martha could live here, too, and help you teach. Of course, if you prefer to live alone, we would understand."

Kulien's heart raced with joy. At last she would be busy again, working with the girls—teaching English. She had begun to believe that her move from the mission house meant her assistance was no longer needed. "Your suggestion pleases me very much. As you know, there are many unused rooms in this large house. I would be happy to be at work again. And, of course, you are most welcome to join me," she said to the young woman.

Martha Johnson flashed dark brown eyes at Kulien and began to speak a halting Cantonese. "I know enough Chinese to communicate with the girls. Mrs. Clark has allowed me to help for several weeks." She glanced at Anna. "She believes that, working together, you and I cannot only teach English, but we can also teach what you call, the womanly arts."

Kulien felt an instant rapport with Martha, answering her in English. "You speak Chinese very well. I, too, had to learn Cantonese as Mandarin was my native language." Her smile seemed to light up the room. "Yes, you would be most welcome here. As I said, this house is much too large for only one person." Kulien motioned to the cook who stood in the doorway with a tray of tea and cookies. "This place could be another stepping stone for some of the girls before they walk through the door of freedom."

Horace Clark seemed to settle down and sipped his tea for several moments before speaking. "This is good news, Kulien; we do need your help. As you know, the girls trust you, and with Martha as your aide, our poor outcasts can be prepared to return to their homeland with the ability to teach girls—girls like themselves—who've been cast aside. They can teach English as well as other subjects."

It was decided then and there to transfer some students to the hill on the following day. "I'll make weekly calls to be sure you're all safe. In fact," he added, "Lord Whitfield told me to hire more guards if I thought it necessary. We don't want to take any chances with the safety of any of you living up here away from civilization."

As Kulien and Martha became acquainted, Kulien knew she had found a friend, who was not only close to her age, but who had similar values and dreams. Martha, too, had lost her husband.

"Michael succumbed to dysentery," she confided one evening as they sat by the fireplace. "He died three weeks before we reached San Francisco harbor. He'd dreamed of going to China to open an orphanage and teach the children about Jesus. Before he died, he said that if he couldn't sail across the Pacific, at least he could be buried at sea." Martha dabbed her eyes with a lace handkerchief. "Whenever I look out across that vast body of water, I feel his spirit telling me not to give up—to continue pursuing our vision." She closed her eyes a moment and looked up, smiling. "Thank you, Kulien, for allowing me to continue our dream of helping the Chinese girls and women."

Over the following months, the two worked tirelessly, teaching English, transforming inept, forlorn girls into vibrant women with hope. Martha, in addition to English, taught history, mathematics, and Bible; while Kulien gave instructions in calligraphy, poetry, and embroidery. As time passed, Kulien's loneliness for Ta Ming was somewhat assuaged by the concern she felt for her charges; but she still watched anxiously for his carefully written letters.

When Ta Ming first arrived in England, he wrote every week, but as the seasons changed, so did her son's disposition. His letters were less frequent, his longings for her faded, and his adaptation to the wealth and social life of British nobility replaced his need for a mother's gentle admonitions and love.

Within the space of one year, Ta Ming's (he now signed his name, "George,") letters had dwindled to less than one a month; but Kulien put aside her sadness, grateful that her son was happy in his new surroundings. Occasionally, Marshall added a postscript to Ta Ming's letter, expressing his concern for her, and his hope that one day he could return to America for a visit. Always she felt disappointed that there were no words of love. Had he turned his affection to Elise?

As the year of 1861 unfolded, Kulien's new country encountered exceptional change. The sixteenth president of the United States, Abraham Lincoln, was inaugurated on March 4th, setting in motion the founding of the Confederate States.

Martha Johnson's interest in the new Southern government kept her reading whatever newspapers she could obtain. "Listen to this!" She stopped reading long enough to attract Kulien's attention away from her studies. "'The Secessionists of South Carolina attacked the Federal troops at Fort Sumter on April 12th, and the fort surrendered the next day.'" She looked up, a frown on her face. "President Lincoln proclaimed a blockade of the Southern ports on April 19th."

"What does it all mean?"

Martha set the paper down. "Our country is at war with itself."

"That's common in my country as well." She thought back to Sunfu's alliance with the Taipings, and his strong disapproval of the Ching Dynasty. "Perhaps it's a good thing for people to disagree. Why are they fighting?"

Tapping her fingers on the newspaper, Martha continued to frown. "The Northern States are opposed to slavery. In the South, the wealthy actually own people as slaves. In some cases, they treat them no better than inhuman objects."

Now Kulien's interest was piqued. "Are the slaves Chinese?"

Martha shook her head, her expression grave. "No, they're Africans. They've been shipped over here like livestock, and sold to the highest bidder."

Kulien's mind wandered from Martha's information to the dark alleys of San Francisco. "Does our state support the North or the South?"

Martha's frown deepened. "I'm afraid California is split as well. There are people living here who come from both the South and the North, so their loyalties are divided." Martha rested elbows on the table, forming a steeple with her fingers. "Who knows what the future holds for us here on the west coast?"

Kulien listened, her eyes widening. "From what I've seen, California *is* a slave state—at least here in San Francisco. The sale of men and women goes on every day. Is there any difference between African and Chinese slaves?"

Martha practically bounded from her chair, almost tipping it over. She ran to Kulien and embraced her. "Oh, Kulien, you've opened my eyes! I felt sorry for the girls in the bagnios and cribs, but I never equated their plight with those of the black slaves in the South. Of course, you're right. There is *no* difference." She pressed her palms together and lifted her eyes. "This will be our cause—that those in California who support President Lincoln and the Union, must also give up the Chinese slave trade!"

A smile spread over Kulien's face as Martha's enthusiasm took hold. Could it be possible that they, two young women, might stir up the Americans to believe that Chinese females in America deserved to be free? Who would listen to a soft-spoken, beautiful woman from Pennsylvania and a "half-breed" female from the Flowery Kingdom?

As news of war between the North and South reached San Francisco, lines of division were also drawn between those who had traveled across the country in search of gold. Brawls broke out at the slightest provocation, and men fought openly in the streets. Even newly formed families split apart, depending upon one's political beliefs.

Several weeks passed before Kulien and Martha decided to go to Reverend Clark with their proposition. The more they discussed the problems in Little China, the stronger they felt about their cause. "The general population of San Francisco must be made aware of the slavery and injustices taking place in the alleys of their own city," Martha told him.

As they spoke, Horace and Anna Clark both nodded with renewed interest. "Perhaps we can begin by having you speak to various local churches and clubs," Horace said, after thinking over their words. "It would certainly stir those who oppose slavery in the South to admit the same evil is being perpetrated against the Chinese right here in the West."

Martha touched the tight curls in front of her ears before turning her attention to Kulien. "Suppose the fair-minded citizens of California could compare a slave girl with Kulien—they could see the Chinese woman is human—even beautiful. Not an animal!" Her voice rose as she imagined the result. "Reverend Clark, you could call meetings of city officials, and Kulien could speak to them about her experience in the barracoon."

With a gasp, Kulien covered her mouth with both hands. "Oh, no, Martha, I could never talk to the Americans. You must do it; or you, Reverend Clark."

Until now, Anna had said nothing. She folded her hands under her chin and fastened her eyes on Kulien. Her head bobbed up and down. "Martha is right. We've done all we can to rescue the poor, unfortunate girls, but Kulien, your presence, your voice at a meeting would do more than many of our words."

Kulien felt the blood drain from her face, and she gripped the arms of the chair. "Surely no American would listen to a woman—especially a woman such as I!"

"That's just the point," Horace interrupted. "The men and women attending our churches, as well as those who govern our city (bless their souls) need to be stirred from their apathy. We've tried for years to interest the citizens in our work among the slave girls, but with little response. We haven't reached their hearts. If we want to eradicate this blight from our midst, it's going to take more than what we've done. We need to rid our entire country of slavery—not just the South, and you're just the person they will listen to!"

A glimmer of hope rose in Kulien's heart. Hadn't she longed for freedom for her sisters since childhood? She had exercised the dormant dream for liberty by defying the traditions of her people; and although her life had been difficult, at least she was free to think for herself.

With a tremor in her voice, she asked, "Do you sincerely believe I might be an influence?"

"Most definitely," Horace answered. "We could let the citizens see and hear you, then bring in a girl who is about to die of disease. Who could ignore such a contrast?"

Quickly processing the images, Kulien spoke with determination. "Then I will do whatever you ask of me so that one day my people will be accepted in this country as equals. And one day, even the women in China will also be able to come and go as they please."

"And, God willing," Horace said with determination, they will know the One who loves them and has the power to set them free!"

As Reverend Clark made plans to call together the leading citizens of San Francisco, the climate of California's Gold Rush went through more changes. Nuggets were no longer found in the stream beds. Individual miners could not make a living, so many gathered up their belongings and moved north and east to new mining frontiers. Silver was mined from the Comstock Lode in Nevada. Colorado, Idaho and Montana also attracted miners. Because "easy" gold was no longer available, the percentage of Chinese miners grew. Their patience and hard work in sifting the sand for the last traces of gold brought them into favor with mining companies; and employers, ready to take advantage of the Chinese' willingness to work for low wages, hired them instead of white men. Even more hostility and enmity rose against the sons of the Celestial Kingdom.

Reverend Clark shared his concern with Kulien and Martha. "The situation is growing worse by the day. We can't delay any longer. Prepare your speeches, ladies. We're about to begin our campaign!"

FIFTY

It was a cold Sunday morning, the week before Christmas; and Kulien and Martha waited off-stage to speak to a large gathering of local leaders and business men. Standing side by side, the women offered an interesting portrait of East and West. Martha's soft brown curls bobbed up and down as her head turned to watch the crowd file into the meeting hall. A ruffled collar at her throat softened the simple navy blue dress that reached the floor; and a lace-edged handkerchief peeked over the top of a pocket.

Kulien's clothing was a strong contrast—a traditional *chipao*, a long green satin coat slit to the knees, that revealed slim black satin trousers. As one of her favorite coats, she wore it with pride, fondly remembering the days she had spent embroidering the intricate stitches while conversing with Lucy O'Kelly. Yellow chrysanthemums graced the upper portion, and pale green leaves trailed around the hemline. Even though she wore flat leather shoes, she was inches taller than Martha in her high-laced shoes with heels.

Martha smiled at Kulien. "You are beautiful this morning! With your hair combed back like that, it accentuates your high cheekbones; and your green eyes are almost the same shade as your coat."

Kulien felt heat rise to her face as Martha spoke. She would never become accustomed to the way Westerners praised one another for their appearance. Of course, as a child, she had heard such words from Jiang; but when another woman her age offered such compliments, she wasn't sure how to respond.

"Thank you, Martha. You look very nice today, too. Anna did impress us with the importance of our clothing today, but I hope we'll be more respected for what we say than how we're dressed."

Holding notes of a speech in her hand, Kulien tried to remain calm. "I can't believe that I, a simple Chinese woman, am going to speak to these influential people about the subject dearest to my heart!" (*That doesn't include my son, of course*) she thought.

Speaking softly, so only Kulien could hear, Martha leaned closer. "You know, you remind me of a woman in the Bible. Her name was Esther. Like you, she was living in a foreign land, and had to make a most difficult speech to the king." Seeing Kulien's interest, she went on. "When Esther told her uncle she was afraid, he said, 'Who knows but that you have come to the kingdom for such a time as this?' Kulien, the same is true of you. Who knows but that you have come to San Francisco for such a time as this—to tell the people of this great city that using Chinese girls as slaves and prostitutes is evil!"

Before Kulien could reply, Reverend Clark stepped to the podium. "We welcome those of you who have taken time to leave your warm homes to learn about our friends from far away China.

"And now," he said, after introducing Martha and Kulien, "I turn the meeting over to these young women who are making a difference in this city."

Stepping first to the podium, Martha's voice quavered as she began her short speech; but after only a few moments, the words rolled easily off her tongue. "As a widow, I'm here in San Francisco today instead of in China because my husband died on our voyage from the east coast." Several women glanced at their husbands, and then fastened their eyes sympathetically upon Martha.

"Our plans were to go to China to help impoverished people who had lost their homes and livelihood through flood and famine. Our primary objective was to open an orphanage in the interior, but. . ." She paused to inhale deeply. "...I go on alone now, perhaps having an even greater influence right here among the Chinese of San Francisco. You can be part of that work by helping Reverend and Mrs. Clark in their mission. They are risking their lives to rescue the slave girls from the alleys of Little China." She turned to Anna Clark who stood in the shadows at the far side of the platform. "How many of you have ever seen a girl who has lived in a bagnio—those little cells of—of iniquity?"

Anna walked over to stand beside Martha with an arm supporting an emaciated shell of a woman. As the stooped figure turned to face the audience, a gasp arose from those seated near the front of the room. The face of the Chinese woman was covered with running sores. Her head was almost bald—the small amount of hair, which had not been pulled out, were no more than tangled strands. When she opened her mouth to speak to Mrs. Clark, her rotted and missing teeth added to the horror.

"This 'girl' standing here is only twenty-one years old," Martha explained. "She's younger than the lovely Chinese woman who was introduced to you as Kuang Kulien Whitfield."

Whispers came from all parts of the room before Martha held up a hand. "Pink Pearl was kidnapped from her loving family when she was only five years old. She has been used by men in the ports of the China coast; and she was mutilated and abused by her owners as she traveled across the Pacific in the hold of a ship. After reaching this country, where she was told she would find hope and freedom, she was sold again to live out her days in a cage on Cooper's Alley. When she was too diseased to use any longer as a sexual object, she was consigned to die." Martha waited as the people registered their shock. "Was she sent to a clean hospital where she would receive medical attention? No! Her 'hospital' was a filthy vermin-infested cubicle without light or water. That is where we found her—at the point of death."

Anna put a protective arm around the woman's shoulders, holding her as a mother would a child. Martha continued, "Pink Pearl could be one of *your* own daughters, except that she was born into a poor family as a Chinese female! She's not pretty to look at; and she still carries disease. This young woman will soon be dead. But she will die with dignity—in a clean bed with people nearby who love her. Pink Pearl could have been a beautiful woman had she not been stolen away by bandits. But there are girls and women like her, not only in China, but right here in our city—girls who, if saved in time, could one day become socially acceptable and contributing members of society."

Anna beckoned at Horace to bring another girl to the podium. The next Chinese girl, though scarred and limping, was clean and bright-eyed. Her bobbed hair shone like polished ebony, and holding back one side was a red satin bow. She wore a light blue padded jacket and trousers. Smiling and bowing to the rows of people, she, too, had missing teeth. Yet there was hope in her face as she spoke in faltering English. "I, Clear Moon, no more slave. I free now. I learn read and write. One day I go China—help my people."

The audience applauded Clear Moon's enthusiastic speech. Then speaking from the front row, a man asked, "What can we do?"

Stepping aside, the Clarks, along with Martha watched Kulien walk up to the podium. Lifting her chin, her strong voice and articulate speech flowed as smoothly as an unhindered stream. "As a sixteen year old girl, living in China, a cruel man—not my father," she added, "sold me to a house of prostitution in Shanghai. I was able to escape and make my way to a nearby Christian mission run by the British. The kind people there tried to help me reach my husband in Hong Kong, but I was not allowed to leave the ship until it reached San Francisco.

"Again, I was sold into prostitution. I ended up in a barracoon, a market for slave traffic, and was destined to live out my life like Pink Pearl. A doctor, who lived near the Chinese Quarter, rescued me, and I eventually came to live with Reverend and Mrs. Clark. Through them I have found my purpose." She waited as women in the room dabbed at their eyes, and men coughed with discomfort.

Kulien's color rose with her voice. "Girls who are rescued from the bagnios are treated with medicine to cure their physical ailments; but they also receive spiritual encouragement from Reverend and Mrs. Clark; and Miss Johnson and I are giving them an education that will enable them to rise above their present status."

All eyes were on Kulien as she spoke. Some appeared dumbfounded at her eloquent use of the English language; others seemed to focus on her graceful posture, her noble features, and her unusual green eyes.

"You can help clean up this city and its slave traffic by writing letters to President Lincoln; you can refuse to support the establishments of those who deal in human flesh; and you can take a stand against slavery! No human being, whether black, white or yellow, was born to be bought and sold as chattel."

Before leaving the platform, Kulien drew the two Chinese girls close to her sides, an arm over each of their shoulders. "These are my sisters," she said. "They're your sisters, too. Can you stand by and close your eyes to their misery? Not one of us could choose our family or nationality, but we can all choose to help those less fortunate. Please," her voice broke with emotion. "Please help us. Although we may be a different color on the outside, inside we are all human beings who have a right to freedom—freedom to breathe fresh air—freedom to live our lives without fear."

Kulien's arms slid off the girls' shoulders. With deliberate slowness, she folded hands at her waist, closed her eyes, and bowed. Just as thunderous applause began to echo throughout the hall, those nearest the platform watched a tear roll down Kulien's smooth cheek and fall at her feet.

FIFTY-ONE

Ten months had gone by since Kulien had made her first impassioned plea to the interested citizens of San Francisco. They had been months filled with more pleas and speeches before women's clubs, political rallies, and service organizations. Always the people seemed interested; they asked questions; they offered suggestions; some even volunteered to join rescue teams. Others provided food, clothing and money. But as the practice of buying and selling slaves continued to prosper in Little China as well as along the waterfront district known as the Barbary Coast, Kulien and Martha became discouraged.

"There've been letters written to Governor Leland Stanford and to the committees formed to protest the sale of Chinese girls," Reverend Clark reminded Kulien. "You and Martha have brought awareness to so many, and have been instrumental in giving life back to at least twenty girls this year. They can now read and write—and learn about life outside the bagnios! You must not give up."

Regardless of Horace Clark's words, Kulien felt disheartened. Although she had been invited to speak at many gatherings, neither federal nor city authorities attempted to interfere effectively with the slave traffic. She had learned that police had occasionally boarded ships from China, and had placed many of the girls into the growing number of mission homes throughout the city. However, instead of diminishing, the population of Chinese prostitutes in San Francisco had grown to over one thousand.

Kulien and Martha sat with Reverend and Mrs. Clark at the dining table in Kulien's home discussing what they should do next. Each one showed signs of weariness: circles under their eyes, drooping shoulders, heavy sighs. Shaking her head, Kulien finally spoke. "You're right that twenty girls have come through our home," she glanced sideways at Martha, "but the problem only grows. Why do the Americans continue to invite *me* to their meetings, requesting that I come alone? I certainly haven't had much success in winning them to our cause! I think Martha would have more influence."

Nodding while glancing at Horace, Anna said, "It will take years, child, for us to see any remarkable changes. People, as a general rule, are selfish. They are more interested in money than in these discarded girls." Her eyes darkened with intensity. "And you say that you wonder why they fawn over you, yet take no heed of your words?"

"Now Anna," Horace warned.

"She has a right to know." Anna Clark stiffened her neck, ignoring her husband's words. "You, the wealthy Chinese woman with the surname of a British lord, are the talk of the town—the *objet d'art*, as the French would say."

Kulien's eyes narrowed and a line creased her brow. "I don't understand."

"Is Martha invited to the meetings and social gatherings?"

"No, but. . .."

"Martha is as concerned as you are, and she speaks well; but Martha is one of us. You, Kulien, are something of a 'party favor.'"

Kulien felt the blood rush to her cheeks. "You mean that I'm being *used* by the barbarians?" She thought a moment before adding, "Instead of prostituting my body, they prostitute my words?"

"Yes, my child, I'm afraid you're right."

"But," Horace interrupted, "at least you're getting the message out to some folks who would never hear. Of course, we know there are those who have clear passage from one ear to the other! But we've gained a few followers—a few staunch supporters from the soirees of the wealthy."

With a sense of sadness, Kulien rested a hand over her heart. "Then do you advise me to continue to accept their invitations?"

Horace nodded. "Unless you are uncomfortable about their unseemly interest in *you*, I suggest you go as often as possible. You're admired by the upper class, Kulien, not only for your beauty and intelligence, but it's true, people are impressed by your wealth—by this house." He swept his arm, taking in the spacious dining room with its priceless furnishings.

"And, I might add, the bored matrons of society find your relationship with a British noble a choice piece of gossip."

Lowering her eyelids, Kulien had no words. Her private life was a topic of conversation among the Americans? What she had believed was a genuine interest in her cause was actually only an excuse to observe and discuss her. Tears formed in the corners of her eyes and she blinked them away.

Horace, seemingly unaware of Kulien's discomfort, went on. "California is making an impact on the rest of the country; and you're part of that driving force, Kulien. Now that the telegraph line has been completed, we have direct contact with New York. And there's word that Congress will approve the completion of the railroad from the Missouri River to the Pacific Ocean."

"Oh, Horace," Anna blurted, "don't bore Kulien with all your facts. Can't you see how upset she is?"

Horace wiped his glasses with a handkerchief, as his neck turned a light shade of red. "Well, what I'm trying to say," he scowled in Anna's direction, "is that there are men and women who listen to you. They're writing relatives in the East about the slave situation here. We must be patient—and trust God."

The following Saturday night, Kulien prepared to attend yet another party, given by the Herbert McKnights, a socially prominent family from Connecticut. Their home, like Kulien's, was situated in the hills rising above the city. As was her custom, Kulien dressed in a traditional Chinese gown and combed her long hair into a roll at the back of her head.

Martha watched her twist the shiny black strands and fasten them with an ivory pin. "Do you think Mr. McKnight will allow you to speak about the slave problem?"

Kulien absentmindedly smoothed the silk gown over her hips as she walked toward the front door. "I never know. I'm sure I'll hear much talk about the War; and I suppose pledges of gold will again be taken to assist the Union."

Martha stood at the front entrance with Kulien, helping her into a long satin coat. "I'm happy about that! I read that over a hundred thousand dollars in gold coin has been sent to

New York in behalf of the sick and wounded." Her voice rose in pitch whenever the subject of the Civil War came up.

Kulien wasn't as enthusiastic about the war. "It would give me great joy if only a fraction of that wealth could be used to change conditions in our city!"

"Who can tell?" Martha asked, as Kulien stepped into the buggy and shut the door. "Perhaps tonight there could be one person who might give time and effort to help us."

Kulien pulled the collar of her coat up around her neck, and sighed. "Even one more would be great encouragement."

As the buggy bumped along the road to the McKnight residence, Kulien recited the words she would say if asked to speak on behalf of her Chinese sisters. Her mind drifted back to those first years in her new country. What a frightened girl she had been—alone and expecting a child; purchased as a slave by the infamous Ahtoy. Her heart ached as she thought about Ta Ming. She had tried not to think of him because her longing was so great. How many months had it been since he'd written? Two? Three? Had he forgotten her? Had Marshall also put her out his mind and heart?

Before she could come to any conclusion the buggy stopped in front of a stately mansion. Kulien's eyes swept over the wide veranda, the massive columns, and the lights shining from every window. Juan, the husband of her housekeeper, opened the half-door of the buggy and extended a calloused hand. The young Mexican not only acted as a driver, he also kept the gardens weeded and took care of incidental problems as they arose. She smiled at him, feeling a kinship with one far from his native land.

As she stepped down from the buggy, a tall man with dark skin beckoned her inside. With a French accent, he said, "I will escort you to the parlor." He helped remove her coat, and then led the way to a room humming with animated conversation. "All of the guests have arrived," he said, "and Mrs. McKnight is eagerly awaiting you."

Through the crowd of men and women who gathered in conversational groups, Kulien could see the swirl of moving color as dancers circled the floor in the adjoining room. Agnes

McKnight, weaving through clusters of conversing guests, fastened her eyes on the latest arrival.

"Oh, my dear, Mrs. Whitfield, we're so delighted you could join us."

A warm flush, at hearing her English name, spread over Kulien's face. "It was most generous of you to invite me." She extended a hand, Western-fashion.

The middle-aged woman crooked a forefinger, motioning to her husband who seemed anxious to escape the men surrounding him. "Herbert, see who we have here. Isn't she a lovely thing?" She enunciated each word as if Kulien didn't understand English. "It's no wonder everyone wants to have this charming young woman attend their parties. Why just look at the attention she's drawn."

Kulien glanced up from lowered lashes to see that most of the people had stopped talking. Even the music in the ballroom ceased as dancers swarmed into the parlor to ogle the richly clad, beautiful woman from across the Pacific Ocean. It was always the same whenever Kulien visited the homes of the Westerners. She was treated with extreme kindness—and curiosity.

Reverend Clark had explained that most Americans had never seen a Chinese woman; all they knew of China were the peasant-class men who lived in the shanties of Little China's alleys. Although she had often felt awkward at the attention she received, tonight she suffered from embarrassment. After what Anna had said about her being a "party favor," she had wanted to refuse any more invitations; and had only agreed to go in order to raise the impressions Americans had of Chinese in general.

Herbert McKnight bowed, welcoming her to his home. "Forgive our ungallant behavior, Mrs. Whitfield," he said raising an arm toward the orchestra in the ballroom. As the sound of a waltz again filtered through the parlor, and people returned to their conversations and dancing, the host fixed his eyes on Kulien. "I assure you, Mrs. Whitfield, the rudeness of my guests is not intentional. As you know, the sight of a Chinese woman is unusual, and word of your intelligence and beauty precedes you." He smiled warmly and turned to his wife. "Has Jonathan Wung arrived? I was so occupied with those gentlemen who came from Washington that I neglected to receive him."

"I believe I saw him at the buffet—talking with Charles Crocker."

"Good, very good," Mr. McKnight said to himself. "Ah, Mrs. Whitfield, I think you might be interested in meeting a Harvard-educated man from China."

"Forgive my ignorance, sir, but I'm not familiar with the institution you mentioned. Harvard?"

Herbert McKnight's smile softened his sharp features. "Harvard University is the oldest and largest institution of learning in America—founded in 1636. My own school," he beamed. "Dr. Wung is among the first Chinese students to be formally educated in America. He has just completed his studies of medicine. I think you would find him an interesting conversationalist—and a possible ally in your cause."

Before he had finished speaking, Jonathan Wung stepped into view. Dressed in Western clothes, the slim young man caught the interest of those he passed. His short black hair, parted in the middle, shone with pomade; round glasses framed his slanted eyes; and his square chin was set with determination. Kulien guessed that his position among Americans was as uncomfortable as hers. Perhaps his role had been even more difficult as a Chinese man attending an American university.

After introductions, Mr. and Mrs. McKnight asked to be excused to attend to their other guests. Kulien, feeling confused and bewildered at how to converse with this Americanized member of her race, watched in dismay as the older couple walked away. She glanced sideways at the man who stood stiffly beside her. Jonathan Wung was truly Chinese, but without a queue and Chinese clothing, he seemed neither a citizen of China nor America.

His voice startled her. "Does my adoption of Western ways disturb you?" The man's full lips hinted a smile. "I, too, find myself in a quandary. It has been many years since I've spoken to a Chinese woman." He bowed slightly before stepping aside. "Would you care to sit down, and perhaps have a cup of tea?"

Without speaking, Kulien nodded her head. How strange to hear well-enunciated English words come from his mouth. She realized, with a start, that since arriving in California she had spoken with no men of her race except her cook. He, as others who had immigrated to America, dressed in loose clothing, wore the long braid of the Ching Dynasty, and spoke either Cantonese or Pidgin.

They sat at a small table near the ballroom and waited for a servant to set delicate porcelain cups in front of them. As the man poured amber liquid from the tea pot into her cup, Kulien wondered what to say to Jonathan Wung. She had accepted the invitation to the McKnight party, thinking it would be another opportunity to enlighten their guests about the plight of the Chinese slave girls. But what would this man think? Did he see the Chinese woman through the eyes of a white or a yellow man?

Answering her unspoken questions, Jonathan broke the silence. "I understand you're working with Chinese girls who have been rescued from slavery."

Kulien set her cup in its saucer, examining the hand-painted flowers before looking up. "Yes, that's true. What else have you heard about me?" Her boldness seemed to catch them both off guard, and they smiled at each other.

His smile broadened, revealing straight, very white, teeth. "To be honest, I've not heard enough. I know that you've been here for many years—and that your work is your life." He tipped his head, studying her features. "You're not from southern China, are you?"

"No. I came from Kiangsu Province. My home was about six *li*, two miles, from Shanghai."

Jonathan leaned back in his chair, relaxing. "I, too, am from Kiangsu Province; but I hail from Soochow, the city of kings—'Beautiful Soo'."

A soothing calm came with Jonathan's words, and Kulien leaned toward him. "From your expression, I believe you long to return to your city. I've heard of its beauty—of its lakes, canals, and exceptional gardens."

With dark eyes shining behind his glasses, Jonathan's lips turned up in a slight smile. "Ah, yes," he said. "On the bank of the Grand Canal, Soochow is the most beautiful of all the cities in China. One cannot speak or write of it with words of any language." The smile crinkled the corners of his dark, shining eyes. "Mrs. Whitfield, would you speak Mandarin with me? I shame myself in showing you my homesickness."

Suddenly, Kulien felt herself transported back in time—to her family compound. Across from her sat a young man very much like her step-brother, Sunfu. Long repressed feelings of loneliness rose within her. She was sharing a table with a man from her own country, a man who spoke her language—but a man who appeared and sounded much more American than Chinese.

She lifted her chin, and with composure she didn't feel, answered, "Of course, I would enjoy that as well. To speak in our common language will be an experience I've not had for many years." Smiling shyly, she said, "I speak English fluently, and Cantonese fairly well, but I still think in my native tongue."

"I do also—think in our native tongue." He bit at his lower lip, pleasure showing on his face. "I dream in Mandarin as well."

Listening to Jonathan speak the familiar dialect, Kulien felt as if a fragrant oil had been poured over her dry spirit. When she realized she was trembling, she laced her fingers together in her lap, and waited for what else this unusual man would have to say.

Completely at ease in his surroundings, Jonathan Wung began to speak about the city of his birth. Listening to him paint pictures with words, Kulien could almost see and smell the ancient city. Sitting quietly across the table with the man from Soochow, she was keenly aware that such an occurrence would never have taken place had they been in China. An unescorted Chinese woman alone in the presence of a Chinese man, conversing as equals, was unheard of—even between adult brothers and sisters. She held onto his every word, every inflection. Occasionally he slipped into the local Wu dialect of Soochow—a melodious, full-toned quality of speech, one Kulien didn't entirely understand.

Acknowledging her quizzical expression, Jonathan stopped his monologue. "Is there a question? Do I talk too much?"

"No, not at all. I understand most of what you say, but you use an unfamiliar dialect, yet one that is quite pleasant to my ears."

Jonathan's teeth flashed in a bright smile. "There's an old saying, 'Argument in Soochow is more agreeable than flattery in Canton.'" His cheeks flushed. "I'm afraid I show unacceptable pride in my ancestry."

"And is that a crime?" Kulien smiled back at him, the dimple in her right cheek visible in the flickering lights of the room.

Jonathan's smile turned to a frown. "I've lived in America for eight years. A man by the name of Julian Somerset is my benefactor. He paid my living expenses and education costs with the intention of sending me back to China as a doctor of medicine. I've learned well what it means to be humbled—but in your company, I find myself relaxing and returning to my old ways—even the dialect of my youth."

Kulien was confused by his words. Had he intimated that she caused him to lose face with his American benefactor? Many years had passed since she had left her childhood home, and to understand the ways and words of a Chinese gentleman—to know the hidden meaning—had disappeared into the forgotten past. "Perhaps you would prefer a different companion to share your pot of tea." Her voice was so low Jonathan had to lean forward to hear.

The frown disappeared, and his words were quick, but gentle. "Forgive me if my speaking was like an arrow. I can think of no one I'd rather be with at this very moment. I'm *not* offended by your company—quite the contrary." He circled the edge of his cup with a long, slender forefinger, his eyes following the motion. "When I look at you, and am able to converse in my language, I breathe the fresh air of my homeland. It has been a very long time since. . ."

Uncomfortable with the direction of their conversation, Kulien attempted to change the subject. "Have you—do you have a wife in China, Jonathan—that is—Dr. Wung?" Kulien stuttered over the name. Did he prefer to be addressed by his American name, or should she have ignored the "Doctor" title?

Seeing her discomfort, the man said, "You may call me Jonathan if you wish. Because the white men call us 'John Chinaman,' among other not-so pleasant names, Mr. Somerset decided that Jonathan would be my English name. In Soochow, I was called Wung Ti Chiu. If you would use my surname, Wung, I would surely believe that I'm at home; but Jonathan suits me well, too."

"Thank you," Kulien said, lowering her eyelids. Looking up, she asked again, "Does your wife wait for you to return to China, Wung?"

"There is no wife." He paused. "Now it is my turn to ask—do I call you, Mrs. Whitfield?"

"That is my English name," she said, without explanation. "But I prefer Kulien—Bitter Seed."

Jonathan Wung's dark eyes met and held hers. "I think you were wrongly named, Kulien!" He shook his head while silently mouthing the words, *Bitter Seed*. "But to further answer your question. There is no family waiting for me in China. Europeans, the British actually, rescued me after my family died of a plague. For ten years, I lived in an orphanage. It was there I learned the English language and Western ways, including their religion. It was also there I decided upon my life's work—to be a physician. Mr. Somerset, the man I mentioned before, is a wealthy American who had been conducting business in China. Through the missionaries who ran the orphanage, he became interested in my progress. When I was eighteen years old, he paid my passage to America. Because I had no family ties, a wife had not been chosen from another Chinese family. After I arrived in America, it was made clear that I was forbidden to make friends with the *white* girls who were invited to the Somerset home." He shrugged his shoulders and smiled. "So, you see, I remain a man alone!"

Kulien smiled back, and then turned her attention to the music flowing from the ballroom. It had been an interesting evening, and she found the conversation stimulating as well as informative. She wondered how much Wung knew about her work. Would he, as Mr. McKnight suggested, consider helping in the rescue of the Chinese slave girls?

Straining her eyes through the crowd, trying to see her host, Kulien doubted that she would be asked to make a speech tonight. She had hoped there would be opportunity to let these carefree people know that only a few blocks away, young girls were prisoners to men's lusts.

Turning to Wung, Kulien announced, "I have a husband in England. My son lives there with his father." Sadness veiled her eyes. "I remain in America to continue my endeavors to help Reverend and Mrs. Clark in their mission."

Before the man could respond, Mrs. McKnight approached their table speaking above the music and laughter that had risen in volume as the evening progressed. "I intended to ask you to tell us of your work, Mrs. Whitfield; but it will have to be another time perhaps. There's so much gaiety tonight—very little talk about the war, or other unpleasant things." She nodded to her husband who stood several feet away. "Herbert thinks we should let our guests forget the darker side of life tonight." Turning away, she added, "Please enjoy the party; we're pleased you could attend."

With the words of dismissal hanging over them, Kulien, looking at Jonathan Wung, rose to leave. "It's been an honor talking with you," she said. "I hope your stay in San Francisco is agreeable."

Rising quickly to his feet, Jonathan bowed. "I came here to learn more about the Chinese immigrants; and it gave me an opportunity to visit a relative." His voice took on a serious tone. "I'll be here for only six months. After that, I will either return to Boston to continue more studies; or perhaps it will be time for me to go home." He blinked his dark, expressive eyes. "My benefactor favors my return to Massachusetts."

"Oh?" Kulien made her way through the crush of people with Jonathan at her side.

"Yes, Mr. Somerset believes I would be wise to take more classes and an internship at a Boston hospital." He took Kulien's coat from the man standing at the doorway, and held it as she slipped her arms into the sleeves. Stepping out onto the veranda, he inhaled deeply of the fresh air. "He says that I would gain necessary experience by practicing medicine. For me to obtain support to back an opening of a hospital in central China, I must show that I'm worthy." His face showed little emotion. "That means another year or more in this country."

Buttoning the collar of the satin coat around her neck, Kulien asked, "Then you will not be returning to Soochow?"

"No. There's a well equipped hospital there. People in the interior need doctors." As they walked to her buggy where Juan stood waiting to assist her, Jonathan added, "It's a difficult decision—to go or to stay." Glancing at Kulien, his eyes partially hidden by the reflection of lanterns on his glasses, his final words lifted her spirits. "Perhaps, if you would agree, I could be of assistance in your work while I'm here."

Kulien's smile from inside the buggy, though not seen, could be heard in her reply, "I'm certain you could!"

FIFTY-TWO

That night as Kulien lay in the quiet of her bedroom, she thought over the events of the day. Two of the girls, Spring Rain and Clear Moon, had passed their tests and were ready to leave. They spoke English well enough to carry on a conversation, and they could read the simplest stories. Spring Rain, who enjoyed cooking, wanted to be placed in an American home as a cook; but Clear Moon's desire was to return to China to teach English. All each needed now were sponsors and a doctor's statement that they were free of disease.

Kulien smiled in the darkness. At just the right time, Jonathan Wung had arrived in San Francisco. Their former doctor, Lionel Forbes, had returned to the east coast one week ago, leaving them to find another doctor. Kulien turned to her side, pulling the quilt under her chin. Yes, Jonathan Wung could be a great help—and he reminded her of her favorite brother, Sunfu.

Kulien had been asleep for several hours when she woke from a troubled dream. She rubbed her eyes and stared through the blackness enveloping the room. Dreams of faceless men swarming through the rooms of her house looking for gold sent waves of fear through her body. She bolted upright in bed, straining her ears. Had she heard screams and shrieks coming from downstairs?

Her heart racing, Kulien tiptoed across the bedroom to crack open the door. Nothing but silence—a deathly hush—fell upon the house. Without lighting a candle, she crept along the hallway to Martha's room, and, as stealthily as possible, opened her door. "Martha," she said in a hoarse whisper. "Martha, I heard something."

A thin ray of moonlight edged around the heavy draperies, revealing Martha as she leaned up on one elbow. "What is it? What did you hear?"

"I'm not certain. It could have been a dream."

Kulien stood over Martha, and the woman grasped Kulien's cold hand. "Tell me what you heard."

"I heard screams," Kulien voice quavered. "They weren't loud—but muffled. Do you think someone has come into the house, and . . .?"

"Juan is here, isn't he? He would have alerted us. And there are guards at the gate!"

Kulien's mouth went dry and she struggled to speak. "Suppose he couldn't call us. Suppose the guards left; they sometimes do."

Martha was out of bed in an instant, and slipped into her robe. She groped in the dark closet to find one for Kulien. "We have to go downstairs to see if the girls are safe." With a gentle pat on Kulien's shoulder, she added, "I'm sure you were dreaming; I heard nothing."

Making their way down the stairway, step by cautious step, they stopped often listening for any sign of life. "The house is quiet," Martha whispered. "I'm sure you were just dreaming," she said again, to reassure herself.

When they reached the last stair, a blast of cold air whipped the robes around their ankles. The front door stood wide open, and from the light of the moon, they could see that something—someone—lay in the doorway.

"What's that?" Martha pointed to the still form.

Shivering with apprehension, Kulien shook her head; and with Martha close behind, she edged along the short hallway to the entrance. Without speaking, they peered down at the unmoving form.

The gardener's wide, unseeing eyes stared back at them, his mouth gaped open in death. Martha touched a shoulder as if to wake him; then gasped as his head drooped to the side, revealing a long bloody gash across the throat.

Kulien had seen death many times, but the sight of Juan's face, frozen in horror, and the open wound still pulsating with blood, left her knees weak. She dropped to the floor, staring in disbelief at the dead man. Juan—such a quiet, peaceful man. Why would anyone kill him? He had never hurt anyone. Then she remembered the girls—her girls!

Martha tugged at Kulien's arm, her voice rising in volume, "Quick! We must see about the girls!"

They backed away from the door, their eyes still fastened on the grotesque expression of a man who had been their protector. "Yes, the girls—we must see about the girls," Kulien repeated in a monotone.

Martha led Kulien down the first-floor hallway to the two rooms occupied by six girls now in their charge. Kulien's breathing was shallow as they approached the back of the house. Would they be gone? Or dead? When they reached the first bedroom, they saw the door was open, but could see nothing through the darkness.

Kulien's fingers trembled as she struck a match and held it to the wick of a kerosene lamp. The flame sputtered an instant before spreading an orange glow across the room—an empty room. The three girls who occupied it were gone! She fixed her eyes on Martha, unsure of what to do. Then without a word, they turned to race to the next room.

That room, too, was empty, but torn apart. Cots had been tipped upside down; blankets and clothing were strewn across the floor. Spilling from the shelves were books with pages torn out and cast aside. Martha began to sob, "Our girls have been kidnapped! Juan is dead! Oh, what shall we do?"

"Stop it!" Kulien, now keenly aware of the situation, spoke with authority. "This is not the time to lose our courage. We must contact Reverend Clark immediately; he'll get the police."

Suddenly, from the corner of the room, came a whimper. "Who's there?" Kulien called in Chinese. "Come out. You're safe now; the men are gone."

The newest arrival, a girl of twelve, poked her head out from a pile of quilts. "It's Silver Bell. I outran the *fankuei*, and hid."

"Foreign devils?" Martha wrapped her arms around the shivering girl. "White men did this?"

Still shaking with fear, and clinging to each other, the three made their way to the kitchen. There was no sign of either Ling, the cook, or Bonita, Juan's wife. Had they too, been murdered? Or had they managed to escape?

"Martha, you must go for help? If you're afraid, I'll do it." Kulien had brought a large tablecloth from the kitchen, and carefully draped it over Juan's body.

Martha shuddered before answering. "I can take the cart; if Chinese women are being hunted, you'd be better off to stay inside with the doors locked."

It took only a few minutes for Martha to put a long coat over her nightclothes, tie on a pair of shoes and run down the graveled walk to the stable. Kulien didn't wait to see her race by in the cart; and with Silver Bell's help, she shoved Juan's heavy body onto the front porch and slammed the door shut.

After latching all the locks, Kulien glanced at the small pale girl sitting on the bottom step of the stairway, tears streaming down her face. "Come, little Bell, don't cry. You're safe now, and the police will rescue our sisters again." Kneeling beside her, she comforted the child. "I know you're afraid, and so am I. But we must be brave, and thank God for sparing your life!"

Kulien wrapped an arm around the girl's shoulders, and led her up the stairs to her own bedroom. "See what a fine big bed I have. Now you get in and go to sleep. The *fankuei* won't return tonight." She rested a cool hand on the smooth forehead and, until the child fell asleep, she hummed a lullaby that Ta Ming had loved. To her surprise, instead of sensing loneliness for her son, she felt only a deep love for Silver Bell—and all the students under her care.

It was daylight before the police had left with Juan's body. There had been many questions, but few answers. In the surrounding woods, police discovered the bodies of both guards, their throats also slashed. There was still no sign of Ling or Bonita.

A red-faced police officer tried to convince them that the servants had simply run for cover. "We'll look for your students," he said, before mounting his horse, "but they're probably already on their way to some mining camp in the mountains." Pointing at the house, he said to Kulien, "Seems they've left another message."

Scrawled across the front of the white house in crude letters still wet with black paint were the words, "China whores go home!"

Both shocked and angry, Martha and Kulien stood staring at the blatant words of hate. "When will it end?" Martha asked.

"Haven't the slightest idea, young lady." The policeman looked down on them from his mount. It's gettin' worse, this opposition to the Chinese. Not only here. The whole state's in an uproar. We fish dead Chinamen out of the sea every day." He shrugged. "Course they use *women* for things other than fish bait." A sly smile twisted his mouth.

Martha's arm tightened around Kulien. "Well, people are going to have to accept our presence here." She emphasized the word, *our*. "We are the salt of the earth!"

Before riding away, the officer chuckled. "Well, salt won't keep the bandits away. I suggest you get stronger locks— and some guns!

It was late afternoon before the blood stains and hateful words had been washed away from both the outside and inside of the house. Silver Bell had been sent to Kulien's bedroom to read a book, while she and Martha cleaned and straightened the disordered rooms. They said little to each other about the tragedy, but endeavored to carry on as usual.

When suppertime arrived, they were surprised by a knock at the door. Bearing baskets of steaming vegetables, and fresh-from-the-oven bread were Anna and Horace Clark. Following close behind was Jonathan Wung, dressed today in a long blue coat and trousers with full legs, the traditional Chinese clothing of the middle class. He bowed courteously before Kulien and Martha, using only his eyes to express the unspoken sorrow he felt for their ordeal.

After Martha and Kulien had set the table and served each person, the group talked little about the disaster, even though it was the foremost thought on all their minds. Performing as hostess, Kulien poured tea, and brought up light topics of discussion. She spoke of the late-blooming chrysanthemums at the back corner of the property, and of the trellis of white roses that reminded her of home.

Jonathan took her cue to tell of an unusual flower, his favorite. "There is a flower, the rarest in all of China, *Chingkuei*, which grows only in Kiangsu Province. I believe the best English translation would be, 'Enchantress'. Are you familiar with this flower?" he asked Kulien.

When she shook her head, Jonathan continued. "Then you are in for a delightful surprise when you return to our homeland. You must travel to Soochow to fully appreciate the delicate 'Enchantress.' It's a small plant that hides itself under other plants. Its leaves are such a soft green that it's not easy to see; and its blossoms, though minute, are the most delicate of colors. But it receives its name from the fragrance. Perfume comes from bell-like sacks that must be crushed to enjoy the sweetness. Some believe *Chingkuei* releases magic. I will not say whether I believe—or not." He smiled at each person around the table. "Although we Chinese greatly appreciate the beauty of flowers, we also cling to our fairy tales."

The others returned Jonathan's pleasant smile, but Kulien only nodded her head, her mind and heart far away from San Francisco.

Later, when they were in the parlor drinking tea, Reverend Clark spoke in a solemn tone. "A desecration of human lives has taken place here today. I fear that those who have murdered and kidnapped will not be brought to justice." His eyes went from Kulien to Jonathan Wung. "Neither of you is safe." Then his eyes rested on Martha, "And you are also in danger because of your alliance to this cause."

"I thought the Americans had begun to accept us." They seemed genuinely interested to hear about the slave problem in Little China." She looked from Horace's face to Anna's

Horace Clark pressed his lips together in a tight line before he spoke. "Governor Stanford has taken a positive stand against the Chinese, Kulien. He maintains that Asia has sent the 'dregs of her population here.' He wants immigration to be discouraged by every legitimate means."

"What about *your* work? Will it go on?" Kulien's frown revealed her deep concern.

Anna lifted her chin and voice, "As long as we're alive, and by God's grace, we'll continue our rescue operations." The usually controlled woman allowed a tear to slide down her cheek. "We have people who secretly help us, so we will find those five girls. I refuse to be frightened away!"

Standing beside Kulien, Martha agreed. "They won't frighten us either! Scare tactics have always been used wherever good is being accomplished," Martha went on. "I know this is where I should be; and as long as Kulien wants me, I'm here to help her."

Suddenly, Reverend Clark turned to Jonathan. "Where are *you* staying, Doctor Wung?" Are you with friends, or in a hotel?"

"I have a distant cousin who lives on Dupont Street," he answered. "I visited with him my first week here. However, he lives in such crowded quarters, that I've now taken up residence in the Grant Hotel."

Nodding, Horace glanced from Jonathan to Kulien. "Would you be willing to stay here tonight? I think a man should be present. Tomorrow we'll find new household help and guards for the gate."

Kulien held up a hand. "Forgive me, but as you know, there were three men here last night, and now all are dead. It would be even more dangerous for Dr. Wung as only one man to stay and associate himself with our cause."

With hands tucked inside wide sleeves, Jonathan stood up and bowed from the waist. "You forget that I am already associated with *your cause*, as you put it." His eyes narrowed behind the round glasses. "I have seen girl children cast out to die on the banks of the Grand Canal. I've smelled the rotting flesh of baby girls who were encased in jars and left along the roadside." Glancing down in shame, he continued, "I abhor the way Chinese females are mistreated. I am not afraid of any danger perpetrated from those who approve such actions!"

Seeing there would be no further argument, Jonathan smiled at Kulien. "So it is settled. I stay for the night—right here on the floor of your parlor."

That night before Kulien and Martha turned to go upstairs Jonathan asked them to join him in prayer for their protection and the safe recovery of the girls. Jonathan Wung's quiet strength and confidence brought peace to Kulien's spirit, though she wondered how the soft-spoken man could be a match against the knives of foreigners.

Kulien slept soundly and without dreams; and when she awoke the next morning she felt a sense of urgency to find her charges. After dressing quickly, she ran downstairs to see that Jonathan had already risen, as he welcomed her into the kitchen with a cup of hot tea and a bowl of rice gruel.

"Forgive my presumptuousness," he said, "but I have not only prepared breakfast; I left before dawn to talk with Reverend Clark. I hope you don't mind that I borrowed one of your horses?"

Kulien was speechless. How else would this man surprise her?

Sitting across from her at the small table, Jonathan leaned forward, lacing his fingers together on the table. "I have news about your students. We now know where they are—and what we must do."

FIFTY-THREE

Kulien waited to hear what Jonathan had to say. His calm tone belied his expression of anxiety. "I want to hear your news," she said. "Whether good or bad, please tell me," she replied in Mandarin

"The police contacted Reverend Clark shortly after he arrived home last night. Since it was too late to make any plans, he decided to wait until morning. When I showed up unexpectedly, he told me that the man who worked here as your cook was the person who made a bargain with the kidnappers."

Placing fingers over her mouth to muffle the dreaded words, she asked, "Ling? Jo Ling? But why? I don't understand."

Jonathan frowned, his voice tender, yet strong. "The kidnappers promised your cook a safe trip back to his home in China—if he would unlock the front door. Your gardener, Juan, must have tried to stop them from coming in—so they killed him.

"After Jo Ling fulfilled his part by unlocking the door, they dragged him away, and beat him, leaving him for dead." Jonathan paused, watching Kulien's reaction. "Your cook, still barely alive, was found last night in the bushes at the far end of your property. Before he died, he told the police that *some* of your students were being taken to a central valley town to the east, *Sam Fow*, Stockton. He said he overheard that the others would be sold to a mining camp near Sonora." Jonathan Wung lifted his shoulders before reaching across the small table to cover Kulien's hand. "That isn't good news; but at least now we know where the kidnappers have taken them."

Kulien relished Jonathan's warm hand on hers, grateful for this man—a friend so like herself. "What should we do?" She moved her hand to pick up the tea cup. "Is there a plan for rescuing them?"

Jonathan's kind smile enveloped her. "Yes, Reverend Clark is getting up a group of men, some police officers, and a judge. I'm also going to ride with them to Stockton. When we recover the girls, we'll bring them back here. We can only pray that they haven't been harmed!"

"I'm going with you." Kulien stood up with hands on her hips, her eyes daring him to disagree.

Jonathan jumped to his feet. "Oh, no you're not! This is not a trip for a woman. And we're taking only one cart for bringing the girls back. It's a long ride and we have no idea what to expect when we get there." He held up a hand. "No, you are not going with us."

Kulien's jade-green eyes burned with determination. "*Excuse me*, Doctor Wung, I'm not accustomed to a man telling me what I may or may not do. Those girls were under my protection—I *am* going to help rescue them!"

Taken aback by Kulien's bold outburst, Jonathan couldn't restrain a smile. "Do you know how to ride a horse? It could take as many as three or four days to reach Stockton; then we have the same distance to travel back." He watched her with admiring eyes, knowing how she would answer.

"Of course I can ride a horse. I rode when I was a child." Kulien turned her face away so he wouldn't suspect her lie. She *had* ridden—a pony—around the courtyard of the compound. Riding a full-grown horse shouldn't be all that different. She had learned over the years that she could do almost anything she set her mind to. And her mind was set. She stiffened her back.

"The girls trust me," she said, speaking Mandarin. "They would be afraid of the police—and of you." She pointed to his eyes. "Especially of you. The Chinese exploit them; but I'm the woman who's been caring for them. They trust me." Kulien smiled, feeling proud that she was so adept at arguing in her own language with this well-educated man.

Jonathan could only watch in amazement as Kulien raced from the kitchen and ran up the stairs to change her clothes. Still twisting her hair into one long braid, she came back a short time later dressed in the dark clothing of a Chinese worker. "I've told Martha where we're going. She'll take Silver Bell to the mission where they'll be safe until our return."

Kulien marched across the room and down the hall, calling over her shoulder, "Are you coming, Doctor? Or do you prefer to stay with the women?"

It was an hour later and the sun had barely risen over the eastern hills when the small group of rescuers was ready to leave. Horses had been rented from the livery stable, and a large covered cart had been attached to one of the more sturdy animals. "Kulien, I think you should ride in the cart. The trip will be long and treacherous." Reverend Clark's words fell on deaf ears.

"I learned to ride as a child." She bit her lower lip before speaking the half-truth. "My honorable father allowed me many privileges denied most females."

"Very well," he said at last. "But we will be on the road for several days. We don't want to be recognized, so we can't cross the bay by ferry. We have a long ride down the peninsula before we head east, and over a low range of mountains." Horace shook his head again, watching Jonathan Wung as he shrugged his shoulders. "It's just not fitting for a woman to travel with men under such circumstances."

Unable to control her emotions, Kulien's voice rose, "You seem to forget that I traveled with men in the hold of a ship for nearly four moons. I'm not bothered about the differences between men and women."

Wung stood at a distance listening, his lips curved in a smile showing his approval of this vibrant woman who argued with such authority. He held up his hands in surrender as the bewildered minister watched Kulien mount a horse that appeared bored with the entire process. "What are we waiting for?" she asked, looking down on the others. "We're losing precious time."

Kulien's horse, though old and tired, seemed to sense her inexperience in riding. Before the others had mounted, it reared up on its hind legs; then, to Kulien's surprise, began to race down the road. She almost dropped the reins, but gripped the saddle with her knees to keep from falling off. Terrified, she shouted, "Stop!" But the horse ignored her command, and began to run even faster. She couldn't fall and die! Not now.

Grasping the reins with one hand, and the saddle with the other, she used all her energy to hold on. Leaning forward, she could feel horse's mane blow against her face. She tried to pull back on the reins to no avail. Jonathan Wung galloped up beside her urging his horse in front of hers until they both slowed to a trot. "So," he said, his voice crisp with anger, "you know how to ride?" His glasses had slipped down on his nose, and his eyes bored into hers.

Although still trembling with fear, Kulien, met his gaze, and managed to sit straight in the saddle. "It has been many years." She feigned an uneasy smile. "Don't tell the others. I *have* to go with you. I'll learn as I go." Her voice quavered. "And—thank you for saving my life!"

After two days of riding, stopping only to eat, sleep, and water the horses, Kulien was certain that her every muscle and bone was bruised. Even through the pain, she congratulated herself on her persistence; and began to enjoy the rhythmic movement of the horse under her. When they stopped for the second night, she couldn't repress a groan as she rubbed her back. Trying to hide her misery with a weak smile, she knew she hadn't fooled Jonathan. His groans were almost as pain-filled as hers. "Oh, I'm not sure I can go much farther," he said, leading his horse to a stream. "I only hope we're not pursuing a lost cause."

"We're all tired," Horace Clark admitted. "It's been a long time since I've ridden this far." He twisted his large frame to relieve the cramped muscles, and slapped at his wide-brimmed hat with a glove. "But if our information is correct, we'll find the girls in Stockton."

Officer O'Day glanced at a map. "I think we've come about two-thirds of the way—maybe farther."

"Oooh," Jonathan sighed. "You mean we have another long day like this?" He reached his arms high overhead, and then bent to touch his fingers to the ground. "I'm not sure I can make it. How about you, Mrs. Whitfield?" His smile was teasing. "Can you survive one more day of this torture?"

"I've asked you to call me, Kulien—remember?" Tossing her head, she answered over her shoulder, "Yes, another day could mean freedom for some of our girls." She slapped the rump of her horse as he dipped his muzzle in the cool stream. "I would even be willing to ride farther tonight. Every hour lost means more danger for them. I'm especially anxious about Spring Rain and Clear Moon."

None of the rescue party agreed with Kulien's suggestion, so after a small meal around a warming fire, Kulien retired to the tent set up for her. Like a protective wall, the men slept on mats surrounding her tent.

As she lay in the stillness of the night listening to the crackle of the dying embers, and feeling the tension melt from her body, she thought of Marshall. Where was he tonight? Did he ever think of her? And Ta Ming? When would she see her son again? They were so far away. After this trip, she would write another letter begging, if she had to, for Ta Ming to come to California. More than two years had passed since that morning he had clung to her neck in tears—years that she missed him—and Marshall.

Shifting her body for a more comfortable place on the hard ground, she closed her eyes, trying to recall the last days she had spent with Ta Ming. It was becoming more difficult to see his features s as the months passed. Adding to her sadness, she could barely remember those final hours alone with Marshall before he turned his back and walked away.

It was almost sunset on their last day of travel when the little party of rescuers sighted the village of Stockton. The inland city had been built on a channel, an inlet of the San Joaquin River. Several steamers waited at the docks to take passengers either west to San Francisco or north to Sacramento. Sighing with weariness, Kulien turned to Horace Clark, riding near her. "Could we have come by boat?"

"We considered that idea, but we wouldn't have been able to keep our presence a secret." He watched Kulien stand in the stirrups to stretch her legs. "You're a brave young woman, Kulien. But now," he turned to call to the other riders; "we must stop here and plan our strategy. Judge Martin, are you familiar with the town? Have you any idea where the Chinese have settled?"

The judge, a tall, balding man pointed toward the mouth of the channel. "When I was here a few years ago, the majority of Chinese lived there; but a fire destroyed most of their buildings this year. We'll just have to take a look."

Motioning between himself and Kulien, Jonathan Wung suggested, "We would be the least conspicuous, so let us go in, on foot, by ourselves. We're dressed as the 'black-haired,' the peasants. We'll pretend to be looking for a place to find relaxation—and women." He lifted his dark eyebrows at Kulien's disguise. "When we know where the prostitutes are kept, we'll come back and return as a group."

Nodding her agreement, Kulien dismounted. Reverend Clark agreed that they would be more likely to be accepted as travelers among their own people. "But," he warned, "don't take any chances. You're both too valuable to risk your lives."

"Our lives are no more valuable than those young women." Jonathan's voice was so low that only Kulien and Horace Clark heard.

Glancing at the tall, slender doctor, she thought, *"This man has deep feelings—a heart for people. He's a little like Sunfu—yet unlike any man I've ever known."*

Kulien and Jonathan walked for nearly a mile before they reached the outskirts of the city. They said nothing for several minutes before Kulien began to speak in her native tongue. "You may think I'm bold, but I enjoy being with you."

Through the dim moonlight Kulien could see a smile flicker at the corners of Wung's eyes. "I, too, feel completely relaxed and content in your company. I've never openly conversed with any woman."

"I was privileged to have discussions with my father," she said, matching her strides with his. "My step-brother, Sunfu, also took me into his confidence. With you, I can remember the pleasant memories of my youth."

Jonathan stopped walking, motioning toward a narrow lane. "Here we take on the appearance of tired miners." Removing his glasses, he put them in a pocket; then he bent over to pick up a handful of dust. He rubbed the soil over his clothes and face. Kulien did the same, smearing her face and clothing with the black earth.

"If you would permit me, I'd like to ask my Heavenly Father to assist us in our purposes." Kulien only nodded, and with open eyes, watched Wung bow his head, and speak softly. "Father, we need you! Please help us find the girls; and keep us safe."

With his head still lowered, and his shoulders drooping, he led the way down a muddy, rutted road. Kulien, following his example, also took on the disguise of a weary traveler.

Most of the area leading into the village was charred from fire; only a few buildings remained—among them a joss house. Several men stood outside the place of worship, smoking and talking in low tones. Carefully, Jonathan approached them, speaking Cantonese. "My cousin and I have come down from the mines." He motioned toward Kulien, standing in the shadows. "We've been away from our wives for many moons, and are looking for women. Are there any for hire near here?"

The men glanced in Kulien's direction before one man, with missing teeth, smiled. He pointed toward the south. "Have plenty good time there. New girls—three, maybe four. Fresh from San Francisco."

Wung thanked them and walked toward Kulien with his teeth clenched, and his eyes straight ahead. "We'll go see for ourselves first. Then we'll make no mistakes when it's time to take the girls out of there."

In order to avoid suspicion, the nondescript figures walked two blocks south of the small business district as leisurely as possible. Familiar odors of China assailed their senses—drying fish, onions, garlic, and an occasional whiff of incense. The general ambience began to change as they went on. Instead of orderly, well-kept houses, the shacks were in disrepair, some practically falling in on themselves.

"All Chinese settlements seem to be the same," Kulien noted.

"The men know their time in America is only temporary," Jonathan answered, "so they care little for comfort or sanitation. I haven't spent as much time in the Chinese sections as you have, but I know there'll be a place for smoking the foreign mud, opium, and that's where we'll find the bordellos."

They walked down one dark alley after another, coming at last to a building that obviously housed a gambling den. They could overhear men playing *fan tan,* calling out the number of coins they guessed were left under a cup. Voices rose as the excitement of the games continued. Kulien and Jonathan stared at one another, certain they had found the house where the girls were kept prisoners. Wung put a finger of warning over his lips, and motioned for Kulien to follow him around the edge of the house. At the rear they found a small ground-level window. Dropping to their knees to peer inside, they discovered that the window was covered with thick tarpaper.

"Do you smell that?" Wung leaned near a crack at the top of the window. "Opium."

Familiar with the pungent odor, Kulien nodded. "Our girls must be in there," she whispered. "We've been through the entire area, and this is the most likely place for them to be."

Jonathan rose to his feet, leaning close to Kulien's ear. "Should we try to sneak inside? Just to be sure?"

Kulien shivered, whether from fear or from the closeness of her companion, she didn't know. Shaking her head, she warned, "No, there'll be guards. We should go back for the others. When the kidnappers are faced by tall foreigners holding guns, they will be quick to surrender."

It was in the darkest hours before sunrise when the entire group made their way to the gambling den. Fortunately a cloud mass had descended blotting out the moonlight, and no one saw the rescue party sneak quietly into the alley behind the building. As they approached the corner of the house Officer O'Day, who was in the lead motioned for them to stop. In a hoarse whisper, he nodded toward the entrance. "Guards."

He was right. Two men stood on either side of the door, speaking in low tones. An occasional laugh punctuated the darkness. For several minutes the rescue party watched, each wondering what the next move should be.

"Now what?" Horace Clark asked in a sigh of exasperation.

"We'll have to take them!" O'Day's voice was low-pitched, but authoritative.

Horace Clark spoke first. "How? What do you mean? I don't want any killing."

"Do you want to turn back then? Leave those girls in there?"

"No." Kulien answered the question meant for Reverend Clark. Her voice was soft, but firm. "I'm not concerned about the lives of those who deal in human flesh. We must get our girls—whatever it takes."

O'Day reached into his coat for a large pistol. He whirled the cylinder, keeping the gun close to his body to muffle the sound. Studying the filled chambers, he asked, "Who'll go with me?"

"I will." Wung stepped forward, drawing a shiny dagger from his belt.

"I'm not much of a fighter," Judge Martin confessed, "but I'll help in any way I can."

"Then you take this." Wung placed the knife in the older man's hand. "I have weapons I learned to use as a boy." He crouched and sliced the air with flattened hands.

"Good!" O'Day pointed at Horace Clark. "You stay here with the woman. We'll put those bastards out of commission."

Kulien and Horace lingered in the shadows near the corner of the building as the three men separated to edge around the house. The waiting seemed interminable as they watched for movement. Suddenly Wung appeared around the opposite side of the house, creeping silently upon a man whose back was turned. From the light of the doorway, Kulien saw the man's startled expression as Wung's arm went around his neck. With a twist and a subtle cracking sound, the man's head lopped to one side, his eyes still wide with surprise. In the same instant, Officer O'Day brought the butt of his revolver down on the other man's head, stopping him before he could shout. Judge Martin rushed for the man's back, driving the knife in up to the hilt. Both guards slumped to a lifeless heap as Wung motioned Kulien and Horace Clark to join them.

"Quick!" he ordered. "We must move before anyone else comes."

With a large hand on Horace's shoulder, O'Day said, "Don't be disturbed. There was no other way to silence them."

Single-file, they slipped through the door and moved silently down a dingy hallway littered with rotting garbage and animal feces. The stench of urine hung in the air overcoming every other repugnant odor. At the end of the hall, they found steps leading under the house. Stupefying fumes of opium wafted up the rickety stairs to assail their senses with yet another offensive stench.

Still holding his gun ready to fire, Officer O'Day watched Horace Clark remove a candle from his coat pocket and light it. "Watch it," O'Day warned. "There may be other guards down here. If the girls *are* in the cellar, you can be sure they aren't alone."

Kulien nodded. It was true that the girls were more valuable than gold to their owners. With women in such short supply, a man would pay a week's wages to spend a few lustful minutes with one of them.

When they reached the bottom of the stairs, they could see that the only occupants of the squalid room were drugged smokers lying on cots like dead men, the long opium pipes still hanging from their mouths. The vapors were overpowering; and Kulien held her breath against the sickening fumes of the potent drug.

In the darkest recesses of the room, the red-haired Irishman stopped. "Here's another door," he said. "I think we'll find what we're looking for in here." His head turned from side to side. "And there aren't any more guards." Shoving his bulk against the padlocked wooden door, he watched it give way.

With the candle held high, the group peered through the darkness, and saw two girls cowering in a corner. Kulien recognized them at once, and dropped to her knees in front of one of them. "You're here! Clear Moon, it is I, Kulien. We've come to take you home."

The girl began to cry hysterically. "You're too late! She's gone! She's gone!" The young girl pointed toward the far corner. Horace Clark shone the light in that direction. The once lively Spring Rain, with eyes bulging and tongue lolling from an open mouth, hung grotesquely from a red silk sash tied to an open rafter. Kicked to the side was a splintery crate.

Ice water filled Kulien's veins, and she leaped to her feet with a scream. "No! Not Spring Rain! Oh, no." As strength drained from her body, she fell to the dirt floor, reaching for Clear Moon.

Without a word, Reverend Clark, assisted by Judge Martin, cut through the red silk and tenderly lifted the limp form in his arms and lowered her gently to the earth. Jonathan Wung knelt over her and pressed his ear against the chest for several moments. Looking up at Kulien, he said sadly, "She's dead. But her body is still warm. If only we had come sooner. . .."

"Why, Clear Moon?" Kulien hugged the girl so close they seemed to be one. "Why did she do this?"

Clear Moon drew away from Kulien's grasp and wiped at her eyes. "She was used all day—by many, many men. When they finally left, I thought she was dead. She was bleeding, and so very pale. She asked me to help arrange her hair and put on her clothes. Then when she set up the crate, I thought she only wanted to sit down. I watched her for a short while, but I must have fallen asleep." Clear Moon's eyes fastened on the still form in the center of the room. "I woke when I heard the crate fall. Spring Rain was gasping and choking, but I couldn't get her down. That's when that man," she pointed at Officer O'Day, "broke through the door."

Clear Moon motioned to the other girl, who seemed to be in a trance. "Ma Wong was used the same way yesterday. Since then, she's not spoken or moved." Clear Moon's voice was barely audible. "I was to be tomorrow's victim."

Kulien reached out to touch Ma Wong's shoulder. "Oh, you poor children! But where are Sweet Flower and Chu Long? Five of our girls were taken, and only Silver Bell escaped." With eyes still on Ma Wong, Kulien watched her rock back and forth, making strange growling sounds.

In a flat, unemotional voice, Clear Moon said, "After a day of traveling, Chu Long began to kick and scream until a man cut her throat and threw her out of the wagon. I heard them say that they were taking Sweet Flower to the mountains where there had been no women for two years." Clear Moon hugged herself and began to shake uncontrollably.

When the group was ready to leave, Jonathan lifted Ma Wong in his arms while Reverend Clark held the sputtering candle. Officer O'Day carried Spring Rain's body while Kulien wrapped an arm around Clear Moon to steady her, and Judge Martin followed as a rear guard. He spoke loud enough for all to hear. "We must leave quickly before more guards arrive. It's almost daylight."

The group returned to their camp by sneaking down alleys and hiding in the shadows, assuring both girls that they were on their way back to Kulien's home. Refreshed after a meal and an hour or two of sleep, they placed the girls on mats in the cart and mounted their horses. Jonathan had wrapped Spring Rain's body in a burlap bag, tied both ends with ropes, and laid her over the back of his horse. "When we find an acceptable place, we will stop to bury her."

Kulien watched the young man with interest. Since being in America she had never seen white men show respect to a Chinese—man or woman. Yet whenever Jonathan Wung spoke, the others gave him their attention. The man carried himself with an air of authority, blended with a show of humility—a most honorable combination, she thought.

After traveling for many hours, they reached a glistening rivulet hidden in a grove of trees. "This is the place," Jonathan announced. "It is off the beaten path—and quiet and cool. We'll lay Spring Rain here where her body won't be disturbed."

Sitting at a distance with Clear Moon and Ma Wong at her side, Kulien watched in silence as the men dug a grave in the soft earth, and carefully lowered the body into the hole. With dignified reverence, they shoveled the piles of soil back into the grave. Leaving the girls beside the cart, Kulien picked some wildflowers to place beside the cross marker Horace Clark had made of branches. Then each person stood quietly as Jonathan piled large stones on top of the grave. "This will deter the coyotes," he said.

Reverend Clark lifted his eyes heavenward. "Let us join our hearts in prayer."

The weary band of travelers stood at the foot of the grave and bowed their heads. "Father, this child has seen too much of men's sin." He wiped at his eyes with his sleeve, and began to recite memorized verses from the Bible: "Jesus said, 'I am the resurrection, and the life; he that believeth in me, though he were dead, yet shall he live; And whosoever liveth and believeth in me shall never die.'" Horace Clark's eyes roamed over those standing beside the grave. Officer O'Day coughed uncomfortably; Judge Martin slapped at his boots with his hat; and Jonathan Wung muttered, "Amen."

"Only God knows if this young girl believed the words of Scripture, but we entrust her to her Creator." Horace turned to walk away with the others where the horses had been tied; but Kulien lingered a few moments to think her own thoughts. *Never again would Spring Rain be the victim of men's passions. I hope she has found a safe harbor.*

Two more days passed before the city of San Francisco came into view. The trip back home, for the most part, had been without incident. Kulien and Jonathan often rode side by side talking of happier days, remembering childhood games, laughing over almost forgotten pleasures. "Before the plague took most of my family, we boys would go to the countryside to fly kites. I often pretended to be that kite, looking down on the canals, floating over the hillsides." A childlike smile played at the corners of his mouth, and Kulien's lips also turned up in a smile as their friendship grew.

She had never had a friend her own age, of her own race. Nor had she ever known such camaraderie in one of the opposite sex, except perhaps with Sunfu. Her mind drifted across the miles to Marshall. As a young girl, she had loved him deeply and passionately, but had they ever been *friends?* They had spoken only a little of their childhoods; and his interest in her had been their marriage relationship and the son that one night had produced. Suddenly, she realized that she was now mature—able to think for herself, to be a woman alone! Her heart skipped a beat as the thought grew. She had been accepted into San Francisco's society; she owned her home; and she was a teacher to eager students. Yet, something was still lacking—an empty spot remained deep within. She shook her head to dismiss the idea. Time would heal the fresh wounds, and, for the present, she would concentrate on educating her students

"You're very quiet," Jonathan said after several miles. "Are you thinking about your husband?"

Kulien's eyes widened. The man even saw into her thoughts. "Yes, among other things. What do you know of him—of Marshall Whitfield?"

"Only that he lives in Great Britain—with your son."

Kulien tugged at her horse's reins bringing him to a stop. "Then you should also know that Lord Whitfield has taken a wife of British ancestry. My marriage is not recognized by the laws of either of our countries." Somehow saying those words aloud released a secret bond, and Kulien smiled.

Jonathan lowered his eyelids. "I didn't know. I ask your pardon if I caused you to lose face."

Kulien waited until his eyes met hers. "No, your words had the opposite effect. You, Dr. Jonathan Wung, have set me free!"

Kulien dug her heels into her mount's flanks, and raced away, her hair flying in the wind.

With the city in sight, but not daring to enter without her American protectors, Kulien slowed her horse to a trot, waiting for Reverend Clark to reach her side. "Are you feeling unwell, Kulien? Your face is flushed. I'm afraid this trip has been too much for you. There was so much violence—and death!"

How do I feel? It was neither the violence nor the long days of travel that most affected me. It was Jonathan Wung. Why such an attraction to the young doctor? And why do I compare him with Marshall Whitfield?

She shook her head to dispel the confusion. Lifting her face to the westerly breezes, she answered her old friend, "I am well, Horace—very well."

FIFTY-FOUR

Over the next two months, Kulien's emotions wavered between grief and joy. After ten days of rest and Dr. Wung's medical care, Clear Moon had recovered from her ordeal, and had begun her studies with enthusiasm. However, Ma Wong, infected with pox, died six weeks after being rescued from the bordello.

Martha and Kulien tried to bring as much encouragement and hope to their charges as possible, decorating the parlor for Christmas with boughs of greenery while their new cook, an African woman, baked cookies, pies and cakes to fill the house with warm, fragrant aromas. More slave girls had been relocated from the "Home for Slave Girls" to Kulien's residence; and the students once again numbered six.

After Christmas came Chinese New Year with further celebrations, and more delicious foods; and the two young women began to relax their frightened vigil and direct their attention to teaching. Two or three times a week, Dr. Wung arrived at the house to examine the girls, often staying long enough to enjoy a meal and conversation with Kulien in their native tongue.

One morning over breakfast, Kulien confided in Martha, "I've never spoken to you about my concern for Ta Ming; but I do worry about him. You've told me how you trust the invisible God; and I was wondering if you have words to help me?"

Martha's soft brown eyes rested on Kulien's smooth face. "I don't know, Kulien. I will help you in any way I can. What is it that worries you?"

Kulien folded her hands on the table, opening and closing her entwined fingers. "My son hasn't written for months. I don't know if he's well, or if he's forgotten me. It's just that I— I'm confused about what to do…." She couldn't continue as she fought back tears.

"The best thing I can do is to pray for you. We've worked together now for many months, and I can see how much you miss your child. I've also noticed your sad expression whenever Dr. Wung leaves. Does he remind you of your son?"

"I don't understand. Why would Jonathan remind me of Ta Ming?"

Martha shrugged her shoulders. "Oh, I don't know—I guess just because he's Chinese—and a male." A self-conscious laugh covered Martha's embarrassment.

Kulien felt her face warm as she acknowledged to herself that Jonathan Wung *was* another reason for her confusion. She found herself looking forward to his visits with great anticipation; and felt disappointed when he didn't arrive.

Two days later, on a dreary February afternoon, Reverend Clark arrived at the front door with mail. "I'll come in for only a minute," he said, glancing over his shoulder at the sheets of rain. "The roads are almost impassable as the ruts fill with water." He shook the drops off his wide-brimmed hat and stepped inside the door. Closing it behind him, he held out the packet. "I glanced through the mail, and I'm sure this delivery will bring a smile to your face."

He waited a moment as Kulien sifted through the bills. When she saw the envelope with stamps bearing the stately likeness of Queen Victoria, her dark green eyes danced with joy. "Oh, thank you for coming through the storm to bring news from Ta Ming! It's been months since I've heard from him."

"I know." Reverend Clark nodded his understanding before he opened the door and turned to walk off the porch. "I hope it's good news," he called, as he stepped up into his coach.

Kulien watched the horse and carriage disappear around the bend before she closed the door and walked across the parlor to the settee in front of the fireplace. Carefully, she unsealed the envelope and removed the crisp parchment with Ta Ming's large printed letters. Pleased, she noticed another sheet of paper with Marshall's elegant script. To treasure the desired correspondence as long as possible, she slipped the letters into the pocket of her jacket and walked to the kitchen. Martha was upstairs reading; the girls were napping, and Farina, the cook, had gone to town to shop for vegetables. Alone in the kitchen, Kulien boiled water for tea, and after placing two thin cookies on a flowered saucer, she walked slowly back to the parlor to sit near the warming fire.

She read Ta Ming's letter first. It had been three years since she last saw her child. He had been only six years old—still her baby. Closing her eyes, she brought to mind his smooth cheeks, the bright blue eyes, and his arms reaching for her neck. Now he was nine—no longer a baby. Was he the same boy, only in a larger body? Was his skin fair; and had he become more European than Chinese?

Dwelling on each word, Kulien hoped to discover a hint of his true thoughts. However, he said nothing about missing her—or wanting to come to California. The letter was simply a report of his education and the social life he enjoyed as the son of a British noble. He had no personal words for her—no expressions of love.

With disappointment, she folded the letter and put it back into the envelope. Her heart and arms ached for him, yet he seemed to have no need of her.

For several moments Kulien sat staring at the flames. She sighed, sipping at her tea, trying to dismiss the troubled feeling. Would Marshall's letter be as cold? Fearful, yet anxious to know what he wrote, she unfolded the smooth paper and began to read, "My dear Kulien," it began. "It has been many months since I've been able to correspond with you; however, when I explain, I believe you will grant me forgiveness."

Kulien refolded the letter, and waited a moment before continuing to read. A sense of impending sorrow swept over her heart. Why would he need forgiveness? What could have happened that he had delayed writing? She opened it again.

The letter went on, "Elise has been extremely ill—at the point of death actually. On the fifteenth of November last, after great suffering, she gave birth to a baby girl. The child, born a month too soon, died the next day."

Kulien dropped the letter to her lap, and clutched at her heart. The woman had a baby? But Marshall had said they would never come together as husband and wife! Hot tears pricked her eyelids before flowing down her cheeks. She could scarcely breathe. *Marshall—you promised! You didn't keep our marriage vows, and you joined your body with Elise!* Bile rose to Kulien's throat and her head began to whirl. She buried her face in her hands and cried. "Oh, Marshall, now it *is* truly over between us."

How long she sat there rehearsing the painful news, she didn't know. When she lifted her head, the fire was only a glowing log. Kulien crumpled the letter to throw it onto the burning embers—then she stopped. Why had he believed she would forgive him when he had disregarded their marriage vows?

Leaning closer to the fire's dim light, she read further. "It is most difficult and awkward to write this letter, but I must explain what has happened since George came to live with us. He and Elise have become great friends. He makes her laugh, and has brought the color back to her cheeks. It was her love for him that strengthened her desire, and mine, for *us* to have a child—regardless of the consequences. Kulien, please remember—Elise is my legal wife. I could not deny her the rightful place she has in my bed."

As anger replaced sadness, Kulien hardened her heart, but continued to read. "After the baby died, and Elise became even more attached to George, her health returned. The doctor was encouraged, and urged her to have another baby as soon as possible."

And of course, you're only too willing to help! That woman has not only stolen my husband, but also my son.

As only a few words remained on the page, Kulien read, "I have no plans to bring George to see you in the near future. I only ask for your understanding and patience."

"And forgiveness!" she said aloud. "No, I don't understand, and I won't forgive!"

Kulien crumpled the letter into a tight ball and threw it into the fireplace. She watched it curl among the ashes, smoke rising from the distressing words. Suddenly, with a flash, the fire consumed it, and sparks rose up the chimney, taking her long-held hopes with them.

Kulien didn't tell Martha about the letters, but kept the hurt and bitterness hidden in her heart. Martha, knowing Kulien so well, continued to work beside her, a question in her eyes. She sensed Kulien's aloofness, but didn't inquire, and ministered to the girls as usual. Both women were involved in preparing their students for life on the outside.

But Kulien was troubled about sending Clear Moon to China; since the abduction and rescue, she had hovered over the girl as if she were her own child. The sense of rejection from both Marshall and Ta Ming drew her even closer to Clear Moon, who was eager to return to her homeland.

"I have received both physical and spiritual life from the hands of missionaries," she told Kulien. "I must return to China to tell the girls not to be afraid of the people with 'big noses.'" She smiled at the expression. "I was told that Westerners plucked the eyes out of children and fried their skin. It's no wonder there are so few who trust them."

"But they *will* trust you," Kulien assured her. "If the people in our own country could understand and believe the worth of their children, whether they're male or female there would be no more slave girls—no losses like Spring Rain and Ma Wong."

Clear Moon's black eyes shone with mischief. "I think you, too, my teacher, would like to go to China. If you would come with me, I would be most happy!" The girl touched Kulien's arm, letting her fingers caress the silk fabric of the sleeve.

Kulien placed a warm hand over Clear Moon's fingers. "Yes, that is my desire. Someday I will return, but the time is not yet. I don't know where I would live."

"I'm sure the Americans who want me to help in their clinic in Shanghai would be pleased to have you accompany us." A broad smile lit up the plain face. "I don't know anything about my future except that Reverend Clark said when April arrives and the flowers bloom, the doctor and his wife will come for me." Her eyelids lowered, and she spoke softly. "Of course, I must pass the health test, and pay my passage."

"We have money for your passage," Kulien answered having planned to withdraw from the savings Marshall had set up for her. Although there was not much reserve after paying the servants and buying food and clothing for all the members of the household, she had managed to put aside enough to send Clear Moon across the Peaceful Sea. "But you must continue to eat and sleep well. Dr. Wung will give you a physical examination soon. He'll be in San Francisco for only two more months."

Kulien sighed as she remembered his announcement, "My benefactor insists I spend at least another year or two here in America before I return to China," he had said the day before. Kulien had listened with sadness, but had shown only happiness on her face. It would not do for him to know that she cared whether he stayed or left.

Later that afternoon, when Clear Moon and the other students had retired to their rooms to practice reading, Kulien alerted the guards and household help to remain watchful because she and Martha had been invited to visit the Clarks at the Home for Slave Girls.

When Jonathan arrived with a large covered buggy that would comfortably seat six passengers, he bounded from the buggy and raced to the front door. "I am to be your escort," he said. "It seems our American friends want us to accompany them on a walking tour of Little China."

Kulien paled. "It won't be safe for me, will it—a Chinese woman walking along the streets of the Chinese Quarter?"

Jonathan bowed from the waist. "You'll be surrounded by the Clarks, a policeman, and another barbarian—Martha," he said with a twinkle in his eyes. "And surely you haven't forgotten my own weapons." He crouched and with flattened hands sliced the air.

Laughing, Kulien and Martha stepped up into the carriage. "And, you may be surprised to learn," he added, "that my medicine has become quite popular among our people. Western medicine, used in combination with traditional herbs, has brought health to *Tong Yen Fau,* the Port of the Chinese."

Kulien, for the moment, forgot the sadness that had been brooding in her heart, and laughed. Jonathan's enthusiasm, and the prospect of spending the afternoon with him in the Chinese Quarter, lifted her spirits. She realized that she had become more homesick for China as the days passed and wondered if it was because she had given up hope for a reunion with Ta Ming and Marshall?

The enthusiastic group, composed of tall white foreigners accompanying a young Chinese man and Eurasian woman, attracted attention as they strolled up and down the streets of the Chinese Quarter. Approximately ten blocks of buildings, streets, and narrow alleys had become not only a living community for the Asian settlers, but it was also a prison to those who found a home there. To step outside the boundaries could mean a barrage of stone-throwing youths or even death at the hands of a drunken Westerner. Some of the Chinese carried a police whistle to attract attention when attacked by thugs, but more often than not, the alarm went unheeded.

People stepped aside to ogle the Chinese couple and their barbarian friends. Jonathan smiled at Kulien as they both understood the words spoken by those who watched the short parade.

"I wish I could be a man right now," Kulien said to Jonathan. "I would be free to go where I wished and become part of the crowd."

"Perhaps, if we're alert, we can escape our protectors," he said with a sly smile. "Would you like to try?"

Kulien's green eyes sparkled with excitement. Could he be serious? Would they dare to separate themselves from the others? "Wouldn't I be in danger?"

"As I said before, the men here know and trust me. They wouldn't attempt to harm you while you're with me." He turned to wave at a group of men who waited in front of a barber shop to have their crowns shaved.

Glancing over her shoulder, Kulien watched Martha and the Clarks peer into a curio shop where silk goods were displayed. Martha beckoned to Kulien. "We want to go in here. Come on."

Kulien nodded, but as the Americans and their police escort disappeared into the building, she turned to Jonathan. "It's time to make our escape!"

Jonathan reached for her hand, and in one fluid movement, they darted into an alley. Running as fast as they could, they passed men hunched over benches making shoes and boots, and a group of peddlers selling live chickens in wicker baskets. Passing open doors of basement restaurants, they smelled delectable aromas of rice, and saw noodles drying in the afternoon air.

Finally, gasping for breath, they stopped to get their bearings. "Are you hungry?" Jonathan panted the words.

"Starved."

"My cousin lives on the next street," he said, inhaling deeply. "He operates a kitchen for merchants. The food is good. Come on."

For the first time in years, Kulien felt the burden of life slip from her shoulders. The sights, the smells, and the black-haired people talking and bargaining transported her back to Shanghai. She had been only ten years old on a promised trip to the city with her father and brothers. On that trip, as on this one, she had dared to break away from her father's protection. That day, Sunfu had been the one to suggest they slip away from Kuang Lufong's ever-watchful eyes. She recalled their excitement as they hid first in one shop, and then another. They had managed to elude their father's search for an hour before he discovered them. The punishment of two days without sweets was worth every stolen minute.

Now, as on that long-ago day, joy bubbled up from deep within, and Kulien laughed as they again broke into a run. Old men with parchment-dry faces smiled at the couple as they darted by. Young men, far from home and lonely for their sweethearts, cheered them on as they ran past street vendors and medicine shops. At last they stopped, and laboring for air, leaned against a building, their hearts pounding from exertion.

Suddenly realizing they still held hands, Kulien drew her hand away and looked up at Jonathan. "I can't believe I'm doing this." Always speaking Mandarin with him, her words were melodic, her face glowing from the exertion.

"Nor I." Jonathan pushed back a strand of soft, black hair, free of pomade, and wiped at his forehead with a handkerchief. He held it up. "Do you mind?" When she shook her head, he dabbed at her damp face. "It's been many years since I've run so fast," he said. "As my legs broke free, so did my spirit." Removing his glasses to wipe them, Jonathan fastened his obsidian eyes on Kulien's upturned face. Her lips parted in a bright smile, and the dimple in her right cheek winked at him. His face flushed, and he quickly slipped the glasses back on his nose.

"My cousin's shop is here." He pointed to an upstairs' window of the building. "As I said, he only caters to merchants, but I know he'll make an exception in our case." He bowed slightly and motioned toward the narrow doorway.

Kulien couldn't move. Her heart still racing from the unaccustomed exercise, she struggled against another emotion. She must face the truth: Jonathan was *not* like her brother, Sunfu; nor was he like Marshall Whitfield. He was a strong, intelligent man—and at this moment, he was extremely attractive to her!

His dark eyebrows drew together in concern and his black eyes softened as he tipped his head, waiting for her to speak.

"Are you feeling all right? Was it too much for you to run so fast?"

"You're the doctor," she said, the smile brightening again. "You tell me."

"I'm going to prescribe a cup of tea and a bowl of noodles. My cousin, who is also from the north, prepares the best noodles in all of Little China."

Kulien hesitated before entering the door that led up a dark stairway. Holding out a hand, Jonathan stepped in front of her. "If you won't think I'm forward, I'll guide you to the dining room."

Had he forgotten that he had held her hand all the way from the busy thoroughfare and through the alleys? Placing her hand in his, she repeated over and over in her mind, *Jonathan Wung is like a brother to me—a brother!* But the tingling she felt race up her arm and to her heart could not be ignored. This man, this doctor, was *not* her brother. He was a man from Soochow—a kind, sensitive man who, she knew, found her attractive.

After being warmly greeted by Jonathan's cousin, Wung Fu Chi, they were directed to a far corner of the crowded room. "What do you suppose is going through the minds of Reverend and Mrs. Clark?" Jonathan asked, after they had settled on the straight-backed chairs.

"And poor Martha," Kulien said, a hint of concern in her voice. "They will surely call for more police to make a search for us."

"Are you sorry about our adventure?"

"Do I look sorry?" Her smile flashed and her eyes shone.

"You look—you look beautiful." His cheeks flushed again. "Forgive me. I'm afraid I've taken on the ways of the West. I didn't mean to be disrespectful. Even though you told me that your marriage is not legally recognized, I know that, in your heart, you're a married woman. I had no right to speak my thoughts."

As she watched Jonathan's distressed expression, the words of Marshall's letter invaded her heart. "Elise gave birth to a baby girl…she's my wife and has the right to my bed." Trying to hold her emotions in check, she paused by scooping up some noodles from the red porcelain bowl.

Slowly, she wiped her mouth with a napkin, and smiled. "You don't offend me. Actually it has been many years since a man has admired me." She set the chopsticks aside with the decision to tell him about her past.

"As you said, I'm not *legally* married to Marshall Whitfield. We betrothed ourselves to each other—many years ago. I was but a headstrong child in my father's house. Would you be offended if I told you my story?"

Jonathan leaned forward on his elbows, his eyes intent on hers. "I would be most honored."

Kulien relaxed her mind and body as she began to relive the past in the presence of her closest friend and ally. "Are you certain you won't be bored—or shocked when I tell you how I came to be here?"

His eyes bright with interest and admiration, he answered, "Of course not. You, and your past, are safe with me."

Kulien began by telling him about her privileged childhood, and how on her sixteenth birthday, her father had revealed *his* past, and how it would affect *her* future.

Jonathan's eyebrows rose as she spoke about her British mother and the contract her father had made with the Kong clan. "May I interrupt for only a minute," he asked.

"Of course," Kulien said, breathing a sigh of relief. "I need to gather my thoughts."

"Did your mother give you an English name? Or have you always been called by the name your grandmother gave you?"

Kulien tipped her head. "You know, I haven't even thought of my English name for years. And I've never spoken it to anyone. My mother named me Grace after her mother. I've not used it because it doesn't suit me."

Jonathan's smile surrounded her with warmth. "Oh, but you're wrong. Grace is a beautiful name for a beautiful woman." His cheeks flushed as he continued. "As you know, I'm a Christian, and I have learned that 'grace' is a term often used in the English Bible. It speaks of God's favor to the undeserving. When I see you, I see a woman on whom God's grace rests."

"I don't understand. I know about your God, but I have not experienced this 'grace' you talk about."

Jonathan rested his elbows on the table, his hands forming a steeple. "I will talk to you more about that at another time. For now, please continue your story. We have no idea if, or when, our American friends will find our hiding place!"

Kulien let her mind revive the memories of her secret heart, telling Jonathan about the meetings with Marshall Whitfield in the summerhouse; and how she had freely given herself to him. She told of her joy when she knew she carried his child; and the shame and horror in Kong Litang's house.

Jonathan listened without comment as her story unfolded: the days in the prostitute shop, then the orphanage in Shanghai. She cried when she related how she and Marshall had been torn apart in Hong Kong; and how she'd been sold into slavery in San Francisco. Her face lit up as she spoke of Ta Ming's birth, and the kindness of the O'Kelly's. Weary from the ordeal of her monologue, she sighed, resting her chin on folded hands.

"Then you came to live with the Clark's?" Before she could answer, he went on, "And haven't you seen the Englishman again?"

"I think you know that part of the story. Perhaps Horace told you."

Jonathan shrugged and nodded. "I hope you don't mind."

"No, I'm glad he did. Marshall came here to meet our son, and persuaded me to let him return to Great Britain with him." Her eyes rested on Jonathan's kind face. "I received a letter from Marshall telling me that his wife, who has been unable to walk for years, gave birth to a baby. The child died soon after birth, but they plan to have another soon!" Kulien lowered her eyelids to hide her emotion. When she lifted them, she said with resolve, "I'm no longer part of Lord Whitfield's life. So I have resumed my family name—Kuang."

The words were spoken with such finality, that Kulien was surprised at the hardness in her voice.

Jonathan reached across the table to cover her hand with his. "Perhaps one day, you will again find room in your heart for love."

Kulien looked out the small window behind Jonathan's head. The sky had changed from pale blue to dark purple; and the room was empty of patrons. Glancing back at his expectant smile, her voice was filled with promise, "Yes, you may be right. Perhaps one day—there will be room."

FIFTY-FIVE

It was late by the time Kulien and Jonathan had walked from the Chinese Quarter to her home on the hill. Their conversation along the way had been enjoyable; but Kulien had tried to focus on ordinary subjects. Her emotions during their meal together had both confused and frightened her. What had been a reciprocal friendship had changed—she had become conscious of him as a *man*—more than just a friend.

"I hope you won't be chastised by Martha," he said, with a smile, when they neared the gate.

"She'll only say how worried she was and that I should be more careful and thoughtful of others' concerns for my safety."

Facing each other, Kulien saw how the moonlight accentuated his fine cheekbones and well-shaped face. His eyes rested on hers, and she inhaled deeply to erase the new awareness of attraction.

"And what will you tell her?"

Kulien lowered her eyelids, suddenly feeling like a young girl. "I shall say that two friends wanted to recapture their love for China."

Jonathan cleared his throat and bowed. "Ah, yes, I believe we accomplished that, and more."

Without answering, Kulien stepped to the gate where an armed guard waited inside. He watched for Kulien's nod before fitting a large key into the padlock. When it snapped open he pushed the gate outward so Kulien could enter.

Jonathan touched her arm. "Thank you for a most enjoyable day." He voice was soft, barely audible. "I will treasure the memory."

"Yes, I will always remember our race through the alleys. It was delightful."

With a smile on both their faces, they parted—he, to walk back to his hotel, and she, to the house where Martha stood on the porch wringing her hands. "Where were you? We were so concerned, and had decided to call for another policeman when Anna convinced us you were safe with Dr. Wung."

Kulien removed her jacket and hung it on a peg near the door before answering, "I'm sorry for causing you anxiety, but we had to escape into our past for just a few hours."

Martha's frown disappeared as she turned to walk up the stairs, "I think I understand." Over her shoulder, she added with a smile, "I believe you and our doctor friend have more in common than either of you have realized."

Kulien did not think of Jonathan during the following week, nor did she allow her thoughts to linger on either Ta Ming or Marshall. Clear Moon was uppermost in her mind because the girl had to pass not only the written tests given by Martha and Kulien, she would also be questioned by Reverend Clark about her understanding of Christianity. In two months, she would leave her refuge in San Francisco to sail to China with a foreign doctor and his wife.

"I am torn between two loves," Clear Moon said one morning after English class. "You are my friend, and it was here in your home that I became a person of worth." Her eyes filled with tears. "Although I knew only suffering and misery in China, I have a longing to return to my homeland."

"I know how you feel," Kulien sighed. "My father once said, 'The fragments of the past remind us of who we are.' At the time I didn't understand, but now I do. Although British blood runs in my veins, I am more Chinese in my heart. I'm like you; I'll never be completely at peace until my feet are once again on the land of my forefathers."

"Do you think you will return one day soon?" Clear Moon asked, with a knowing smile.

"There's still much for me to do here. As long as there are slave girls in San Francisco, there's a need for my help."

Frowning, Clear Moon added, "But perhaps you could do even more if you stopped the problem where it begins—in China."

Without responding, Kulien turned to walk out the back door to gather some lilacs for the house. *She's right,* she thought, lifting a blossom to her nose, *but what can I, a half-breed woman, do in a vast country steeped in centuries-old traditions?*

As the days grew longer, Clear Moon's time in America grew shorter, and soon the missionaries would arrive to take the young girl to Shanghai with them. Kulien wondered who these people were who wanted Clear Moon to accompany them; but when she asked the Clarks about the missionaries, they only shrugged their shoulders and didn't answer.

One Saturday night, Horace Clark arrived at the front door with a question, "Would you be willing to come to church with us tomorrow? We would like the people to meet Clear Moon before she leaves, and it would be a good opportunity for you to speak about your work." His dark gray eyes bored into hers. "Dr. Wung is our guest speaker; and I think you'd like to hear what he has to say."

The next morning after everyone was seated Reverend Clark stepped up to the podium. "It is our privilege this morning to hear from Dr. Jonathan Wung, a citizen of China and a graduate of Harvard University." His eyes met Jonathan's with a smile. "This young man will give you new insight into the people of China. Most of you are familiar only with the hard-working peasants who have come to our land—some in search of gold—some in search of gainful employment. This gentleman has come for a more lasting treasure—education." He motioned toward the front row where Jonathan sat next to Kulien. "Please welcome Dr. Jonathan Wung of Soochow, China."

There were whispers among the people as the young doctor smiled and bowed to the audience. When he removed a small black book from an inside pocket, he said, "It is an honor to be here, and I give my heartfelt gratitude to you, the citizens of America—and to the God who rules this new country. My people are much like you: they love their families; they toil in their fields; and they hunger for peace of mind and soul." He paused and inhaled deeply. "It is my desire to return to China with the knowledge I have gained here. I want to teach them to value women—and to end the practice of footbinding. I will also bring Western medicine and a new way of life."

Jonathan opened the book and began to read a story told by Jesus about a farmer who sowed seed in his field. "I want to be that farmer in the wide fields of China. Some of the people, as in every country, will disregard those seeds of truth, but some will believe and be changed." Jonathan's eyes searched the upturned faces of the congregation. "I urge *you* to forsake your lives of ease and share your time and wealth with your neighbors who still live in darkness and sin. You know who you are—living in richly furnished homes, never satisfied—always looking for more to gratify your longings."

Several people spoke to each other in low tones and then got up and left the room; but Jonathan stood firm, his eyes shining with love.

Kulien wiped away the tears that rose to her eyes as she listened to his every word. *I'm like most of the people in this room—I live in luxury and freedom while my sisters are sold into slavery.* She struggled within herself, trying to justify her position in the community. She had been but the recipient of all the fine gifts Marshall had bestowed on her. She had used her home and possessions to alleviate the suffering of others; but since Marshall was no longer part of her life, she had no right to continue living in his home.

When Jonathan spoke her name, inviting her to the platform to tell of her work, she touched a finger to her lips and bowed her head. He seemed confused by her response and glanced at Martha, who sat with Horace and Anna Clark. "Miss Johnson, perhaps you would be willing to bring Clear Moon to the platform, and tell what you and Miss Kuang are doing for the slave girls of 'Little China.'"

Jonathan returned to his seat beside Kulien, his arm brushing against hers. Then with a slight movement, he placed a handkerchief in her hand and turned his attention to Martha and Clear Moon.

On the way home from the meeting, no one mentioned Jonathan's speech or Kulien's refusal to address the congregation. They only talked about Clear Moon's imminent departure, and what still needed to be done. When the buggy stopped in the front driveway, Kulien asked, "Won't all of you come in? Farina has prepared a turkey for our dinner, and there's plenty for all. The other girls have already eaten and are in their rooms.

Pleased that everyone had agreed to stay, they were soon seated around the long table in the dining room. Lively conversation centered primarily upon Clear Moon's final preparations, and in only the next two days, she would take her written examinations in English and Chinese history. "On Thursday," Jonathan said to Clear Moon, "I'll give you a complete physical examination before I sign the papers of release. You'll need an inoculation to protect you from the disease of smallpox."

Reverend Clark leaned forward on both elbows. "I understand that there has been a fast-spreading epidemic of the disease in the north of China. We can be thankful that a vaccine, made from the virus of cowpox, has been discovered."

"Yes," Jonathan nodded. "I hope one day the Chinese will accept the vaccination process. They don't believe they need anything other than their gods—whose name is legion: the Kitchen god; the Fire god; the god of Wealth; and the god of Medicine, just to name a few. But they have learned in the past months that the Goddess of Smallpox lacks power over the dread disease. It's not yet known how many have died." Jonathan's voice rose with enthusiasm. "They not only need the one true God of every nation, but they also need Western medicine."

After they had finished their meal, and Anna and Horace rose to leave, the older woman put an arm around Kulien's shoulders and drew her close. A soft fragrance of lavender drifted between them. "Kulien, my dear, we thank you for your hospitality—and for all that you've done for our rescued girls." She lowered her voice to a whisper, "Forgive me if I intrude on your privacy, but I could see that you were moved by Dr. Wung's words this morning. If Horace and I can be of help, please come to us. You know," she said, squeezing Kulien ever closer, "you're like a daughter to us!"

After Reverend and Mrs. Clark rode away in their buggy, Jonathan walked to the door and began putting on his coat when Kulien placed a hand on his arm. "Please don't go yet. Will you walk with me in the garden? It's so beautiful and I know that you love flowers as much as I do." Her face lit up with a smile. "At the back of the house are bushes, loaded down with deep purple lilacs, and the paths are bordered by a variety of colors. There are roses, tulips and lilies in many shades." She tipped her head, "And there's a small open house with stone benches where I often go when I want to be alone."

"A summerhouse! How delightful. I'd be honored to walk with you."

Kulien winced at the word, "summerhouse," but shook the images of the past from her mind, and said, "There's something I want to tell you."

But as they walked down the steps and around the side of her home, she wondered how to tell him of the impression of God's presence she had received that morning.

Neither spoke as they walked side by side, stopping now and then to gaze with appreciation at a brilliantly-hued flower, or to lower their heads over the fragrance of the lilacs bushes. When they reached the small frame building, Jonathan looked it over and smiled. "My benefactor has such a structure on his spacious property. He called it—a gazebo."

Kulien repeated the word in her mind before speaking. "Gazebo. That is a most difficult word to pronounce, but it is a pleasant place to sit." She sat on the stone bench, and patted the place next to her. "Will you join me?"

Jonathan's manner was modest and unassuming as he sat beside her, careful to keep an adequate distance between them. He folded his hands in his lap, and waited for her to tell him what was on her heart.

As the afternoon sun disappeared behind a cloud, Kulien shivered from the cool breeze blowing from the west. Instantly aware of her discomfort, Jonathan stood to remove his coat. "Would you accept my jacket?" When she nodded, he draped the padded garment over her shoulders, allowing his hands to rest on her arms for a lingering moment.

"You have something you want to tell me." Jonathan's words were a statement. "I'm ready to listen."

Kulien trembled under his gaze before turning to face him. "Today when you spoke about your concern for the women and girls of China, and of your calling to sow seeds of freedom, my heart was stirred. I have told myself and my friends that I wanted to return to China; but I confess that I have been reluctant to relinquish the wealth and honor I have received since Lord Whitfield came to America." Pulling the jacket closer around her shoulders, she gazed out at the garden. "For many years I was treated with scorn, not only by family members in my compound; but here, in this country, I have been maligned and hated because of my race and my gender. Finally, I have been recognized as a woman of substance; and my place in the community is respected. I told myself that, at last, I'd found freedom, but Jonathan…." Kulien's voice choked with emotion, and she wiped at the corners of her eyes with a forefinger. "…and I must be honest with you—pride, not liberty has controlled my heart. I didn't truly desire to return to the land of my birth; there I would be as I was before—a despised female." She paused again before going on. "Today, as you spoke, something happened to me. My possessions and prestige no longer seemed of any importance!" Kulien lifted teary eyes to Jonathan.

He didn't speak, but waited for her to finish her thoughts.

"When I was a child, I thought I must be naughty to unloose the bonds of propriety practiced in my compound. In my marriage year, I believed the only way to freedom was through the love of an Englishman." Her cheeks warmed as she spoke, but she persisted, wanting Jonathan to know more about her. She turned to face him. "What I've done, how I've lived, has not brought me the liberty I've been searching for. My bondage has grown more restricting with each passing year." She tipped her head, a frown creasing her smooth brow. "Do I make myself clear?"

"Yes," Jonathan agreed. "Education was my god, Kulien. When I put aside my selfish desires to find a higher purpose in life, I found peace through my trust in God."

Kulien and Jonathan smiled at each other, a deeper relationship growing between them. Without speaking, he stood up and drew her to his chest, holding her close. "Perhaps today you will begin a new life," he whispered into her hair. "You were made for more than this world has offered you. You are not a Bitter Seed—you are a woman of *grace.*"

Relaxing in his embrace, Kulien looked into his dark eyes, glistening with tears. Her heart swelled with unfamiliar emotions as they stood in that quiet place. Kulien took his face in her hands while looking deeply into his eyes. "You speak only good words to me; and my joy is…almost complete…."

Her remarks were interrupted as Jonathan lowered his head and covered her lips with his. With his arms encircling her waist, he drew her closer to his body. The kiss, reserved and tentative at first, answered to her response with hunger—desire.

Breathlessly, they parted—surprised, yet pleased with each other's nearness. Jonathan's expression of astonishment caused Kulien to laugh nervously. He touched her full, expressive lips with his fingertips. "I am not worthy of you, Kulien. I've been an orphan, secluded away in private schools for most of my life. I know so little about women. If I've offended you in any way, I ask your forgiveness."

Kulien could hardly believe her ears—he was apologizing? Hadn't she returned his kiss with abandonment? "It is I who am unworthy. You are a pure man—untouched by the vileness I've seen. You could never offend me! You only honor me."

Jonathan's smile captured her like a helpless bird caught in a net. She lifted her arms and wrapped them around his neck. As they held one another, Kulien could feel his heart beating in rhythm with hers. He brushed her forehead with a kiss before tipping her face with a fingertip. "Kulien, as you know, Clear Moon leaves for China next week; and I must return to Boston. But I have an important question to ask you." He brought his face close to hers and kissed her again.

Long-forgotten feminine powers surged through her body, and she was moved with longing for him. Was this the same desire she had felt for Marshall Whitfield? Confused, she closed her eyes—thinking. No, there was something different— better even than the physical relationship she'd had with Marshall. As a young, inexperienced girl, she had surrendered herself with abandon to the foreigner—but here was a man of her own race—a man who loved her with pure motives.

"Jonathan," she said, releasing herself from his embrace, "let's walk in the garden again. I'm overcome with troublesome thoughts. I told you how Marshall Whitfield and I performed our own wedding ceremony." She watched him nod, a crease on his forehead. "There has been no other man. Even though I was forced into prostitution, I never had to do business with a man.

"I thought I was wed for eternity; but Marshall has taken another wife, and they hope to have a child. Please tell me, if you know, am I free to love another, or does your black book say I'm still Marshall Whitfield's wife?"

Jonathan stepped off the path and broke a white lily off the tall plant. "You must find the answer for yourself. I only know that this blossom," he handed it to Kulien, "will always bear the likeness of its mother-plant, as you will always bear the events of your past. But the flower is severed now from the branch; it's free to be taken into the house, or to be discarded on the trash heap."

He removed his glasses and slipped them into a pocket of his shirt. Taking Kulien's hand, which still held the flower, he spoke in a low tone. "Today you have a future awaiting you. As I said, you'll continue to bear the results of your past life; but you must move forward in your new faith, and not allow your life to be cast aside. Your marriage, though genuine in your eyes and heart, was not recognized by either your country or his. Marshall Whitfield has a legal wife who wants to give him a child. I believe you are free from that marriage vow—free to love again. However, you must be assured of this in your own heart."

Kulien had no words to say as they continued around the edge of the house and into the warm parlor. "I must go now." Jonathan bowed, keeping his eyes on Kulien's face.

"Yes, I know. I thank you for your kind words; but you said earlier that you had a question for me. What is it, Jonathan?"

A moment of tension hung in the air before he answered. "When you are convinced of your freedom, I hope you will consider what I have to say."

"I will, of course. What is it?" Kulien sensed his discomfort as he began to pace back and forth in front of her; and to put his mind at ease, she held out a hand, urging him to stop in front of her.

Jonathan inhaled deeply and in one burst of air blurted, "When I leave for Boston, I would be the happiest man in the world if you would accompany me as my wife!"

FIFTY-SIX

After a light supper and Martha's reading of the same scripture passage that Jonathan had read that morning, the girls, along with Martha, retired for the night. Kulien was too tired and confused to talk about the events of the day. She knew Martha would be happy to hear about her new awareness of the One God; and she would be especially surprised to hear of Jonathan's proposal of marriage. But the news would wait until morning; all she wanted now was to go to bed and mull over the past hours.

When she turned down the lamp, and pulled the quilt up under her chin, Jonathan's face and words filled every thought. More than she could fathom, she had enjoyed his closeness and the delight of his full lips pressing on hers. His eyes, the tone of his voice, and the gentleness of his embrace sent shivers of joy through every part of her body. Did she love him as a woman loves a man? Did he love her in that intimate way? Could she imagine their being together as she and Marshall had been? She touched Marshall's signet ring, still hidden under her gown. It was time to return the ring to its owner. Perhaps he would give it to Ta Ming.

Oh Marshall. The tears rolled down her face, dampening the pillow. *We never worked together the way Jonathan and I have. We were never friends—only lovers.*
The revelation brought more tears, more questions.

She let her mind soar to the possibility of accepting Jonathan's proposal of marriage. He had looked so sad when she had responded, "I am most honored that you would consider me worthy—but I cannot give you an answer yet."

His face had flushed. "I embarrass myself for speaking so rashly. It's only that I will leave soon, and I—I feel a great admiration for you. Perhaps it is love, though I confess, I'm unfamiliar with the emotion."

Kulien had stepped into his arms and lifted her face, her lips meeting his. "And I esteem you more highly than any man I have ever known," she had said when they drew apart. "I believe that it *is* love that grows between us; but so much has happened today, that I'm not sure how to answer."

She had opened the front door leading onto the veranda, and stood within the circle of his arms as they watched the rain fall in a gentle shower. "I must go then," he said, after several quiet moments. "Please do not be troubled about your answer. If it is ordained by God that we be together; we will have no doubts. If not—then we must accept our destiny."

With tenderness, his hand had brushed over her smooth cheek before he darted down the steps and disappeared around the bend.

He would want an answer soon—before he left for Boston. What would she tell him? After today's decision regarding her future with the women of China, could she wait two more years before returning to her homeland?

Through the early hours of the night, Kulien tossed and turned with unanswered questions—unsolved riddles. At last, too weary to think another thought, she fell into a troubled sleep.

Heat. Unbearable heat. Kulien felt suffocated. She couldn't get her breath. She was sitting in the red bridal sedan, bowed down with the weight of the beaded headdress, bouncing and swaying on the hot, dusty road to Hangchow. She tried to peer through the opaque covering of the small window, but she couldn't open her eyes. Where was she? How much longer must she be subjected to this intolerable heat? There must be a way to escape—to break out of her prison.

Flailing her arms, she gasped for air, and tried to open her eyes. They felt dry and crusted—impossible to open. When she finally forced them open, she realized that she wasn't in the bridal chair, after all. She was in her own bed; but something was wrong—terribly wrong. Her face burned with fever; and her throat tightened with every scorching breath. Straining to see through the darkness, she felt, more than saw, the room filling with smoke—thick, blinding smoke.

Suddenly, she was fully awake. She threw off the bedclothes and ran to the door, reaching for the knob. It was so hot, she could barely grasp it, but she opened the door to a wall of flames. Fire singed her hair and licked at her nightclothes.

Slamming the door shut, she backed away. What should she do? She couldn't get into the hallway to see about Martha and the girls.

There were no sounds in the house other than the roar of the fire and the crash of falling timbers. Glass shattered somewhere in the house; but there were no sounds of anyone calling for help. Where were Martha—and the girls? How about Clear Moon? What should she do? Where could she go?

Returning to the door, she watched smoke pour around the edges like water from a broken cistern. By now, the brass doorknob glowed with heat; and there was no escape except through the window.

With all her strength, she yanked down the heavy velvet drapes and unlatched the window. But it wouldn't budge. Kulien began to panic as a crackling snapping sound drew her attention to the door. Tongues of fire, like deadly serpents, crept into the room and across the carpet, devouring first the wood-paneled door, then everything in its path.

Perspiration ran down Kulien's face as the heat enveloped the room; and her fear grew beyond anything she'd ever known. She had to get the window open. Glancing around for a heavy object, she grabbed the desk chair, which was already beginning to burn. The chair was so heavy, she could hardly lift it; but she managed to raise it high enough to heave at the window. As splinters of glass flew through the air, Kulien turned her face away.

Fresh air flooded the area; but it only fed the fire. The blaze hurtled across the room, surrounding Kulien on all sides. She had to get out. She couldn't stay there and burn to death. Wrapping her hand in the hem of her nightgown, she beat at the jagged pieces of broken glass still adhering to the window frame. Afraid to look behind at the raging fire, and wary of looking down at the drop from a two-story window, she closed her eyes and climbed onto the ledge. She could see that flames, like fiery swords of ancient warriors, flashed from every window. Beyond the sound of the roaring inferno, came a clanging of bells. Horse-drawn fire engines raced up the hill, followed by a gang of volunteer firemen.

The fire had caught a corner of her gown and she felt the heat on her back. If she waited any longer, she wouldn't be able to get away. She had no other choice. "Help me, God!"

She closed her eyes—and jumped.

"Kulien, wake up! Don't you hear me?"

"No. Go away! What do you want?"

"It is I, Jiang, your *amah*. Today is the first day of spring—the day we celebrate your birthday. Come now, little ladybug—wake up!"

"Jiang? But I thought you were dead."

"Wake up! Wake up!"

Pain—excruciating pain held Kulien in its grip. With each shallow breath, searing pangs of severe pain ripped throughout her body. Kulien groaned, and cried out, "Oh, Jiang, I'm so glad you're not dead. I've had a horrible dream."

A cool hand stroked Kulien's head; a damp cloth sponged her face. But the pain continued. Her ribs felt like they were splitting; her hands burned and throbbed. As she lay there, she realized that there wasn't a single part of her body that didn't hurt.

"Wake up, dear. You must wake up and have something to eat."

The voice was no longer Jiang's; but it was familiar—a voice from the past.

"Oh, Horace, I'm so worried! Do you think she'll live through this?"

"Yes, I do. Look, her eyelids flicker; she's coming around."

Kulien opened her eyes, and through a murky haze, she could see white faces hovering over her. A man's face; and a woman's. Who were these foreigners? What were they doing in the compound? Did Lufong know they had invaded her apartment?

Suddenly, another face projected itself in her vision. A kind face—one with slanted eyes. Sunfu! Her brother must have invited them to their home.

"Kulien—Grace." The Chinese voice, speaking Mandarin, was gentle. "Don't be afraid. We're your friends.

You're in a hospital." He leaned closer. "You've been here for two days."

Kulien blinked her eyes. *Grace!* How did this man know her foreign name? She tried to focus on his face; he wore glasses. The man was not Sunfu; but he said he was a friend.

She tried to move her arm, and noticed that her hand was bandaged. What had happened to her? Why was she in so much pain; and why were these people hovering over her?

The man lifted her bandaged hand and touched his lips to the white cloths. He spoke to the foreigners. "She's still disoriented. Falling, or jumping, from such a height was a great shock to her system."

"Are you certain her injuries are not life-threatening?"

The man leaned over her again—lifting her eyelids. "She'll recover—in time. Three of her ribs are cracked, and she needed stitches in her forehead. The palm of her right hand is burned; and she has surface burns on her legs and feet—along with many bruises." He sighed heavily, looking down on her with concern. "If those lilac bushes hadn't broken her fall, she might be. . .." He didn't finish his sentence. Touching her forehead, he added, "She has a slight concussion; that would account for her confusion."

As the voices droned overhead, Kulien closed her eyes. She wanted only to sleep—to forget the pain. But the moment her eyelids shut, the kind voice probed into her mind. "Kulien, you must not sleep any longer. You've slept enough. It's time to come back into this world." His voice dropped to a hoarse whisper, "You survived the fire—you're alive. Now you must force yourself to accept the tragedy you have escaped."

Fire? Tragedy? Kulien turned the words over in her mind, attempting to match them to a faded picture which seemed to elude her grasp.

The woman's voice spoke again. "Dr. Wung, is there anything we can do?"

"You can pray. Go home and pray. I'll stay here with her until she's lucid."

"But Doctor, you've been here day and night for two days!"

"She is my patient."

Kulien opened her eyes to see him nod at the couple. "She's more than my patient. I hope to make her my wife."

Another word to decipher—wife. Of whom was the man speaking? And who was this doctor who claimed to be her friend?

Minutes passed. She no longer heard the voices of the man and woman. Kulien summoned all her energy to lift heavy eyelids. She turned her head to one side. The man with black hair and glasses sat on a chair beside the bed. Long, cool fingers brushed over her forehead. "You will be all right, *Chingkuei,* my Enchantress."

Enchantress? She had heard that word only recently. She sifted through her memories. Yes, the man from Soochow had spoken about the rare flower. Enchantress was a delicate white wildflower with a fragrance that cast magic on those fortunate enough to find one. Why did the man call her by that name?

"Kulien," he said, speaking softly, "you are *not* a Bitter Seed. You are an Enchantress, the rarest wildflower of China. I could have searched a lifetime and never found you. But here you are—and I've come under your spell."

Kulien sighed at the words, beautifully spoken in her native tongue. She focused her eyes again on the man. Jonathan Wung! Her friend. Color rose to her cheeks. Ah, she remembered now. This fine-boned man with the gentle touch was more than a friend.

"Do I see a blush of roses on my Enchantress? I do believe she is on the road to recovery."

Jonathan carefully slipped an arm under Kulien's shoulders to lift her head enough to sip warm tea. Before lowering her, he spooned a few noodles, flavored with chicken broth, into her mouth. His eyes never left her face as she swallowed. "There now, you'll soon be good as new."

Gently, he laid her back on the pillow, talking her through the pain of movement. "You've been bound very tightly because your ribs are fractured. I know you are uncomfortable, and if you need it, I'll give you some laudanum, tincture of opium, for your pain."

Kulien opened her mouth to speak, but her throat felt gritty, full of sand; and she coughed.

Pain! Cutting, ripping pain!

"Here, another sip of tea will soothe your throat."

"I—I heard you say that I'm in a hospital." Her voice was hoarse. "But I don't remember anything. Have I been ill?"

"There was a fire," Jonathan said, waiting for Kulien to absorb the words. "You jumped from the second story window." Again he waited, his eyes reaching into her spirit with compassion.

As if reading an unfolding scroll, Kulien saw the smoke hanging over her bed; she inhaled the acrid pungency of burning timbers and furniture; she heard the crackling and roar of flames out of control.   There was heat—suffocating, searing heat. Suddenly, she began to shiver, ice water rushing through her veins. Her teeth chattered—her head shook—tears poured from her eyes.

Jonathan put an arm under her back and gently lifted her. He held her as carefully as if she were a baby. "There, there, my wildflower," he whispered in her ear. "You've had a great shock; but don't fear, you'll be able to face it all soon. And when you do, the healing will begin."

After several minutes of his soothing voice, Kulien relaxed. She lay back and closed her eyes. It was coming back to her. There had been a great fire. Her house had fallen around her; and she had jumped from the window ledge of her bedroom to keep from burning to death. But what about Martha? And Clear Moon? Had the other girls and servants escaped? She didn't think she could face the answers yet. First, she must sleep. She looked up at Jonathan, "May I sleep now? I'm so very tired."

"Yes, you're out of danger now.   Close your eyes, delicate flower. Tomorrow will come soon enough."

Kulien felt a gentle pressure on her lips—a soft, delicious kiss. She sighed, too weak to respond—but for now, she was content. Aware than Jonathan Wung continued to watch over her, she slipped into a comforting oblivion.

FIFTY-SEVEN

The next morning, Kulien was awakened by the touch of a cool cloth on her face and neck. A woman in white clothing was at the bedside giving her a sponge bath with something that had the scent of tea. She smiled briefly when Kulien opened her eyes. "So—you're awake. And about time, I might say."

"Where is Dr. Wung?" Kulien's eyes darted from the nurse to the door.

"He's been here for three nights and two days; Dr. Miller insisted that he go home to sleep."

Kulien took in the information, feeling sad that Jonathan wasn't there. "I'm very hungry," she said, at last. "I smell tea. May I have some?"

"You're getting a tea bath." The nurse's tone was filled with compassion. "That doctor of yours says the tannic acid is good for burns. One of those old-fashioned home remedies, I suppose."

"Well," Kulien said, a hint of a smile on her face, "I wouldn't like to drink my bath water; but a cup of hot tea and a bowl of rice would please me very much."

"Good—that's good. If you eat well today, and have another full night's sleep, you might be able to go home tomorrow."

Home. Did she have a home? If her house wasn't totally destroyed, she was certain it was too damaged to be livable; and she would never ask Marshall for help. She grasped the nurse's wrist with her good hand. "Do you know what happened to the others in my house? Did they escape the fire?"

The woman frowned before patting Kulien's shoulder. "I'm sorry. I know nothing about your home. Dr. Wung will tell you all you want to know."

"But I want an answer now. He's not here; so I demand that you tell me! Where is Martha Johnson? Where are my students? I can see by your expression that you can answer my questions."

The woman turned away without speaking and left the room, leaving Kulien to imagine the most dreaded circumstances.

Several hours had passed, and she had fallen back into a restless sleep when footsteps sounded on the tile floor. Anna Clark leaned over the bed. "Kulien, how are you feeling today?"

Kulien opened her eyes, glad to see a familiar face. "I'm better—really I am. I want to leave; but I don't know if I still have a home."

Anna nodded, but her eyes welled with tears. "You have a home with us as long as you want, my child. You know that."

"Then what I've imagined is true. My house is gone, isn't it?"

Anna clucked her tongue. "Yes, I'm afraid so. There's nothing but rubble. I'm so sorry Kulien. But that's not the extent of the loss." The tears spilled onto her cheeks, and she wiped at them with a handkerchief. "I'm not sure you're well enough to hear the news."

"I think I know what you have to say; and I've prepared my heart to receive your words."

Anna inhaled deeply, fortifying herself. Her face paled and she bit her lower lip. "Martha, Clear Moon, the other girls, and the servants—they're all gone!"

Although Kulien had supposed the worst, to hear the dire words drained her of all strength.

"I'm so sorry, "Anna said, again. "They were all found in their beds. They must have died of smoke inhalation." She paused to bow her head. "They never knew what happened."

Many minutes passed before Kulien could bring her emotions under control enough to speak. "Why was I left? Why, Anna? Clear Moon was so excited about going to China; and Martha was such a beautiful and sweet young woman!" A sob escaped her lips. "And my little girls. They had hope for a new life. I don't understand why this happened to them."

Kulien wanted to turn over and bury her face in the bedclothes, but her tight bandages and the pain in her ribs held her fast. She lay flat on her back and stared at the ceiling. She knew there were tears, many tears; but they wouldn't come. Her heart was stone.

The hazy fog lifted and bright rays of a spring afternoon slanted through the small window of Kulien's hospital room.

Dust particles danced on the sunbeams before vanishing into the shadows. A bird chirped from a tree branch, announcing the arrival of five blue speckled eggs. Kulien turned her head toward the sound.

Her house was gone; her dear friends were dead, forever gone. She had put to rest the once-cherished hope of a reunion with Marshall; even the remembered joy of Ta Ming's arms around her neck had disappeared. But life would go on. The sun would continue to shine. The birds would keep building their nests and teaching their young ones to fly away. She, too, would pick up what was left of her life and step into the future.

She closed her eyes again, and turned her thoughts to China. Was her father still alive? Did he ever think of her with kindness? That part of her life was also past. Now she must look to tomorrow and the days following. Jonathan Wung would soon leave for Boston, and he had asked her to go with him as his wife. Many of her problems would be solved if she did as he wished. He was a good man, a pure man, and she did feel a growing love for him. They understood each other, and had much in common. She could try to be a proper wife for him; and she knew that he would always be considerate and faithful to her.

Wrapped in her thoughts, Kulien didn't hear him enter the room. For several moments, Jonathan stood at her bedside, gazing down on her face. When he spoke, it was a soft soothing tone, "You smile in your sleep."

Comforted that he had returned, she opened her eyes, and the smile broadened. "I'm not sleeping, only thinking." She lifted her bandaged hand and he held it tenderly.

"And what thoughts bring such an expression of delight to your face."

"I was thinking of you." She lowered her eyelids, suddenly shy at her boldness.

"I'm pleased that you smile when you think of me." He leaned over her face and looked into her eyes as doctor to patient. "Your pupils are normal today; and I've been told that your appetite has returned. I believe you're ready to leave this place. Would you like to go home?"

Kulien's heart skipped a beat, and she sighed. "As you know, I don't have a home of my own anymore. But Anna said I could stay with them as long as I wish."

Jonathan strode to the window and stood for several minutes before turning to Kulien. "This isn't the best time to bring up another decision for you to make; you've had a traumatic experience, and you need time to heal. But," he pulled a chair near the bed and sat in it, leaning close to Kulien, "as you may remember, I leave for Boston in three days—and I want you to come with me. Reverend Clark will marry us—if you're willing, of course." His cheeks flushed and his eyes sparkled behind the glasses. "You do remember that I asked you to be my wife, don't you?"

Kulien reached up a hand and rested it on his smooth cheek. "I remember." Her fingers moved to the back of his neck, and she drew his face to hers.

As their lips met, his scent reminded her of China on a spring day. The kiss was gentle, yet fervent. She felt whole, satisfied, and wanting more.

Jonathan pulled away after touching his lips to her nose and forehead. "Does this mean you have come to a decision? Am I to believe that you love me Kulien—that you will be my wife?"

Her hesitation caused a shadow to pass over Jonathan's face. Was she ready to marry Jonathan—to forsake her work with the slave girls of San Francisco? Could she wait the two years of his internship before returning to China? She lifted sad eyes to his. "You honor me, and I know I would be happy with you, but I can't make such an important decision today."

Jonathan bowed his head. "Of course, I understand." Then taking on his role of a doctor, he turned back the light quilt, and gently touched the bandaged ribs. He unwound the gauze from her ankles and feet, and applied a salve before rewrapping them. "I think your burns are healing well, and," he said, leaning over to peer at her forehead, "we can remove those stitches today."

"Then I may leave soon?"

"How about tomorrow morning?" Jonathan's former ease had been replaced by a cool exterior. "The American doctor and his wife arrive tomorrow afternoon from China. They'll be sad and disappointed to learn of Clear Moon's death."

"Yes." Kulien swallowed deeply, fighting back the despair. "I have trouble believing she's gone. She went through so much to get this far, and was so excited to go back to China to serve with the missionary doctor and his wife." Kulien frowned, reaching to take hold of Jonathan's sleeve. "What have you heard about the missionaries who had planned to take Clear Moon to Shanghai? Anna and Horace behave as though they have eaten bitter fruit whenever I ask about them."

Jonathan smiled. "I think they want you to be surprised." He shook his head at her questioning gaze. "I will say no more than that. I believe you'll be strong enough to meet the ship when it arrives. Then all your questions will be answered."

The next morning Kulien was ready to leave the hospital. Though there was pain in her ribs when she moved suddenly, she could walk stiffly without help. The burns and cuts stung and the bruises were tender to the touch, but the anticipation of returning to a normal life was enough to sustain her. She hadn't arrived at an answer to Jonathan's proposal yet, and knew she needed to tell him her decision soon.

Anna and Horace Clark made Kulien's homecoming as festive as possible. When the buggy stopped at the front door of the house on Sacramento Street, more than ten young girls rushed out to greet her. They waved red and green streamers, and held cards with ideograms denoting, "Good Luck," "Health," and "Long Life." Jonathan stood quietly in the background, his eyes searching her face.

After a sumptuous feast of Kulien's favorite foods: fried prawns, golden brown dumplings, bamboo sprouts, and spiced almonds, Anna entered the dining room bearing a large soup tureen. "This is the best surprise of all," she said, setting the bowl in front of Kulien.

As Kulien lifted the lid, her eyes filled with tears. Lotus seed soup!

"Dr. Wung says it's an old remedy that would surely bring health to your bones." Anna folded arms over her starched apron and smiled.

Kulien glanced from Jonathan to Anna, then with her eyes on the plump seeds, she exclaimed in an awed voice, "Thank you! This is a wonderful surprise. My *amah* prepared it for me when I was a child in my father's home. Dr. Wung is correct. A bowl of this ancient medicine is a perfect conclusion to a most splendid homecoming."

After the meal, and at Jonathan's urging, Kulien retired to rest for an hour before the group would be ready to go to the docks. The estimated arrival time of the American missionaries was five o'clock. The trading ship, *Flying Cloud*, was known for its speed, and could be counted on to anchor near the posted time.

Two buggies were employed to transport the new arrivals back to the house. Jonathan and Kulien rode together in a buggy behind Reverend and Mrs. Clark. They were silent as the horse plodded down the hill to the bay. Kulien still had no answer for him, and was grateful that he didn't press her for one. When the buggies rumbled over the wood planking of the wharf, they saw that the clipper ship had arrived ahead of them. The crew hung from masts pulling and tugging at sails. There were shouts and high-pitched whistles as large crates were lowered in giant nets. Men ran to and fro over the wharf unloading the cargo and stacking bundles in tottering piles.

Kulien strained her eyes over the activity to the gangplank where passengers disembarked. The crowds made it impossible to see, and Kulien found herself growing more impatient with each passing moment. Who were these people? And why had Anna and Horace kept their identity a secret?

Finally, as the crowd seemed to clear a pathway for the debarking passengers, Kulien gasped, a rush of pleasure warming her from head to toe.

This was a surprise! A delightful one! Walking toward them were her old friends, Benjamin and Evelyn O'Kelly. Their faces were wreathed in smiles, and in their arms, they held identical baby girls wearing ruffled sunbonnets.

FIFTY-EIGHT

Kulien stood quietly beside the buggy watching Anna and Horace Clark make their way through the crowds to greet the new arrivals. Her heart moved with love when the familiar faces smiled in her direction. Evelyn and Dr. Ben—and their little family.

She recalled the years of friendship with Dr. Ben: the joy, the pain, and the heartaches. And she would never forget the close bond she and Evelyn had formed as they worked together to teach the slave girls. Now only a few feet away, Ben waved a hand, and Evelyn called, "Kulien, Kulien, I can't believe we're actually here!" Evelyn's smiling face was as sweet and beautiful as it had been seven years ago.

Her eyes met Kulien's, and she thrust the child she carried into Ben's free arm, and reached for her. "Oh, my dear friend, it's so good to see you again!"

Kulien winced at Evelyn's embrace, only too conscious of her fractured ribs, but she quickly recovered and returned the hug. "I'm too amazed to speak. I wasn't told that you were coming."

"I know," Evelyn answered. "We wanted to surprise you. And I can see that we have." She turned to Ben. "Just see who we've brought for a visit—our delightful little twins, Kathleen and Maureen."

Ben's face, shining with pride and happiness, looked down on Kulien with a wide smile. "Ah, Colleen, it has been a very long time." A slight flush appeared on his cheeks, and Kulien wondered if he was thinking of those long-ago years when he had expressed his love to her.

"But what is this?" Dr. Ben asked, glancing over her face. "You've been hurt. And your hand," he said, lifting it tenderly to look over the signs of burns.

"We can talk about that later," Kulien said, before introducing Jonathan Wung. After a brief exchange of pleasantries, Ben and Evelyn, each holding a child in their arms, rode back to the mission house in Jonathan and Kulien's buggy.

"Where is Clear Moon, our new helper," Ben asked. "We're certainly looking forward to meeting her. We really can use her help!"

Kulien lowered her eyelids before leaning toward the couple. "There was a fire, a terrible fire—my home was burned to the ground."

Evelyn gasped and a frown marred her smooth forehead, but she said nothing.

"A home can be replaced," Kulien said softly, "but Clear Moon, I fear, is gone forever."

"What? Are you saying that the girl died in the fire?" Ben's thick red eyebrows rose with his voice.

"Yes, it's true." Kulien's voice cracked with emotion, but she sat back with a sigh when Jonathan took up the conversation.

"Kulien was also injured, as you noticed," he said to Ben. "Only today was she released from the hospital."

"Oh, no," Ben and Evelyn said in unison. Their expressions showed their concern, and for the next few blocks, no one spoke about either the fire or the devastating news of Clear Moon's death.

Although the air outside had grown warmer with each passing day, inside the big old house it felt damp and cold. After the group had eaten a light meal and the twins had been put to bed, Horace set a fire in the parlor and invited Kulien and Jonathan, along with the O'Kellys, to retire to the formal room for further discussion.

"We've been in China for only one year," Ben said when they were seated near the fireplace, "but we really believe we've found our home." He smiled at Evelyn. "Kathleen and Maureen are just beginning to talk—and speak Chinese as well as English. Our patients love them."

"I had no idea how busy a two year old could be." Evelyn rolled her eyes and laughed. "And to think I've been twice blessed!" She turned to Kulien, and lowered her voice. "Anna wrote that Ta Ming is in Great Britain with his father."

"Yes, that's right. He does well in school, and one day will be a fine gentleman." Kulien forced the painful words from her lips. "But tell us more about your work," she said, changing the subject. "Do the people accept your Western medicine?" Glancing at Jonathan, she added, "Dr. Wung hopes to return to China after spending another year or two practicing medicine in Boston."

For several minutes, Benjamin engaged Jonathan in a discussion of medicine while Evelyn spoke of the joys of motherhood. Then she gestured toward Kulien's forehead. "I hope your injuries weren't serious. I know you've suffered a great loss—not only in losing your home, but also Clear Moon. We were so looking forward to having her return with us."

Kulien nodded. "Yes, she was a delightful girl, and longed to return to China as a woman of self-respect." She sighed as the horror of the fire played across her mind. "It was a tragic accident. The fire claimed five of the young girls under our charge, as well as two of the servants." She fought back the tears. "And Martha, my very dear friend, also died. I've tried to understand what could have caused such an uncontrollable blaze."

"But Anna, didn't you tell me a few minutes ago that the fire was deliberately set by enemies of the Chinese?" Evelyn looked at the older woman, who wore a frown. Covering her mouth, Evelyn realized she had spoken out of turn. "Oh, I'm so sorry," she said, her cheeks flushed with embarrassment. "I didn't know I was betraying a confidence."

Kulien saw the expressions exchanged between Anna and Evelyn and knew that she hadn't been told the entire truth. "Now I understand. Why wasn't I told this news? How long have you known the fire wasn't an accident?"

Anna rose from her chair, and gently rested a hand on Kulien's shoulder. "We learned the truth only this morning. You've had enough grief, child. Dr. Wung thought we should wait until you were stronger before we told you about another vicious attack on the Chinese."

Her heart pounding, she struggled to control her emotions. "I'm certain Dr. Wung meant well; however he knows that I don't fear the truth." Her eyes met Jonathan's, and she spoke with a cold firmness to her voice. "It's better to die for one's beliefs than to forfeit life through a piece of bad luck. It gives me some comfort to know that Martha and Clear Moon died for what they believed—that their deaths were not by accident or chance."

Jonathan said nothing as Kulien continued to hold his attention. Evelyn broke the tension. "What will you do now, Kulien?" Her soft curls framed her face in a halo, and her eyes were moist with concern.

Feeling even more confused about her future, Kulien studied her fingers. "Dr. Wung has asked me to accompany him when he returns to Boston the day after tomorrow." She looked up at him, her expression softening. "As his wife."

"Oh, what wonderful news," Evelyn said, as she looked back and forth from Kulien to Jonathan. "I'm sure you'll both be very happy." She turned to smile at Benjamin. "There's nothing more satisfying than to be married to a man you love."

Not wanting to hurt Jonathan, Kulien swallowed the words, *Yes, I know*.

When the grandfather clock, in the corner of the room, struck ten times, Anna covered a yawn with her handkerchief. "It's late and Horace and I must get our sleep. The girls demand all the strength we have. She held out a hand to Horace, beckoning him to join her. "Will you excuse us?"

"I, too, must leave," Jonathan said, bowing. "Tomorrow will be my last day in Little China. I begin my rounds early." He nodded at Kulien. "Perhaps my newest patient also needs a consultation before my departure."

Kulien followed Jonathan to the front door and onto the porch. "And what is it that my doctor wishes to say? Have you medicine for me?" She shrugged her shoulders, hugging herself. "I'm so glad to see my old friends. They seem to be very happy in China." Her voice was wistful, and she smiled as she rested a hand on his arm. "Do you like them?"

He nodded. "They're fine people; and your old friend, Ben, is filled with laughter." He brushed a strand of hair off her cheek with his fingertips. "You like them very much, don't you? When they speak, your eyes shine. Does your heart yearn for old friends—or do I see China reflected in your face?"

"You're too wise," she said in a playful voice. "I don't need to answer because you already know my thoughts." A sense of peace wrapped around her as Jonathan put a firm hand on her back and tenderly drew her closer.

For several minutes he studied her upturned face in the light of the moon, caressing her with his dark eyes. "I don't know all your thoughts, Enchantress—wildflower."

"Nor do I," she confessed, returning his gaze. "I know you wait for my answer to your proposal, and the time is short. I'll give you my decision tomorrow. I hope your God will guide me to the right decision."

"And I hope the day comes soon when you confess that 'my God' is your God, too. Kulien, I know that you want to believe in Jesus, but you are still bound to your family's beliefs." Jonathan brushed velvet-soft lips over her forehead, and she lifted her mouth to his, savoring the moment of the warm kiss.

"Tomorrow afternoon, then," he called, walking down the steps. "I'll be back tomorrow afternoon for your answer."

When Kulien entered the parlor, she was surprised to see Evelyn and Ben waiting for her. "I thought you would have retired for the night. I know you must be exhausted after your long voyage." She placed her hands on her flushed cheeks, hoping the pleasure of Jonathan's kiss didn't betray her emotions.

"We needed to talk to you alone," Ben said. His voice was low, his jaw clenched. "We have news of your family."

"My family? What do you know of them? Is my father alive? Oh, please, tell me your news." Kulien's cheeks flushed again, this time with hope, and she began to shake as images of the past crowded into her mind.

They sat in a close circle, their faces reflecting the rise and fall of a flickering lamp. Ben reached into a pocket to withdraw a parchment scroll. He glanced at it several times before speaking. "Kulien, have you heard of the epidemic that has invaded China?" He watched her nod and went on. "Smallpox has claimed the lives of thousands of men, women and children throughout Kiangsu Province. It's spreading to the south. We foreigners are protected by a vaccine; and as many people as we can reach, we vaccinate." He tapped the scroll on his knee. "We took our medicine to the countryside hoping to stop the plague before it reached the landowners and their villages."

Kulien stiffened and clenched her hands into a ball.

"When we approached this one compound, we saw that death had already been there. The white banner of mourning flew over the gate, but we rapped for admittance. An old man answered. He was weak and scarred, but had survived the disease. He told us that the majority of his family had moved north to escape sickness, but that his servants, one remaining son, and the son's mother had succumbed to smallpox." Ben glanced at Evelyn, then at Kulien's somber face.

"I asked the man if there was anyone else in the family that we might help. He said, 'My elder son passed beyond the Yellow Springs many years ago; and the daughter of my beloved wife disappeared soon after her marriage. There is no one left.'"

Evelyn leaned forward to grasp Kulien's cold hands. "I asked him to tell us the name of his daughter because I remembered what you had told me about your family. And there was something quite different about the old man. When he mentioned the daughter, there were tears in his eyes." She paused. "He said, 'My daughter was named, Kulien, Bitter Seed. She was my only natural child.'"

At the unexpected news, tears of joy pooled in Kulien's eyes. "My father lives! He has not forgotten me."

"We told Kuang about you, Colleen. That his daughter resides in America—and that she has a son."

Evelyn interrupted Ben. "He wanted to believe us, but kept shaking his head and repeating, 'It cannot be. It cannot be.'"

"He invited us into his home," Ben said, taking up the story, "and showed us his garden. He said he often sits there recalling more pleasant days. He is a lonely old man, Colleen, and wants to believe that you still live." He leaned forward. "He said that he needs proof. He is dying and said he cannot rest until he is certain that you are his lost daughter."

"We found his behavior most unusual for a Chinese man, and that he would care so much about a daughter."

Kulien's smile was radiant. Yes, that's my father. We're similar in many ways. We have difficulty fitting the pattern designed for our race." She looked from Ben to Evelyn. "As I told you before, he married an English woman, my mother, against all tradition."

Benjamin fingered the scroll again before handing it to Kulien. "This is a message from Kuang Lufong to you. He wrote it shortly before we left Shanghai. He brought it to the clinic himself. We don't know what he wrote. As you can see, the seal has not been broken."

Kulien received the roll with trembling hands. Her heart pounded in her ears, and her eyes refused to focus. "I thank you," she said, rising to leave the room. "I will wait until morning to read this, as I need to make a most important decision."

FIFTY-NINE

The next morning, a pearly mist rose from the bay to drift over the city. It flowed past the crowded buildings to settle on the surrounding sandy hills. Wildflowers of various colors and hues dotted the landscape with new life. Tall grasses, bent by constant westerly winds, sparkled with dew. Birds, small brown ones, and large white ones, dipped and soared over the California countryside. In a small, darkened room, a woman of mixed race lifted her spirit heavenward. She was about to break the wax seal on a parchment that had traveled across the Peaceful Sea—a letter from her father. What story would the ancient characters tell? What answers would they bring to her many questions?

Kulien had spent a restless night. Her dreams had taken her to a spacious hall filled with innumerable paintings. She had paused before each picture, sometimes smiling, but often crying. She gazed on splashes of color depicting a compound garden; she shuddered at the crimson slash across a swan's white throat; and nausea overcame her when she approached a painting of little girls with tortured eyes, while old men, with serpents' fangs, crouched in the background.

She had awakened only to drift into another, more frightening dream. She saw herself perched on the upturned eaves of a pagoda. From her vantage point, she could see across a wide blue expanse where a young boy sat on a golden steed. The horse galloped away when she called to him; and the boy watched her over his shoulder until he was out of sight. As she waited for him to reappear, a willow tree grew out of the blue, and a man with glasses stepped out to greet her. He opened his arms, calling for her to come to him, but the roof was so high, and she was afraid to jump. However, when she noticed the roof was on fire, she flung herself from the building; but instead of falling into the man's arms, she spread giant wings and began to rise into the sky.

Now as Kulien sat thinking about the dreams, she turned the scroll over and over in her hands. Her father lived and wished to see her! And Jonathan Wung had asked her to marry him. Her longing to see and be forgiven by her father would be a most precious gift; but to be the wife of a truly fine and

454

honorable man, who shared her vision, was also a most surprising and welcome proposal! And then there were Jonathan's words about her growing faith in the One God. Oh, there were many decisions to make!

Finally, with a small knife, Kulien broke the wax seal that bore the chop mark of her father's name. She moved her chair closer to the window where a pale light encircled her. Unrolling the crisp parchment, she inhaled deeply, half afraid to read her father's words. Bold black characters, formed with precision and grace, greeted her from behind the compound wall. "*Baba*," she said under her breath. "It has been ten years since I have heard your voice, or seen your writing."

Kulien studied the scroll, rereading each character through tears, until the sun's rays pierced the veil of mist. Her heart was moved as she read, stopping a moment to smile, and then allowing the tears to fall. After rereading the letter several times, she rolled up the paper and stared at it for long, quiet minutes.

Her father wanted proof that the woman Benjamin O'Kelly had spoken about was his only daughter. What proof could she give? Then she remembered the red silk bag that held her mother's brooch. She and Jiang had buried it in the garden shortly before she left to become Kong Litang's wife. Could it still be there? That would be proof—proof that she was Kuang Kulien, daughter of Kuang Lufong and Marguerite Howard. As she considered the possibility of a reunion with her father, or marriage to Jonathan Wung, she finally made a major decision— she had the answer. Closing her eyes, she surrendered her life and concerns to the Most High, and suddenly a deep peace poured through her spirit.

Today she would tell Jonathan what she must do; and beg for his understanding and forgiveness in hurting him. She knew now that she truly loved the man from Soochow. He had expressed his deep commitment to her, and for a time, she wondered if she could possibly return that same depth of love. These last few days, however, she knew that her love for him had begun to blossom into a beautiful relationship.

Jonathan had touched her soul with his kindness and gentle ways. Her physical response to him, while stirring her femininity and longing for fulfillment, had been pure and patient, very unlike the kind of passion she had shared with Marshall Whitfield. But knowing Jonathan as she did, she was certain he would understand her choice—and he would wait for her. Their time apart would only deepen the strong affection growing between them.

As serenity covered her like a warm blanket, she reached into a large chest of clothing that Anna had gathered for the slave girls. She selected an appropriate outfit for this most important day—an emerald green silk tunic with matching trousers. Kneeling before an ebony toilet case, she opened the lid and surveyed her reflection in the mirror. She was no longer a young impetuous girl who demanded her own way. In ten years, she had learned that patience is the greatest virtue, one that can only be learned through suffering.

She smiled at the woman in the mirror. The dimple in her cheek reminded her that she had retained a sense of humor and playfulness. With a wooden comb, she smoothed her long hair, watching it shine and glisten like polished ebony as it spread over her shoulders. She was ready—ready to voice her decision to Jonathan and to her American friends.

The rest of the morning and early afternoon passed quickly. Kulien wore a smile of mystery, but said nothing of her plans. She asked Evelyn and Benjamin questions about their work; and she played with Kathleen and Maureen, delighting in their baby antics, remembering Ta Ming and Katie as babies. While playing with the little girls, she glanced up to see Ben watching her. As their eyes met, the years of separation washed away. She was again on the floor of the small frame house, still a child herself, laughing at toddlers falling over each other while learning to walk. Kulien smiled up at Ben, glad for his contentment with Evelyn—happy that he now had two little girls to fill the emptiness left by Lucy's and Katie's deaths. Perhaps one day, *she* might even have another child—a girl—yes, many, many little girls.

As the other members of the family came into the parlor, Anna began to tease Kulien. "Your face is a mask, but I perceive joy behind that inscrutable expression."

Evelyn sat on the floor beside Kulien and leaned close enough to whisper, "Are you going to marry the doctor? Oh, I know you are! And you'll be so happy!"

Kulien's eyes twinkled as she faced Evelyn. "Yes, I know I will be happy."

"Then your answer to his proposal is 'yes,' isn't it?"

"You will know my answer after I've spoken to him. It would not be honorable to make my intentions known to you before he hears my decision."

Evelyn squealed with delight, and Ben shook his head, his eyes betraying the love he felt for his petite wife. "Leave Colleen alone," he said with a laugh. "She said she won't tell you until she sees Jonathan." He turned his smile on Kulien. "I've known this young woman for many years, and one thing I've learned is that when she makes up her mind, there's no moving her."

It was late afternoon when Jonathan arrived at the mission house. He wore American clothing—a dark suit and white shirt. A dark blue bow tie at his throat moved as he spoke. "I apologize for my tardiness," he said, taking in the group gathered in the parlor. "I've packed my belongings, and have come directly from the ticket master." His eyes rested on Kulien's. "I have purchased passage for two—but," he said, a slight frown between his brows, "if necessary, I can return one in the morning."

Jonathan sat in the chair nearest the doorway, and studied Kulien as she moved slowly from one person to the next, pouring tea into the delicate porcelain cups that had been set on small tables beside the chairs. After she finished pouring tea for everyone, she glanced at each face with a smile before stepping in front of Dr. Ben and Evelyn. "Benjamin, she said, her eyes meeting his, "if you had not found me in the street and taken me to your home, my son and I would have died. But you and Lucy cared for us as if we were members of your own family. I will never forget you." She reached for Evelyn's hand. "And you, Evelyn, have been like a sister to me. I thank you for sharing your pain and your happiness with me."

Stepping in front of Anna and Horace Clark, her voice was soft and filled with emotion. "You are my mother and father. I have lived in your home for many years; and you taught me that love is not to be hoarded, but given away. You gave me your unconditional love, and you showed me that I can also know the love of your God." She dropped to her knees. "In my country, reverence is shown by the kowtow. Please do not be offended as I offer my respect to you." Kulien touched her head to the floor three times. When she rose from her knees, there were tears in her eyes as well as in Anna's and Horace's.

Slowly and deliberately, she turned and approached Jonathan. When she held out her hands, she smiled as he took them in his. "What I have to say to you, I will say in private." Standing beside Jonathan, she asked, "Will you please give me permission to leave the house with Dr. Wung—and to take the buggy?"

All nodded their agreement, and Kulien smiled over her shoulder as she left the room with Jonathan close beside her. When Jonathan went outside to hitch up the horse, Anna joined Kulien at the doorway. She draped a white woolen cape over her shoulders. "The afternoon breezes are cold coming off the bay, my dear. This will keep you warm." There was a lilt in the older woman's voice. "We will try to be patient as we wait for you to return. You know that we all love you, and are praying that whatever decision you have made will be one that makes you happy." Anna brushed her soft, powdery lips over Kulien's cheek. "May God go with you," she added, as Kulien walked out the door and down the steps.

SIXTY

As the buggy rattled over bumpy roads and out to a point overlooking the ocean, neither Kulien nor Jonathan spoke. A quiet peace pervaded the ride with the only sounds, an occasional snort from the horse, and the intermittent squawking of seagulls. When they reached the destination Kulien had in mind, she put a hand on Jonathan's arm. "Here is where we will stop."

Jonathan tugged at the reins, and turned to Kulien. "Why here? Have you been to this place before?"

Kulien's eyes swept over the jagged rocks jutting out over the sea. Looking back to that day when she had surrendered her son to Marshall Whitfield, she knew that as on that day, today would also be a moment when her life would change.

Without waiting for Jonathan's aid, she stepped out of the buggy and walked to the edge of the steep cliff. A gust of cold air whipped the cape and lifted the hair from her shoulders. Her voice was husky as she held out a hand. "Jonathan, you are a patient man, and I believe you are the kindest, most generous person I've ever known." As she spoke in her native tongue, the words flowed like oil. "Because of you, I have found the peace and freedom I've searched for all my life. Through your words and actions, I've seen and understood God's purpose for my life."

A lock of shiny black hair blew over Jonathan's forehead, and he nodded. "Your words please me beyond my deepest hopes, for as you know, my spirit is joined to yours." His eyes searched her face, resting on her parted lips. "I find that I'm incomplete without you." He stepped toward Kulien, but didn't touch her. He waited for her to go on.

She took the scroll from a pocket in her tunic. "Ben and Evelyn brought word from my father." Holding it out to him, she added, "He is living, but not for long. I am his only heir, and as a woman divorced by the man chosen by my family, I've learned that I'm permitted to return to the compound of my youth." Watching Jonathan take the scroll, she said, "Please, read it. I want you to know my father's heart—and mine."

Jonathan and Kulien sat opposite each other on large boulders near the edge of the cliff, and she watched him as he read the Chinese characters. He seemed to be holding his breath as his eyes traced the characters up and down the page. When he had finished reading, he sat with his head bowed for a moment before rolling up the scroll and handing it back to Kulien.

His eyes glistened with unshed tears and he drew in his bottom lip as if not wanting to speak his thoughts. Kulien watched him carefully, trying to read his unsaid words. When she spoke, it was in a questioning tone. "Jonathan, I thought I knew what I must do after I read my father's letter. But being here with you, and sensing the love and patience you show toward me, I'm confused." She walked the few paces to where he sat and edged next to him on the boulder. As their shoulders touched, she felt a thrill race through her body, and more than anything wanted to give herself fully to him.

After several tense moments, Kulien rested her hand on his. Turning to face him, she said, "As you can see by my father's communication, he asks, even begs me to return to China. Of course, he also insists that I prove I'm his daughter. On the anniversary of my sixteenth birthday, he gave me a brooch that had belonged to my mother, as well as a small picture of her. Before I left my home, my *amah* and I put these treasures in a jar and buried them in the garden of my private quarters."

She waited for Jonathan to respond, but when he didn't, she went on. "If the jar is still where I hid it, I can show him the proof he's looking for." Inhaling deeply, she added, "But just knowing that he's willing to forgive me means more to me than I can express. Having his acceptance is much greater than receiving his inheritance."

Jonathan's words broke into her thoughts, "Is the inheritance great?"

"Yes, my father owns not only an expansive compound, but his estate includes farmland as far as the eye can see."

"Then you would have a place to care for many young girls."

"Yes, but I need you to help me know the right thing to do."

As Jonathan rose, he lifted Kulien to her feet. "I know what you want me to say, but I'm asking *you* to speak plainly.

What is it that *you* truly want? It is your decision to make, not mine."

The roar of the surf echoed in Kulien's ears; salty spray misted her lips as she faced him. "You have asked me to be your wife; and that is my greatest desire. You are a man of great integrity; and we share many values. I know our life together would be one of great contentment." Her heart pounded as she spoke. "I can think of nothing that would make me happier than to spend my life with you. I do love you."

Jonathan's eyes sparkled, and his mouth opened in a broad smile. He drew her closer and looked deeply into her eyes. "Then are you saying that you will be my wife? Are you willing for Reverend Clark to marry us—today?"

Kulien sighed, and putting her arms around Jonathan's neck, she pressed her body against his. Oh, how she loved him! She longed to be his wife and to be joined with him in the purity of the marriage they both wanted. His breath against her face was warm, and she felt his arms press her even closer. She reached up to touch his smooth cheek, and then lifted her lips to his. Long-denied emotions raced through her as she returned his kiss with passion. When they pulled away from each other, they were both breathing heavily. Kulien took his hand and led him to the crest of the cliff.

"Jonathan, my dear Jonathan. You know that I have been with another man—only once." She felt her cheeks warm even though the wind had turned cold. "I would come to you as a soiled dove, not as the pure woman you deserve."

"But Kulien, I know all that. I. . . ."

"Please, let me finish." She glanced out at the sun as it began to sink into the blue horizon. "I've told you about my past: about Marshall Whitfield, and the son who was born of our love. You know about Kong Litang and how he sold me into prostitution. While I was at The Blue Chambers, I saw and heard things that would sicken you, but I was able to escape before I was raped. I also lived among men for four months while sailing to America, and again I was spared from their plans to ravish me. Ahtoy, a well-known and respected madam in this city, gave me a home where I could wait for the arrival of my child."

Jonathan slipped an arm around Kulien's waist and held her as she retold her anguished past.

"As you know, Dr. Ben found me on the street when I was in labor, and took me to his home where I gave birth to my son. He and his wife, Lucy, cared for Ta Ming and me. When Ahtoy came back to claim us as her property, Benjamin told her that my child had died; but he still had to turn me over to an old woman who sold girls as sexual slaves."

"Oh, my Enchantress, I don't know how you could bear such treatment. You don't need to relive all that again!"

"Yes, I do," she answered. "I want you to hear why I'm confused today. I have seen so much evil and sordidness, that I'm afraid I would bring it into our marriage."

"No! I would be all you need. I, along with *our* Lord, would help you forget the past, and look only to the future."

"Jonathan, I know you mean well, but who I am today, the woman you love, is the result of my past. You reminded me of that; and I can't deny it or run from it. And neither can you." She closed her eyes as he brushed his lips over her cheek. "I almost gave in to my desire for Marshall when he came to San Francisco for Ta Ming. I told myself that we were married, and that even though I'd learned from the black book that the Most High frowns on that kind of behavior, I wanted to lie with him."

Jonathan lifted Kulien's chin to look into her eyes. "Did you?"

"Would it matter to you if I did?"

"No. I love you. I love you today, and for all your yesterdays. I will love you until I have no breath left in my body!"

Kulien touched his lips with a fingertip and smiled into his eyes. "No, I didn't. Although I had no idea of your being in my future, I believe now, that I was saving myself for you—and for our marriage bed."

"Then what is your answer? Are you staying here to marry me? Or are you returning to China with the O'Kelly's?"

"My heart is divided." Kulien's words rose above the roar of the surf, but Jonathan leaned closer to hear everything she had to say. "I long to go to Boston with you as your wife; I think you can tell how much I want you for my husband. But there is an even deeper longing to return to China and be reunited with my father." Her eyes filled with tears as she reached to touch Jonathan's smooth cheek.

"It isn't just because of my father, though it would give me great comfort to be forgiven by him—to see him again. No, I believe my desire to return is from the memories I carry from childhood—memories of discarded girls. Unwanted females. I'm angered, as I know you are, by the mutilation of women's feet! I despise the crippling and deforming of healthy toes."

Jonathan released her and folded his arms at his waist. "Now I know what you're going to say. You are returning to China, aren't you?"

"If I listened to my deepest heart, I would go with you, for that is what I truly want—to be your wife. But I hear another call, one that has echoed across the years and miles—and perhaps even from Heaven."

She inhaled deeply, looking first at Jonathan, then at the horizon. "When I was young, I thought I could find freedom and fulfillment by doing as I pleased, but I know now that true freedom comes by surrendering my plans—my right to order my destiny. Since Clear Moon has passed on, I know that I must return to China with Dr. Ben and Evelyn. Then when the time is right, I will open the Kuang family compound to girls who have never had a home—never known love." Kulien's eyes sought Jonathan's. "Can you understand? *This* is my destiny."

She reached for Jonathan's hands and held them to her face. "It may be that my influence will be no larger than a seed—a bitter seed. But, I have to go. Please say that you understand and agree that I'm making the right decision."

Jonathan loosed his fingers from hers and cupped her face in both hands. His eyes swept over her face, resting first on her eyes, then on her small nose, and finally to her full lips. He seemed to devour her every feature, trying somehow to make her a part of himself. When he finally spoke, his voice was a hoarse whisper. "I believe you've made the right choice; and I can only admire your courage."

His hands slid over her shoulders to her waist, and a thrill danced through her body as she waited for what would be his last kiss. He pulled her closer, careful not to hurt the still painful ribs, and pressed his lips against her forehead.

"Kulien—Grace, I accept your decision even though it's not what I had hoped to hear." He leaned back to gaze into her eyes. "But know this, my Enchantress, I haven't given up. When I return to China in two years, I will be at your gate, again asking you to be my wife." He lowered his face to hers, and she knew she loved him with all her heart. Their lips found each other, sending a spiral of ecstasy through her entire being, and she responded with a hunger, a fire that could not be quenched—at least, not for now.

When they parted, their faces were wet with tears, but they couldn't speak. They both turned to gaze at the western horizon; their hearts across the Peaceful Sea; their hopes on that day in the future when they would seal their love with marriage vows.

After several moments of silence, Jonathan's arms dropped to his sides. "I want to walk back to town. I need the time to think. You take the buggy." He lowered his head, his expression tight with strain. "My heart goes with you, Wildflower! I know we'll meet again because you've cast your magic over me, and I am forever under your spell."

Jonathan Wung reached the crest of the hill and turned to look back at the figure silhouetted in the glow of the setting sun. Her green silk trousers appeared as a long slender stem rising from the ocean's depths. Suddenly a gust of wind, carried by the surf, lifted the white cape to surround her in a billowing reflection of the rose-tinted sky.

Jonathan brushed a hand over his eyes and stared in wonder. As Kulien faced the land of her heritage, her beautiful life unfolded before him; she was no longer a bitter seed, or even an enchanting wildflower. The woman who had captured his heart was an elegant and graceful lily—*Wong Yu,* a most favored flower of China!

I will see you again, my dearest. Wait for me.

~~~~

And Jesus said,

"...unless a grain of wheat falls into the earth and dies, it remains by itself alone; but if it dies, it bears much fruit. He who loves his life loses it; and he who hates his life in this world shall keep it to life eternal." (John 12:24-25 NAS)

"...How shall we picture the Kingdom of God?...It is like a mustard seed which when sown upon the soil, though it is smaller than all the seeds that are upon the soil, yet when it is sown, grows up and becomes larger than all the garden plants and forms large branches so that the birds of the air can nest under its shade." (Mark 4:30-32)

13752857R00261

Made in the USA
San Bernardino, CA
02 August 2014